AN... ...THE PRIVY GARDEN

This is the second novel in Janet Laurence's new historical series, following *Canaletto and the Case of Westminster Bridge* (also available in Pan Books).

Janet Laurence is also the author of the successful series of culinary mysteries featuring Darina Lisle, the most recent being *Diet for Death*, *Appetite for Death* and *The Mermaid's Feast*.

Janet began her career as a cookery writer, producing a weekly column for the *Daily Telegraph*. She has written four cookery books, contributed articles to a number of publications, including a series on historical cooking for *Country Life*, and is the author of *The Craft of Food and Cookery Writing*. Under a pseudonym she also writes contemporary women's fiction.

Canaletto and the Case of the Privy Garden is her eleventh crime novel.

D0488889

Janet Laurence

Canaletto

AND THE CASE OF
THE PRIVY GARDEN

F/475297

PAN BOOKS

First published 1999 by Macmillan

This edition published 2000 by Pan Books
an imprint of Macmillan Publishers Ltd
25 Eccleston Place, London SW1W 9NF
Basingstoke and Oxford
Associated companies throughout the world
www.macmillan.co.uk

ISBN 0 330 39037 6

1 3 5 7 9 8 6 4 2

A CIP catalogue record for this book is available from
the British Library.

Phototypeset by Intype London Ltd
Printed and bound in Great Britain by
Mackays of Chatham plc, Chatham, Kent

To

Christian and Toria
with love

Acknowledgements

As usual many people and various sources have helped me to tell this story. I would like to thank particularly Rosemary Baird, Curator of Goodwood House. She made available many details regarding Richmond House and its furnishings including showing me some, now at Goodwood House, where Canaletto's two paintings, *London, Whitehall and the Privy Garden from Richmond House* and *London, the Thames and the City of London from Richmond House* can be seen. The staff at the British Newspaper Library, the London Library, the London Metropolitan Archives (where the Foundling Hospital records are kept), and the Westminster City Archives were all most helpful. I spent many happy hours touching the past in their care. Rhian Harris, curator at the Thomas Coram Foundation for Children, also co-operated with information. David Bomford and Gabriele Finaldi, curators at the National Gallery, gave enlightening talks on Canaletto in connection with the gallery's fascinating 1998 exhibition *Venice Through Canaletto's Eyes*. John Symes gave me valuable information on cabinet making and Robert Avery and Jeffrey Deaver were illuminating on various aspects of swordplay. As always, my husband, Keith, was wonderfully supportive and put up with almost total

Acknowledgements

disruption to his life during the last stages of the writing. However, we both paid an enjoyable visit to the filming of *Aristocrats*, the BBC Classic Serial based on Stella Tillyard's book of the same name, which tells brilliantly the story of the second Duke of Richmond's family. I had already written the first scene set in the Privy Garden for this book when we heard that *Aristocrats* was to be filmed by the BBC as a classic serial and that my step-daughter-in-law, Serena Gordon, had a starring role as Emily's older sister, Caroline. An amazing coincidence!

Chapter One

March 1747

The storm arrived with shocking suddenness.

There had been little warning that the weather was to darken so dramatically. True, the early March air had been warm to the point of clamminess, but the temperature had been a delight after the previous chilly weeks. It was almost possible to believe in the arrival of spring. Also true was that the light had vanished early that day, but then the atmosphere was so often smoke ridden. The rooftop jumble that was the ever-growing, thrusting city of London sprouted chimney pots like an exuberant vegetable patch. They created a heavy pall that constantly veiled the sun and shrouded the streets.

Canaletto and his friend and colleague, Owen McSwiney, had set out dressed in their best. McSwiney, complaining endlessly of the rubbish-strewn streets and damage to the polish on his shoes, had wanted to travel by chair. Canaletto had insisted on walking. He watched every penny of expenditure with the care of a widow guarding her mites.

Canaletto also liked to see more than could be viewed from a chair's small windows. He was always eager to study the London scene, so very different from his native Venice. Here, down a side alley, for instance, was a gin shop. It had none of the cheerful bonhomie of a tavern or the sophisticated charm of a coffee house. Its customers sought no companionship, only the oblivion granted by cheap spirit. Canaletto stepped nimbly out of the way of a drunken fellow of disgusting appearance and unsteady gait only to collide with a woman whose breath reeked of the juniper-laced spirit. 'You're a pretty fellow,' she slurred at him. He tripped and nearly fell into the lane's drainage channel, loaded with the sordid detritus of city life, but her ample arms caught and cradled him. 'I'd be happy to service you,' she cooed into his ear. Canaletto's nose was in her cleavage, two swelling hills of flesh that reeked of offensive body odours. 'I like older men,' she added, narrowing her eyes suggestively.

Older men, indeed! Was fifty such an age? 'Begone, wench,' Canaletto spluttered as he struggled to disentangle himself.

McSwiney laughed. 'I'll wait,' he offered, leering suggestively.

Canaletto shot him a disgusted look, ignored the lewd words the woman sent after him and walked on.

It was a few minutes after that that the rain started. Fat drops began first to patter then to pour. Both men swore and ran for an arched passageway as the streets quickly emptied of homebound traffic.

'A pox on your English weather,' Canaletto cursed as muddy rain bounced off the dusty road and splashed his silk stockings. 'In Venice now sun and warmth. Why Canaletto stay here?'

'Because this is where your market is,' Owen McSwiney said jovially, slapping the painter on his slim shoulders with such force that Canaletto staggered against the dank stone of the passageway. 'Who was buying your paintings in Venice, eh?' Another encouraging blow to the shoulders.

The stone wall gave off a sour smell that reminded Canaletto forcibly of his old home. Nostalgia for the lambent light and faded splendours of Venice filled him and he felt afresh the worst of the grievances that he held against this tall Irishman.

'Four paintings I do since I come! Four in one year! In Venice in same time fifty, perhaps a hundred. Where are patrons and commissions you promise?' he grumbled. 'Cannot live with so little work.' Then he jumped as a fork of lightning cut through the driving rain and dramatically deepening darkness. It was followed by a clap of thunder that sounded as though buildings had collapsed. '*Dio mio*, what storm!' He looked anxiously at the ancient stones that sheltered them, took in the crumbling mortar as it was lit by more lightning. 'I think this not safe.' He would have gone out into the street, now aswirl with water, but McSwiney caught his sleeve.

'Don't be a fool! Do you want to drown? Or be ridden down?' Through the all-engulfing rain came the sound of a horse ridden hard. It swept by the entrance to their shelter, rider and mount blinded by the weather. It was as well all traffic had vanished, anything in their path would have been mown down.

'Tonio, be of good heart.' McSwiney still sounded in the best of moods. 'This storm will ease and we can be on our way. Soon we shall enjoy an evening of gaiety with your fellow painters. They have all been longing to meet you, why have you been so, so *reclusive*?'

'Reclusive?' Canaletto was flattered that McSwiney

felt they could talk together in English but would have been happier in his native Italian.

'You meet no one, go nowhere, do nothing!'

'I work!' Canaletto was irritated. Why hadn't McSwiney been working to find him commissions? What had he been up to? It was several weeks since Canaletto had finished his last painting. Since then he'd spent his time walking London, sketching buildings, the river and its traffic and the streets with their milling throngs of people, always assessing possible viewpoints, skylines, accessories. Later his capacious memory would hardly need his sketchbook to build one of his famous scenes in the studio. But for that there must first be a commission. Canaletto's funds were almost exhausted and he was beginning to feel desperation.

'Come, how is little Miss Fanny?' McSwiney said teasingly. 'You are comfortably situated there, I think?'

Canaletto felt a complex mixture of emotions. Anger that McSwiney should refer to his apprentice, Fanny Rooker, so, so slightingly, as though she was no more than a woman of the town, accommodating his demands, together with a familiar frustration that he had laid himself open to such a charge. But above all he was worried. For months he and Fanny had dealt famously together, yet now he hardly dared speak without her snapping back at him. What had happened?

Sheet lightning flashed, silvering the driving rain and illuminating the shuttered shops opposite the entrance to their shelter with an eerie brilliance. Automatically Canaletto noted details of the carving on the lintel above one of the doors, then staggered backwards

4

as a small flood swept into the passage. He couldn't afford to have his shoes ruined by the swirling, refuse-laden water.

One of his heels met an obstruction and he staggered, saving himself from falling by clutching at the damp wall. As automatically as he had noticed the carving on the lintel, Canaletto's mind registered that whatever had snagged his heel had a give, a softness that said it couldn't be a piece of wood or brick or a stone outcrop of the wall.

Another flash of lightning. This far down the passageway the light was diluted to little more than a candle beam but it was enough. Canaletto could see the crumpled figure of a woman.

Holding the skirts of his best velvet coat around his waist, Canaletto crouched. Darkness once again engulfed the scene. All he'd registered was the form of a female body huddled against the base of the wall, as though the woman had lacked the will or the energy to remain upright. Was she drunk? Sleeping herself to sobriety? But there was no sound of drunken, stertorous breathing.

He bent nearer, trying to catch a sound of life over the beat of the rain and the menacing rumble of thunder.

There was nothing.

Canaletto slid out a nervous hand. Her hair was abundant and felt simply arranged. Around the neck was a soft kerchief. His sensitive fingers groped for a pulse below the ear and could find none.

'Owen,' Canaletto called, his voice high and nervous. 'Here!'

Behind him he heard McSwiney cautiously ease his way along the dark passage.

Then another great flash of lightning lit the scene just long enough for Canaletto to see the woman's face.

'Good God!' It was McSwiney's voice, deeply shocked. 'What the devil!'

Once again they were in darkness but Canaletto knew he'd hold the memory of that face until the day he died.

She'd been young, maybe even comely, before she'd met evil in this cold, sepulchral passageway. Now her face was a ruin, slashed from either side of the wide, staring eyes to the corners of once soft lips, and again down from the small nose to the same corners of the mouth. Blood dripped from the cuts. Canaletto registered that it was only drips, not a flood.

He slipped his hand down the slight figure, encountering whaleboning beneath cheap cloth. Then he met sticky wetness below the left breast, a breast that still swelled with lost promise.

Canaletto found a handkerchief in his coat pocket and wiped his fingers. 'Stabbed,' he said in a neutral voice. 'Someone stab her here then he do that, that vileness to her face. After death do it.' Automatically he scanned the darkness. Did the perpetrator of this foul deed still linger?

Chapter Two

A frustrated Fanny Rooker lit a rushlight at the small fire in the corner of the studio. It wasn't often she had the chance to work at her painting uninterrupted by Canaletto's unceasing demands; why had it got dark so early?

She put the tall candle holder on the long trestle table that ran down one wall and watched its flickering light throw shadows across her painting. It was an attempt at the frontage of the Silver Street lodgings where Canaletto had his rooms and studio. The windows of the building were large, arranged across each of the four floors, and the brick was almost yellow. She had tried to make the most of both of these features. What would Canaletto think of his apprentice's effort?

Fanny kicked her stool in sudden temper. What was the use of wondering what Canaletto thought? She couldn't remember the last time he'd taken an interest in her progress. Had he forgotten she was his apprentice?

She walked around the whitewashed studio in a temper. Masters were supposed to teach their apprentices in exchange for their work. She worked for him all right, everywhere was evidence of her efforts. Lumps of colour were neatly arranged in their small bags, ready to be ground for pigment, first in the bronze mortar with its pestle that stood at the end of the table, then crushed even finer on the slab of porphyry with the glass maler, gradually mixing in the oil until her exhausted arm produced paint smooth enough to satisfy Canaletto's critical standards.

There were the bottles of linseed, olive and walnut oils that were used as the painting media. Fanny wrinkled her nose as she thought of the smell that accompanied the long heating needed to refine them down. Brushes, arranged as to size, stood upright in pottery jars. There were brushes of delicate miniver and squirrel hairs together with those of the more robust hog's hair; all had been checked and were ready for use. A box held sections of quill from various birds in a variety of sizes, all ready for when a new holder was needed for the hairs. A range of knives was to hand, from large to small, all honed ready to cut canvas, chop pigment, sharpen pens or blend pigment with oil.

Canaletto's palette was cleaned and waiting, as was his painting stick, which helped steady his hand as he applied the oils. Over a peg on the door hung his smock, as clean as Fanny could make it; even she couldn't remove all the smudges of paint that so liberally decorated its front. On the easel, protected by a cloth, stood a canvas, primed and base-painted, first in red, then in beige, the way he liked.

The canvas had been prepared in anticipation of another commission from Canaletto's new patron, Sir Hugh Smithson. Sir Hugh had been mightily pleased with the two paintings he'd commanded, particularly the view of Windsor. Fanny herself had preferred the lord mayor's procession on the Thames. Was it because of the fun of the gaily coloured boats that crowded the river scene, or because she'd actually been allowed to paint in the basic shapes of a few of the smaller ones?

She'd been so excited.

Canaletto had watched her prime her brush with dark paint, had gently put his hand over her trembling one. 'Very gently, very softly, little at a time,' he'd said quietly. 'Paint must be fine, very thin, very smooth. Not great slashes, not thick.'

The sound of his voice had quietened her, the trembling had stopped and she'd been able to stroke in the background of first one, then two little boats. No one but the two of them would know that they hadn't been painted by the master. But Fanny didn't need public recognition. It had been enough that Canaletto had felt she was worthy of even a tiny bit of one of his canvases.

'Hmm,' he'd said as she finished the first little shape. 'You progress, Fanny, you progress.'

She'd hugged the words to herself for days afterwards. They were worth all the drudgery of preparing pigments, refining oils, bargaining with suppliers, not to mention the housework that also had to be done.

With those two tiny boats she'd felt that she'd graduated onto a different level of apprenticeship, that the day mightn't be too far away when Canaletto would maybe trust her to paint in background water or some other minor detail of one of his works whilst he concentrated on more important effects.

But that was before he'd become so difficult. Before matters progressed to the stage she hardly dared address a word to him in case it brought a sarcastic remark, or be dismissed with a disdainful flick of his hand. Oh, the expressiveness of those graceful hands!

Still on the wall were pinned the sketches he'd made for his last painting, the one of Windsor. Fanny had had nothing to do with that one. No, while Canaletto had painted, she had cooked their meals and mended his shirts! Even after he'd finished the picture, there had apparently been no time to instruct her in technique.

'Fanny?' The studio door opened without so much as a knock and Betty Spragg entered. 'I thought as how Donald is out this evening, you and me might drink some mulled ale together,' she said. 'I heard Signor Canaletto go out, I'd not presume else.' There was a sly look as she said this.

'I'm free of an evening at any time, Mrs Spragg,' Fanny said brightly, trying not to remember the times when Canaletto had taught her to play cards, talked of his life in Venice or allowed himself to be coached in English, merry flames leaping from the fire. Before Christmas they'd roasted chestnuts in a small brass pan, the nuts leaping noisily inside. Fanny had burned her fingers and Canaletto had been all concern, anointing them with butter.

It seemed a long time since they'd been comfortable with each other in that way.

Betty Spragg had a way of hovering that suggested she had only alighted beside you for a moment, like a butterfly on a leaf; her little feet seemed about to dance away, her hands fluttered. 'Well then, girl, do you come? Or can you not drag yourself away from your little kingdom here?' Betty's tone expressed perfectly what she thought of Fanny's domain. Her glance took in its ordered simplicity. Was it Fanny's imagination or did her eyes linger on the little bed that stood not far from the fire? If they did, it wasn't long before she was looking at the shrouded canvas. 'Started another painting, has he?'

Fanny recognized purpose behind the casual remark. Daniel Spragg made a good living as a cabinet maker but his income was greatly increased by the letting out of the upper floors of the handsome building that had his workshop on the ground floor and the studio in the garden behind.

Income that no doubt had paid for the new dress of sprigged muslin Betty wore this evening, the latest fashion, with fine ruffles at the elbows. Fanny wondered that her landlady should have donned such splendour to mull ale with the painter's apprentice. But Betty had recently acquired a small maid of all work, perhaps she was at a loss to know how to amuse herself with her husband out on the town with friends.

No, Betty would not be pleased if Canaletto failed to pay the rent on time. Fanny had seen the way her fingers closed over coins and the look she gave them. It was the sort of look Canaletto reserved for his precious paints. Charity was not a close companion of Betty Spragg's. If the rent couldn't be paid, all her friendliness would vanish and Canaletto and Fanny would be out. Then where would they go? Where could they find equally comfortable and suitable accommodation?

'Mr McSwiney takes care in selecting Signor Canaletto's next commission,' she said airily, wishing she had any confidence in the tall Irishman's ability to produce the work that was so urgently needed. Too fond of his alcohol, his playgoing and his cards to worry about what should be his main concern. After all, Fanny had no doubt but that he took a generous cut of Canaletto's fee, if and when it was paid.

'Of course, my dear. Wouldn't do to let any Jim-cum-easily worm a valuable painting from your famous signor. And there are such up-jumps around these days, more money than sensibility,' Betty said smoothly, never lost for a word or phrase. A dainty hand twitched at her apron, which, like the scarf that veiled the swell of her breasts, looked freshly put on. The smile which constantly played on her lips deepened and a dimple appeared in one plump cheek. 'My Daniel has just been asked to make a secretaire for one of the gentry in Golden Square, 'twill not be the last from that quarter, I fancy. No parvenus there, all such smart and settled folk. This is a diplomatic gentleman,' she preened, giving Fanny another of the flashing smiles that never seemed to light up her chill, grey eyes.

Canaletto had told Fanny that the nearness of the Spraggs' accommodation to Golden Square had been one of the reasons for choosing the lodgings. 'Not area where patrons live but area where patrons not reluctant to come,' he'd explained.

But Sir Hugh Smithson was the only patron who had found his way to Silver Street and it had been a long time since Canaletto had suggested meat pies for their dinner. Indeed, the amount of money he gave Fanny for the housekeeping had dwindled week by week over the last couple of months. She'd grown used to bargaining with the friendly butcher round the corner for scrag ends of meat and begging leftover vegetables from the market.

'I'll be with you directly, Mrs Spragg,' Fanny said

firmly. 'A gossip this evening will be most pleasant and I thank you for the invitation.'

'I'll be mightily pleased to see you. I'll set the ale a-warming right now with my own mix of spices. 'Tis a chill evening and a storm on the way I wouldn't wonder.' With a last, lingering, possessive look around the studio, Betty Spragg left.

Fanny found a clean muslin scarf in the small box that sat at the foot of the narrow bed. Newly ironed, it didn't fold as neatly as she liked. Her fingers twitched impatiently at the material and she failed to be soothed by its fresh-air smell, washed and dried as it had been in the yard outside the studio.

Fanny sighed as she fastened the clasp that held it in place over her small breasts. There was no point in worrying too much about her appearance. She had no illusions about her looks, plain she was born and plain she'd die, that was for sure. She smoothed down her skirts, found a clean apron, tied that neatly round her waist, and allowed herself a moment's complacency. Her skin might be freckled, her hair ginger, her mouth too large and her bosom too small but at least her waist was tiny.

As she snuffed out the rush light, a flash lit the darkness. Fanny jumped, then put her hands over her ears as the thunder came. Heavy drops of rain resounded on the roof. Fanny hated the thought of crossing the small area between the studio and the Spraggs' house – suppose she was to be struck by lightning?

Another flash of lightning almost convinced Fanny to remain where she was, until she realized how much she hated the thought of staying alone in the empty studio for the rest of the evening.

Once the place had held such promise, such excitement. Now it seemed all she was allowed to do there were menial tasks. The arrangement between Canaletto and herself had been unofficial, no papers signed, no money paid to him, but surely she paid for her tuition in other ways?

Neatly folded in a corner of the studio was a piece of sacking, remnant of some packing. Fanny snatched it up, held it over her head and dashed across the yard to the small flight of stairs that led to the Spraggs' private quarters. Blinded by the sacking and the driving rain, she crashed into the back of a man with all the force of a barrel into a beer cellar.

Fanny clutched at his coat to keep her balance. 'I'm sorry, sir, the rain!' she gasped.

The door opened and he pushed her inside. 'Apologies can wait,' he said. 'My coat must be drenched.'

There was hardly room in the tiny space at the bottom of the narrow staircase that twisted its way up the house for the man, Fanny and Betty Spragg's hesitant little maid, Jenny, all to stand together.

'Cursed weather,' complained the visitor, splashing Fanny with water from his broad tricorne. 'Well, girl, are we to stand here all evening?'

Jenny coloured and gave a quick dip of her knees. 'M-m-mistress says to come upstairs,' she stammered.

'Lead away, then!'

Nimbly Jenny went up the steep steps. There was no doubt who followed her first. No doubt any man with so fine a coat would take precedence and Fanny found it no slight that he went ahead of her. The only light came from a dim lantern on the stairs and Jenny's candle. It flickered as she climbed, throwing weird shadows, but Fanny could see that the coat was cut in the newest style, its skirts full and stiffened. There were silver buckles on his shoes and his wig was the neat peruke that the most fashionable men favoured, not the old-fashioned, full-bottomed version older men so often preferred. Yet his voice had had the bluffness of a trader rather than the smoothness of a man of gentle breeding.

'Why, Mrs Spragg,' he said, all warmth and expectation, as he reached the tiny first-floor landing, 'how good of you to receive me thus.'

'This is Mister, this is Mister,' the hapless Jenny said. 'Nay, I have forgot the name,' she added dolefully. Then brightened as Fanny came up. 'Mistress Rooker,' she ended thankfully.

'Thank you, Jenny, that will do,' Betty said sharply. The girl ducked behind Fanny and fled down the stairs, the candle spluttering and leaving a trail of smoke.

'Sir, may I introduce Miss Fanny Rooker?' said Betty with a nervous smile. 'Fanny, this is Mr Jonathan Wright.' He turned, displaying a jutting chin and slightly beaky nose. He looked well over forty.

Fanny dipped in acknowledgement of the introduction; Mr Wright gave her a slight nod of his head, a nod that signified she could be nobody of importance.

'Mr Wright is to order a table from Daniel,' Betty said. She'd led them into the small room on the first floor she and Daniel used for sitting, though there were few occasions the busy cabinet maker had time for idleness. Sconces on the wall and a three-branched candelabra on a candle table gave welcoming light. Three

15

straight-backed chairs had been placed ready. Heating on a trivet by the corner fire was a jug and a tray with three pewter mugs sat on a small, tilt-topped table. The only other furniture in the room was a remarkably fine cabinet.

Betty bustled around, commanding them to sit, saying she had mulled ale at the ready, complaining about the storm that had so suddenly arisen. As she attended to the drink, Jonathan Wright inspected the workmanship of the cabinet with its breakfront cupboard set atop a chest of drawers. The doors each carried a panel of mirror-style walnut veneer. One stood open, revealing sets of movable small shelves and slots to hold papers.

'Mr Wright has recently taken a house in Golden Square,' Betty proclaimed proudly as she handed first him and then Fanny a mug of warm, spiced ale. 'He is a hosier with a large business and has removed here from Derbyshire.'

Something in the set of his shoulders told Fanny that Mr Jonathan Wright was not amused at this artless outpouring of information.

'Now we are comfortable,' added Betty as her two guests sat themselves on the chairs.

Fanny felt her situation was awkward. Instead of acting as some earpiece for Betty, a convenient recipient of her plans for Daniel's advancement or her views on a new play, she found herself an unregarded third.

'And how is dear Mrs Wright?' enquired Betty, as though the woman was a close friend.

Fanny found it difficult to believe that Betty could be intimately acquainted with any inhabitant of

Golden Square. It was the home of diplomats, minor society and those with wealth if not necessarily society connections. Her artist's eye noted the ordinary line of his cheekbones and the dissipated pouches under the watery blue eyes that weakened the impact of his beaky nose and jutting chin, all was such a contrast to Canaletto's neat features, his hazel eyes that saw everything and his finely shaped mouth.

'Mrs Wright fares somewhat better, I thank you, Mrs Spragg. We have hopes her ague will soon be gone.' He glanced in Fanny's direction and she had a definite sense he was surprised to find she sat there.

'She must enjoy so the luxury of life in Golden Square, such spaciousness, such salubriety, such modishness!' Betty's hands fluttered at the wonder of it all.

Jonathan Wright shifted his legs. 'Aye, she likes it well enough,' he said bluntly then deliberately turned towards Fanny. 'And what be Miss Rooker's concern, other, that is, than hurtling into strangers?'

'Hurtling? Hurtling? Why, Fanny, what is this?'

'It was the rain,' Fanny said pleasantly, refusing to allow herself to feel set upon. 'I ran that I should not become wet.'

'You arrived from nowhere,' Jonathan Wright said aggressively. 'Not from the street as I did.' He made it sound a criminal act.

'Miss Rooker assists Signor Canaletto, the great Italian painter, and his studio is in our yard,' Betty said, showing evident pride in her tenant's stature. 'Fanny and I are such friends.' She gave Fanny a speaking look, one that said they knew all each other's secrets.

Fanny stiffened.

'Famous Italian painter, eh?' Jonathan Wright said

17

in a considering manner. 'Perhaps I may be needing a work to adorn the walls of my new drawing room. I may well patronize your master,' he said to Fanny.

'All the great aristocrats have paintings by Signor Canaletto,' she said with dignity. 'He is the height of fashion.'

Betty rose and went over to the cabinet. 'Signor Canaletto greatly admires Mr Spragg's work, I assure you, sir. Now, I will show you Daniel's portentous designs for your table. Mr Spragg is sorry not to be here this evening himself but there are so many demands on his time.'

Demands on his time? Daniel had gone carousing with friends, an often indulged pleasure and hardly something to keep him from attending on a valued client.

'Designs?' queried Mister Wright as though nothing had been further from his mind. 'Ah, yes, Mrs Spragg, the designs.' His voice was colourless, he glanced at Fanny. 'I am anxious to see them,' he said with more animation. 'If the work proceeds as well as I've been led to hope, it's possible I may be able to put some additional business Mr Spragg's way.' He stood a little taller, his chest filling out. 'I am, you know, a governor of the Foundling Hospital.' He paused, as though expecting some comment. None came. 'The first building is completed but the second will soon be commenced and there will be numerous items to be commissioned by way of tables, chairs, benches and the like.'

'Foundling Hospital?' said Fanny, feeling bound to say something as Betty appeared strangely reluctant to explain that Daniel was a master craftsman who would not be interested in such business. 'I know nothing of such a place.'

'Indeed not? I am surprised. It is a charity of the highest social standing. Dukes, earls and others are amongst the governors. It was a mark of the greatest respect that I was elected to their number.' Again the puffing out of the chest.

'Oh, it is of all things commendable, I'm sure,' Betty said.

'And the foundlings, where do they come from?' asked Fanny.

'Why, they are the poor, the deprived, the flotsam and jetsam of London life, and not only of London, many come from further afield,' said Jonathan Wright, his voice sonorous. 'We offer these desperate babes a secure future, provided they are healthy enough,' he added hastily.

'I've heard that some high-born ladies take advantage of your handsomeness to hide their peccadilloes in your portals,' fluttered Betty.

Mr Wright's nostrils flared. 'Upon my word, what a calumny! Put about such lies and slanders and our charitable funds will dry up, dear lady.'

'Oh, dear sir, I'm sure I meant no such thing, just a story, no doubt floated by some malefactor. Now, let me show you the designs. I declare Fanny, Miss Rooker, will be wondering else what we are about.'

As Betty opened a drawer, took out a sheaf of papers and brought them over to her husband's client, Fanny caught a look that passed between the two of them. It was challenge on her part, grim understanding on his.

And suddenly Fanny saw why she had been invited

along. This was a rendezvous. An occasion for the client to dally with the wife whilst the husband was away. But for some reason Betty had deliberately asked Fanny to play gooseberry.

Fanny's opinion of Betty Spragg, never very high, fell even further. Jonathan Wright was not a man to stand for such a game as this.

Chapter Three

Canaletto couldn't believe he'd heard Owen McSwiney aright. 'Go to Artists' Club? Now, after this?' He would have gestured towards the pitiful figure on the ground but the dark made such a move useless. Then a long flash of lightning lit the mutilated face and Canaletto just caught the other man's shrug.

'Is there life in her? No! So, what can we do?'

'But,' started Canaletto. Used as he was to McSwiney's cavalier attitude to life, he was still startled that he could propose to walk away from this pathetic remnant of a woman.

'Pshaw, man, what's a dead doxy? If you worried about every lifeless corpse you encountered in London's alleyways, you'd have no time for living. I fell over an infant's body only the other day.'

The sound of the pounding rain outside their sheltering arch beat upon Canaletto's mind. It was true, death was an all too common phenomenon. Sad bundles of rags that revealed themselves to be covering the last vestiges of some poor soul were frequently encountered in the stinking stewpots of London's worse areas. And it wasn't always disease or homelessness that carried them off. Violence could erupt at any time and even when the officers of the watch arrived

on the scene, they were usually powerless to prevent the inevitable result.

Another long flash of sheet lightning illuminated something Canaletto had missed. He bent down and felt the girl's hand. She couldn't have been dead long, her flesh wasn't yet waxy. Thunder cracked and rolled right overhead, making him jump. The right hand was curled into a fist. Gently he straightened the unresisting fingers, noting the lack of calluses, the neat fingernails. She'd been holding a scrap of paper. Hopeless to try and discern whether it contained writing so Canaletto slipped it in his pocket. Then he managed to remove the ring that had glinted in the lightning flash as though it was made of gold. 'See, McSwiney, ring!'

'I cannot see anything in this cursed night. Cease your wretched obsession with that damned body, Tonio.'

'This not robbery or ring be taken. This some, some damned crime.' Damned wasn't the right word. What with the pounding of the rain and the outrage he felt, Canaletto's English was deserting him. He took a deep breath and switched to Italian, reaching for McSwiney's arm, sinewy and tough beneath the velvet of his coat. 'My friend, admit this is a dastardly killing. Someone used a knife on this poor girl. Then mutilated her face.'

'So, she cheated some client and he took his revenge! Probably diseased, certainly after his money. Why should we worry?' McSwiney's Italian was fluent, the product of several years living in Venice. 'Come, the rain is lessening, let us leave this noisome pit and find some civilized entertainment.' His rich voice, his Irish accent that heightened Italian's musical cadence, was soothing.

22

Canaletto wanted to be soothed. There was little in his life that was going well at the moment and the present situation offered increasing discomfort. Rainwater was running around his shoes, cold was seeping into his bones and an unusually strong smell of rotting ordure was beginning to overpower his senses. More than anything he wanted to get away from this impromptu morgue.

Yet he couldn't just leave the huddled, abused body for the dogs to nose at, some beggar to strip off her clothes for profit and heaven knew what other indignity to befall her before a reluctant authority took action. 'Find Watch!' he said obdurately, switching back to English.

McSwiney sighed with exasperation. 'What an obstinate Venetian you are!' He edged cautiously out of the arch. The thunder was now rumbling some distance away, the rain was lessening and a grey light was replacing the extreme darkness. 'I'll search out the officer of the Watch,' he said resignedly.

Canaletto waited by the body, feeling the damp seep through the stonework. He peered out of the other end of the passageway. As far as he could see in the dim light, it led into a courtyard lined with tenement buildings of the most mean sort. In the centre of the courtyard there seemed to be a midden heap, piled with refuse that was obviously the source of the appalling odour. Had the girl lived here? Or was it sheer coincidence she had met her end in this place?

The passageway seemed to Canaletto a no man's land between two worlds; one where mankind at least

23

pretended a respect for others, and this dark and seamy underworld where at any moment life could be lost to an assassin's knife or, at the very least, your purse to a footpad. Canaletto was a small, slight man whose weapon of choice was a paintbrush. Amongst the low life of Venice, he had learned to melt into the background, to appear a figure of no account. This evening, dressed in his best clothes and armed only with a dress sword, he felt very vulnerable.

Something rustled in the passageway. He whirled, only to see in the dim, grey light a huge rat scampering past him. He knew he had been right to insist on finding the Watch. Leave the girl's body here and who knew what rats would gnaw on her remains. Just under a year ago, on his arrival in London, Canaletto had been attacked and left for dead in an area very like this. Then it had been brave Fanny who had guarded his unconscious body.

Canaletto suddenly realized why he was concerning himself so with this poor corpse. It could have been Fanny lying there. She never worried about dangers as she darted about London on his errands. She claimed she could look after herself.

Now Canaletto was seized with something like panic. If it had been Fanny who had been murdered, how would he be able to continue in this town that was so different from Venice, where he knew so few people? All at once the breakdown of their relationship hit him even harder. Why had Fanny lost her quick, cheerful smile?

'Here we are, did you think I was lost?' McSwiney's tall figure loomed out of the dirty grey light. He was followed by a small, stooped and wizened man with a face like a walnut beneath an aged and broad-brimmed hat that looked as though only the dirt was holding it together. His coat was capacious; so capacious he seemed lost in its folds, but the cloth was worn to the threads. He carried a sturdy stave twice his height in a hand that seemed too frail to wield it to any purpose. In his other hand was a lantern that shone with a light as feeble as the old man himself.

'A body, you say?' he wheezed.

Canaletto, speechless at this apparition of the law, pointed to the dead girl.

Arthritic joints creaked as the man bent to examine the dead girl.

'This can't be the Watch,' Canaletto said to McSwiney in Italian. 'He has not enough breath left in his body to accost a criminal, let alone arrest him.'

'I can only agree with you, Tonio, but such remnants of life are all the parish can afford to employ even though the pay is miserly.'

'I am amazed they will take the job if the wage is indeed so low. The dangers must be considerable.'

'At least it keeps them from the workhouse and most of them learn quickly enough that there is little they can do if villainy comes their way.'

'She's dead, masters,' the wavering voice said in a tone that suggested he had made a great discovery.

'Indeed,' McSwiney said jovially. 'That is why we brought you here.'

'And do you know the malefactor? If so, I can report him to the magistrate. Then he will conduct an examination of the facts.' Once the man must have had some smattering of education, now Canaletto doubted he had wits enough to apprehend a child stealing a kitten.

'We know nothing,' he said roughly.

'Her name, do you know that?'

'No.'

'Don't know her name, don't know who killed her. How do you expect us to proceed?' The man had placed his lantern on the ground and leant his stave against the stone wall. Now he felt the dead girl's clothing, patting the folds of skirt, feeling round the waist. 'No purse, probably killed for that. Clear case of theft followed by murder.' The wavery voice was stronger now.

'Would a petty thief bother to knife his victim?' asked McSwiney.

'Oh, sirs, some be foolish enough to withstand the assault, to fight. Such be this poor girl, I think. Look how her face was scratched.'

'Not scratching,' Canaletto almost shouted. 'Knife do that after death.'

'Say you so?' the officer ruminated. 'Couldn't tell that myself.'

'You will question those who live around here?' Canaletto asked with no great hopes.

'Question?' quavered the officer. 'Who, sir, should we question? One of life's poor wretches she was, few will mourn her passing.'

Anger built in Canaletto at the careless way this girl's death was dismissed. What if it had been Fanny lying there? He felt for the ring he had removed. 'Her clothes poor but, look, she had this!' He held it out to the officer. 'A thief take this, I think.'

The man hauled himself to his feet by clawing at the stonework. The lantern was picked up. 'Ring, is it, sir? You'd best give it here.' He held out a hand that was grimed and trembling. Reluctantly Canaletto placed the little band of gold on the dirty palm.

The officer inspected the ring carefully in the light of his lantern and drew in his breath as three small blue stones set in the metal winked at him. After a couple of attempts, he managed to slip it into a pocket of his heavy overcoat.

'Her hands not hands of poor woman. Her hair, her skin, that of woman of quality.'

'Didn't you say you knew nothing of her?' the officer asked suspiciously.

'Use eyes! All there to be seen. Look, must look!' Canaletto was exasperated.

'We knows our job,' the man said stubbornly.

'Quite,' McSwiney said hastily. 'And my friend and I will leave you to it.' He grabbed Canaletto's arm and started to pull him away.

Canaletto wrenched his arm free. 'Your direction?' he demanded of the officer before McSwiney could force him away from the scene.

'My direction? As to that, masters, you can apply at the magistrate's house in Bow Street. Any information will be there.'

Canaletto was very tired as he entered Daniel Spragg's Silver Street house and started to climb the twisting stairs to his lodgings on the third floor. After McSwiney had finally dragged him away from the mutilated body, Canaletto had been shocked to realize the Irishman still intended to visit the Artists' Club. He had refused to accompany him. McSwiney had cursed his bad temper and then gone off there on his own and would no doubt regale them all with this evening's tale.

Canaletto was still angry at the other man's lack of sensitivity. Between that and his exhaustion, he failed to hear little Jenny's steps coming down the stairs. She, too, apparently had her mind on other matters for they collided and the tray and basin she was carrying clattered down, spraying water. Canaletto, apologizing profusely, helped Jenny to pick up the broken basin and the tray, then realized he also had hold of a bloody rag. He peered at the thankfully few splashes that had landed on him. His dark brown velvet coat, bought with the proceeds of his last painting and the colour chosen to wear well, showed nothing more than a slight additional dampness, but the muslin ruffles at the end of his shirt sleeves, nicely displayed by the broad cuffs of the coat, were marred with spots of pink.

'There has been an accident?' he enquired politely, fastidiously placing the bloody cloth back on the tray.

Jenny's face in the flickering rushlight was worried, but then she lived life in a constant state of anxiety. With the way that Betty Spragg continually shouted at her, it was a wonder the girl had any wits left. Now Jenny clutched the tray even tighter. 'No, sir, no! That is to say, Mrs Spragg, she says it was nothing. And I wouldn't know, I wasn't there. All I did was show them in.'

'Show who in?' Canaletto enquired, now intrigued.

'Why Miss Fanny and the gentleman. I always forget his name. I was sure Mrs Spragg would be letting me know my stupidity. But when she shouted for me, it wasn't for that.' She suddenly clamped her mouth shut, looked down at her burden and said in a rush, 'Thank you, sir, and there's nothing I've said I'm sure that could be held against me and I'll be obliged if I can go down.'

Canaletto stood aside and let her pass, then followed her downstairs and went outside to the studio. For a moment he hesitated, then saw a shadow pass behind the curtained window. Fanny hadn't yet gone to bed. Would she greet him with curt words? Should he leave this until the morning? But too many questions were hammering inside his head; he needed to talk to someone and Fanny had been such a good listener.

He knocked gently on the door of the studio then entered.

Fanny was walking down the length of the room, her back to him, her steps hurried, as though she would rid herself of disturbed thoughts through exercise. A rushlight stood on the long trestle table, spilling a small pool of gold onto the scrubbed wood but making little impression on the shadows that crowded the corners of the large room.

Then she swung round, saw him and hurried back, her hands reaching out. 'Oh, signor, I am so pleased to see you!'

At the warmth of her voice, Canaletto felt as though an invisible burden had been lifted from his shoulders. For an instant he forgot about the body he'd found earlier that evening as he took her hands in his. He was shocked at how cold they were and started to rub them gently between his. 'Why, Fanny, what is matter?'

With the wayward light behind her, he couldn't see her eyes clearly, only that they seemed larger than usual. She clutched at his hands, 'Oh, it's been such an evening! First the mulled ale with Mrs Spragg and that man being there, then my leaving and then, and then . . . Oh, signor, she blames me for it all!'

'Come, sit and tell me slowly. You know, my English not good, you must speak very plain.' It wasn't often Canaletto could bring himself to suggest his understanding of the English language could be less than perfect. He drew out a couple of stools from beneath the trestle table, sat her on one and took the other himself. 'Now, little Fanny, you tell me, yes, this thing that has happened?' It was no doubt some stupid misunderstanding on the part of the supremely silly Mrs Betty Spragg.

With hesitations, stops and starts, Fanny related her story.

As he managed to piece together the ridiculous tale, Canaletto relaxed. 'Dear Fanny,' he said as she stopped for breath after explaining how she had left the small party. 'This nothing to concern you. Mrs Spragg be very silly, you do right thing.'

'No, sir,' Fanny's mouth trembled, 'you haven't heard all. After I came back here, I was so cross. With Betty Spragg for being so idiotish, with myself for accepting her invitation, only, only I was glad of the company,' her voice caught and Canaletto suddenly realized that his competent, busy Fanny could be lonely. 'Well, anyway, I went, more fool me. And, as I said, I left them to it. Which I should not have done.'

'But what has happened?' Canaletto said impatiently, his sympathy dissolving into irritation. Why couldn't the girl tell her tale?

Fanny had recovered much of her equanimity. She sat straight on her stool. 'I was in here, thinking I should go to bed but not yet ready, when there came a scream. The storm had passed, it was quiet outside, no criers, no traffic, no drunken merrymakers, so it came clear as clear and I was sure it was Betty who screamed so.'

'Indeed,' murmured Canaletto, reminded of the basin filled with bloody water. 'So what did you do?'

'Why, I ran across,' said Fanny simply, as though anyone would have done the same.

'And found?'

'Mr Wright rushing down the stairs. He pushed his way past me, as though I was some piece of dirt.' Fanny was indignant at the memory. 'But that is his manner. I think in his estimation, everyone in the world is less than Mr Wright, unless it might be the king. Or you, sir! He was mightily interested to learn you had your studio here, I think he seeks a work for his walls in Golden Square.'

A hosier! A dealer in stockings and underwear! Canaletto could think of few patrons who would do his cause less good. He would have to be approaching destitution before he accepted a commission from such a one, even if his prices could be afforded. 'So you went to Mrs Spragg,' he prompted Fanny, fearing the light would expire before they had the full story.

'Oh, signor! She was on the floor, blood flowing from her cheek. He had hit her and his ring had cut to the bone, so hard he'd struck.'

Canaletto had a sudden vision of a powerful man backhanding the face of a woman who had made him look a fool. Such things happened every day, many men were predisposed to violence when thwarted. A shiver ran through his slight frame as he remembered the violated face of the murdered woman.

'I helped her to a chair and tried to staunch the flow

with my scarf.' Fanny looked down at her hands, the fingers linking and unlinking.

Canaletto noted that the neck of Fanny's light wool gown was bare, revealing the vulnerable curve of a small bosom.

'She pushed me away. She was hysterical, shouting that the fault was mine, that had I stayed, Wright would have left. She fell to cursing. She has always sounded so proper before! Then she said she could not abide the sight of me.' Fanny's voice wobbled for a moment. 'Jenny had come, so I left her. Oh, sir, what if she gives us notice?'

Canaletto took her hands again in his, feeling the strong, supple fingers that were learning to apply paint in a way that promised well. 'Fanny,' he said in a stern voice that had her raise her head in surprise, 'you very silly! More silly than I, who expect all women to be silly, would expect. No one gives Antonio da Canal the notice to go!' he said grandly. 'Better we go ourselves. Not only studio in London.' He glanced at his surroundings, knowing that the last thing he wanted was to find himself other lodgings. 'But Mrs Spragg not landlord. I talk to Daniel, he master of house.'

Fanny's face showed how little she agreed with this.

'Anyway,' Canaletto added quickly, 'Betty better off than poor woman McSwiney and I found tonight, dead in passageway.' He launched into an account of his evening. Soon it was clear that Fanny's horror at what he had to tell had driven out her concern regarding Betty Spragg.

'So, you see, violent men everywhere take revenge on women.'

'You think this woman was murdered for some cause?'

Canaletto shrugged. 'Of course! Why else her face marked so?'

'How, exactly, was it cut?' Fanny asked slowly.

Canaletto reached inside the skirts of his coat and removed his sketchbook from the back pocket. He reached for a lead stylo from the drawing implements on the table and quickly drew the dead girl's face. His memory, always capable of retaining what he saw, had no trouble at all in recalling every line.

Fanny drew a sharp breath as she saw him draw in the slashes from the temples and nose to the corners of the mouth. 'You say these cuts were made after he'd killed her?'

Canaletto nodded. 'He stab her first.' He demonstrated and Fanny drew back sharply as the lead threatened her ribs. 'Clean, quick, not much blood. Then, he cut her face so.' He tapped the sketch. 'Again, little blood so she must be dead. Bodies do not bleed when dead.'

'How strange,' Fanny mused, looking at the sketch. 'I'd have thought the blood would pour out whether alive or dead.'

'Not so,' Canaletto said positively.

Fanny traced the slashes with her finger, down from the temple to the mouth, up to the nose, down again and finally another up stroke. 'It's almost as though he drew a W. What does it mean?'

Canaletto shrugged. 'Do not know. Maybe he sign his work?' He suddenly remembered the piece of paper he'd removed from the dead girl's hand, felt in his pocket and brought it out. It was a corner of a larger piece, probably a letter. 'This evening' was on one line with 'help you' beneath. The other side was blank. He handed it to Fanny, 'Was in her hand,' he said. 'Maybe it had directions for meeting. Maybe killer don't want it found.'

'You think he tried to take it from her but she was holding it so tightly, it tore?'

Canaletto, as so often before, admired the quickness of Fanny's mind.

'The hand is educated,' she added, studying the words again.

Canaletto nodded. He stood up, feeling very tired now. 'In morning I see officer of Watch, maybe he have information, her name.'

Fanny looked doubtful.

Canaletto looked at his soiled ruffles. 'And in morning you clean shirt, yes?'

'No,' said Fanny firmly.

Canaletto was astounded. 'No?'

'No, not unless you give me proper lessons in painting.'

Canaletto was outraged. Who did this girl think she was? He saw the determination in her face, the way her arms were crossed, the belligerence in her stance. He realized he was too tired to deal with such insubordination now.

'In morning we talk,' he said, trying to sound determined and in command.

'Fine,' was all Fanny said. She remained standing, confronting him.

Canaletto sighed, went out without another word and climbed the stairs to his rooms, wondering whether a night's sleep would bring him the energy to deal with what faced him in the morning.

Chapter Four

Dawn edged itself circumspectly round the generous windows of the boys' dormitory at the Foundling Hospital.

Charles Lennox, six and three-quarter years old, known to his fellow foundlings as Charlie, slipped out of the bed he shared with another boy and hurriedly dressed. Willy turned over but didn't wake. No one in the big room stirred. Carrying his shoes, Charlie walked on tiptoe out of the room and down the stairs. Not for the first time, he glanced regretfully at the narrow rail fastened just above the broad surface of the banisters. Without it, sliding down would have been such a quick and easy way to reach the bottom.

As he descended, Charlie looked nervously around. His bottom still smarted from the thrashing he'd got the previous day after he'd challenged William Beckwith and Robert Walpole into racing him down the colonnaded walkway where the boys were making ropes, Mr Birchem having been called away from overseeing the work.

The rest of the boys had whooped and hollered, goading the runners on until they reached the end of the long, long passage, Charlie in the lead, Robert on his heels; then William, a close third, had cried that they must run back again, so they'd turned and done a second lap, racing alongside the endless length of twisted rope they'd spent the morning constructing on the stone floor of the colonnade and dodging the piles of hemp while they ran. It had been no use William thinking he could catch up because Charlie had won the second leg of the race also. But at that moment Mr Birchem had arrived back.

It wasn't the caning he and the two others had received that was behind this dawn exodus. Charlie didn't reckon he lacked 'bottom', as Henry Birchem had called it as he'd commanded the three boys to drop their breeches and to behave like men. Willy and Bob had snivelled, trying to swallow their fear but Charlie had faced the hospital officer with his lips firmly clamped together and eyes wide. No one, particularly not Mr Birchem, would have known how his insides had turned to liquid until he was afraid he would disgrace himself. But the blows had come swiftly, the breeches had been raised and the boys made ready to depart.

Mr Birchem had stopped them. 'I want you to remember', he'd said, 'how lucky you are. Many a boy out there in London today would give much to be in your places. You are fed, clothed, given a bed to sleep in and trained. You have a future, not like those unfortunates, starving without a roof over their heads and scavenging for a living with no prospect for the future.'

No prospect for the future? Charlie had wondered at that. At least those other boys could do what they wanted. In the hospital, everything was decided for you.

The stair treads were polished under his stockinged

feet. This building was new, the foundlings had moved here from their previous home less than two years earlier. The change had been a brief excitement in their ordered lives.

But the greatest change as far as Charlie was concerned had been that Mrs Pleasant had taken over responsibility for teaching the boys to read. From being a penance, the lessons had become a delight. For Mrs Pleasant had a way with her that made the hard business of learning one's letters an adventure. 'Think what you'll be able to do when you can read,' she would urge in that soft voice of hers. 'The world will be open. You might even become a lawyer or, if you heed your lessons in figures, a banker maybe.' They'd all laughed at that, Willy's silly bray rising above all the rest. They knew about bankers, and about lawyers. They were among the fine folk who came to look at the hospital and see what their charity had provided. And the foundlings knew they could not look to join such circles, they were expected to keep to their station in life.

Most of the boys didn't seem to mind but Charlie hated it.

He hated being on display. Hated the way sweetly smelling ladies with soft skins and rich clothes would put a fastidious finger under his chin, turning his face to theirs, looking earnestly into his eyes then say something like, 'Why, here's a pretty lad. Such large blue eyes! Such a sweet straight nose, such a neat chin. Surely, Amelia,' or Prudence, or Charlotte or Anne, 'you need a page?'

The first time it had happened, hope had leaped

within him and he'd gazed hungrily at the richly dressed lady and her companion.

'Faugh,' had said the companion. 'Have you lost all reason, dearest? A page without parentage or background? Only imagine how long it would take to train him to run the simplest of errands!' There had been a silvery tinkle of laughter, a wave of perfume and the ladies had passed on. He'd soon learned never to place any reliance on the flattering comments that came his way.

Charlie reached the bottom of the stairs. Still no one was about. The wide hall was empty and there, before him, was the front door and freedom.

Matters had come to a head a couple of months ago. He'd been told to report to the Court Room to help with some arrangements. Charlie had never been in the Court Room before, that was for the governors of the hospital. Greatly excited at being so privileged, he'd opened the door and then gasped at the glorious panelling of the walls and the ornate plasterwork of the ceiling. This was so different from the rest of the hospital. That was spacious, yes, but all so plain. Until that moment, Charlie hadn't realized how plain.

In the room were two men. 'Ah, boy, at last!' said one of them. He had a snub nose, bulging forehead and protuberant eyes. 'Come here, help Mr Hayman to hold this painting against the wall.' Charlie ran across, took one end of an elaborately framed picture and struggled to hold it as instructed while the snub-nosed man stood back and assessed the effect.

'Come on, Hogarth,' pleaded Mr Hayman after a little, 'you must have made up your mind by now.'

And it seemed he had, for Charlie had been allowed

to lower his end to the ground. At last he could see what it was that he'd been supporting. There were several people in the painting. One was a pretty lady, prettier even than Mrs Pleasant, reclining in some rich seating and holding out a hand to a small, unhappy looking child who was grabbing at the robe of the woman standing beside him. There were other figures as well but Charlie's attention was held by these three. He knew exactly how that child felt. The lady was like the gentry that came and gawped at the foundlings. She was wanting something from the child and the child didn't know what. He was grabbing at the robe because that was what he knew and was comfortable with.

'Well,' said Mr Hogarth, sounding amused. 'What do you think, son?'

So Charlie told him.

The other man, taller and slimmer with an intelligent face, had laughed. 'Hogarth, you've done it! He's got it exactly!'

Then the painter, for so apparently he was, had explained that the picture was of Pharaoh's daughter claiming Moses, who'd been found in the bulrushes as a baby and been looked after by the woman whose robe he was clutching. 'She was, in fact, his mother, though he didn't know it,' the painter added. The foundlings were regularly fed tales from the Bible but this was a new one.

'His mother?' Charlie exclaimed. There were two great topics of conversation amongst the boys. The first was their wet-nurses, the women with whom the Foundling Hospital had placed them as babies when they were first admitted and with whom they'd lived in the country until the ages of three or four. These women remained for each of the foundlings a source of warm memories, their loss a constant sorrow. The other was the question of who their mothers could be and why they had abandoned them. It didn't matter how many times they were told they'd been brought to the hospital because it offered a better life than their mothers could give them, they never lost the hurt of knowing they'd been given away.

'What is your name, son?' asked the painter.

'I'm Charles Lennox.'

'Oho, are you, indeed? Then the Duke of Richmond's your sponsor.'

'Sponsor?'

'He gave you his name when you were accepted by the hospital,' Hogarth said with a broad smile. 'There are others here with aristocratic names but few have such a powerful one.'

'He's powerful?'

'The grandson of King Charles II,' said Francis Hayman.

'On the wrong side of the blanket,' Hogarth said with the same sort of sarcastic voice Mr Birchem often used.

'Tush, man, with royalty such matters are unimportant.'

Charlie had no idea what all this meant. He fastened onto the detail that concerned him most. 'A duke gave me his name? Does that mean he, well, sort of adopted me?'

The other man laughed and Hogarth smiled. 'I suppose it does in a way. Well, Francis,' he turned to the other man, 'that's my work done, how about yours?'

'Did you paint this, sir?' Charlie blurted out before the other man could answer.

Francis frowned at such impertinence but Mr Hogarth said, 'Yes, do you like it?'

'William!' expostulated Francis, 'you can't ask a child what he thinks of your painting.'

'Why ever not?' asked Hogarth in a reasonable manner. 'Well, Charles Lennox, does it please you?'

Charlie gazed at the pretty lady and the unsettling small boy. He remembered his wet-nurse. She'd been jolly, had taught him to recognize birds and trees, had held him on her ample lap, cuddling him against her soft bosom. There'd been animals for him to play with and a man with a rough voice but kind manner who'd cuffed him when he'd chased the cat and pulled the tail of the dog. Then someone had taken him to London and delivered him to the hospital. When he'd asked to visit Nana, the name he'd known his wet-nurse by, Mr Birchem had said in a not unkindly way, 'That was when you were a baby, Lennox. You aren't a baby any more.'

Looking at the woman with the little boy in the picture, Charlie could almost taste the gush of sweet milk in his mouth, feel the hand that had held his head against the billowy softness of the breast. Against his lips was the curiously muscular sensation of the nipple.

Then he looked at the glorious colours in the pretty lady's robes, at the way light seemed to stream out of them. He felt drawn into the picture, lost in its beauty. 'I'd like to paint something like that,' he said simply.

Francis Hayman shouted with laughter but William Hogarth said gently, 'Would you indeed, Lennox? Well,

I hardly think you'll be able to persuade us governors of the hospital to apprentice you to a painter.'

Mr Birchem had been scathing when Charlie had asked if it wouldn't be possible. 'Painter, is it? Painter of houses maybe; painter of pictures, never. You need a proper training that will equip you for life, young Lennox. The sea it is for you. To be a sailor in His Majesty's fleet is a great thing.'

A sailor! Stark before Charlie's eyes was the time he'd been taken on a boat by Nana and her husband. They'd lived near the sea and had told him it would be a great experience. But a wind had got up unexpectedly and blown fiercely. Charlie and Nana had been sick. So sick, Charlie had thought he'd die. In fact he'd wanted to die. When they'd finally got back to shore, Nana had spoken. 'That's enough of that, Walter,' she'd said to her husband in her no-nonsense voice. 'You won't get me in a boat again, not if it were to save my life.'

Charlie had wholeheartedly agreed with her.

And now he was being told he'd be sent to sea!

He'd applied to Mrs Pleasant but even she had not been encouraging. 'A painter? Oh, Charlie, you don't understand, it's a very hard thing, you have to train for a long, long time and even then, you need a very special talent. I would love to have been an artist and someone once told me I was very good. But I would have needed to dedicate myself and forget everything else. I couldn't do that, there was someone who meant too much to me.' None of this made much sense to Charlie. 'And you, you aren't being taught how to write, let alone how to draw.' Her eyes had been very sad, as though she would have liked to make his wish come true. But she'd looked sad for quite a bit. Perhaps,

Charlie had thought, she had some trouble of her own. When she didn't appear after that to take them for their lessons, he reckoned that was the case.

While Charlie wondered when she would be teaching them their letters again and tried to think of a way he could become a painter, a Captain White arrived at the hospital to tell the boys the attractions of life as a sailor. At the finish, Charlie was more in despair than ever. He went over what Mr Hogarth had told him and eventually he realized there was only one way out for him. That was why he'd crept downstairs at dawn. Why he was turning the big brass handle of the front door.

Only to find that the door was locked.

Only to hear behind him Mr Birchem's voice. 'And what, may I ask, my lad, are you doing?' A hand grabbed his ear and twisted it painfully. 'You will come with me, young Lennox, and learn what's good for you.'

Chapter Five

Canaletto woke in the morning with rat claws of worry tugging at his mind.

He lay in his bed for a moment, watching the light as it made its way through the skimpy curtains. Light had always fascinated him. What it could reveal, what it could conceal, how shadows could define a view.

The shadows in his mind now retreated and he remembered what was worrying him. He rose and drew back the curtains. Looking down at the yard, he saw the studio door open and Fanny emerge to fill a bowl with water from the pump. Canaletto frowned. How was he to resolve the problem of his apprentice? It was insupportable that she should refuse to wash his shirts. On the other hand, maybe she had a point about his neglect of her training.

The matter was too frustrating. If only McSwiney would produce another commission, surely everything would fall into place? He'd be too busy to worry about Fanny or dead girls or what a foolish woman Betty Spragg was.

There came a knock on the door and Daniel Spragg entered with the morning jug of hot water for Canaletto's ablutions. The sight of his landlord shocked Canaletto.

'Ill, Daniel?'

The carpenter was a well-set-up man in his mid-thirties. At least, he had been when Canaletto had first taken lodgings in his house. Now the painter realized Daniel had lost a considerable amount of weight. There were dark shadows under his eyes and the vertical line between his thick, dark brows was deeper than he remembered it. How long had this been going on? Had Canaletto been so wrapped up in his own troubles he had failed to see that his landlord and friend was wasting away? What had happened to his ability to notice everything?

'Plaguey flux. It will pass. Day is nice.' This, for Daniel, passed for loquacious conversation. Canaletto tried to feel reassured. If Daniel felt as bad as he looked, he'd not have said anything.

Daniel disappeared, leaving no chance for further enquiry.

As Canaletto washed, he pushed worries about his landlord to the back of his mind and planned his day.

Shaved, dressed in a serviceable grey coat and breeches, his linen carefully arranged, Canaletto picked up his wig and sighed as he saw what a mess last night's storm had made of its powdered curls.

Carrying wig, brush and powder horn, he went downstairs to the studio.

Fanny was dusting the painting implements. She looked up as Canaletto entered. There was a determined sparkle in her eyes.

Summoning as much authority as he could, he said, 'Fanny, my dear, wig!' He held it out. 'You better with brush, yes?' and gave her his best smile, the one he found it difficult to produce too often.

She gave him a long, level look.

'Please?' he said with another smile.

Slowly she put down her dusting cloth and reached for wig and brush. 'You should send it to the wigmaker,' she said. 'It's too long since it had attention.' But she sat on one of the stools and started carefully removing flakes of dried powder from the stiff hairs. Her lips were pressed together and Canaletto decided he had better remain silent.

After a little she gave the wig a good shake. 'Now, signor, it is ready for more powder.'

Canaletto produced his powder horn and aimed it at the wig.

Fanny snatched the wig away, scandalized. 'Not in here, signor! Not when I have just dusted!' She marched outside and Canaletto meekly followed.

Fanny held out her arm with the wig on her raised hand. 'Now, signor, puff away!'

He carefully blew the fine white powder over the cleaned curls while Fanny turned the wig this way and that until each part was evenly coated.

Finally Canaletto arranged it on his bald head. He was properly dressed. 'Now, Fanny, go out.'

'Me?'

'No, I.' Canaletto thought he would never master English pronouns. 'Fanny draw.'

She looked surprised but excited. 'Draw, signor? Draw what?'

He had given the matter some thought. 'A view from southern end of Golden Square. Sketch what you need then return here and prepare finished drawing, yes?' A nice little test for her. It would be interesting to see what she needed to note down and how she could develop the initial sketch. 'While I not work, time to instruct Fanny, yes?' he smiled benignly at her, full of good intentions. 'And perhaps persuade butcher friend for, what call it, scrag end? For dinner, yes?' He produced a few coins and handed them to her, his fingers hovering over them as though he found it difficult to leave them exposed in the bright sunlight instead of reposing in the dark of his pocket.

He saw some of her excitement vanish. But cooking a dish of stew wouldn't take much of her time, surely? In any case, it was part of her duties.

He bid her good morning and set out. Soon he'd forgotten about Fanny and the conflicting demands of the tasks he'd set her as he ran over everything he could remember about the dead woman from the previous night.

The magistrate's house in Bow Street did not prove difficult to find. Adjacent to Covent Garden, the street ran north to south and was, indeed, curved like a bow. Tall and narrow, the house seemed to admit a constant stream of people. Canaletto followed in a large and verbose woman, who announced to any who could be bothered to listen that her purse had been snatched not ten minutes earlier and she would make sure the malefactor was arrested.

Inside, a clerk received complaints. Criminal activity was obviously high, for there was a disorderly queue who pressed to give their details together with a number of burly men who appeared to have apprehended wrongdoers. Thief-takers they'd be, self-appointed and in it for the reward. There was no one as well dressed as he, no one who appeared such a gentleman. Had this been Venice, he would undoubtedly have been given priority, but in London there seemed to be a greater independence of spirit. Glances were cast at his well-cut coat and his immaculate wig, but few gave way. Canaletto flirted with the idea of pushing to the front of the queue regardless, then decided to wait his turn. After all, he had little else to do that day. So he amused himself by studying the various characters around him, noting their dress and manner: the nervous, the confident, the humble, the proud, those who proclaimed their innocence, those who appeared resigned to their fate.

Eventually it was his turn to approach the clerk's desk. The fellow wore a small, untidy wig and a worn brown jacket of inferior cloth. His linen was none too clean and his fingers were ink stained. 'Yes?' he said wearily. He dipped his pen into the metal ink pot sunk into a corner of his desk and prepared to scratch yet more entries into his large book.

Canaletto carefully explained his purpose.

'Hmm, dead girl, you say?' said the clerk, flipping through a pile of papers on his desk. 'You have information regarding her attacker?'

'No,' Canaletto said patiently. 'Seek information from you.'

The man's questing fingers lodged on a sheet of notes. These were quickly scanned. 'We have no information,' he said curtly. 'Next!'

'But,' expostulated Canaletto, 'conduct enquiry, no?'

The fellow looked at him sharply. 'If you mean, will we institute an examination, yes, if a suspect is identified. Until then, there is little that can be done.'

The clerk cast another glance at the scribbled notes. 'Don't even know her name.' He glanced up. His eyes were reddened and bloodshot, whether from constant perusal of his entries or a fondness for spirituous liquor, it was impossible to say. They gleamed with sudden calculation as for the first time he seemed to take in Canaletto's appearance. 'Should you be prepared, good sir, to underwrite the cost of an enquiry, it might be that we could garner some information that would lead us to an arrest.'

It took a moment for Canaletto to understand exactly what he was saying. 'You mean, pay money?' he demanded, his voice quick and hot.

'Now you have it, sir,' the clerk agreed happily. 'Without finance, what can we do?'

He should have known. Nothing bought nothing. 'Have no money,' Canaletto muttered, thinking of the precious coins he had left with Fanny for their food. His miserly hoard had to be eked out for who knew how many days and weeks before he earned more. He could not afford to institute expensive – and he had no doubt but that they would be expensive – enquiries about the death of some unknown woman.

Angry and exasperated, he swung round and pushed his way through the crowd that pressed behind him.

He should not care, he thought, as he made his way out of the magistrate's house, but he could not get the vision of that mutilated face out of his memory. He wondered what had happened to the gold ring. Had that been pocketed by the Watch? Canaletto turned and thrust his way back to the clerk's table, ignoring the cries and protestations. With an effort he displaced the tradesman who had taken his place in front of the clark. 'She had ring on finger. What happen to ring?'

The clerk gazed at him. 'Ring,' he repeated without expression.

'Ring,' reiterated Canaletto. 'Gold ring with blue stones.'

The crowd grew interested. Jewellery they could understand. 'Taken it has someone?' enquired the man Canaletto had displaced. 'There's scoundrels will take advantage of anyone, dead or alive, but easier when they're dead.' There was a general murmur of agreement at this.

The clerk consulted the notes again then, reluctantly, drew out a drawer from his table, leaning back in his chair to accommodate the movement. He scrabbled around then removed a gold band tagged with a small white label written in a crabbed hand. 'This the ring? It was handed in by the officer of the Watch last night.' He gripped it between thumb and forefinger as he showed it to Canaletto.

But his grip was no match for the speed and strength with which Canaletto seized it from him.

'Hey!' shouted the clerk, levering himself up from his chair and trying to snatch it back.

But Canaletto had moved back from the table. Surrounded by the interested crowd, he examined the ring. Yes, as he'd thought, it was gold, with those little stamps the English used to guarantee its quality clearly to be seen on the inside. And inset into the precious metal were three small stones that looked like sapphires. The workmanship was good, the ring was valuable. He wondered that the girl should have been so poorly dressed when she wore something as fine as this.

Canaletto handed back the ring with a flourish. 'Examine only,' he said graciously.

The clerk's fingers closed over it with the speed of a card-sharper. 'You had no right to do that,' he said sullenly, 'it's evidence.'

Necks were craned as the ring was dropped again into the drawer and the crowd sighed as it was then slammed shut.

Evidence, yes, Canaletto thought as he once again pushed his way towards the entrance. It could no doubt identify the girl. If, that is, she hadn't stolen it herself. But he was somewhat reassured to find that the ring had indeed been handed in.

'Good sir,' said a voice as he reached the door. 'I have information that could help you.'

The speaker was a middle-aged, middle-sized, middle-everything seeming man. You would not notice him in a crowd but he had a knowing look in his eye as he laid a hand on Canaletto's arm. 'Come outside,' he said ingratiatingly.

That had been Canaletto's aim but, instantly, he wished to do anything but find himself on the road with this fellow. He could only want money and it was highly unlikely he had anything worth the price. There was, however, little option.

'I knows where the body of the girl what you's interested in is. Worth something that would be, wouldn't you say?'

The body of the girl? What could this fellow know?

Canaletto waited. He'd conducted many an enquiry back in Venice, usually on behalf of the milords who

commissioned his paintings. He knew the city and
its buildings, bridges, waterways, petty thieves, confidence tricksters, prostitutes and other criminal types
as few others. And he knew it was always best to
appear less than keen when anyone wanted to sell him
information.

'Terrible mess her face was,' the chap added,
looking horribly cheerful about it.

At least he appeared to have the right girl.

'No identification, no money for burial,' he continued as Canaletto still held back from offering any
encouragement. 'Pauper's grave, charge on the parish,'
he said as though that explained everything.

Canaletto waited, idly scanning the hustle and
bustle of the street, feeling, despite himself, a certain
excitement. For who knew what a proper examination
of the body in the clear light of day might show?

'You come with me an' I'll show you.' For the first
time there was a note of anxiety in the fellow's voice.

'Lead,' commanded Canaletto with a throwaway air.

'First you pay,' insisted the man.

There ensued a protracted bargaining session that
finally ended with Canaletto handing over a small coin.

The fellow looked at it grudgingly, bit it to test the
metal then slid it into his pocket. 'Follow me,' he said
with resignation and set off at a rapid pace.

Canaletto's expectation grew as they dived down a
dark passageway past a set of stables and a gin shop.
Even that early in the day, several happy souls leaned
against the wall downing their pennyworth of oblivion.
Then Canaletto's guide stopped at a carpenter's workshop, the carpenter planing a long piece of wood. It
was nothing like Daniel Spragg's, the workmanship

here was rough and ready, the wood of the poorest, the organization minimal. No surprise, perhaps, when Canaletto saw that the principal product appeared to be coffins of the crudest kind.

'In the back,' said the fellow, who then melted away into the maze of backstreets the district afforded.

Canaletto was left with little choice but to approach the carpenter. 'Seek body of girl killed last night,' he said, feeling vaguely foolish. Yet, if this was a coffin maker, maybe he had somewhere where bodies rested.

The carpenter hardly paused in his work. 'Back there,' he said, jerking his head towards a door at the rear of his workroom.

Canaletto turned the handle with caution, which was as well for it opened onto four steps leading down to a large, flag-stoned floor. In its centre was a table. On the table was the naked body of the dead girl, her mutilated face plain in the light thrown by an unexpectedly wide window.

Beside the girl stood a large man wearing a capacious apron. He held a knife and as Canaletto watched, he raised and then thrust it into the body.

Chapter Six

The morning air, freshened by the previous night's storm, was clear and bright. No hint today of the smoke that usually hung, pall like, above London's forest of chimney pots, it had all been blown away by the wind and for once river, houses and parks glistened and glimmered in the sun.

The Privy Gardens in Whitehall looked particularly attractive. Once the queen's private play and exercise area, two devastating fires had driven the royal court to St James's Palace and now the area was public property; that bit, at least, that remained after various aristocrats had built large and impressive houses on the part of the previously parterred land that ran beside the River Thames.

The recently constructed London home of the Duke of Richmond could well be named the largest and most impressive of the private dwellings. Classically proportioned, with lush lawns running from a generous terrace down to the river and round one side of the building, it occupied an enviable site, protected from the hurly-burly of London life by the stretch of Privy Gardens that lay between house and public thoroughfare.

The well-polished front door of Richmond House

opened and out came two girls. Both pretty, both fashionably dressed in sprigged muslin. They ran down the steps, laughing. Behind them came a maid, a slender girl in a plain dress with a shawl around her shoulders, anchored about her waist by its ends. Her skin shone with the rich gleam of cleanly hewn coal and her fine features were emphasized by the colourful turban she wore around her head. She walked with a lithe freedom very different from the tripping steps of the girls, following them like a young panther slightly contemptuous of a pair of cubs but nevertheless conscious of a certain responsibility for their safety.

'Lady Kitty,' she called as the girls ran onto one of the paths that led through the grassy expanse of the gardens, 'mind your hat.' Her voice was low and resonant.

Lady Kitty Manners clutched at the straw a stray breeze threatened to remove from her blonde curls. 'Oh, Emily,' she said. 'isn't it a wonderful day? The sort of day one could meet one's fate! Of course,' she added, turning to her companion, 'you already have your fate.'

'You mean, Kitty, I'm already married?' A dimple deepened at the side of Emily's mouth.

'Oh,' sighed Kitty, 'it's too romantic. To be fifteen and married! But, then, your family is romantic! Tell me again about your father. And you listen to Lady Kildare, Purity, they'll have no stories like this in Africa.' She laughed back at her maid, who appeared to take no notice but continued her fluid progress several steps behind the two girls.

'Oh, Kitty, I know I have told you before,' sighed Lady Kildare. 'And so has my father. And I'm sure your father will have told you before you came to stay with us, such a friend of my father's as he is, even though he hardly visits London these days.'

'Tell, please,' pleaded Kitty, pouting prettily. 'He was the Earl of March then, was he not? And his father, the first Duke of Richmond, promised him in marriage to your mother in exchange for a gambling debt, was it not so?'

'And was highly discomposed to find himself, as he puts it, contracted to such a dowd. Of course, mama was very young then, not above thirteen years of age.'

'So off he went on the Grand Tour,' interposed Kitty eagerly.

Lady Kildare looked severely at her friend, 'Do I tell this story or do you?'

'Oh, you, Emily, you. Only do hurry.'

The other girl laughed with a healthy exuberance. 'Well, on his return, three years later, he was more anxious to visit the theatre than my mama. And there . . .'

'He saw the most beautiful girl!'

'Kitty!'

Kitty stopped abruptly on the path and gagged her mouth with both her hands, looking at her friend over them in such a beseeching way that Lady Kildare could only laugh again. 'He asked a friend who the beauteous creature was, cursing himself that he wasn't free to pay her court.' She paused as though expecting Kitty to interject once more but Kitty still held her hands across her mouth. 'And was told he must be a stranger to London if he did not know the beautiful Lady March.'

'Oh, it must have been such a moment! Do you not think so, Purity?'

The black girl had remained standing also, looking

around the bustle of Londoners disporting themselves on the grassy expanses of the Privy Gardens with its paths and carriageways, trees and shrubs softening the lines of the buildings and walls that continued to make it a private area. She said nothing.

'Come, girl, you must have some comment,' Kitty stamped a little foot in its kid slipper on the path.

'Why, then, Lady Kitty, I'm wondering what Lady March had been doing, going around town so that all the young men knew who she was!'

'Why, Purity, what a thing to say!' gasped Kitty. 'Apologize this instant to Lady Kildare.'

Purity turned her calm, level gaze towards the other girl. For a moment it seemed she wouldn't speak, then she said in a toneless voice, 'If I have offended, my lady, I am sorry. I only spoke as I thought.'

'Indeed, so it would seem,' Emily Kildare said frostily. 'I can assure you no hint of scandal has ever attached itself to my mother.'

'No, indeed!' Kitty said hastily. 'She would not be a lady of the bedchamber else. Society is not so large that its most prominent members are not known to all.'

There seemed nothing further to say on that and the girls resumed their walking, Purity remaining ever further behind them.

'You must not mind Purity,' Kitty said to her friend. 'She sees things differently from us. Coming from Africa, you know.'

'I wonder you can have a slave for a maid.'

'Oh, she is quite house-trained. Indeed, apart from her frank way of speaking, she has better manners than some girls of breeding I have met.'

'It wasn't that I meant,' Emily said, a little sharply.

'Why, what then?'

'Only that for anyone not to have the freedom to be where they would must be so, so ignominious.'

'Ignominious? What long words you use, Emily.'

'I think people must have freedom,' repeated Emily, a trifle stubbornly.

'Freedom to starve?' asked Kitty, astounded. 'Freedom to be homeless? Ask Purity which she would prefer. I can assure you what her answer will be.'

Emily glanced back at the maid, but Purity's face was expressionless. It appeared she had not heard. Emily opened her mouth, seemed as if she would make a further remark, then closed it, made a small, helpless gesture and asked instead, 'How come you have her as your maid?'

'Why, black maids are all the fashion! Papa's younger brother has some interest in the West Indies. He gave her to us; apparently she was a princess in her country,' Kitty said proudly. 'Uncle gave her to my mother. It was he who named her Purity.'

The two girls walked in silence for a little, then Emily said pleasantly, 'I am happy to shop with you, Kitty, but why, pray, are we to visit haberdashers and mantua makers when we could so easily have them call?'

Kitty, who had been conscious she had said something to her disadvantage but was unable to work out what it could have been, cheered up immediately. 'Oh, but that would be no fun at all! Why, who knows what adventures we might meet? And if I do not have an adventure soon it will be too late. You will be off to Ireland with your wonderful Jemmy, your family will go down to Sussex and I, I will be back to

Cheshire! What chance is there of finding romance in Cheshire? You have no idea how boring the company, how *ordinaire* the pursuits, how desperately dull the entertainments. Indeed, one could hardly call them entertaining in any sense. What possessed my mama to bury herself there, I cannot conceive. If I were her I'd have worked on my father until he provided me with a house in London so we could meet society, visit the playhouse, attend court and, oh, all the activities your mama and papa enjoy.'

Emily wrinkled her nose and stepped lightly aside from a ball thrown in her path by a couple of children exercising with their nurse. 'Do not think attending court such a pleasurable activity. I long for Ireland, it will be such an adventure.'

'Oh, it's all very well for you to complain court is dull. You have the entrée everywhere and are well married. My father scans every man who so much as speaks to me. His demands for my husband are as stringent as, as, well, as though I was a royal princess instead of the daughter of an earl of no particular significance,' Kitty sniffed. 'If it had not been for your mama's invitation, I should never have been allowed to travel to London. And when I get back I shall find myself married to someone old and cantankerous but with a lineage dating from Adam and Eve!'

'Cheer up, Kitty, the days are past when girls were forced into unions distasteful to them. You may even, like me, be able to persuade your parents your happiness lies with a man of your choice not theirs.'

'You think so?' Kitty did not seem to think the prospect was likely. 'And easy enough for you when your Jemmy is so rich and landed gentry even if Irish. What

if he had no pedigree? Or was poor?' Kitty enquired
with a hint of petulance. She really was a very pretty
girl, her features regular, her nose delightfully tiptilted,
her upper lip a trifle short, which gave her an engaging
air of someone perpetually breathless with excitement
at life, an impression heightened by the mischievous-
ness of her astonishingly large and deeply blue eyes.
'And you will have had any number of suitors, Lady
Emily Lennox, daughter of the second Duke of Richmond, great-granddaughter of a king. Who would not
wish to ally themselves with your family?'

'My sister and I have not found romance an easy
path,' Emily said. 'You remember she had to elope to
marry her Henry Fox? And now Mama and Papa will
not receive her. And as for me, I had to wait a year
before I was allowed to marry my Jemmy.'

'Oh,' sighed Kitty. 'To elope! And to meet your fate
at fourteen! I said your family was romantic, not even a
novel could offer more. I would give a fortune to have
your background.' Kitty flashed an automatic smile at
the handsome young guardsman lounging against
railings.

Emily giggled and drew her friend onwards. 'Tush,
Kitty, save your smiles for more worthy recipients.
Marry for love by all means but do not bestow your
hand where there is nothing. And you have several
weeks with us before the court goes to Hanover, when
Jemmy and I will leave for Ireland, and Mama and
Papa go to the country, to Goodwood.'

'Oh, Ireland!' Kitty sighed. 'And, Emily, do tell, is
marriage as exciting, you know, as one thinks it must
be?'

'Kitty, are you meaning what I think you are?' Emily tried to sound severe but it was beyond her.

Kitty stopped in the middle of the gardens. 'Nobody will tell one anything! When I asked Mama, she cut me short, as though it was some silly secret. And cousin Constance, who used to giggle with me and showed me how to tie my ribbons, and wedded the most boring man in the whole wide world, how she could! Well, when I asked her, she became so, so adult! And said I must wait for marriage, when I would find that life always disappoints.

'Oh, Emily, marriage isn't a disappointment, is it?' Kitty pleaded. 'Only sometimes, when I meet a man who is really handsome and he smiles at me, well, I feel such things.' Kitty wrapped her arms around herself and hugged her slim frame. 'And I think that that must have something to do with marriage.'

Emily smiled joyously. 'Yes, Kitty, it does! And, oh, you are right, it is exciting. My Jemmy makes me feel, oh, one can't explain, not to someone who does not know. I shall be like your mama and say you will have to wait.'

'But if he's ancient and fat and heavy breathing, well, Emily, surely then it isn't exciting?' Kitty wailed.

'Are you being asked to marry someone who's ancient and fat and heavy breathing?'

'No,' Kitty said uncertainly.

'Then do not worry,' Emily said carelessly. 'Kitty, you should not look for troubles where there are none. Come, let us enjoy our shopping.' She slipped her arm through her friend's but at that moment a dog bounded up, barking excitedly and thrust an impertinent nose in Kitty's skirts. She backed away with an exclamation of disgust. Emily laughed and gave the dog a friendly cuff across the nose. 'Off with you,' she said authoritatively. The dog bounded away, narrowly missed being run down by a carriage and pair, then cannoned into a tall, distinguished-looking man approaching from the direction of the Banqueting Hall. With an exclamation of disgust, the man whacked the dog across the hindquarters with his cane and it ran off, yelping, its tail between its legs.

'Why, Lady Emily,' the man advanced towards the girls. 'No, I should say, Lady Kildare. Forgive me, my dear, I had for a moment forgot that you are no longer the most eligible girl in London.'

'Lord Maltravers,' Emily acknowledged with the slightest bow of her head. 'How do you?' The question was asked with the barest of courtesies and Kitty looked inquisitively at the elegant figure, dressed all in black apart from a white silk waistcoat, and the whitest of white linen, lace at his cuffs. His highly polished shoes were decorated with diamond buckles.

He returned her stare with a questioning glance that demanded an introduction.

'Kitty, this is Lord Maltravers,' Emily said without warmth. 'Lord Maltravers, may I present Lady Katherine Manners, daughter of the Earl of Cheshire, who has been visiting with us these last few weeks.'

Kitty bobbed a little curtsy, peeked at the tall stranger under modestly lowered eyelids, and offered a languid hand.

He took and held it in his like some precious piece of porcelain. 'Lady Katherine, I am sure you must be known as Kitty.' He had a dark, flexible voice that made everything he said seem more interesting than the actual words suggested. 'For you are all kitten cat, all sleek softness but, I am sure, with sharply pointed claws about you.'

Kitty gazed full at him, her eyes startled and delighted.

'Once I knew your mother, Lady Charlotte Rouse, was she not?'

Kitty nodded.

'You promise as great beauty as did she.' He released Kitty's hand and turned to her companion. 'I visit your mama, Lady Kildare. I hope she is at home?'

'Yes, my lord, she is,' Emily said briefly.

Lord Maltravers gave the two girls a graceful bow, holding his cane elegantly on the ground with his right hand while he swept the air with his hat in his left.

The girls dipped their heads in acknowledgement and continued on their way.

'Who is he?' Kitty enquired eagerly as soon as they had moved out of earshot. 'I have never heard Mama mention a Lord Maltravers.'

'He has been abroad many years,' Emily said as though that explained everything. 'Mama says he was a well-known gallant in his youth.'

'Why, Emily, you do not like him. Why so?'

Emily walked a little faster and for a moment it looked as though she would not answer. Then she burst out, 'I find him hateful! He looks at one as if, as if he would eat one!'

'What an extraordinary thing to say! I thought he looked excessively romantic. Why, if he wasn't so old, I dare say a girl might find him amazingly attractive.' Kitty thought for a moment, then added, 'He must be as old as Mama at least, which would make him nearly forty. Perhaps it is that which makes you dislike him so.'

'Kitty, what nonsense you do talk. Lord Maltravers must indeed be as old as you say if not older but my dislike has nothing to do with age. It is more that I fear he is as unprincipled a man as there exists.'

Kitty slipped her arm through her friend's. 'Really? Emily, do tell.'

Emily shook her head, setting the ribbons on her little hat a-dancing. 'I know nothing to tell, it is all a matter of insinuation; a few words heard here, a few there; the way Papa mentions his name, something Mama once let slip when first he arrived back from the continent.'

'What was it?' Kitty pleaded, almost dancing with impatience.

'Merely that she would not care to see a daughter of hers squired by such a man.'

'Oh, how delicious! He must have such fascination!'

'You read too many novels,' Emily said severely.

'Why, Emily, I would never have thought to hear you sound a prude!'

Emily stopped in horror. 'Me, a prude? Kitty, never say so.'

'Then admit you read as many novels as I and stop sounding so righteous about a man who seems to me more interesting than almost any I have met in London so far.'

Emily laughed. 'Almost any? Why, Kitty, who would you rate above the fascinating Lord Maltravers?'

'Ah, now that would be saying!' Kitty firmly closed her enchanting little rosebud mouth and refused to say more.

The girls had skirted the classical elegance of the Banqueting House and emerged from the Privy Garden into a wide thoroughfare. Some twenty minutes later, followed by Purity's graceful figure, they entered an emporium in the Strand.

'Oh, look, Emily, such materials!' cooed Kitty, waving a hand at the bolts of muslin, cotton, silk and velvet displayed on the shelves around the walls of the shop. A fire burned welcomingly in a back room and Purity unobtrusively edged her way there and stood where it could warm her.

'Would mademoiselle care to see some materials?' asked a salesman, coming forward.

But Kitty explained they had come to find ribbons to trim her new gown.

A pleasurable half-hour was spent comparing the merits of a watered silk in emerald green with one in coquelicot pink. After the choice had been made, the purchase charged to an account and delivery promised within the hour, Kitty expressed a wish to see a bolt of silk in a deep blue.

'Did you not want to visit the mantua maker?' Emily asked.

'Patience, we have time enough. The blue is pleasant but how about that one in pink, above the striped red and white?' Kitty said, pointing. The salesman hurried to bring another bolt down for her inspection. ''Tis vastly pretty,' Kitty said, her hand caressing the lustrous material.

'The first matches your eyes,' said a male voice provocatively behind them.

Kitty spun round, her blue eyes, which were indeed a shade of speedwell as deep as the silk, full of laughter and delight. 'Why, if it's not Mr Wright! How come you to be here? Emily, may I present Mr Thomas Wright? Mr Wright, Lady Kildare.'

Emily Kildare gave a small nod to the young man and offered him one delicate hand, looking him over as he bowed low and almost brought his mouth to her fingers. 'Do we have your acquaintance, Mr Wright?' she asked in a somewhat haughty voice.

Thomas Wright was a man of obvious attractions, chief amongst them a tall, commanding figure, a face that rivalled a Greek statue's and a graceful manner. His clothes were so fine he might have been en route to some great rout. His coat blazed with gold lace, his waistcoat with fine embroidery, his breeches, cut uncommonly tight, were of the finest cloth, his shoe buckles as he bowed before them winked with the patina of true silver.

'The promise of your acquaintance is a light that has guided me hither,' he said with yet another graceful bow.

Emily gave Kitty a look that said she had much to explain.

Kitty said hurriedly, 'Mr Wright and I met in St James's Park just after I arrived here. You were preparing for your wedding. Purity and I took a stroll there and, well, a dog tripped me and Mr Wright helped me up.' This was said with an air of studied innocence. 'Then, such a coincidence, we found Mr Wright also had a slave for a servant.' Kitty glanced towards the door of the shop.

Unnoticed until then, there stood an African of impressive-looking strength in a dark green livery plentifully adorned with silver lace. High cheekbones, full mouth, a broken nose and close-cropped hair were all emphasized by the dusky hue of his skin.

'Such a noble savage, don't you think?' said Kitty excitedly.

The noble savage moved his weight restlessly from one foot to another.

'Oh, Brute's no savage,' laughed Thomas Wright. 'But he's a devil with his fists. I say if I need money, I'll enter him in prize fights.'

'Brute?' enquired Emily, one eyebrow lifting expressively.

'My father called him John, but such a name's no use for a fellow like that. Ladies, do you shop further? Can I be allowed to walk with you?'

'Emily, what do you think?' Kitty asked lightly, sending her friend a look under her eyelashes that was almost pleading. 'Shall we allow this forward fellow to accompany us? I am sure he has excellent taste in wraps.'

After a slight hesitation, Lady Kildare agreed Mr Wright might walk with them to the next shop, then contrived to be between the young man and her friend as they made their way through the busy crowds towards their next port of call.

Behind the three of them walked Brute and Purity. They didn't speak but Purity's face wore the look of someone unused to food who had been sat before a laden table and Brute's shoulder moved so near to hers they almost touched.

Chapter Seven

Fanny added herbs to the scrag end of neck she had wheedled out of the butcher. In with it were the cheapest vegetables she could find, mostly cabbage with a few turnips. Then she went to the pump and fetched water. She bitterly resented the time she had to spend on this task.

As she pulled up the bucket, Betty Spragg came into the courtyard. A filmy scarf was arranged around her face but it couldn't hide the blue bruise round one eye.

'Good day, Mrs Spragg,' Fanny said, attempting to sound as though nothing had happened between them. 'A fine one it is, too.'

'I've hardly had time to consider the weather,' Betty said fretfully, 'what with Daniel being so wretchedly ill in the night and my own constitution to think of as well.'

'Master Spragg ill? I am right sorry to hear that. Does he need medication? Can I go to the apothecary for you?' Fanny liked the quiet carpenter. He always had a smile for her and would listen whenever she needed someone to talk to. In a way he had taken the place of her brother, Ned. Fanny wasn't welcome at Ned's these days, his wife had made that plain, and she missed being able to boss him around and tell him her troubles.

Betty fiddled with the ends of her scarf. 'Nay, I went myself last week, when Daniel first took sick. But potions do not seem to help,' she added peevishly. 'Fanny, I . . !' her voice trailed off. Then, not quite looking her in the eye, Betty said, 'I am sorry I said those things to you last night, it was just that I, that I . . !'

Fanny took pity on her. 'We will say no more about last night, Mrs Spragg,' she said firmly, giving the pump handle an energetic push. Water gushed out and splashed Betty's dress.

'Clumsy girl!' shrieked Betty, attempting to brush away the water. 'No wonder Mr Wright did not take to you!'

'I do not care to be thought of by such as Mr Wright,' Fanny said firmly. 'And if you've a morsel of sense, you will leave the business of his table to Daniel.'

A stain of colour washed through Betty's face and she dropped her gaze. ''Twas an accident, nothing more,' she said sullenly, examining the damp patch on her gown. 'And I'll thank you to keep your opinions to yourself. And,' she added, looking Fanny straight in the face, 'not to share them with such as Mister Spragg.'

That, Fanny realized, had been her sole purpose in coming out to speak to her.

'I'll not interfere between husband and wife,' she said briskly, picking up her jug.

Betty retreated nervously. 'There is no need to take such a tone with me, young Fanny.' She hurried back into the house.

What was it about Jonathan Wright that had

attracted Betty? His solid figure and unexceptional face had made no impact on Fanny. Why, she wondered, did men and women make such fools of themselves over one another? There was Betty's maid, Jenny, mooning over Daniel's lump of an apprentice, Betty apparently losing all sense over a bully of a hosier and her own brother, Ned, married to a girl who was making his life a misery.

Fanny picked a couple of bay leaves from the tree by the studio, plucked up her jug and went inside wondering whether to feel glad or sorry she had never fallen under the spell of any man. Oh, there had been kisses, mostly fumbled, from young men. Some she had even enjoyed, but nothing that could make her lose her senses or she would risk her reputation for.

Fanny added the water and the bay leaves to the stew, gave it a stir and reckoned it was probably as well no male had captured her heart. She needed to keep all her energies for building her career. Becoming a painter was so much more important than enjoying moments of excitement with a member of the opposite sex. Especially when it seemed that dalliance could lead to disaster. There was, for instance, the poor girl Canaletto had found the previous evening. All Betty had sustained was a black eye, little enough when compared with a face mutilated in such a dreadful manner and a fatal knife wound. No, men were best not thought about.

As Fanny started to lift the heavy pot, there came a knock at the door of the studio. On the step was a young man with a most open and manly face.

'I seek Signor Canaletto,' he said. Then, as Fanny

said nothing, he added, 'I was told this was his direction.'

Fanny swallowed hard. 'Indeed it is. But I am afraid he is not here presently.'

'Alas, he is the most elusive of mortals.' The young man took off his hat and sketched a quick bow. 'Richard Thompkins at your service.'

Fanny bobbed a little curtsy. 'Fanny Rooker at yours. Perhaps if you tell me your business? I am Signor Canaletto's apprentice,' she added with a touch of aggression.

'Say you so?' The young man looked at her in surprise. 'Why, then, well met. I am also a painter.'

Whatever Fanny had been expecting, it was not that. This charming fellow had an air of fashion about him, he looked a young man about town. His maroon coat and grey breeches were well cut from fine cloth. His linen was clean and his wig a neat little peruke. His attractions, though, went beyond fashion. Nature had endowed Richard Thompkins with features that were in complete harmony. The deep-set, golden eyes, gold as topaz, were balanced by high cheekbones, the straight nose was perhaps a smidgen too long, but the wide mouth was perfect and the chin was finished with a small cleft that deepened when he spoke.

As Fanny took in his appearance, Richard Thompkins shifted his feet uneasily and rubbed his chin. 'Have I smuts?' he enquired anxiously.

Fanny realized she was staring at him. 'You have no smuts,' she said gravely. 'Will you come into the studio and tell me what it is you require from Signor Canaletto?'

'Can I help with that? It looks heavy,' he said as she

picked the stewpot up from the table and came and took it from her. He was so close, she could see the shine of a recent shave on his cheeks.

'It's to go on the chain,' she said a trifle breathlessly, pointing to the fireplace, where she had built up a goodly fire.

Carefully he carried the pot to the grate.

'Let me,' Fanny said, snatching up the old piece of sacking she used to protect her hand from the heat of the iron links. She grabbed the chain and held out the hook. Gingerly he guided the pot as she let the chain swing back until it hung over the flames. 'There,' she said with satisfaction, 'that will do nicely. Thank you for your help, sir. Now, tell me your business with my master.'

He looked round the studio, his eyes greedy. Fanny wished he would look at her with the same appreciation he showed for the tools of Canaletto's trade. 'I would work with him,' he said. 'Tell me, Miss Rooker, do you think I might?' He swung round to her, his expression eager. He had a light voice with an accent that she thought might come from the north of England.

'But I am his apprentice,' Fanny said, dismayed. If it came to a choice between this young man, who looked as though he could afford a hefty fee, and her, who had been unable to offer Canaletto anything beyond her efficiency and knowledge of London life, there could be no doubting whom Canaletto would choose.

'I do not ask to become an apprentice!' Richard Thompkins sounded shocked. 'Indeed, I have just finished such a position with the portraitist, Mr Francis Hayman.' He hitched a leg onto the trestle table and

half sat, talking earnestly. 'I have already a commission.'

'Indeed!' Fanny was greatly impressed. 'But my
master is not a portraitist, he is a painter of scenes, of
vedute,' she said the Italian word carefully.

'Of course he is,' the young man said impatiently.
'Does not everyone know of Canaletto's skill and reputation? There is no one like him at painting light. That
is what I want to learn. I thought if I offered a fee, he
could teach me, perhaps in the afternoons; I shall need
to work at my portrait in the mornings.' There was an
air of easy authority about him.

Fanny wondered how Canaletto would react to this
suggestion. If he had a commission on hand, she would
have had no doubt, but did he want to make public the
fact he had no work at present? On the other hand, she
knew he needed money and this attractive young man
was offering to pay him, no doubt handsomely. 'I will
tell the signor what you wish,' she said carefully. 'Leave
me your direction, or', a better thought struck her,
'perhaps you would care to return later today? He may
well be here this afternoon.'

'And if not, you could maybe have news for me?'
the young man said with a smile that was so charming,
Fanny felt a shiver go through her. 'You will be here?'

She nodded, too breathless to speak.

'Why, then, I shall return.' Richard Thompkins
replaced his hat on his head, gave her a quick bow and
left.

Fanny sank onto one of the stools, feeling as battered as though she'd been flung against a brick wall.
'Ridiculous!' she said out loud. 'Quite ridiculous. It

must have been the effect of the sun, so unexpected as it was.'

Fanny went and inspected her stew and decided that if she dampened down the fire a little, it would do very well while she went and did her sketching in Golden Square. She reached for the poker and raked away some of the burning coals, poured a little water on the rest, then picked up her bag of sketching requirements and left.

Fanny settled the folding stool Daniel Spragg had made for Canaletto at the south end of Golden Square, sat down and considered her viewpoint.

Canaletto had such a thing about viewpoints. 'Is most important,' he had said more than once. 'Sometimes you onlooker, standing back, sometimes boatman, sometimes looking out of upper window. Viewpoint contains whole drama of painting.'

Whole drama of painting? Fanny looked at the regular frontages of the houses around what was more of an oblong than a square. The regularity of roofs and windows was broken by some of the houses being taller than others. In the centre of the square was a circle of grass within an octagonal arrangement of railings. In the middle stood a statue. The area around the garden was cobbled but in front of the little railings guarding the houses was a paved path, protected from the traffic by posts. It was an elegant scene yet there were no decorative flourishes to any of the houses, no nice arrangement of parterred lawns to the central garden, nothing for a viewpoint to focus on. Even the sun had vanished, replaced by a sullen and overcast sky.

Fanny rose and walked first to one end of the paved southern path and then the other, seeking an angle that would make the northern aspect of this not particularly distinguished square more interesting.

Finally she returned to her stool. If she faced the houses squarely on, she could at least capture the full frontage. Then she had an idea. If Canaletto wanted drama in the viewpoint, perhaps she could give him drama. Carefully she opened her bottle of ink, placed it on the pavement and examined her pen. Reassured as to its condition, she settled down to sketch. As she drew lines of windows, doors and architraves she began to wonder which of the houses belonged to Jonathan Wright.

The square could hardly be described as bustling but from time to time well-dressed ladies and gentlemen issued forth from front doors. Occasionally they stepped into carriages, more often a sedan chair; sometimes they walked, usually followed by a servant. Could one of the ladies be Mrs Jonathan Wright?

'That is a very handsome sketch,' said an elderly voice.

Fanny turned. Out of one of the houses behind her, for if they had come from anywhere else she would have seen them, had appeared two ladies. The speaker looked some seventy years with a back as straight as the Monument. Her hair was iron grey under a black bonnet and she wore a black silk ruffled mantua over a black silk gown. Her face was sharp, intelligent, with thin lips, a slightly hooked nose and petal-fine skin stretched over excellent bones. Her eyes were deep blue and uncommonly large. In her youth she must have been exceedingly handsome, if never pretty. 'My daughter was quite an artist and her daughter, my granddaughter, also has considerable talent. But your skill is exceptional.'

'Thank you, my lady,' said Fanny, rising from her stool, somewhat taken aback at being spoken to by such an imposing figure.

'Mrs Truscott will do nicely. I have no title nor wish one. And what might your name be, pray?'

'Fanny Rooker, madam.'

'Hmm, would you be related to the engraver Rooker?'

Fanny was startled but extremely pleased. 'Why, yes, madam, he is my brother.'

'I bought an engraving of his the other day, a pretty river scene, ideal for the upstairs landing, isn't it, Patience?' she turned to the other woman.

'Oh yes, Nancy, quite ideal,' she agreed happily. She was a little younger than Mrs Truscott and her dress proclaimed her slightly inferior, being of grey wool trimmed in black, her bonnet similar, her face lively but wrinkled, round and weathered.

'I worked with Ned until I became apprenticed to Signor Antonio Canal,' said Fanny proudly.

'Indeed!' Mrs Truscott sounded impressed. At that moment there came a commotion from the house on the corner. The front door was flung open and out came a tall, heavy-set man, moving rapidly. Behind him followed a girl dressed in a dark blue gown of some fine stuff, with a light blue petticoat beneath a large white apron of fine linen. Red-gold hair was nicely dressed under a muslin cap.

'You treat me like this and you'll suffer for it,' she

shrieked after the man, her eyes narrowed like some wild cat. 'You'll find no better worker, nor more skilful.'

The man turned and Fanny saw without surprise that it was Jonathan Wright. 'I'll have no more of your insolence. Be gone afore I return or it'll be the worse for you.' He raised a hand and the girl instinctively shrank back. Then he seemed to become aware that he had an audience. His face contorted in a fresh rage, he turned on his heel and disappeared round the corner.

The girl stuck hands on hips. 'Good-for-nothing son of a whore,' she shouted after him. 'May the devil take you!' The door slammed shut behind her.

'Is poor Mrs Wright to lose yet another maid?' enquired Mrs Truscott.

'I fear so,' said Patience with a sniff. 'The servants say that Mr Wright has behaved towards her in a way quite unbecoming to a gentleman, if you understand me, Nancy, dear. Quite properly, she will have none of him.'

'Hmm!' Mrs Truscott gave a cynical sniff.

'And to think that it was you who introduced Mr Wright to Golden Square!'

'I never said he was a gentleman!' pronounced Mrs Truscott with authority. 'Now, young Fanny Rooker, you say you are apprenticed to the Italian painter, Signor Canaletto?'

Fanny bobbed a little curtsy. 'I am, madam.'

'I would be interested to see some of your work. Would your master be willing for you to come round to my house, say tomorrow afternoon?'

Fanny bobbed another curtsy. 'I think so, madam.'

'Send word if he is not. Otherwise I shall expect you around two of the clock. This is Mrs Partridge, she lives with me.' She waved a hand at her companion. 'Come, Patience, we must be on our way, the park awaits.'

Fanny returned to her sketching. Suddenly the view of Golden Square took on an added interest. Surely Mrs Truscott would not ask to see her work unless she was interested in a view of the place where she lived?

As she continued sketching, Fanny glanced from time to time at the severe frontage of the corner house from which Mr Wright had emerged so precipitously and wondered just what dramas were taking place inside.

After a little, the red-haired girl re-emerged, a shawl around her shoulders and a carpet-bag in her hand. She slammed the door behind her then stood on the pavement facing the house, stuck a thumb to her nose and waggled her fingers, pushing out her tongue.

Fanny couldn't help but laugh.

The girl dropped her hand. 'What you staring at, then, young miss?' she demanded. But her tone was friendly.

'A girl who does not like Mr Wright,' Fanny said with a smile.

The girl took a firmer grip on her carpet-bag and came closer. 'You know him?' she asked curiously.

'I met him, once.'

'Once is enough for such as he.'

'You work – worked for him?'

The girl put her bag on the pavement beside Fanny's stool and looked with interest at her sketch. 'Worked is right. And glad I am that I do so no more. You have caught him well.'

Surprised, Fanny looked at her pad and saw that a

caricature of Jonathan Wright had appeared in the corner. There he was, strutting as though he owned the square, if not the whole of London, his big nose in the air, a hand lifted as though to command the attention he obviously thought should be his.

'You do this for a living?'

'I shall do, I am apprenticed to Signor Canaletto, the great Italian view painter.'

The girl was unimpressed. 'I know nothing of painters or painting. I would be an actress.' She spread her arms wide, as though to embrace the world, and her large eyes sparkled. For a moment it was as though the square was a stage.

'Indeed? Well, Fanny Rooker is my name.'

The girl dropped her arms. 'Marie Boucher,' she said grandly with a French accent, then gave an engaging grin. 'My professional name that is. Actually I'm called Mary Butcher. But as a lady's maid it's profitable to be French.'

'That is what you are? To Mrs Wright?'

Mary nodded. 'Well, I was. Poor lady, she is in floods of tears at losing her so dear Marie.' Her expression sobered for a moment. 'In truth, she is the only reason I have stayed so long in this house.' Then she brightened again. 'But I would have left shortly in any case. So she might just as well find a new maid sooner rather than later.'

'You have a new position in hand?' Fanny asked curiously.

'Ah, that would be telling.' Mary looked at Fanny. 'Have you time? I would like to talk of my plans with someone and why not you?'

It was hardly the most compelling of invitations but

there was something exhilarating about Mary Butcher's insouciance. Fanny decided she had all the details she needed to work up a finished drawing. 'I live not a step from here. Will you come with me? You can talk whilst I work.'

'Oho, can't afford a break, eh? You must learn to take more liberties with life!'

'I enjoy my work,' Fanny was indignant.

'Little Miss-Work-Hard!'

'I wonder you wish to come back with me,' Fanny said tartly, packing away her drawing tools and folding up the stool.

Instantly her arm was seized. 'Don't be such a grouch, I would so like to talk with you. You must not mind what I say, my mother told me my mouth would be my downfall. Look at the way I railed at old Wrong John.'

Fanny giggled, instantly forgiving this odd girl, aware that she liked her. As they approached the house in Silver Street, she had a moment's thought. Could Jonathan Wright possibly be with Betty Spragg? But there was no sign of the burly man as she took Mary through to the studio.

Ridding herself of bag and stool, Fanny went first to the fire to inspect her stew.

'You do the cooking? You said you were an apprentice to a famous painter,' said Mary, suspicion and disgust mingled in equal quantities.

'I am. I also do the cooking so we may eat,' Fanny responded with as much dignity as she could muster. She pulled her skirts back from the fire, added more salt to the pot, then turned her attention to her guest. 'Will you have some small ale?' she asked.

Mary's nose wrinkled. 'I would prefer some apricot shrub.'

'You've been living the high life. Here is no shrub, no, nor cordial either. Only ale, unless – I could go to the gin shop if that is what you would prefer.'

'Gin! I'm no street doxy, thank you. I'll take the ale.' Mary dropped her bag and wandered restlessly around the large studio. 'My, how many things are here!' She picked up a brush from its mug, inspected the hairs without much interest, let it fall to the table, then opened one of the bags of pigment. She ran a finger over the lump of colouring matter within, then looked curiously at the smear of yellow left on her skin. 'What do you do with this?'

Fanny brought over two tankards, put them on the table and removed the pigment from Mary's hand. 'It is ground very fine and mixed with oil for paint.'

Mary's eyes took in the row of bulging bags. 'They are all different?'

Fanny poured ale. 'Yes, indeed.'

'Upon my word, so many colours!' Mary marvelled.

'They are the basis for many, many more when mixed together in various proportions.' Fanny handed over a tankard. 'But you do not wish to talk of such things. Tell me what you plan to do now that you no longer work for Mr Wright. Do you have another position as maid?'

Mary drank deeply. She might sniff at humble ale but she was not averse to its taste, thought Fanny. 'Lord love you, no! Not that I could not obtain a much better position tomorrow, if not today,' she added hastily. 'London offers a wealth of opportunities to a well-trained lady's maid and there is none better than yours truly, who speaks French and can sew and dress hair beyond anything.'

Fanny looked at her sceptically.

Mary looked back with a good deal of comprehension in her fine eyes. She put down her ale, placed her hands together, demurely dropped her gaze and bobbed a little curtsy. 'I have starched madam's best apron,' she said in quiet, well-bred tones. 'May I suggest madam wears her blue brocade? 'Tis so becoming to madam's complexion?' She looked up with an impish smile. 'Now see me act the fine lady!' She straightened her shoulders, adopted a haughty look. 'I'll thank 'ee, Marie, not to dictate me my wear. I desire you should refurbish my pink silk with coquelicot ribbons. As for my blue brocade, 'tis yours, I shall never wear it again, it quite washes out my eyes.' Then she stuck her hands on her hips, threw back her head and gave a brazen laugh, 'Why, varlet, dare you cheat me? You're a whoreson knave and I'll have the Watch on 'ee.' She gave a triumphant laugh and twirled around, her skirts billowing out. 'I can play any part I like! Maid, mistress, common woman, ingénue. I shall be the toast of the town!' She twirled again then sank onto a stool and drained her tankard dry. 'You should see your face,' she spluttered, reaching for the jug and pouring herself more ale.

'Where did you learn to act the part?' asked Fanny, marvelling at the quicksilver transformation the girl could achieve.

Mary leaned back against the table, spreading her arms along its length, the tankard held in one hand. 'My mother was a dancer, in Paris. Alas, she became ill and was turned off for being unreliable. She told me the stage was too uncertain a life and trained me in the arts of being a lady's maid, which she had learned in her youth.'

'She was French?'

'Nay, a Londoner, born and bred who loved to dance and met a Frenchman who said he'd make her a star in Paris.'

'And did he?'

'Do pigs fly? His mama commanded his presence in Brittany and off he went, leaving my mama with me about to be born.'

'No! That is shocking!'

'That is men for you. He left her with money, he said enough for my upbringing and education, my mama said it hardly kept us both more than a year.'

'You did not go on the stage in Paris?'

For the first time, Mary looked sad. 'No, mama died, there was no money and the only stage offers I received were for sleeping parts – from impecunious fellows,' she added bitterly. 'So I applied for a position to an English aristocrat staying in Paris whose maid had fallen sick of the pox and died. And so I came to England.'

'But that lady was not Mrs Jonathan Wright?'

Mary laughed. 'No, indeed, she was a titled lady of some pedigree. I shan't bore you with details of all the households I have worked in. I tell you, being a servant opens you to so many insults, you cannot conceive. Those that employ think they only have to withhold a reference and you are their slave. But we have such tales as we can tell of them and their doings, they would not dare!' She emptied the tankard of ale once again. 'I envy such as you with your freedom.'

'Freedom!' Fanny gave a snort. 'I have no freedom, I am bound to obey my master in all things. And I earn nothing.'

'But you learn a skill! One day you will have your independence.'

'So will you when you are an actress,' Fanny said, wondering just how likely that was.

Mary instantly recovered her spirits. 'Why, so I will! And in the meantime, you have no conception what a neat arrangement I have made.'

Chapter Eight

With one supremely easy stroke, the man with the knife opened up the mutilated girl's body from neck to pubis.

Canaletto had experienced many distasteful moments in life but few that revolted him so much.

Yet, after the initial shock, he found himself fascinated – and disliking himself for such an emotion. Reluctantly but unable to stop himself, he moved to stand on the opposite side of the table. 'Surgeon, I think,' he said to the man. 'Such skill with knife. Much more than man who did that.' He indicated the cuts to the face.

The surgeon looked up. He was above average height and seemed to tower above Canaletto. His thoughtful, questioning face had a rumpled look. His clothes under the large apron were good but carelessly worn. 'Interesting that,' he agreed. 'The strokes seem very deliberate, this was no artist of the quick slash. Look how carefully drawn the cuts are, the pattern replicated each side of the face.'

Canaletto leaned forward. 'Replicated' was a new word to him but the sense was clear enough. He studied the face, conscious that the surgeon was watching him. Soon, though, he lost all sense of the other man. The large windows of this dank room let in enough light for him. The staring eyes – none had thought to shut and weight them – had irises an unusually deep blue. The lashes were long and thick, the same golden brown shade as the luxuriant hair.

Her skin had lost the fine bloom it must once have had, it was waxy now and displayed that lifeless pallor that resembled nothing so much as pale mud, the edges of the cuts gaping in horrid fashion. Now that Canaletto studied them, he could see exactly what the surgeon had referred to. Yes, they had indeed been carefully drawn, as carefully as he himself delineated the lines of a building.

His gaze moved down, trying to avoid the terrible opening that ran the length of the torso, and concentrated on the much smaller cut under the left breast. 'He kill with one stroke?'

The surgeon looked up. 'May I ask, sir, your business here?' His tone was interested rather than aggressive. Here was someone who sought information instead of warning a stranger he was unwelcome.

'I find body,' Canaletto said concisely. 'I now involved in finding,' he paused while he sought to remember the word the officer of the Watch had used the previous night. 'I find malefactor.'

'Indeed?' The surgeon looked at him in an interested way. 'Well, your malefactor was either skilful or lucky. He despatched this poor girl with one swift stroke. There is no sign of any struggle.'

'How can you tell?'

The man shrugged, almost apologetically, as if such matters were not properly his concern. 'I have examined various corpses found as this one was. As a medical man, I seek bodies to dissect,' he added. 'When the magistrate has an unidentified corpse destined for a pauper's grave, he allows me to practise my art and widen my knowledge. In return, I examine for him bodies that have met a suspicious end. It is not often a violent death comes so cleanly.' He picked up one of the well-cared-for hands and slipped the point of his knife under a neat fingernail. 'On occasion I have observed skin caught under the nails, indicating a victim has scratched the face or hands of their attacker. Not so here.' He showed the clean blade of the knife. 'Nor is there any bruising on the body.'

Canaletto was impressed with the man's perception. This was someone who used intelligence in his approach to his work. 'And the knife stroke that killed, skilful – or lucky?'

The surgeon rested the point of his knife on the table and looked thoughtfully at the cadaver. 'If I was seeking to kill someone in this way, I would choose exactly this point, between the ribs, straight to the heart. You see the angle of the knife.' He laid the point of his own in the cut and moved it slightly up and down, demonstrating how well the blade fitted when it was pointing at an angle.

'But the knife used was larger, no?' suggested Canaletto.

'Indeed,' the surgeon agreed and made another slight movement that showed how much wider the cut was than his slim blade.

'What sort of knife?'

The surgeon shrugged. 'I cannot say. Butchers use a wide knife, yet I would not say the entry point is as big as one of their weapons would make; also from the edges of the wound I can tell it was double bladed, no butcher I know uses such. But the stroke did not penetrate through to the back, so it was unlikely to have been a sword. I would judge this was done by a knife with a short blade.'

It sounded a singular instrument. 'He use dagger?' hazarded Canaletto.

'Maybe,' the surgeon agreed. 'Perhaps a foreign weapon. And it might not have been a man who killed her. A woman of determination could have done this. Judging by the angle of the knife as it entered, she, or he, would have to have been at least the same height but more probably considerably taller. Here, may I show you?' The surgeon grabbed hold of Canaletto, towering over him, and struck upwards, pulling his knife just short of entering Canaletto's jacket and burying itself in his bosom.

'I understand,' he gasped, taking a hasty step backwards.

Canaletto studied the length of the dead girl's body, and judged that she had been almost as tall as he was. The killer was therefore likely to have been taller than him by several inches. There were many such, Canaletto was sensitive about his height.

'You are hunting the malefactor, you say. You are perhaps an investigator of such incidents in your own country?'

'Ah, no,' Canaletto said apologetically, wondering how he was to justify his interest. 'It is that I find body, as I tell you.'

'Indeed?' The surgeon looked even more curiously at him. 'And that would have been in some muddy street, I'll warrant. In the storm perhaps?'

Once again Canaletto was impressed with his perception. 'How tell?'

The knife was pointed at a pile of clothes folded neatly in a corner of the room. 'The skirts were wet and streaked with dirt. The back of the bodice is also stained, as though she'd been pressed against a damp stone wall and had then slid down.'

'Very seeing,' approved Canaletto. 'May examine, yes?' He gestured towards the clothes.

'Nothing to do with me. My only interest is in the body. You will excuse me if I go about my task? I have other business to attend to later today.'

Canaletto nodded. He wasn't sorry to have something to occupy himself with while the surgeon continued with his gruesome investigation of the body.

He didn't need long to examine the clothes. They contained little of interest, though Canaletto noted that the underclothes were of better quality than the dress. No sign of a reticule: had she not felt one was necessary, perhaps because she was only slipping out for a short time, or had it been stolen? Had the killer been a thief after all?

No, he decided. Not with the ring still on the finger and that scrap of paper clutched in the hand. Canaletto looked again towards the body. The stomach had been opened and the surgeon was peering into the cavity. 'What do you look for?'

'I take every opportunity to extend my knowledge of anatomy. If there is no obvious cause, I look to see what has brought death. I examine heart, liver, kidneys and entrails to find signs of disease. Come, tell me of your interest. I cannot believe you to be so keenly involved merely because you stumbled over the poor creature's cadaver.'

How to explain that he felt he owed a duty to a girl who'd saved him from death not once but twice, but a girl who was even now very much alive? The man would no doubt think him mad.

The surgeon's eyes narrowed. 'Don't tell me you have some morbid turn of mind that brings you to my post-mortem examination?'

That suspicion, at least, could be dealt with easily enough. 'I painter,' Canaletto said carelessly. 'I also like to study anatomy.' There were indeed many painters who undertook detailed studies of the human body to aid its depiction with their brush.

'Painter, eh? Italian, I'll be bound. Your name, sir?'

'Antonio da Canal, at your service,' Canaletto gave a small bow, using his hand to make a graceful gesture, not quite as deep as he would have given in polite society but deep enough to acknowledge an equal.

'Canal?' the man repeated. 'Signor Canaletto, perhaps? I am honoured to make your acquaintance. I have patients who from time to time show me their artistic collections, including mementoes from Venice. Matthew Bagshott at your service.' He gave a small nod. No flourishes from this man.

Canaletto waited for some comment about the small part figures paid in his paintings, but the man returned to his work. Canaletto watched in horrid fascination as the surgeon set aside his knife and plunged his hands into the stomach cavity.

'Aha!' Bagshott said triumphantly. 'Signor, I think you will be interested in this finding.'

Chapter Nine

'An evening at Ranelagh Gardens?' said Purity, carefully hanging a blue silk skirt on a peg by a loop from its waist. 'What is that?'

'Why, Purity, do you know nothing?' Kitty said in a bored voice. 'Ranelagh is a pleasure garden. I vow I was dying to visit Vauxhall but Lady Kildare says it is too early in the season. Even Ranelagh only opens for special events. At Vauxhall all the boxes are open to the elements but Ranelagh offers the Rotunda, a delightful pleasure dome for dancing and mingling. And, Lady Kildare says, so much more select than Vauxhall. It sounds quite divine!'

Purity examined a small tear in a lace ruffle that belonged to one of Kitty's evening dresses and said nothing.

'But Emily and the earl will not take me yet for another sennight, when there is to be a dance there. It is closed until then. Oh, seven days! How am I to wait so long?' Kitty squirmed her little body in her chair, twisting round to see Purity and stetching out her arms in a pretty show of exasperation. 'And this afternoon', she went on, collapsing back into the chair with a sulky look on her face, 'it is decided that we shall visit St Paul's cathedral. Purity, what could be more boring?

Oh,' she sighed, 'to be married and free to do what you want whenever you want it.'

'As long as your husband agrees,' Purity said tartly. She put the torn lace on one side, then hung a petticoat onto another peg, unconsciously caressing the luminous white silk that was so prettily embroidered with pink roses.

'Oh, James is mad for Emily, he'll do anything to please her. Well may I have such a complaisant and handsome husband one day.' Kitty was dressed in a loose morning sack, her hair unpowdered, her fingers busily investigating a paper poke of candies. Then she cast it aside. 'Purity, cease that primping with those clothes, I need you to run an errand for me.'

Purity came out of the cupboard. She distrusted her mistress when in this mood. In fact, she hardly ever trusted Lady Katherine Manners. Kitty's mother, the Countess of Crewe, had had serious words with Purity before the two of them had left for London in the earl's coach. 'I'm trusting you, Purity, to guide my daughter. You have some sense, I think. I would that this invitation from the Duchess of Richmond had come some other time but, as it is, it is impossible for me to travel,' she'd laid a careful hand over her swelling stomach. 'My lying in is all too close and I pray that this child will survive.' Her eyes had filled with tears. So many confinements, so many tragedies. Purity knew that only Kitty, the second child, had lived more than a few years. 'My lord's steward will take you to London. The duchess will have a care for you both, I know. But my Kitty can be, shall I say, determined at certain times?' The question was left hanging in the air.

Purity had dipped a small curtsy and muttered

something about doing what she could but she'd told herself that determined wasn't quite the word for her young mistress. Headstrong, obstinate, self-centred, all those, and a right termagant when she didn't get her own way. Many was the time Purity had had to dodge a well-aimed blow; there was strength in those slender arms. If she'd wanted, Purity could have told the countess many a tale about her indulged daughter.

But Purity had feelings of loyalty to Kitty. They went back to the days when she'd arrived at the Earl of Crewe's gloomy northern pile in the pouring rain, a gift from his younger brother, who was making a fortune for himself out of growing sugar in the West Indies. 'A princess, eh?' the earl had said when she'd arrived and stood, shivering, a ten-year-old girl, hardly alive after the terrible journey in a leaking ship that had corkscrewed around on the ocean until Purity had been convinced they would all end up on the seabed. However, they hadn't and the voyage could be said to have been sweetness and light compared with the one she and her mother had endured between Africa and the West Indies. Every time she had heard her mother relate the dreadful details, Purity had thanked the good Lord she couldn't remember the journey.

'My father was ruler in his country,' Purity said to the earl, repeating the words her mother had taught her. 'He was powerful and had many slaves.'

'Yet he allowed his family to be taken in slavery!' The earl had looked sceptical and for the first time Purity had wondered just how it had all happened.

'My mother says', she repeated carefully, 'that we were bathing in a stream and men came and took us. I was only little,' she added.

'And where did my brother find you?'

'He bought the plantation where we lived.' Purity didn't like to think of the way she and her mother had worked, walking behind the men, hacking down the ripe canes, picking them up from the ground, helping to strip off the outer leaves then pushing them through the crushing machine that squeezed out the sugar juices, all back-breaking work under a remorseless sun. Even worse was the work in the refining plant in its suffocating heat.

To become the new master's concubine and leave that life behind had been a pleasure, Purity's mother had said. And surely it was better for Purity to travel to England than to work in the sugar fields?

'He says you are adept at various household tasks and a quick learner,' the earl continued, scanning the letter he held in his hand.

Purity nodded dutifully, taking in the badly lit, draughty hall with the half-alight fire in a large, stone grate, in front of which slumbered two huge dogs, one dribbling down a slack muzzle. The walls were panelled and ragged flags hung from a great height. She pulled her thin scarf round her shoulders. She had never been so cold in her life, not even on the boat.

Then she'd been taken up to the nursery, where Kitty had been eating her supper in company with a strict-looking woman in a white cap and large white apron. 'I'm Nanny,' she'd said to the shivering girl. 'But you will address me as Mrs Comfort. And if you're to be companion and maid to Lady Kitty, you'd best start by clearing away the supper things and ringing that bell over there for Hawkins to take them away.'

Then Kitty had looked up, deep blue eyes curious in her neat little face. 'You're black,' she'd said.

'Now then, Lady Kitty, we don't notice personal details,' Nanny said sharply.

'But you are,' Kitty had persisted. 'Will it wash off?' As Purity had reached out to gather together the plates, she'd licked her fingers then rubbed them on the back of her hand. 'Why, you're frozen,' she'd said in astonishment. 'Nanny, this girl needs more clothes. Take her to my wardrobe and let her choose something, but not my sprigged challis wool,' she'd added hastily.

'No, indeed!' Nanny had said, her eyes narrowing. 'And I'll thank you, Lady Kitty, not to take such things upon yourself.'

'Then I'll go to Mama.' Kitty had got up from the table and would have run from the room except that Nanny caught her.

'No need to go upsetting her ladyship, I'm sure we can find something for the girl.'

'My name is Purity,' Purity had said, standing very straight, holding the pile of dirty crockery.

Kitty had clapped her hands together. 'That's a lovely name,' she'd said. 'We shall be friends.' Purity had been Kitty's slave, in fact and in affection ever since. An affection that did not prevent her from recognizing all her mistress's faults as well as her virtues.

Now she took the letter held out to her. 'Mind, it's to be delivered immediately,' Kitty said imperiously. 'And you're to give it into no one's hands but the person to whom it is addressed.'

Purity did not need to glance at the name on the letter.

'And you must wait for an answer and watch and

tell me exactly how he looks and what he says,' Kitty continued. 'You can find your way?'

Purity nodded and it never occurred to her mistress to question such familiarity with Golden Square.

The good weather had given way to drizzle. Purity tried to shelter in the depths of her hooded cloak as her feet took her through the Privy Garden to the mire of Whitehall with its constant stream of carriages, horses, chairs and general traffic, up to Charing Cross then up Haymarket and across Piccadilly to Golden Square. Noise and smell assailed her as she went. London was so different from the country around the Earl of Crewe's seat. Even their largest local town offered but a fraction of the buildings, traffic and general commotion that went on in London. It was a relief to reach the relative calm of Golden Square.

Purity made her way to the corner house and banged the big brass knocker on the dark-blue painted door.

For several minutes nothing happened. Purity stood on the doorstep, straining her ears. Was that the sound of someone coming to the door? Or should she try again? Her life was full of these tiny decisions. Should she tell Lady Kitty once again to rise, or leave it for a few more minutes? Should she remind Lady Kitty it was time to send her mother a letter, or not? And how could she divert Lady Kitty from ordering a thoroughly unsuitable gown?

Just as she was about to give the knocker another thump, the door swung open and a bent man stood there in the household's green livery laced with silver. 'Yes?' he said wearily.

'Mr Thomas Wright, if you be so pleased,' Purity said, trying to combine a soupçon of humility with more than an ounce of authority. In her experience, grovelling got you nowhere. Even Kitty responded to a touch of severity. 'I have a message for him.'

The bent figure held out a hand, 'If you will give it to me, I will see that it is delivered to Mr Thomas.'

Purity kept her hands locked within her cloak. 'I am directed to deliver the message in person,' she said firmly but pleasantly.

'Indeed?' Wispy eyebrows raised themselves and rheumy eyes inspected her more closely.

Purity was used to being looked at. People of her colour, she had found, were not common in the north of England. There it had taken time for the Crewe household to adjust to her exotic quality and she became accustomed to stares whenever she went out. But in London she had noticed many, many coloured folk, not only dressed as servants but also going about their business in a way that suggested they were free and independent, so she wondered that she should still call forth stares. It never occurred to her that it could be because she was exceedingly attractive.

Something akin to a leer crept over the man's face. 'If you'll wait in here, I'll see if I can find Mr Thomas,' he said, stepping back so that Purity could cross the threshold. He opened a door off the hall into a room that looked as though it served as an office, furnished as it was with a large, ornate breakfront cabinet with heavy-looking leather-bound books behind the glass doors, a writing table complete with silver inkstand,

and two chairs. On the walls were a couple of dark and inscrutable paintings.

Purity stepped haughtily inside and eased back the hood of her cloak from her short, dark curls.

Sometimes Purity allowed herself to dream that she was not a slave, tied forever to a headstrong and foolish girl but would one day have her own life and home. Not as grand as this, of course, but . . . Her imaginings got no further before in came, not Thomas Wright but his manservant, John – Purity refused even to think of him by the name he'd been given by his young master.

Purity had seen girls blush when an attractive man looked at them, the rosy colour rising in their pale skins, and been glad that hers could not betray her in such a way. Yet she could feel the heat flush up into her face as this man gave her an intimate smile. 'My master asks if you will not give me your message,' he said in the sort of voice that is meant to be overheard. Even as he spoke, their hands were reaching for each other, their bodies drawing close together.

Tears pricked at Purity's eyes at the sound of his dark voice. How she'd missed that reverberative quality since leaving the West Indies. Englishmen's voices were too sharp, too defined, carried no comfort in their crispness.

'Nay, I regret but my mistress has sworn me to give her message to no one but your master,' Purity said loudly, loving the way John was kissing her fingers, feasting her eyes on the width of his shoulders, the sculptured quality of his head.

'Why, then, I'll tell my master so,' John said and his face split into a wide grin, the white of his teeth gorgeous against the steel blue darkness of his skin. 'I will return and acquaint you with his decision on the matter.' Purity admired the way he talked as though he liked words, as though he had studied their sounds and meanings.

He clasped her to him, pressed a passionate kiss on her mouth, released her and left the room. She gazed at the door he had closed behind him and felt she'd been abandoned once again in a cold place. Had she really only known him for just over a month? It seemed like for ever.

She would never forget the day she and Kitty had bumped into Thomas Wright and his servant. The hustle and bustle of London had bludgeoned at her ever since their arrival three days earlier. Combined with the necessity to get on terms with the Richmond household, itself in an uproar with arrangements for the marriage of Lady Emily and the Earl of Kildare, and to listen to Kitty's excited chatter of all that had been promised for her, Purity had found it hard to keep her wits about her.

No doubt she should have cautioned against the expedition into St James's Park. But it was only just across Whitehall and such a fashionable place for a daytime stroll, or so she'd been assured. Kitty had been so determined to be seen amongst the *beau monde*, Purity would have had a hard time dissuading her and neither Lady Emily nor her mother, the Duchess of Richmond, had been around to say her nay.

So they'd gone. And for a time all had been well, they'd walked on the grass by the central canal, admiring those who were similarly taking the air, Kitty speculating on who everyone was and looking forward to the day when she would be able to greet friends and acquaintances. Then a large, ill-disciplined dog had dashed across the grass in pursuit of a ball and had tripped, not Kitty, but Purity. She had fallen to the ground, hit her head on a stone and for a moment lost consciousness. Kitty had had hysterics.

That was when Thomas Wright and his servant had come to the rescue, Thomas to soothe Kitty and John to attend to Purity.

She'd regained her senses to find him laying a wet handkerchief on her forehead, his face deeply concerned. It had been such a relief to see another African, someone whose skin was the same colour as hers, and to hear that deep, vibrant voice asking how she was, that Purity had clutched at his hand as though it was all that was keeping her alive.

He'd helped her to her feet, Kitty and Thomas Wright had been all concern but Purity had brushed aside any suggestion she needed assistance to return to Richmond House. Her only concern was to see her fellow countryman again.

It had not proved difficult, for young Mr Wright had been all afire to arrange a rendezvous with Lady Kitty and Purity had not sufficient wits about her to warn of the dangers of encouraging someone who lacked a proper introduction. An assignation had been arranged in the park for the next day. With all the excitement in Richmond House, it had been easy for Kitty and Purity to escape again to the park.

While Kitty and Thomas had walked and flirted, John and Purity had talked first of their respective households, then of themselves. During the second rendezvous, Thomas had told Kitty he had to leave town on business for his father for several weeks and

John had asked Purity to meet him alone. It seemed he was not to accompany Thomas but fulfil errands for Jonathan Wright, something he said he did often. There were many times Kitty did not require Purity's attendance in the evenings, apart from being ready to undress her when she returned, nor did John seem to have duties then. Purity was not allowed callers at Richmond House, but there seemed no such restraints on John. Or was it that no one had noticed her slip into the Golden Square house and retire to his back room with him? They'd only met there once, though. After that it had been in public, a trip to the play-house, a visit to a coffee house or a tavern. Once Thomas had returned to town, however, he required John's attendance most evenings and there had been little opportunity for such treats.

After a few minutes, the door opened and in came Thomas Wright, dressed in waistcoat and breeches, his cravat untied. Behind him John grinned broadly at her.

'You have a message for me, I think?' Thomas said eagerly.

Purity was sure this young man had nothing to recommend him to the Crewe family beyond looks, an easy manner and, if the furnishings of this house were to be believed, a certain fortune. Or his father had. Oh, Kitty, Kitty, she sighed, you have fallen for a pretty face. Where will all this end?

Purity would have liked to withhold the letter but she had promised her mistress and could do nothing less than hand it over.

Thomas Wright went over to the window and stood reading the missive. Then he turned round, his face alight. Casting around for a suitable simile to describe its look to her mistress, Purity decided that winning a horse race could not have made him look happier.

'Why, tell Lady Katherine that I shall be her servant at St Paul's. And I shall see that Brute attends me. I take it,' he added with a droll look at her, 'I take it that you will wait on Kitty at the cathedral?'

Purity dared not look at John. 'Indeed, sir, as always,' she said in a disinterested voice.

Thomas Wright tossed the letter on the writing table, came closer and picked up her hands, much as John had earlier. He held them in his and looked down at her. 'She is fortunate to have such an attractive companion.'

Purity pulled away. Something in his eyes made her feel uncomfortable.

'You are very lovely,' Thomas Wright said, his voice low and confiding. 'A ravishing contrast to Lady Katherine, is she not, Brute?'

All expression vanished from the African's face, but Purity could see a pulse beating hard by the corner of his jaw. 'As always, you have *les mots justes*, sir,' he said stiffly.

'Get off your high horse, man!' Thomas Wright cuffed his servant lightly round the ear as he left the room. 'And make sure we have all the details of this rendezvous.'

'You do not like him,' Purity said as the servant closed the door behind the master. They had not discussed Thomas before.

'You are very perceptive,' John said quietly. He stood close to her. Purity could feel her heart beating like a bird caged for someone's entertainment. 'They care for nobody, this man and his father! The young master seeks nothing but gratification of his senses and I must facilitate him in everything. His father is no better. I spit upon them!' With an elegant movement, John turned his face and actually did spit. Purity saw the tiny globule resting, shining, on the highly polished boards that lay outside the rich, dark-red Turkey rug with its sombre yet glowing patterning. She shivered. The room was cold and small droplets of rain ran down the window pane. She longed for the warmth of an Africa she couldn't remember and the West Indies, where her mother was.

'Do you have to stay with him?' she asked in a small voice.

John looked away from her. Some of his self-assurance ebbed. 'I have not my freedom,' he reminded her.

'Nor I mine,' she whispered.

'When I was brought to England, fifteen years ago, I thought I would be free, I thought that every Christian in England was free. But it is not so.'

'No one suggested I might be free,' burst out Purity. She had grown so used to being grateful for not being abused, the way her mother had been abused, for not having to toil in the cane fields, the way other Africans had to, for having enough to eat and nice clothes to wear, that the idea she might be able to choose where to go or what to do had been firmly kept in its place. Until she'd met this man. 'But you have been educated,' she said. It wasn't a subject they had discussed before, other matters had demanded their attention. Purity had also been educated, taking her place alongside Lady Kitty, trying to help her concentrate while Kitty had her mind on more pleasurable activities.

John stuck his hands in his pockets and leaned against the door. 'My first master in England sent me to school. I learned Latin and French and mathematics, how to write and read.' He looked at Purity, his eyes burning, 'I know not what for. What did he intend, that master? That I should do his business for him?' He laughed bitterly. 'He left it too late, all disappeared through his incompetence then he turned to gambling. Finally he lost everything including me to Mr Wright over the fall of a dice and shot himself. He had no courage.' He looked at Purity, his eyes burning. 'Why could he not have freed me?'

Purity could feel the emotion rising in him, feel his self-control, usually so rigid, slipping. Just as it had slipped the first time she had met him alone in this house. The passions banked up inside this man were so powerful. When they swept her along, she felt wonderful. When they seemed directed elsewhere, Purity found them almost frightening.

'Will Mr Wright free you?'

'Will your mistress free you?' he retorted. 'No, they like the power they have over us. Other servants can leave, can seek higher wages, better conditions, prettier uniforms.' He dashed a dismissive hand down the silver braid on his green coat. 'We have to stay, unless we wish to be chased through the hovels of London as runaways.'

'Brute!' roared a voice from the floor above. 'Stop pleasuring that wench and attend me!'

One more snatched kiss and Purity left, her heart full of both despair and hope.

Chapter Ten

Canaletto was finding it difficult to keep his temper. 'You are apprentice,' he told Fanny. 'Apprentices prepare pigments.'

'Tomorrow, please,' Fanny pleaded.

'Tomorrow I start painting.'

Fanny's hazel eyes suddenly lost their exasperation. 'You have a commission at last?' she said. 'Oh, signor!'

That 'at last' so infuriated Canaletto he ignored her change of mood. 'Is important Canaletto has pigments, no?' he said balefully, staring at her, drawing himself up to his full height to try to ensure their eyes were on a level. 'What else you have to do this afternoon? Visit young man?'

'No, signor,' Fanny sounded shocked. Canaletto was mollified but wary. He knew the young were always prone to be carried away by their feelings for the opposite sex. It was only a matter of time before Fanny fell under the spell of some tiresome stripling.

'Do not, what is word? Canoodle? Yes, canoodle with Daniel's apprentice?'

Fanny laughed, a gay, carefree sound that, again, reassured Canaletto. 'What, that great lumpkin of an Adam? Nay, signor, he is not to my taste, nor I to his.'

Canaletto began to feel easier. 'He look very hot upon you, I think, when we first come.'

Fanny waved an airy hand. 'That was before Jenny arrived, signor. I assure you he has had no eyes for me nor any other girl since.'

'Say you so?' Canaletto grunted. 'A nothing of a girl!'

'She's pretty enough,' Fanny said carelessly.

'So,' Canaletto returned to the main matter in hand, 'why not want prepare pigment this afternoon? Canvas ready, I start painting tomorrow.'

Fanny took a deep breath. 'Signor, yesterday, as I sketched in Golden Square, a Mrs Truscott admired my work and asked me to bring other examples to her this afternoon.' She looked pleadingly at him. 'I thought you would not mind; if she commissions me, the payment could help.'

Canaletto was taken aback. He did not regard his apprentice as anywhere near skilful enough to be commissioned. The name Truscott did not suggest a woman of discernment or fortune, but one never knew with the English, the most unlikely people had money these days. 'Fanny does not tell me this,' he said sternly. 'Says nothing to me, why?'

Fanny looked stubbornly at him. 'Signor, you sent me out yesterday morning to sketch but when I tried to show you what I'd done, you would not look, would not comment on my work.'

Canaletto sighed. He had handled this matter badly, even he could see this.

'I come back to find carousing and chatter,' he said sternly. 'My apprentice entertains, not works. Dinner not ready.'

Fanny dropped her gaze. Ah, at last he had made

her conscious of her dereliction of duty. 'I'm sorry, signor, that was Mary. I tried to tell you about her, but you would not listen,' she added a touch resentfully. Then out spilt a stream of words Canaletto had difficulty in following. It seemed to be some tale of how a maid had been turned off by the man who had given Betty Spragg the black eye. He had to calm her down, make her speak more slowly and carefully so he could follow.

Certainly he could not forget the vivid girl he had found with Fanny the previous day. At first she'd tried to charm him, laughing, smiling, fluttering her eyelashes at him, moving her body in such a way as to display her considerable physical attributes. Canaletto had refused to be attracted. He'd wanted to tell Fanny of his morning's activities and he was hungry. He could smell the stew cooking on the fire, could see appetizing steam rising from the pot. The last thing he wanted was to share his meal with this girl who made her availability so obvious. He had been curt and unwelcoming.

The girl had picked up her bag and left, a queenly twist of her head and neck displaying exactly what she thought of his attitude. He'd heard her and Fanny whispering outside the studio door, Fanny's voice apologetic, the girl's hard and flippant. Fanny had returned all sulks and when Canaletto had started on his tale of his morning's doings, she had more or less accused him of rudeness to a friend of hers. They had eaten in silence, which had spoilt the flavour of the really excellent dish she had put before him.

Was it any wonder he had had the indigestion? The wind in his stomach had been so uncomfortable that when she had brought out her sketchbook, Canaletto had told her she must wait until later for him to look at her work.

And later had come the young man with his so welcome request for tuition. He had spoken to Canaletto's apprentice that morning, he'd said, at which he had glanced at Fanny.

Canaletto had seen her blush. 'Fanny,' he'd said sternly. 'Not tell me?'

She'd blushed again. 'There's been no opportunity,' she said lamely.

Of course there had been. There had been the whole dinnertime when they'd eaten in silence. He'd stared at Fanny, who'd muttered something about having to go and check with their supplier whether the new consignment of linseed oil they needed had arrived and whisked out of the studio.

Canaletto had gazed after her in amazement for a moment, then mentally shrugged off her extraordinary behaviour and turned his attention to his visitor.

His name was Richard Thompkins and he'd been apprenticed to Francis Hayman. 'A most respected portraitist,' the young man assured him.

Canaletto admitted that he had heard the name. 'Seen no paintings,' he'd added.

'You should visit his studio,' young Thompkins said eagerly.

Canaletto had no desire to visit any English artist's studio. In his opinion, the English learned from the Italians, the French and the Dutch, they taught nobody. He eyed young Thompkins and his fashionable dress. There was nothing of the struggling artist about him. Canaletto marked him down for an amateur with the money to persuade a professional to take him on as an apprentice, not a serious career painter.

'Father supports son's endeavours?' he suggested when the young man had finished a flattering account of how he longed to study with the great Italian master of the painting of light.

The golden eyes suddenly hardened. 'I have no father, sir. I am an orphan.'

Canaletto's interest was caught. 'Orphan? Pity. But father left you well provided for, yes?' he said inquisitively.

'My guardian did, sir,' Richard Thompkins said quietly.

'To study with Canaletto will cost,' the painter told him brutally.

'I have money,' the young man said happily.

'And Signor 'Ayman?'

'I have completed my apprenticeship but, in any case, Mr Hayman is happy for me to study with you,' Richard Thompkins said with a sunny smile. 'He is anxious to see me succeed in all things.'

Fleetingly Canaletto remembered his nephew, Bernardo Bellotti, who had been his apprentice in Venice. He had taught the boy everything he knew until Bernardo had emerged as good a painter as Canaletto was himself, skilled in the views and with a style so modelled on his uncle's it made Canaletto both proud and heartsick to see.

Proud to have nurtured such a fine talent, heartsick to realize how much he himself had lost in his mad dash to produce enough paintings to satisfy the market, to amass a fortune. And what had happened? The market had vanished with the European war that had made it hazardous for the English milordi to travel. And when Canaletto had tried to follow his market to England and invest the monies he had carefully collected, he'd been set upon, the fortune stolen and his life almost lost.

It would do no harm to take on a pupil such as this eager young pup. Canaletto could not believe he could show much promise, but if he was willing to pay highly for the privilege, did it matter?

Accordingly he arranged with Master Thompkins that the young man would attend at Canaletto's studio after dinner in two days' time. 'I work on new painting,' Canaletto said grandly. 'Thompkins follow progress, yes?'

'And, dare I suggest, assist you, sir?' The young man's tone was pressing.

He had promised an extremely useful sum of money. 'We see,' Canaletto said guardedly. 'Bring sample of work, yes?'

'Of course, sir. Thank you, sir!' Bowing with gratitude, Richard Thompkins had made his way out of the studio.

When Fanny had returned, it had been to find Canaletto deep in his sketchbook, studying the possible views he'd jotted down, deciding which could most profitably be turned into a finished work. He'd been far too involved with planning to talk to Fanny. He'd stifled her nervous attempts at conversation and had taken his sketchbook off to his room to be able to think in silence.

Sadly he realized now that he had made a great mistake in not looking at the task he had set her yesterday. 'Bring me sketchbook,' he commanded.

Fanny, sullen, fetched it, found the right page and handed it over.

Canaletto laid the book on the long table under the cold light that fell through the generous windows. Never, he thought as he studied Fanny's work, would he get used to the unforgiving quality of the light in this country. There was no brilliance, no warmth, no heart to it. The weather could be cold in Venice, oh, indeed, yes! Canaletto remembered winter days when his fingers had lacked blood enough to grip his pen. But the light even then had scintillated, had bathed buildings and piazzas with a quality that made them sing, had refreshed the eye, made the heart dance.

Here buildings seemed to absorb the light into themselves and give nothing back.

With an effort Canaletto banished all thought of the light, looked at Fanny's sketch and sighed.

She was by his side in an instant. 'It is no good, signor?' she said nervously.

'You have interesting viewpoint.'

'Yes?' Fanny said, even more nervously.

'Perhaps the view of a dog? Or very small child?'

Fanny wilted. 'I thought it would make the picture more attractive,' she said in a low voice. 'The houses are so very dull.'

She had a point there. Indeed, after the problem of the light, Canaletto's main disappointment at being in London was the lack of architectural interest for his brush. How he missed the grand palazzos of Venice, the constant interest of canals and their boats. There were sights in Venice you could paint again and again, and he had. The regatta with its fantastic assembly of boats, the square of St Mark, the Bridge of Sighs, to name only a few. Nothing in London matched them for majesty and interest. Yes, there was something to be made of the Thames, but the normal traffic there lacked the romanticism of the gondolas on the canals with their colourful boatmen. Everything in London was more, more – he searched for a word that would suit and finally decided that 'everyday' had to be the nearest he could get to pinning down the quality or, rather, lack of quality, that he sought.

He decided Fanny needed encouragement. 'Makes view interesting,' he agreed. 'No wonder this Signora Twister – '

'Truscott,' corrected Fanny.

'This Signora Truscott interested see more work. But, Fanny,' he said more sternly, 'proportions of coach in foreground all wrong. With that viewpoint, should be huge, enormous.' He pointed up to the ceiling. 'Would hide all houses! And where is sun?'

'Sun?' asked Fanny in a small voice. 'There wasn't any sun. The morning brightness had all disappeared. Most days in London are overcast,' she added a touch despairingly.

'But picture must have sun, how else achieve liveliness, action in stone and brick? In grey light like this', he flipped the back of his fingers over the sketch, 'all is dead, lifeless.' He watched while Fanny made several attempts to speak, failed, then sat on a stool beside him and studied the sketch despondently. 'But houses captured well, details good. Redraw, with proper viewpoint, with sun, shadows and sketch will be good.'

Fanny's face remained desolate.

'Write letter to Signora Twister.'

'Truscott,' she corrected automatically.

'Saying call next week. Tomorrow prepare pigments, redraw sketch.' He thought for a moment; there
was a lot of work to be done in preparing the colours,
cutting lumps, chopping, then grinding, finer and finer
and finer, working in with the oil. 'No, sketch next day.
Have new apprentice coming then.'

Fanny looked up at that, her face aflame. 'You have
taken on Mr Thompkins?'

'Very keen, offer much money.'

Fanny wilted, her expression dismayed, no, devastated. She rose like a woman twice her age. 'I'll get my
things together,' she said. 'After I prepare the pigments,
I'll leave.'

'Leave?' Canaletto was stunned.

'You told me you have a new apprentice now, so
you do not need me.'

He stared at her in exasperation at her stupidity.
'Thompkins only come afternoons, special arrangement. Fanny my apprentice.'

She still looked uncertain and nervous. Canaletto
lost his temper. 'Fanny, Canaletto cannot work without
his apprentice, that is you! It is you make me comfortable, make painting possible.'

She gave him a baleful look. 'You mean I prepare
your pigments, cook your meals, wash your clothes.
That does not make me an apprentice.'

Canaletto sighed. How was he to handle this difficult girl? 'You progress,' he said in a conciliatory voice.
'And I train you. Once pigments prepared, you finish
sketch, then prepare canvas and paint Golden Square
view, yes? Colours will be all ready.'

Her face lit up. 'I am to paint a picture at last? Sir, I
will write a note to Mrs Truscott saying I cannot visit

today, and your paints will be the best prepared of any artist. Trust me!'

'I do, little Fanny, I do.' Canaletto felt there had been enough emotion, it was not good for the atmosphere of the studio. He cast around for some way to defuse the situation.

'Such interesting talk with surgeon yesterday,' he said. 'Over body of dead girl. You remember me find dead girl?' he asked encouragingly.

Fanny was sitting at the table penning her note to Mrs Truscott. 'Indeed, signor, I do. Please, one more moment and I will have finished this and perhaps I can prevail upon Adam to take it to her house.'

While she finished her note and took it to Daniel's workshop, Canaletto helped himself to a tankard of ale. She returned, went straight to the studio table, unwrapped a lump of cinnabar, cut it in half and started to crush it in the mortar, wielding the pestle with concentrated force. Vermilion wasn't the choice Canaletto would have made for the first pigment, but he decided to let the matter pass.

'Tell me, signor, did you find out who the girl was?'

'No,' Canaletto said gloomily, remembering his frustration over the interview at the magistrate's house. 'But surgeon, he cut her open.'

'Heavens,' Fanny stopped her pounding and looked at him in horror. 'Why?'

'Study inside, improve medical knowledge,' Canaletto said impatiently. He went to the main point of his story. 'Surgeon make discovery.'

'Yes, signor, what did he discover?' Fanny asked expectantly as he paused, tasting again the desolation of the moment.

'Girl with child.'

'With child?' Fanny's face was a picture of confusion and distress. 'How terrible. She died and the baby died too?'

'Surgeon say baby perhaps four, five months old. Not old enough to live.' Canaletto winced as he remembered the foetus the man had drawn from the body of the dead girl, so perfectly formed, almost like a wax model. 'Boy,' the man had said abruptly before laying it carefully, almost with tenderness, in a pail under the table. 'If the killer had known, maybe he would have spared her his knife.' Then the surgeon had gone back to his internal investigations.

'I remember Lucy, my sister-in-law; you remember Lucy, signor?'

Canaletto nodded grimly. Lucy Rooker was a silly, malicious girl who had caused Fanny much pain.

'When she was five months' gone, she hardly showed at all. Could it have been the same with this girl? Was that why you didn't notice she was with child when you found her?'

Canaletto had wondered about this point. He remembered the knife wound, just below the girl's left breast. He remembered the feel of the swelling flesh. Had he missed that other swelling? No, he decided, he had felt something but had assumed it had been the way the body had been lying, slumped at the bottom of the dank wall. But he'd seen the curve on her naked body before it had been ripped apart by the surgeon's knife. The news had not come as a total surprise, either to him or to Matthew Bagshott.

Fanny continued crushing the pigment but she

looked thoughtful. 'You said she was wearing a ring, signor? Was it on her marriage finger?'

'No, on a middle finger.'

'So, she was not married.' Fanny made it a statement rather than a question. 'Perhaps she was seeking marriage from the father of her baby? Perhaps she was killed *because* she was carrying.'

'I think you ask right questions.' Canaletto saw the pleasure in her face.

'Or perhaps he was a married man and she threatened to tell his wife?' Fanny went on. 'And he killed her to protect his marriage.'

'That, too, probable,' Canaletto agreed gravely.

'I think you mean possible,' Fanny told him gently. 'Probable means it must very likely be so, possible that it could be so.'

'Ah!' said Canaletto. 'Probably right.'

Fanny laughed delightedly and after a moment, as he understood, Canaletto followed. Then he sobered. 'Why no one ask about her? Why no one come to magistrate and ask where she is?'

'Perhaps those who know her think she has gone to visit somewhere,' suggested Fanny. 'Why don't you, signor, draw a picture of her face and I'll get my brother to engrave a poster asking anyone who knew her to come to you? We could put it up around the area where you found her.'

'Fanny, good idea! I do sketch now. Words you add, yes?' Without waiting for her answer, Canaletto sat down, reached for his sketchbook and summoned up his memories of the dead girl's face, first as he had seen it lit in the unearthly brightness of the lightning and then on the surgeon's slab. Could it be that no one had realized she was dead? And what of the fact that she had been with child? Had that been the reason for her death or would the killer have spared her had he but known of her condition?

Chapter Eleven

Mary Butcher, or Marie Boucher, as she preferred to be known, brushed the flame of her hair until it floated and crackled around her face. As she brushed, she watched her reflection in the dim and cracked grey of the mirror that stood on the little round table in her room.

A smile played around her mouth. She opened her arms wide, relishing the freedom of her naked body. She felt the warm air from the room's coal fire playing on her long legs and high breasts, their nipples alert like raspberries. She was pleased with her body, with everything about herself. And, much more than this, pleased she no longer had to bend to the whims and demands of another woman.

'Not that I wasn't sorry for my poor mistress,' she said, giving another stroke, watching the hair lift with the brush, as though the fiery gold had a life of its own and could not bear to be parted from something that caressed it so skilfully. 'And she'll not find a maid to look after her better than what I did.' She turned her head. 'Has she found anyone else yet?'

Lying in a mess of bedclothes, slack-featured, a nightshirt rucked around his hairy chest, Thomas Wright grinned. 'She's found a right old harpy.' Then he grew sober. 'Poor Mother, she is not well, Mary, but then you know that better than anyone else.'

Mary said nothing; in her view, Mrs Wright made too much fuss about too little. Elderly ladies – for to Mary ladies approaching their fifties had to be elderly – who had borne nine children, even if four had died in infancy, had by nature's law to suffer from diseases of the stomach and other parts of the body. It should not make them turn from their husband's approach and plead the vapours. No wonder then if that husband turned to other comforts.

'I trust, harpy or not, she knows how to stroke your mother's forehead to bring relief from her crippling aches.'

'Oh, as to that, Mother never stops complaining that no one can relieve her of pain the way her precious Marie could,' Thomas said petulantly. 'She blames my father for your flight. And I think she more than suspects the way you have bewitched me.' He gave her a sidelong glance. Then he added, 'I believe Mother decided to choose as your replacement someone neither Father nor I would give a second glance to.'

Mary dropped her brush and leaped onto the bed, pummelling Thomas with light fists. 'You're not to even think of glancing at another woman. Not, do you hear?'

'Whoa!' He grabbed her wrists, twisting and turning her arms behind her, holding her poised above him, his barrel chest rising and falling with the effort.

She looked into his dark eyes, saw herself reflected, a miniature, passionate creature, liked what she saw and collapsed in giggles onto him.

There followed a pleasant interlude during which

Thomas discarded his nightshirt. It ended in a groaning, thrusting, triumphant climax.

Afterwards Mary drew a slim finger through the sweaty curls on Thomas's chest. 'Swear you will never look at another woman,' she demanded in a throaty little voice. 'Swear or I will make you pay!' She tweaked a little cluster of hairs and smiled at his sudden intake of breath. She felt superbly confident of herself. This was life! Whyever had she spent so much time tending to the wants of women richer and more fortunate than herself when she could have been enjoying herself like this?

Then she found herself flung on her back, wrists pinned to the bed, Thomas towering above her, his face anger-flushed. 'Are you threatening me, Mary?' he breathed out through clenched teeth.

'Threatening?' she said in a dulcet voice. 'And how could I threaten the man who keeps me in luxury? Who could no doubt find five women as beautiful in five minutes if I told him never to come to my door again?' Her voice was honey sweet, her eyes sparkled with humour. He collapsed by her side, breathing fast, still holding one of her wrists, his eyes fixed on hers.

She released herself then placed his hand upon her breast. 'There, whoever is going to understand your moods as I do?'

With a moan, he fastened his mouth on her hardened nipple and suckled passionately while Marie held his shorn head close and smiled fiercely to herself.

Should she tell him that for one terrible second she'd seen his dreadful father shine out of his eyes as his hands cruelly gripped her wrists? How would he react? There seemed little love lost between the two.

Old Jonathan was always ranting at his son, calling him an idle, good-for-nothing layabout, but he supplied him with a more than decent income and had given him that handsome slave. Mary's eyes gleamed for a moment as she thought of Brute's powerful body, no man was ever better named. She wondered, though, what twisted emotions lived within him that he could so completely shun her attractions. Could he be one of those men who preferred his own sex? Mary knew they existed, scorned though they were by society. Or was it something to do with his race? Could he conceivably find her pale skin and vivid hair ugly?

Then she forgot her chagrin at being so ignored as she gave herself up to the delicious sensations Thomas was inflicting upon her. She slid a hand between his legs and was rewarded with instant attention from his manhood.

'Tell me, Thomas,' Mary said idly a little later as, sated at last, he lay back on the ample pillows sipping a glass of burgundy. 'Do you find black skin attractive?'

'Black skin?' he asked guardedly. 'You mean slaves?'

'Some of the girls are very attractive,' she murmured, hooking her leg over his companionably. 'But they look so different, with that dark skin and woolly hair. Yet,' she added ingenuously, 'I have heard men find them devilishly attractive.'

'And you wondered if I am one?' Thomas rested the glass upon his naked stomach. 'Some, as you say, *are* devilishly attractive. There's something about dark meat!' He grinned at her, 'But, upon my word, you have no need to worry, Mary my dove, my present taste is for white, and I'm particularly fond of breast.'

Chuckling, he dipped his head and licked her nipple with a wet tongue.

Mary wriggled away from him. She'd found that statement deeply unattractive. Of course he must have consorted with a slave at some time. There were enough of them in London, she'd even heard there was a brothel solely devoted to providing what he had so unpleasantly described as dark meat for hungry males.

Thomas put down his goblet and sent an idle hand down her body, tracing the curves. 'How much better this is than snatching odd moments in my mother's powder closet,' he said with a louche look. Mary slid down the bed a little as she realized she had under-estimated the effect her availability could have on his potency. 'Why did you not suggest setting up this little nest earlier, eh?' His mouth nuzzled at her ear, his tongue slipped inside and acquainted itself with its private places while his hand moved with luxurious slowness over her hips and belly, working its way towards the hot centre of her sex.

What a fool the man was, Mary thought, circling his nipple with her finger, relishing the way it hardened under her touch. Why could *he* not have suggested it? Why had it taken that row with his father to make her realize she had to arrange things herself?

'You have the touch of a witch,' he said, raising his head for an instant, his eyes heavy lidded, his words slurred. 'Your delights grow ever more, more delightful,' he ended lamely and buried his face in her stomach, giving her navel the same treatment as her ear. 'Your flesh is, well, fleshly,' he slurred on, his hand active between her legs. 'It grows more luscious every day.'

Mary knew her body was growing fuller. Was it because she no longer had to run around a demanding woman? Or could there be some other reason? If so, was it something she could profit from?

'I tried to see Mr Garrick yesterday,' she told Thomas, when he once again fumbled for his goblet of wine. 'But he is ill and sees nobody.'

'This stupid fancy of yours to be an actress,' Thomas said languidly. 'I would not like it, you know. I would have you here at my beck and call.'

'Would you?' she looked at him teasingly. 'But how if all London was at my feet and you were the only man to enjoy my favours?' She dipped a finger in his wine and held it up for him to suck. 'I saw the sweetest buckle as I went. Diamonds set with the prettiest skill in silver. 'T'would look ravishing on my new emerald silk that you bought me the other day.'

Before he could promise her the trinket there came an urgent rap on the door. 'Master Thomas,' came Brute's voice. 'Master Thomas, your father desires your presence, immediately.'

Thomas sighed. 'Damnation! What can the old man want?' Dragging on clothes, he went to the door and opened it, careless of the fact that Mary lay naked on the bed. 'Come in, Brute, tell me the worst.'

Mary watched as the dark man entered. He could not help but take in the sight of her body as she lay, flamboyant, on the bed. He averted his eyes from the sight but not before she had registered an emotion that chilled her so much that she, who delighted in shocking the world, felt constrained to pull up the bed-clothes to cover herself. What she had seen was a mixture of disgust and hate.

Chapter Twelve

Charlie ran and ran. His legs weren't long but they were fast. How long before the staff realized he wasn't with the rest of the boys? Ever since he'd been caught by Mr Birchem at the front door, Charlie had been waiting for the right moment.

It had come whilst the boys were out in the fields next to the Foundling Hospital. A wild dog had suddenly appeared and chased Robert Walpole up a tree, then had sat at the bottom, hysterically barking at him, foam frothing at his mouth.

The other boys had scattered, many screaming. Mr Birchem and his assistant, intent on dealing with the dog, had to content themselves with shouting at their charges to return at once to the hospital.

Charlie melted away, across the fields to the road where he'd seen carts and carriages pass. He knew it must lead to London because from here he could see the smoke that everyone knew hung over the town. He'd heard how big London was, how easy it was to lose oneself in its network of streets and passageways.

The rutted surface of the road was hard to run on, and the long grass beside was equally difficult. Soon Charlie had to stop and bend over, a stitch in his side. Behind him he could hear a cart. He didn't hesitate.

'Please, sir,' he said as the carter drew his weary-looking horse to a halt beside him, 'I've a most urgent need to be in London. Can you give me a lift?'

'Urgent need, is it?' The carter sniffed in a dubious way that had Charlie afraid he was going to be scooped up and taken back to the Hospital. But perhaps the man didn't recognize the Foundling brown breeches and jacket with the red flashes, for after scrutinizing him from top to toe with sad eyes set in a face so creased and dirty that Charlie swore you could sow seeds in the crazy patchwork of lines that covered cheeks and forehead, he nodded. 'Jump up, young un, we'll see if we can take 'ee.'

Charlie scrambled up beside him, clutching first the wheel and then the backboard, grabbing at the hand that was reached down to him and which hauled him up the last bit with surprising strength. 'There, sit 'ee down and don't frighten t' 'orse, 'e's not used to young uns larkin' around up 'ere.'

Above the creaking and thudding of the cart as it jolted over the rutted road came another, quite different series of squeaks and cheeps. Squirming round, Charlie found the flat bed of the cart was piled with square baskets, each filled with several chickens, brown feathers fluffed out as they crouched in their cages, bright eyes surveying all they passed.

'Where are you taking them?' Charlie asked, shuffling on the hard bench as he tried to get comfortable.

'Market,' the carter said laconically.

'Are they yours?'

'Noah!' the carter chuckled, not an entirely pleasant sound. 'But don't be thinkin' it don't matter if a couple falls off the back, they's all been reckoned up and I 'as to count for every one.'

'I am not a thief,' Charlie said, a touch indignantly.

'Noah?' A rheumy eye looked him over in a most suspicious way, 'Well I 'opes not.'

There was silence for a little while Charlie studied the way the carter controlled his horse, occasionally pulling on a rein to guide the animal around a particularly large crater in the road, or allowing the leathers to slacken when the horse seemed to be happy ambling along.

Charlie soon reckoned he'd sorted out the secret of driving a cart and started looking about him. They passed several brickworks, the chimneys standing up like gnarled fingers pointing heavenwards to a better life (for a moment Charlie wondered whether Mr Birchem had managed to get Bob down from the tree without the mad dog savaging either of them), stacks of bricks in shades of red and purple piled around them.

Soon they were in the thick of building works with elegant houses rising all around. Not as large, of course, as the Foundling Hospital, but with the same regularity of feature, generosity of windows and neatness of appearance.

'Where is it 'ee be going on this matter of great urgency?' the carter asked as they continued to bounce and jolt along through heavier and heavier traffic. Charlie thought all the world must be coming to London, there were so many carriages, horses and carts.

'Duke of Richmond,' Charlie said falteringly. While he'd been in the hospital, the task had seemed so simple. Charlie only had to reach London and anyone would know where a man with the power and riches of the duke lived. Now he saw that London was vast and filled with many houses that could be afforded by dukes and suchlike.

'Duke of Richmond, eh?' The carter hawked phlegm over the side of the cart.

Hope grew in Charlie.

'Would that be round the back of Covent Garden Market? I knows there's the duke of something there,' the carter pulled on the reins as the horse seemed in danger of mounting a sidewalk after a tray of buns carried on a street trader's head.

Charlie had to admit he didn't know if that was right or not.

'No direction, eh?' the carter said ruminatively. 'Expecting you, is they?'

Charlie squirmed on the seat. 'Not exactly,' he admitted at last.

'Not expecting you,' the carter repeated, even more ruminatively. 'Oo is it, then, 'as sent 'ee orf wivout direction or word?' It was said so casually, and Charlie by now felt so easy with the carter, he found himself saying, 'As to that, good sir,' for all the foundlings were educated to be most polite to their seniors, 'it was my idea.'

The carter swung round and looked him in the eye and for a moment Charlie felt uneasy, for the man full face was a ferocious sight. 'Your idea?' he asked softly.

A horrible suspicion that he had not been very wise struck Charlie most forcibly and he shrank slightly away from the figure that now seemed positively sinister. 'Well, that is to say, of course, Mr Birchem knows my destination,' he said bravely.

'Mr Birchem, eh?' the carter said even more softly. 'But he didn't give you a direction?' A claw of a hand, so grimy no one could have identified the colour of the skin, rested on the worn but clean sleeve of Charlie's brown jacket. 'A nice boy like you loose in London without a direction. Methinks 'ees a runaway and 'oo ever knows what becomes of runaways, eh?' He grinned into Charlie's face, his breath stinking horribly.

'The duke's my sponsor,' Charlie blurted out desperately.

'A public 'ouse for a sponsor?' the man cackled. It wasn't a nice sound.

Charlie decided he'd be better off without his lift. He made to leap off the cart but the claw-like fingers gripped his arm. 'Oh no, my bully boy. You's not going nowhere. There's folks I know will pay good money for a sweet little lad like 'ee an' all the public houses, or dukes,' the words were thrown in as a richly amusing afterthought, 'or dukes,' he repeated with even greater delight, 'is not going to do 'ee one bit o' good. Cos we're nearly 'ere now. 'Igh 'Olborn this is.'

The cart had left behind the elegant buildings they'd met earlier. It was passing through narrow streets packed with traffic, houses bending towards each other above the road so that the windows were nearly touching. Street traders called out their wares, gentlemen edged carefully through mired sidewalks, their steps precious in an attempt to keep their shining shoe leather clean. Horsemen barged their way through carts and carriages, their mounts liberally adding to the stinking conditions in the road. People argued, barracked and shouted.

Above Charlie's head, a window opened. 'Gardee loo,' shouted a voice.

The carter cursed and whipped his horse. To no avail, an increase of speed in this traffic wasn't possible. A stream of hot, stinking water came down, missing the driver's seat but splashing a section of chickens, who rose in their cages and squawked protest.

Charlie wrenched at the hand that held him, hoping that the carter's attention had been sufficiently distracted that his grip had loosened.

Alas, it was as tight as before.

'Help,' cried Charlie. 'Help, I'm being abducted!'

The hand jerked him down on the seat with cruel force, banging his head against the wood so that stars exploded in his eyes. 'Whoreson lad that you are, I'll tell yer mother when we see 'er this night what a rogue and devil 'ee be,' he cried.

It seemed that that was enough to satisfy anyone who might have been inclined to investigate the situation.

Charlie felt more frightened than he had ever been in his life. Waiting to be caned by Birchem was nothing compared to the unknown horrors that he could expect at the hands of this dreadful man. Carefully he worked himself upright again.

Coming towards them was a large coach drawn by four horses that the coachman was having difficulty controlling through the crush of traffic. There was hardly room for the two vehicles to pass each other. The coachman shouted, gesticulating for the cart to get over and the carter was pulling on the reins, trying to move his ungainly vehicle to the side of the road, his horse reluctant to drag the load out of the ruts.

Charlie dived forward. The carter's hand prevented him from moving off the wooden bench but not from grabbing the reins. Frantically he pulled on the right one, forcing the horse's head around so that he was aimed straight for the approaching carriage.

With a bellow of rage, the carter hit Charlie a dreadful blow that stunned him for a moment. Shaking his head to clear it from the mists that threatened consciousness, he came to just in time and screamed loudly.

The startled carter's horse flattened his ears, neighed loudly, flung up his head and charged at the coach.

The coachman could do nothing to avoid the collision.

There was a terrible crash, horses whinnied and reared. The cart faltered for a moment, then tipped over, bringing carter, Charlie and chickens all down. Baskets rolled and bounced, broke open and released a frightened flock of birds, hipping and hopping everywhere – under the feet of passers-by, under the hooves of horses frantically being reined in by riders and drivers. Youngsters whooping with joy went chasing after them, seizing one, two or even three with astonishing speed then melting away from the scene clutching their unexpected prizes.

And what of Charlie?

Sliding down the bench as the cart tipped over, he stamped on the carter's head with his small shoe, wishing he was a grown man and could do proper damage, then slipped through the press of people exclaiming and goggling at the accident. Two footmen had come down from the coach and one made a grab for the boy but Charlie ducked and weaved and such was the crowd that had now gathered, plus the distractions of the birds, that he was able to make his escape.

Shouts and imprecations following him, Charlie elbowed his way out of the throng, found an alleyway and dived down it. Behind him he heard the pounding of pursuing footsteps. He ran through a courtyard and out into another alley but still his pursuer followed.

Flying through a further courtyard, he tripped over a mangy cur and sprawled to the ground. A hand grabbed his shoulder and forced him upright.

Charlie groaned; it had to be the carter. Helpless, he twisted around, bracing himself for the sight of the lined and begrimed face.

And saw instead a man dressed in a long brown coat of old canvas over leather breeches. It was impossible to tell his age, his olive skin was smooth but it didn't seem the smoothness of youth and his dark, deep-set eyes had an expression that was chilling. A gaily striped bandanna was tied around his head and there were gold hoops in his ears.

The man smiled at Charlie, 'Well,' he said, 'what have we here, eh? A runaway?' His voice was very deep and there was nothing reassuring about the smile. Charlie began to tremble.

Chapter Thirteen

'Anaconda?' called a fresh, young voice.

Through the passageway came a girl carrying a sack. She was dressed in a gown as gaily striped as the man's headscarf. Her hair was a tangle of black curls tied back with a straight piece of the same material as her gown. 'There you are, I thought I'd lost you.' She was breathing fast, as though she'd been running. She lowered the sack to the rubbish-strewn courtyard at Charlie's feet and ran a hand across her forehead. 'What you want to rush off like that for?' she whined. 'What if I hadn't picked up your precious ones, eh?' Her eyes slanted oddly, giving her features an exotic look that was accentuated by her dress.

The man's fingers dug cruelly into Charlie's shoulder and made him squeal a little. The fingers pressed harder and he stopped squealing. Charlie felt this character could be even more dangerous than the carter. 'After a right bit of goods, I was. And be careful with me beauties,' he added curtly.

The girl gave a kick towards the sack that stopped well short of connecting with it. 'You think more of those varmints than you does of me,' she complained. The sack wriggled and heaved as though whatever was

132

inside could hear her. Charlie instinctively moved back, against Anaconda's hard legs.

'And a good deal of trouble you'd be in without them,' he spat at her. 'Come on, pick them up, we're going home to Ma. And glad she'll be to see what I've got for her.'

The girl looked at Charlie and a smile edged up one corner of her mouth and warmed her face. 'Why, he's a lovely lad!' She came nearer, lifted up his chin and looked him over carefully. 'He'll do, see if he don't. What's your name?'

Caught between fear of the man and a feeling that this girl could be someone who might help him, Charlie told her.

'Charles Lennox, eh? That's a nice name,' she purred at him. 'Now, I bet you're called Charlie, ain't yer?'

Charlie nodded hopefully.

'Well, Charlie, you come with us an' we'll give you a good meal. Reckon you could use that, couldn't you?'

Already Charlie's stomach was rumbling. It was the hour of dinner at the Hospital. And it was a meat day, Charlie realized with something like nostalgia.

'I'll take the lad,' said the girl. 'You can carry your misbegotten brood.'

The man slowly removed his hand from Charlie's shoulder, so slowly that the boy knew if he tried to make a run for it, the fingers would immediately clamp down again.

The girl threw an arm around Charlie and moved him towards another passageway. Charlie looked back nervously. The man was picking up the sack and seemed to be talking to it.

'Come on,' said the girl impatiently. 'Ain't got all day.' Her arm removed itself from his shoulders and her hand grabbed his. Charlie was pulled along, through animal droppings, refuse, a dead dog and inhabitants who hurried about their business. No street-sellers in these ramshackle courtyards and passages, these weren't areas where folk bought food or other necessities.

At least, thought Charlie, they must have left the nasty carter far behind. No chance of him catching up with them. He felt somewhat easier, then wondered how he was going to find the Duke of Richmond now. Little though Charlie knew about the world, common sense told him the folk who lived in these surroundings would not know much about dukes and suchlike.

They came to a courtyard where a woman was drawing water from a well and a couple of children played in a corner. Then he saw that they fought over a chicken bone. More refuse filled the area, windows were dirty and broken and many were hung with sacking to keep out the weather. A screeching voice drifted down from one of the upper storeys. Charlie couldn't make out the words but the malevolent tone sent a shudder through him.

The girl dragged him over. 'Up them stairs with you.'

As they started to climb, an individual came down. He might have been handsome but for a nasty scar that ran down one side of his face. He looked in an ugly mood.

'Brought Ma some pickings, Jack?' the girl said as the man pushed past them.

'I thought so but she 'ad other ideas,' he ground out. 'Real mean she is today, I'd watch it, Bella.'

'We brought 'er a little present,' Bella sang out as she pushed Charlie further up the roughly made stairs.

At the top Bella shoved open a door that sagged on its hinges. ''Ere we are, Ma. Got you a real treat we 'ave.'

'You've been long enough about it, thought the Watch must 'ave taken yer.'

Bella dragged Charlie across a wretched room with floorboards that gaped so wide you could see the room below through them, then jerked him to a stop in front of someone sitting in a chair with the light behind. For a moment he couldn't make out the figure.

''Ere 'e is, Ma. Ain't that the goods?'

Charlie tried to jerk back as a claw of a hand reached out and felt his face. 'Young 'un, that's good, Bella. Where's Anaconda?'

It was a voice that hovered somewhere between a screech and a whisper, as though some injury had meant the person couldn't talk as other people did. Then Charlie's eyes adapted to the light and he stood appalled at the apparition that confronted him. His skin scrawled and he shrank back.

'Don't like Ma, is that it, dearie?' the terrible voice said in a steely purr every bit as frightening as the previous screech.

You've got bottom, Charlie repeated silently as he forced himself to look at the creature pawing at every part of him. It was difficult to believe it was human. The skin's surface seemed to be encrusted with scabs, some weeping pus but mostly dry, like gravel ground into mud. Grey hair hung around the travesty of a face like cobwebs off an unswept ceiling. Her mouth was no more

135

than a gash that showed a single tooth as she spoke. But most frightening of all were the eyes. They were horribly cloudy and discoloured orbs that stared at him and seemed to grow. Charlie swore they grew, swelling till all he could see was the dirty egg-white veiling of the irises that were directed in different directions, one to the right-hand ceiling, the other at the floor. Impossible for either eye to see yet he had the feeling they took in everything about him. She must be a witch.

'Well, it's a well-dressed little scamp, ain't it? And one that's clean and cared for. Short 'air, I do likes short 'air.' Charlie shuddered at the caressing note in the evil voice. 'Tell me, Bella, where d'you find 'im?'

The witch's gaunt frame was wrapped around in a loose gown of what had once been some splendid brocaded material that was now grey with age and dirt. Out of the open sleeves came two sinewy arms that ended in the claw-like hands.

'I found him, Ma,' said Anaconda. He came into the room and eased his sack into a corner, where it heaved for a moment then lay still. 'Running away he was, from a right old hue and cry. Reckoned he'd be glad of a helping hand.' He flung himself down into a chair beside Ma. 'Jack bring anything worth speaking of?'

'Jack? That whoreson bugger brought nothing but junk. 'E's 'olding out on us, Ana.' Ma's voice went even quieter, like a sword scratching at the ground. ''Oo was it as rescued 'im from Newgate, an' set 'im up as an 'ighwayman, eh?'

'You did, Ma,' said Anaconda, sounding bored.

'An' all 'e 'ad to do was bring us 'is gains an' for a slice we'd move 'em for 'im. After all, what does 'e know about getting a good price for good things? An' now 'e brings me a few nothings, says that's all 'e can get! As if I don't know wot 'e's up to. 'E thinks 'e can do better 'imself.' The sibilants hissed through the sinister whisper. 'You'll 'ave to deal with 'im, Ana, you know that, don'cha?'

'Consider it done, Ma,' the man said.

'An' what 'ave you and Bella brought me today, eh? Besides the boy.'

'You'll like it, Ma,' said Bella, bringing forward a rickety table that stood at Ma's elbow.

Charlie drew in a sharp breath as she put her hands into deep pockets either side of her gown and pulled out coins of all sorts, not only silver and bronze but also gold, plus brooches and watches, silver buttons and buckles, reticules that once hung from a lady's waist on cords, and wallets from gentlemen's pockets. Ma's hands moved amongst the hoard, picking up coins, biting and laying them down with a nod of approval, or with a tetch of disgust putting them to one side. She picked up buckles and buttons, felt, licked and bit them too, crooning over them, hissing when she found something that wasn't to her liking. 'Paste that is,' she said of one buckle. Then, 'Nice bit o' work that, Solly will like that,' of a brooch.

'That's all,' Bella said finally.

'She did well today, did Bella,' said Anaconda, standing beside her. She looked up at him and smiled, revealing several missing teeth. He put out a hand and ran it down her cheek, then held her by the neck, his thumb under her chin pushing back her head in an incredibly powerful movement. 'And you wouldn't hold back anything, would you, me little darling? Charlie, feel in her pockets.'

Charlie gulped. The man couldn't mean it, surely?

A moment later he knew he had for Ma whipped her hand across his face in a blow that rattled his teeth and sent exquisite pain through his body. 'You'll learn to do what you're told,' she hissed at him. Charlie felt the wound, looked at his hand and saw he was bleeding. There was a ring on one of Ma's fingers with a large, cut stone.

'Move, boy,' said Anaconda viciously.

Charlie moved but Bella was before him. 'Well, what d'yer know, there's somethin' else at the bottom,' she said nervously and drew out two gold coins.

'Sovereigns,' said Anaconda. 'That's what she was keeping back, Ma.'

'Chip off the old block, ain't yer, girl?' Ma said nastily.

Bella retreated nervously. 'Didn't mean anything by it, Ma, you knows I didn't.'

The sightless eyes stared at her. 'Do I, girl? Do I?'

'They got caught in the stitching, that's all, swear by all that's sacred, Ma.'

Anaconda laughed unpleasantly. 'Ain't nothing sacred to you, Bella. But you'll not try that again if yer knows what's good for yer. Bad enough I've got to deal with Jack. Wouldn't like to have to have to do the same with you.' His voice was quiet but full of menace.

Bella went white. 'You wouldn't, Ana.'

'Wouldn't I, girl? Don't test it, that's all.'

Charlie felt sick. He wasn't sure what all this was about but he no longer felt here was someone who could help him.

Anaconda fixed him with his sharp gaze. ''Ere's the thing of it, young Charlie. You 'elps us and we looks after you. You'll get food and a bed. Only straw but it's clean enough. During the day you'll go out with me and Bella and we does our act.' He paused. Charlie waited, unable to say a word. 'You'll want to know what our act is.' He went over to his bag and brought it into the middle of the room and undid the cord that ran around the top. Then he sat down, cross-legged, his long coat splaying out around him, and brought out a pipe.

Strange sounds filled the room, sounds such as Charlie had never heard before. Music he'd heard, the organ in church and someone who'd once played the fiddle when he was very small, but nothing like this. It was unearthly, wailing.

The sacking moved, undulating. Then with a hiss a triangular head appeared and darted upwards. Then another joined it, and another, and another, writhing around, their narrow heads flicking and turning as though seeking their prey.

Charlie had heard about snakes. The foundlings were warned to be careful in long grass and never to approach one. Now, with a cry of terror, he leaped backwards.

Ma screeched with laughter. Bella hooted too. Anaconda continued playing. All at once he stopped, lowered the pipe and laid it in his lap. Then he reached out to the snakes and picked up first one and then another, sending them sliding and slithering around his chest and neck, their forked tongues licking around his face. He raised his head, moving it caressingly against a snake whilst Charlie watched, mesmerized.

Then Bella moved behind him, swishing her skirts. 'This is Anaconda, folks, wonder of the Orient.

Immune to snakes, he is. Them as would kill any normal person, folks like you and me. Only Anaconda knows the secret of it. Give generously, folks, this is a sight as you'll not see again.' She had a little open bag in her hand and passed it around, as if to a crowd of people.

'Of course,' she said to Charlie, confidentially like, 'afore that I'd been working them, see? Whilst they's watching. I mean, did you notice me nick that button orf yer?' She flicked at the back of his jacket. Squirming round, Charlie saw that one of the two buttons that were supposed to be there had gone. She held it up to him. 'Now I suppose I'll 'ave to sew it on again! But if they'd been silver, well!'

Anaconda was putting the snakes back in their bag. 'Sometimes, boy, we'll go out in different mode.'

'Look,' Bella said and whipped the black curls off her head. Underneath was fair hair pinned flat against her skull. She removed Anaconda's scarf to reveal a shaved head. 'With a wig, 'e looks quite a gent. Then we picks pockets. With you to distract our marks. Or you can pass the hat while Anaconda does 'is business with the snakes. I can pretend I'm nothing to do with either of you. Then we'll get much richer pickings. We 'ad another lad once an' it worked a treat. Jeremy that was.'

Something about the way she said his name made Charlie ask, 'What happened to Jeremy?'

'Thought he could escape,' Anaconda said, rising with one supple movement to his feet. With his bare shaved head he looked very tall and very dangerous and once again Charlie shrank back. 'He climbed out of the window upstairs, reached the roof and escaped.' He bared his teeth in a travesty of a smile. 'He didn't last

long. We know everyone, see? An' everyone knows us.
They knows as 'ow it's to their advantage to keep us in
the know. We looks after them and they looks after us.'
He stood with his hands on his hips, holding back the
skirts of the flowing coat. 'Word came to us of where he
was and, well,' he drew a finger across his throat in a
graphic gesture. 'No more Jeremy.'

Charlie gasped in horror. He looked round at Bella
and was astonished to see she was crying. "E was such
a nice boy,' she said, flicking away the tears. 'I really
liked 'im and I thought as 'ow 'e liked us. An' then 'e 'ad
to pull a trick like that.'

Charlie's insides lurched and for a terrible moment
he thought his bowels would liquefy. He clenched his
buttocks together, shut his eyes and took a deep breath.
If he didn't think at all, he might be able to remain
upright and decent.

Ma gave a hiss. 'See you remembers that, young
Charlie. Wouldn't want yer to go the same way. But yer
a good boy, I sees that. So you'll be orl right with us.
We's your family now. Bella's my daughter, Anaconda's
'er man and now I'm yer ma, unnerstand?'

Charlie nodded his head.

'Well?' Ma said in her awful whisper.

'Yes,' Charlie managed to get out. It sounded like
the squeak of a terrified mouse. Ma smiled, her thin
lips dragging back to reveal two teeth, one either side of
her mouth. For a chilling instant she looked like a
snake herself.

At that moment Charlie wished he was back with
the carter. Now he'd never find the Duke of Richmond.

Chapter Fourteen

Fanny pasted up the last of the posters. It had taken her three days to cover the area between Covent Garden and Soho Square. Canaletto had discovered the girl's body more or less in the middle, not far from Slaughter's Coffee House, that favourite location for London's artistic set.

'She must live or work near there. Killer must arrange meeting. That piece of paper in her hand, it say "this evening" and "help you". She went to assignation, to meet her killer,' he'd said. 'Someone must see her, recognize her.'

The first morning Canaletto had come with her and together they'd applied the flour and water paste Fanny had made up and placed in an old milk pail. She'd carried the pail and brush, Canaletto a bag of the posters. They'd stuck these on walls, posts and pillars, anywhere people could see them. But Canaletto had soon itched to be back with his painting. So the second and third mornings Fanny had set out alone. She didn't really mind. Canaletto had kept up a series of complaints, about the weather, it was drizzling, the condition of the streets, vile as always, the rudeness of the people, no worse than usual, and the way the glue stuck to his hands and soiled his clothes. For a painter, he was decidedly clumsy with the paste brush.

Fanny had found doing the job on her own a good deal more relaxing. She worked quickly and neatly, using an old cloth to secure each poster to its location, often on top of other bills and advertisements. Few people bothered her and few showed any interest in the sketch of the dead girl. Fanny quite soon decided her task was a hopeless one but she continued just the same. Each time she passed her cloth over the face Canaletto had drawn, she understood a little more what had decided him to make this effort. It was a sweet face and hadn't deserved its end.

Finally the last poster had been affixed to the last wall, that of the Rose Tavern to the east of Covent Garden and Fanny went to fulfil her next task, which was to replace some of the pigments that she had been crushing to make Canaletto's paints. The supplier wasn't far from Fleet Street. After that was done, Fanny decided to visit her brother. If she was lucky, Lucy, her tiresome sister-in-law, would not be around the shop and they could enjoy one of their all-too-rare conversations.

Ned was bending over a copper plate but dropped his burin as soon as he saw Fanny enter. 'Sister! What a pleasure, I can take a rest from this plaguey landscape and enjoy your company for a little.'

Fanny came over and inspected what he was doing. Once she had been Ned's apprentice and was no mean hand with the burin herself. She saw what Ned meant immediately. He was copying the painting of a stretch of valley and woodland with few distinguishing features. Even worse, she saw that the painting had not

143

been supplied in a mirror image and Ned was having to do this himself.

'How is my nephew, young Michelangelo?' Fanny smiled, and continued to smile through a recital of the babe's first attempts at walking and the trouble they were having with his teething. 'I'm so sorry Lucy has taken him to see her brother's family, you would dote upon his prattle, almost words now. And, Fanny, he is to have a brother,' Ned said happily. 'Lucy is once more in an interesting condition.'

Fanny tried to express suitable congratulations. All she could feel, however, was that selfish, lazy, stuck-up Lucy had no right to be bearing children to a husband so complacent and loving as Ned. Such thoughts made Fanny feel mean and empty. Also ridiculous. For whatever was wrong with her life, it was not going to be cured by a husband and certainly not a baby. Babies insisted on a great deal too much time and attention.

'Do you remember how mother and father used to fight?' she asked abruptly.

Ned looked startled, as well he might; since the fever had taken both their parents within a few days of each other, the subject had never been discussed between them. It was as though they had decided they must remember only the good things about their family life. He scraped some more at his engraving. Fanny said nothing.

'I remember him kissing her after she threw ink at him one time,' Ned said slowly.

'Do you never feel like shouting at Lucy sometimes?' Fanny thought of the number of times she had spoken sharply to her sister-in-law and how Ned always avoided confrontation.

Ned threw down his burin and looked straight at his sister. 'Fanny, what has got into you? Why are you bringing this up?'

'Well, do you? Aren't there times, however much you love her,' she added diplomatically, 'when you'd like to tell her how stupid she is?'

All at once Ned groaned and dropped his head into his hands. 'Oh, Fanny, you don't know how much I long to.'

Fanny should have felt triumphant but found instead she was sad.

'But I remember the fights between mother and father in our childhood, how hateful for us it was. Do you remember the time father hit mother and she fell and knocked her head and father thought he'd killed her?'

'I did, too,' Fanny whispered.

'And there were other times. Fanny, whenever Lucy drives me to distraction, I remember the agony of living with them, never knowing when the next fight would come – and then I swallow my hasty words and work or go out to the tavern.'

Fanny remembered the times Ned had disappeared when she'd railed against him. She'd always thought he took the easy way out, now she wondered at his self-control.

'Why are you bringing this up now?' Ned repeated, looking at his sister closely. 'Have you found a man you want to marry and are you worried you will fight with him in the same way? I always thought that was why you didn't marry Sam.'

Fanny was amazed. 'Why, no, Ned. I didn't marry Sam because we had nothing in common. I would not have made a good wife for him.' Had that really been the reason, she wondered now, remembering the large, good-humoured master carpenter who had courted her and who did whatever she asked of him far too easily. 'And I wanted to be a painter,' she continued hastily.

'Fanny, how goes your painting? You had no time to talk the other day when you brought the sketch over for me to engrave.'

Fanny gave a small shrug and produced a bright smile. 'I am learning, Ned, learning.'

Ned looked worried. 'There is something amiss, Fanny, I think Signor Canal takes advantage of you.'

'No!' said Fanny sharply. 'That he does not!' Canaletto was not to be criticized by anyone but herself.

Ned seemed to decide their conversation needed a different direction – avoiding the issue once again, Fanny later decided. 'Has that poster I did for you brought results?'

'It has only just been printed and put up, Ned,' Fanny protested. 'There has been no time for a response.' But they'd affixed the first posters two days ago. Surely someone might have seen them who could recognize the girl?

'A nasty killing,' Ned said. 'She looked to have had a sweet face.' Who else was going to study it? Fanny wondered. How soon would the rain, the weather or urchins destroy the posters? Had all her hard work been for nothing?

Ned's eyes wandered back to his work. He picked up the burin and carefully filled in the leaves of a tree.

Fanny sighed, kissed Ned, said she would be sure to visit again before too long, and left, making her way back along the familiar street, exchanging greetings with old friends but refusing to spend time with any of them.

This was the area she had grown up in, knew so well. Yet now she felt distanced from her old home. Her parents had died when she'd been fifteen. War between themselves as they had, no one since then had shown such interest in Fanny. One minute her mother would be chastising her, the next listening to her chatter and encouraging her in some activity.

Arriving back at Silver Street, Fanny paused as she passed Daniel's workroom. She was reluctant to go through to the studio. She knew what she would find there: Canaletto and Richard Thompkins painting together.

The young painter had been coming round in the afternoons now for nearly a week. It had been a week of torture for Fanny.

The first afternoon he had arrived, he had brought with him several paintings that Fanny could see had impressed Canaletto. Now Richard Thompkins became more than a source of much-needed cash. He was set painting exercises: masonry, brickwork, windows, pillars, a huge repertoire of building parts to be painted in sunshine and shadow. Occasionally Fanny was allowed to participate. More often she was employed in crushing yet more pigments, mending brushes or preparing a canvas.

And always she was conscious of the nearness of Richard in a way she resented. Never before had a man made Fanny feel like this. And his concentration as he worked was total. She had no wish for him to be interested in her. Apart from her reluctance to become involved with a man, he was, after all, clearly far above her in social status. He had, however, only to look at her with his tawny eyes and her knees turned to water. Furious with her lack of control, resentful of the attention he was receiving from Canaletto, Fanny was aggressive towards them both. She had welcomed her poster sticking because then she could spend more time away from the studio. All the time, though, she found herself wondering what instruction she was missing.

In short, Fanny was miserable.

She pushed open the door to Daniel's workshop and went through. A chat with the cabinet maker always put her in a better mood.

The workroom was filled with the resinous odour of raw wood. Daniel was turning a chair leg while Adam, his large apprentice, pulled on the leather drive to the pole lathe. Tiny shavings of wood filled the air and the floor, already thickly strewn with discarded pieces of wood. Against the walls leaned more wood awaiting attention, untouched planks or half-used, some of the shapes curious.

Fanny waited a moment, watching Daniel apply his chisel to the spinning length of wood to produce a series of seductive curves. There was a comforting rhythm to their work, Adam pulling the leather down and allowing it to be pulled back up by the whippy pole, Daniel applying his chisel to the spinning wood, then waiting for the lathe to turn back before it could spin again.

'Why, Fanny, what's the matter?' Daniel asked, gesturing to Adam to take a rest. The young giant sank onto a stool and wiped a drop of sweat from his eyes.

'Nothing,' Fanny said brightly, feeling tears sting at the back of her eyes. 'I have been to see my brother.'

'Ah,' said Daniel with a wealth of understanding – he knew all about Ned, Lucy and their baby. 'And no doubt Signor Canal is now instructing young Master Thompkins?' There, again, he seemed to understand how matters stood.

Fanny nodded, not feeling able to say anything without bursting into tears. This made her even crosser.

'Daniel,' said Betty Spragg, coming through from the other side of the workshop, 'have you heard yet from Mr Wright about his table and chairs? I vow the man is a meanscraper who never intends to order.'

Betty's black eye was fading now to a marvellous cacophony of greens and yellows.

'If'n he don't want them, there's others who will,' Daniel said peaceably.

'But you designed them especially for his convenience,' Betty said crossly, giving a small, dismissive nod to Fanny. 'I declare I have a mind to go and enquire of him why he keeps honest folk a-dangling on his sufferance.'

'Now, Betty, you knows the way of society folk. It's all for their convenience and none for ours.' Daniel stretched out his arms, easing his shoulders and Fanny suddenly saw how thin he'd become. He started to cough, hacking away until it seemed he'd cough his lungs up.

Betty tutted and went away to fetch him a drink of water. 'You're working too hard, Daniel, you know you are,' she said, rubbing his back.

Gradually the coughing eased and Daniel wiped his eyes. 'Then don't chase more orders,' he wheezed as he closed his eyes and leaned against the wall.

'What can I do with him?' Betty enquired of Fanny with a helpless shrug of her shoulders.

Fanny left her telling Daniel how he should go on to save his health. The familiar sound of Betty chastising her husband was oddly comforting. Fanny wondered whether it reassured Daniel in the way that it did her. Perhaps not. Relationships between men and women were strange. Would Fanny ever understand what could hold two people together?

Mary Butcher had tried to explain some part of it. She had called round after the painting session had ended a few days earlier, resplendent in a gown of golden silk, her red hair ablaze under a lace cap of unquestionable quality.

At first all Fanny could think was that Mary had got a job as an actress and was being paid large sums of money. Mary had hooted at this suggestion. 'My dear Fanny, what a little innocent you are!' she mocked, rustling up and down the studio, turning around and around at every opportunity, surely just for the pure pleasure of hearing that sound, like the rustle of leaves when a soft wind blew through trees. 'Why, you have started a painting,' she said, stopping in front of Canaletto's easel.

'Not me, my master.'

Mary studied the canvas. 'It don't look very interesting.'

'It is only the start. He always begins with the sky.'

'What will it be?'

'A view of London.' In truth, Fanny did not know more. Canaletto had neglected to tell her his plans and his working sketches were all in his room. Fanny assumed he did not yet need these to paint in sky.

Yet the plan was odd. The edges of sky were raggedy, the priming paint showing around the corners, top and sides of the painting where Fanny would have expected the sky to continue. But Canaletto was touchy when he began a painting. He hated being questioned so Fanny, beaten into silence by the caustic response to her first eager query, had little choice but to wait and watch for the gradual unfolding of the design.

'Where is your master?' Mary looked about her as though Canaletto could be lurking in a corner of the spacious, uncluttered studio.

'Out,' Fanny said briefly. Canaletto and Richard had gone off together for an evening of carousing.

'Tell me what has been happening with you,' Fanny urged.

'I look well, do I not?' she said, swishing her skirts from side to side, angling her head to admire the embroidery on her white satin petticoat. The outfit must have set someone back a pretty penny and Fanny realized now it was impossible that Marie could have earned enough in a few days to have paid for such splendour.

'Very,' Fanny said admiringly.

'My mistress gave it to me as a leaving present. It has hardly been worn. A trifle loose around the waist, perhaps, but I can soon find a seamstress to attend to that. Mrs Wright ordered it while we were still in Derbyshire, so she could cut a fine figure in London. Alas, since she arrived, she has lacked the strength to go about in society.' For a fleeting moment she lost some of her ebullience. 'Her health has deteriorated further since I left. I fear she is near to death.'

'You have been in touch?' Fanny was pleased.

Mary laughed, all sparkles once again. 'Silly! 'Tis Thomas Wright, her eldest son, who has set me up in the neatest lodgings you ever did see. He keeps me informed.'

'Set you up? I thought you wanted to be an actress,' Fanny said sternly, a trifle dismayed to learn that Mary was now a kept woman.

'Oh, as to that, Garrick is ill and sees no one. When he is well, then I will bring myself to his notice.'

'How will you do that?'

Mary smiled, her mouth curving provocatively up and in at the corners, her eyes narrowing slightly, the lids falling in a way that made their green sparkle even more compelling. It was the smile of a witch conscious of her powers. 'Oh, Fanny, there are any number of ways a maid can employ to attach the attention of a man. Garrick will have no choice, I assure you, but to offer me employment with his company.'

Fanny was fascinated. 'And Mr Wright, will he be content to have you disport yourself upon the stage?'

'If not, he will no longer be my bed companion,' Mary said airily.

Fanny fetched them both a mug of ale. 'What is it like', she asked curiously, 'to admit a man to your bed?'

The green eyes narrowed once again. 'You have never lain with a man? But, Fanny, you are more than grown, and,' shrewd eyes assessed her, 'more than comely.'

'Thank you, Mary, I have not lacked for offers. Most pressing some of them, indeed.'

'But you have held back?' Mary laughed. 'I congratulate you. To reserve your charms for one who can pay properly for them is the action of a wise woman.'

'It's had nothing to do with economics!' Fanny protested.

'Ay me, what a romantic!' Mary sat herself down on one of the studio stools and sipped daintily at her ale. 'Listen, Fanny, one lies with a man in order that he shall supply you with something. With some it is marriage. With me it is a life that I can enjoy.'

'You have not lain with others, then, before young Mr Wright?'

'Well, I think that is my business, not yours,' Mary said and laughed in such a way it made clear she had taken no offence. 'And as to how it is, well,' she looked into her mug with a private smile, 'what shall I say?' Her head came up. 'You understand about the coupling of a man and a woman?'

Fanny nodded. You could hardly grow up in a crowded and bawdy society such as lived around Fleet Street, not to mention the dogs and cats, without witnessing enough to educate yourself. There were men who would satisfy themselves with women of the town under arches and in doorways with no regard for the inquisitive eyes of a child. 'It has seemed to me, well, to give more pleasure to the man than the woman,' she said frankly.

Mary gave her a slow smile, her eyelids dropping again till she looked half asleep. 'Ah, Fanny, you do not understand the half of it. With time, a man can bring a woman to such pleasure she can swoon of it.'

'Swoon of it?' Unbidden a vision of Richard Thompkins's wide mouth and golden eyes rose before Fanny.

'And a woman can make a man in thrall to her, till he will give her everything that is his and rob and murder for more,' Mary said with theatrical emphasis.

'You jest!'

'I do not jest about such things, not when my life depends upon them,' Mary said with such a droll look Fanny dismissed it all as exaggeration such as only Mary could produce.

Mary leaned forward, laid a hand on Fanny's knee and spoke more seriously, 'I cannot help but make a pantomime of life, Fanny. Why, otherwise, how dull and earnest everything would be! Yet, believe me, love, a woman can bring a man to such ecstasy he will do anything for her.'

'And will the woman do anything for the man?'

'Why, as to that, it depends on the woman,' Mary said airily. 'All are different. I myself am indifferent to a particular man. I can like what he does well enough but to believe it is only he who can so please me would be to place too much reliance upon his presence.' She spoke calmly, little now of the stage actress about her. Fanny sensed detachment and she could not imagine Mary Butcher in confusion over a man.

'What about marriage?' Fanny asked, though she wondered who would marry Mary, a girl who openly acknowledged being kept by a man.

Mary flung up her hands, linking them above her head and gave a small yawn; it was a feline movement, full of lissom grace and sensuousness. Fanny knew that never in a million years could she project that sort of a look. 'If a man is enraptured enough by me and if I am willing, who knows?' She lowered her arms again and leaned forward towards Fanny. 'But marriage, Fanny, can be a trap. It robs a woman of her freedom and her independence. She has to do everything her husband says, she has no will of her own. And husbands do not like their wives to enjoy themselves in bed, they take what is theirs and spend no time on the enjoyment of the woman lest she should seek such pleasures else-where as well.'

Fanny ignored this and thought of Lucy and Ned. It seemed to her that it was Ned who had lost his freedom and Lucy who had gained everything. 'Does not a woman gain security through marriage?'

Mary gave a short laugh. 'Security? My dear Fanny, what is security when a man can lose everything on a turn of a card? When a runaway cart can rob him of the limbs that are his livelihood? When disease can rack him through until he dies in your arms? Life offers no security. That is why you must grab and mould it to your will. Your will, Fanny, not that of some man.'

She stood up. 'I must away. If Tom can leave his mother's side, he will be coming by.' She did not seem to be too concerned with the state of Mrs Wright. 'You must come and see me Fanny, my lodgings are most excellent, you will adore them. I have writ down their direction.' She placed a small piece of paper on the studio table.

Fanny realized that, despite everything, Mary was lonely. She promised she would call. Then, in a drift of heady perfume her friend was gone, and the studio seemed a dull place.

Fanny could not hope for Mary to be there this afternoon. She braced herself as she pushed open the door to the studio. Paintbrushes in hand, Canaletto and his new pupil stood before their easels.

Canaletto had finished his sky and was painting in a frame of laced wooden scaffolding around the edge of the picture. Instantly Fanny knew the subject. It was the view of London through an arch of Westminster Bridge that he had wanted to paint when he first arrived but had failed to find a patron for.

'Oh, signor,' she said, 'I am so pleased to see you have a commission for that painting.'

Both men turned and Richard hurried to help her with her purchases. 'You have everything?' asked Canaletto.

'Everything but the Prussian blue. He awaits a new consignment.'

'*Dio mio,*' he groaned. 'How long?'

'A few days, no more. I think you have more than enough for your present purposes, signor.' Unless, that is, he was intending to paint a madonna in a blue gown in Renaissance style. But Fanny did not put the thought into words, he would not appreciate the joke. Canaletto never painted figures. Oh, he peopled his paintings but only with sketches. He would never do a portrait, or any sort of painting that relied for its effect on people. His speciality was townscapes.

Fanny unpacked her bag. Having stowed away her purchases, she found she had no option but to look at what Richard was working on. It seemed he had finished with exercises and was painting on the canvas Canaletto had instructed her to prime the previous day. It was quite small and he was intent on painting in sky, just as Canaletto always started. On the wall beside the easel were a couple of preliminary drawings.

He noticed her interest. 'Signor Canaletto has suggested a view to me, one in which I am to use light to define architecture. Do you like it?'

Fanny could say nothing. She was gazing in horrified fascination at the drawings.

They were of Golden Square, done from the same geographical point she had chosen, but taken from the viewpoint of a low flying bird rather than a mouse.

Chapter Fifteen

Out of the corner of his eye, Canaletto saw Fanny flinch and knew he had to act quickly. 'Is good idea, yes? You and Thompkins both learn importance of viewpoint and how light works.' He moved to the other end of the studio table. 'Here is canvas for Fanny. Prime myself, yes?' He gave her a small grey rectangle securely nailed to a frame (grey was better for a beginner than the red he favoured). The effort he had made to prepare it without her knowledge was worth it when he saw her face. She knew enough about preparing canvases already.

'Oh, signor!'

'Perhaps you manage paint on table, yes?' He sensed the interest of the young Thompkins as Fanny said she could easily find some way of supporting the canvas that would allow her to work.

'Have palette for you,' Canaletto said proudly. Daniel Spragg had prepared it for him, delighted to be able to do something for the young Fanny.

'And here are brushes.' He handed over the small selection he had sorted out as suitable for her to use. And all were of the same quality as his own. Canaletto always insisted tools should be of the best. Just as the paints had to be most carefully prepared from the finest materials.

Already feeling guilty over his lack of instruction for Fanny, Canaletto was rendered even more so as he saw her delight. 'Now,' he said sternly, 'we all paint together. You and Thompkins both work on view of Golden Square, yes? Learn together.'

He watched for a moment as Fanny went and fished out her sketchbook, found the preparatory sketches she had made, then sat at the table, making sure that the light fell full on her canvas, carefully propped up against a heavy pewter jug and held in place by two stones she had found in the yard. It was not the best idea to sit to paint, the painter lacked the freedom to step back from his work to see the whole, before concentrating again on a small area, and different brush strokes required a different amount of room, only easily achieved when one was standing, but when an easel couldn't be obtained, the posture was possible.

And it was with particular pleasure that Canaletto saw Fanny begin to mix the blue she required for the background painting of her sky in just the way he employed himself. She was a bright and observant girl.

For a little time the three of them worked in silence.

Canaletto forgot for a while to monitor his pupils, he was so keen to progress with his painting. He couldn't understand now why he had felt it imperative to wait for a commission. Once completed, he was certain the picture would find a purchaser.

Halfway through the afternoon, he took time to explain to both his pupils how to scumble thin layers of paint to achieve a translucent look, and showed them how a fine layer of Prussian blue and a few touches of thick white finish to clouds balancing a creamy hint of ochre in their depths could bring a sky alight. Thompkins had talent and worked intensely, but his brushwork wasn't free enough. He tended to jab at the canvas. Fanny had a much freer touch, but her unfamiliarity with the brush was blindingly evident. However, Canaletto could see that soon, if she worked hard enough, he would be able to use her to good effect when the commissions started to pile up.

If the commissions piled up.

He began to wonder what had happened to McSwiney. The big Irishman had not been around for some time. Canaletto vowed to send a note round to his lodgings reminding McSwiney of his existence. Perhaps he would agree once again to visit the Artists' Club with him. Not long after this there came a knock at the door.

Fanny reluctantly laid down her brush and opened it.

Standing outside, large and all of a dither, was a woman with a hat pulled over one eye and a huge mantle billowing around her ample shoulders. She peered suspiciously into the interior of the studio.

'Can I help?' Fanny offered with more than a touch of impatience.

The woman dug into a spacious reticule and Canaletto saw her bring out a piece of paper he instantly recognized.

So, the poster had brought a result! He placed his palette and brushes with care on the table and came over.

'Says 'ere there'd be a reward. That true?'

'Indeed, madam,' Canaletto said. 'Enter.' He stepped aside and waved her into the studio.

Fanny gave him a resigned look and went back to her canvas.

'Here, you see, we paint.'

The woman continued to peer around. 'Pictures, is it?' she said with a loud sniff.

Looking at the three canvases, Canaletto could see cause for doubt. Three areas of sky and some wooden scaffolding did not offer much scope for an onlooker to accept as art. 'We commence,' he said cheerfully, then gently took the poster from the woman. He placed it on the table and smoothed out the paper. It had been roughly printed at little expense but Ned had done an excellent job on the engraving. Even though the ink was slightly blurred, Canaletto's sketch of the dead girl's head was accurately depicted, perhaps helped by the fact that he had himself drawn the mirror image to aid the engraver. But Ned was skilful, no doubt of that.

'Please, sit,' Canaletto said, drawing out a stool. The woman looked at it as though doubting its ability to sustain her weight and she was, indeed, a very large woman. He could see that the voluminous skirts were inhabited by hips that could match a carthorse's and that the billowing mantle was supported by breasts that rivalled the watermelons he so seldom found in this country. These massive protrusions rose and fell in a way suggestive of extreme agitation and her eyes, set in a face that could have been composed of potatoes and dough, flashed their currant brown in a manner that said the woman had either lost her breath through the speed of her passage to the studio, or was not at all sure that she should have come.

Canaletto smiled reassuringly at her. 'I am very pleased to meet you,' he said with great care. Such women, he knew, almost always distrusted foreigners. The more he watched his grammar, the more likely it was she would tell him what she had come to say.

After a little hesitation, she settled herself on the stool and sat eyeing the poster and twisting her hands in her lap. They were a working woman's hands. Canaletto put her down for a laundrywoman, the red chapping and roughness looked as though it was the result of much immersion in hot water and wielding of soap and brushes. Her clothes, though, were of a reasonable standard though undoubtedly purchased second-hand considering their bad fit. No poor labourer, his visitor, she probably ran a small business employing others besides herself. 'This woman, you know?' he asked, tapping the poster with his finger.

The bosom had stopped heaving in quite such an alarming way. 'Yuss,' she said, then shut her mouth with a snap.

'Fanny, do we have a sip of ale?' Canaletto asked. 'Time for refreshment, no?'

Obediently, she laid down her brush again and went to the corner cupboard.

Canaletto dispensed small amounts of ale into mugs for the four of them. 'Mr Thompkins, you join us?'

'You are very kind, signor,' Richard said, coming over.

'And, your name, if be so good?' Canaletto held out a mug to the woman.

'Mrs Gotobed,' she said, reaching with barely disguised eagerness for the mug. Her voice was unusual. From her shape you would expect something low and rasping. Instead it was high, hesitant and sounded shy. Canaletto wondered how she managed to control a workforce, if indeed he was right about her business. The ale disappeared in a moment. She put the mug down with an audible sigh and wiped her mouth with the back of a hand. 'Thanks, sir, right nice of you.' The words minced. Canaletto could see that Richard Thompkins was as fascinated by their visitor as were Fanny and himself. He had ceased painting and perched himself with one buttock on the studio table, sipping his ale and obviously prepared to enjoy whatever scene was to be played out.

Canaletto tapped again at the poster. 'You know?' he repeated.

Richard angled his head to see. Canaletto slid it along towards him.

'Came to me asking for work and somewhere to live.'

For a moment Canaletto was so surprised he couldn't bring his English to mind. With a huge effort he managed, 'This girl, she ask for job?'

'Wot I said. And somewhere to live. As though I'm in the business of running a lodging house.' She sniffed disparagingly.

Canaletto tried to grapple with the unlikely picture of the murdered girl working as a laundress. Her clothes had not been fashionable, the material had been serviceable, the style unmemorable but everything about her, the condition of her hair, the softness of her hands, the smoothness of her facial skin, where it had not been cut, all said that here was someone who lived a genteel sort of life. She mightn't be a gentlewoman but she surely lived amongst such folk. Perhaps a lady's maid or some other upper servant. Never a laundress!

'You gave her job?' he managed to ask.

Mrs Gotobed heaved and made an extraordinary sound, a sort of high-pitched keening. For a moment Canaletto thought she had burst into tears, then he realized that she was laughing.

'Job? That one? Give me strength, mister. That one wouldn't have known one end of a washtub from the other.' Ah, thought Canaletto, he'd been right. 'And as for ironing, oh, dearie me, she'd 'ave burned the frills and creased the shirts. I'm known by the skills of my girls, trained most of 'em meself but they all start with some idea of what's what.' Her bright round eyes fixed themselves on Fanny. 'Nah, take you, my dear. You've the look of someone as knows 'ow long to 'eat an iron.'

Fanny, looking totally fascinated by their visitor, nodded.

'Fanny very good with iron and with washing,' announced Canaletto, then saw how Richard Thompkins looked at her. Had he been less than fair, letting this young man who seemed to want for nothing know that she performed such menial tasks for him? Painters' apprentices weren't usually called upon to demonstrate such skills. 'She help sometimes when laundry fail,' he ended feebly.

'Oh, yers? Yer can't use a very reliable woman, then. If yer want ter send it dahn ter me, I'll guarantee yer'll be satisfied every time.'

Canaletto, who couldn't afford to send out his small

linen at the present time, tried to look grateful. 'So, you told her you had no job for her?' he suggested.

'Cors I did. But you never 'eard such a to-do. Such weepin' and wailin',' Mrs Gotobed was relishing her tale. 'Said as 'ow there was nothin' else she could do. Wot she meant was,' Mrs Gotobed looked at Canaletto craftily. 'Wot she meant was as 'ow she was expectin' and as 'ow no respectable 'ouse would employ 'er. For it was clear as daylight to them as 'ad eyes she was some sort o' lady's maid or governess. She talked nice enough for a governess, I'm sure.'

'You see she was with child?' asked Canaletto, determined to get every detail of the story straight.

'Reckon she was five or six months gorn. Could get away wiv it wiv a bit o' clever dressing 'nother few weeks praps, no longer. Carrying 'igh she was.' Mrs Gotobed sighed gustily. 'An' no wedding ring.'

'But wearing a ring,' Canaletto stated.

'Yers,' Mrs Gotobed said, a trifle reluctantly. 'Not on 'er marriage finger, though.'

Canaletto thanked heavens he had an observant witness here. 'Did she tell you her name?'

Mrs Gotobed shook her head. 'Never arsked, didn't seem no point, not when I didn't 'ave no job to give 'er. Which I 'adn't, even if she 'ad been sootable.' She said this in a righteous tone of voice, as if to excuse herself of any failing on her part.

'So know nothing more?' asked a disappointed Canaletto. At the end of this rigmarole, they knew very little more about the dead girl, except that she was desperate for a job and had no doubt been turned off her last because her condition had been discovered. 'Is not much to tell.' Already he was deciding this was not worth any sort of reward. There would no doubt be a great argument and Mrs Gotobed would attempt to bully money out of him but he would be determined.

'Nah wait a minute, 'ave you arsked me if I knows anyfink more?' demanded Mrs Gotobed, raising her massive shoulders in a belligerent way. Her mantle billowed over the watermelon breasts.

'And so?' said Canaletto after he'd waited a moment or two for further details to be given.

But Mrs Gotobed was not to be hurried. 'Well, as I says, Miss Wivout-an-ounce-o'sense in 'er wants somewhere to stay. I can't 'elp 'er wiv a job but I says there's a friend o' mine 'oo might just 'ave a room she could use in return wiv 'elp in 'er 'ouse. So she gets all grateful like and asks me for the direction. Which I gives 'er,' she added portentously.

'And?' prompted Canaletto, by now realizing that Mrs Gotobed needed the participation of her audience in her tale. 'She went to your friend?'

'Ho yers she did,' was the satisfied reply. ''Oo was grateful to me as she 'ad great need of a reliable bit o' 'elp. Wiv dressin and so forth. And a bit of 'elp wiv the place, keepin' it tidy an' all that.' Mrs Gotobed let her eyes drift around the studio, as though assessing whether help was needed there as well. Apparently satisfied, she fixed her currant eyes once again on Canaletto's and waited.

'And friend, she give news of girl to Mrs Gotobed last few days?' he prompted.

'I'll say she 'as!' Mrs Gotobed's expression became quite lively and for once she continued without waiting for a reaction. 'The girl 'as disappeared! Gorn, wivout a word!'

'With things?' asked Canaletto.

'Not a thing. Not 'er things, not wiv nothin' that aint 'ers neither. Me friend doesn't know wot to fink. But I reckons the girl 'as found a protector and didn't reckon she needed 'er fings, cos they wasn't up to much.'

Canaletto felt he knew now just what sort of woman Mrs Gotobed's friend was. 'Met protector perhaps at place she sent to? With friend?'

Mrs Gotobed beamed at him. 'Knows you to be a sharp gentleman the moment I sets eyes on yer! Yer got exactly the rights of it. 'Cept it wasn't the rights of it at all. Cos the moment I sees this bit o' paper,' she nodded towards the poster, now being studied by Richard Thompkins, 'I recognizes 'er. It's 'er to the life. So I goes along to me friend's and tells 'er. Gave 'er ever such a shock it did,' she added in a very satisfied manner. 'But she said she knowed Smith would come to a bad end.'

'Why think girl come to bad end? Poster not say why ask for information.'

'Why say give reward? Must 'ave stolen somefink or done somefink bad.'

Mrs Gotobed seemed uninterested in exactly what nefarious end the girl had met.

'Name was Smith?'

'As to that, that's wot she told me friend but I doubts it meself. Trying to 'ide 'erself that one, I reckoned. And,' Mrs Gotobed stopped her flow whilst she rummaged again in her reticule, 'I went round to see amongst 'er fings, in case there be somethin' that could tell us somethin'.'

Mrs Gotobed obviously fancied herself as something of an investigator. Canaletto watched while she pulled out a piece of fine linen from the drawstring bag.

''Ere it is, fought for a moment I'd left it behind, but, no. See?' She thrust the square at Canaletto.

He took and examined it. A handkerchief of quality workmanship, and, in one corner, the initials P B.

'Well, I knows me letters, and if Smith begins wiv a P or a B, I'm a duchess. An' she didn't look like no Smith, neither.'

'This friend, you give me name and direction?' he asked.

Mrs Gotobed's expression turned cunning. 'Paper said as 'ow there would be a reward for information received,' she said, speaking the last two words slowly and with emphasis.

Canaletto sighed but he knew that he couldn't palm this woman off with either honeyed words or by down-grading her information. She knew the value of what she had given him all right. He fished a piece of silver out of his pocket. 'Mrs Gotobed, story most interesting. If friend confirm details, tell us more, maybe I give another of these.'

Mrs Gotobed gave one of her loud sniffs, inspected the coin closely, attempted to bend it on the table then, satisfied as to its authenticity as legal tender, slipped it into her reticule. She looked straight at Canaletto, her small, bright brown eyes hard. 'I'll give yer name and direction and I'll expect extra payment afterwards.' There was a bite and weight to her high voice that left him in no doubt as to how she controlled her work-force, or that she wouldn't take measures to extract the additional coin from him if it wasn't forthcoming. He nodded pleasantly at her.

'Mrs Casement in Covent Garden next to the sign of the Crescent Moon.'

Covent Garden was a hotbed of high-class prostitution and not too far from where he had found the body of the girl who called herself Smith, Canaletto noted. All his trampings around London sketching possible viewpoints and assessing skylines and buildings had given him a knowledge of its layout that would rival that of a hackney carriage driver.

'But yer best watch the time yer go to her, she has a powerful number of callers. Late morning's best.' Mrs Gotobed gave a high-pitched cackle that resounded through the studio. 'When she's up and the gentlemen not yet started.' She looked at him with a gleam in her eye, 'I did 'ear, mind you, as 'ow she was planning on going to Ranelagh this very evening. If you was to go, you couldn't miss 'er, she's the tallest woman I ever did see. Now I must be going. Lord knows what's 'appening back at me workplace. Them girls can't be left to work on their own, not if yer want the work done proper.' Mrs Gotobed struggled to her feet, Fanny helping by hauling on one arm as the other used the studio table as a lever. For a moment Canaletto feared it would break. But it held and Mrs Gotobed was upright. 'Most pleasant meeting yer,' she said in her high, mincing voice. 'Remember, yer wants good laundry work, come to Mrs Gotobed. 'Ere's me directions.' She laid an engraved piece of card on the table.

Canaletto thanked her and walked her to the door. He stood watching her waddle across the yard, through the little arch into Silver Street, then turned back into his studio.

Richard Thompkins still had the poster in his hand

and Fanny, in an excited voice, was telling him the story.

'Poor young woman,' the young man said, and laid the paper on the table with a gentle hand, smoothing out the creases it had gained in Mrs Gotobed's reticule.

'Will you go to Ranelagh?' asked Fanny.

'I think you should,' said Richard. 'What say we all go together?'

Canaletto could see that Fanny was greatly taken with the idea and, indeed, it could have been a pleasant occasion, a mixing of business with pleasure and a welcome chance to see little Fanny enjoying herself, but Canaletto had no intention of spending any of his dwindling funds on such frivolity. He wished he could say they must continue working but, though it was nowhere near dark, the daylight had lost its clarity. It was a dangerous time, when a less than alert eye could be fooled into thinking it could see well enough but the next day would reveal faults. There would be no more work this evening.

Just as he was concocting some excuse to do with a prior engagement with Owen McSwiney, the man himself walked in the door.

'Tonio! My friend!' He swept the little painter up into a bear hug. 'I have done it!'

Clasped to the entrepreneur's bosom, his wig slipping and forehead tickled by McSwiney's beard, Canaletto's head swam, not only from the way his narrow chest was being squeezed but also by the alcoholic fumes surrounding the man.

He was returned to the floor. McSwiney took a step back and flung out his arms. 'Here you see your saviour. A greater organizer of your career than even Consul Smith in Venice.'

Excitement began to build in Canaletto's breast. Had it come at last, the commission he had been waiting for?

'Tomorrow you present yourself at Richmond House. The duke wishes you to paint a prospect from there.' McSwiney looked as triumphant as the winner of some prestigious race.

Fanny clapped her hands. 'That is wonderful! Oh, signor, is it not wonderful?'

Canaletto collected himself and summoned his best English, pronouns and all. 'I expected no less,' he said calmly, very conscious of the way Richard Thompkins was regarding him. He had no intention of betraying to this apprentice painter the depths of his concern over the lack of commissions. 'Duke was one of first patrons in Venice, naturally wishes a Canaletto of his London view. Now, my dear,' he turned to Fanny. 'You ask if I visit Ranelagh tonight? Why not we all go?' he held out a hand to the ebullient Irishman, still preening himself on his negotiating skills. 'Come too?' Canaletto suggested.

'Why not?' McSwiney ran a hand through his greying locks, he scorned a wig. 'A small celebration will not come amiss.' He looked at the young painter standing beside Fanny. 'Thompkins, is it not? From Hayman's studio? I think we met at the Artists' Club one evening.'

Richard nodded.

'McSwiney's the name. If I can ever be of help with commissions, I'll be delighted. I have contacts the like of which you'd not believe.'

'Come,' said Canaletto impatiently. 'Attend me while I change.' He would have been happy to go dressed as he was, minus his painting smock, but was sure Fanny would want to do something to her appearance and needed the studio cleared of men before she could do so.

'So,' said Thompkins as they made their way across the yard. 'We combine a celebration of your commission with pursuing the investigation you have instigated into the death of that poor girl.'

'By all the saints,' boomed out McSwiney as they started climbing the stairs. 'You're never still on that nonsense? You won't have time for that now!'

Chapter Sixteen

Dark clouds scudded across the sky and obscured the moon. A breeze rustled through the trees and stirred the silks and satins of the ladies' dresses, lifting them as though with calculated intent to show a gracefully turned ankle.

The night was chilly, there was no doubt of that, and all the arboreal protection of the walkways couldn't prevent delicate shoulders from needing the warmth of velvet wraps and cashmere shawls.

Kitty drew a ruffled silk mantua closer and wished she had worn the less flattering but infinitely warmer velvet lined with squirrel that Purity had tried to press upon her. The boat ride from Richmond House had taxed her ability to maintain the high level of excitement she had felt all day that the long promised treat had actually arrived. All London, Emily had said, would be going to Ranelagh tonight.

'Cold?' asked Emily.

'Not at all,' Kitty lied. 'But why could we not have gone by coach?'

'My dear Kitty, such will be the press of coaches we would have been forced to wait with nothing to do for maybe three-quarters of an hour. And Richmond

House is directly on the river, what more natural than we should travel by water?'

The boat arrived at the landing steps. 'Cheer up,' Emily said, holding a hand out to Kitty, 'Ranelagh has a huge fire in the midst of the Rotunda. You will be warm enough there.'

Kitty thought it was all right for Emily to be so casual about the temperature, she had her husband's arm around her shoulders, holding her close. Yet another of the manifest advantages of being married.

'I think you shiver, can I loan you my coat?' murmured Lord Robert, Kitty's escort, a young aristocratic sprig chosen for her by the duke and duchess for his impeccable credentials.

'How kind,' Kitty flashed him a sweet smile. 'I could not rob you so.'

'Nay, it would be my privilege,' he said seriously, shaking his arms out of the sleeves and placing the heavy velvet coat around her shoulders as they walked towards the immense round building that was their destination.

The welcome warmth of the coat was rendered less welcome by the stale smells that assaulted Kitty's nostrils. She ignored them. 'Why, thank you, Lord Robert, what a cavalier you are.' She took another sideways glance at him. If he didn't have that wart on the end of his nose and if his chin didn't disappear into his neck in quite that way, she supposed he might be thought by some to be almost handsome. After all, the shape of his face was regular and his nose, with that unfortunate wart, was straight. His eyes were pale blue, not icy like some pale blues, more a washed-out shade, as though he'd cried too much as a baby.

There was something wrong with his figure, Kitty decided, taking the inventory of Lord Robert's appearance much as a steward might note the attractions of a piece of furniture. His top half was too long for his bottom half. She was reminded of ducks on her father's estate, so deft and decorative floating on the water, so odd-looking off. Sitting down, Lord Robert would seem a tall, elegant figure. Walking beside her, he was hardly more than her height, and she was not overly tall. Nowhere near as tall, for instance, thought Kitty, as that woman coming towards them, the crowds seeming naturally to part to allow her and her companion through.

She was indeed a striking figure, dressed in a splendid gown of gold brocade with a petticoat of silver tissue liberally displayed by the turned-back edges of the skirts. Her powdered hair was piled high upon her head and she carried it as though she gloried in the fact she was so much taller than other women. Her face was lively, the strong cheekbones emphasized by a large beauty spot set just below the right eye. There was another beside the left corner of the laughing mouth.

Kitty, fascinated, watched her address a remark to her companion, placing a hand on his arm. Then, with a slight sense of shock, she realized that the companion was none other than Lord Maltravers, the distinguished gentleman she and Emily had met in the Privy Gardens and whom Emily so disliked. As tall as his statuesque lady companion, he was looking amused at whatever it was she had said, his right eyebrow raised in a devastatingly attractive way.

Kitty prepared herself for their party to be recognized by this fascinating couple.

'Kitty!' called Emily – rather sharply, Kitty thought – 'we enter here.' It seemed there was more than one entrance to the Rotunda and they were to take one whilst Lord Maltravers and his companion were heading for another. The suspicion that Emily had deliberately avoided Lord Maltravers grew when it appeared that the Kildare party had to walk a long way to find their box in the gallery that ran round the Rotunda. 'I don't know how you so mistook things,' complained the Earl of Kildare to his new bride in a fond voice. 'You are usually so *au fait*.'

'Oh, la, 'tis the distraction of your presence, darling Jemmy,' Emily said cheerfully and popped a kiss on her husband's cheek. He took her hand in a most telling way and kissed the tips of her fingers.

Kitty sighed. She couldn't see Lord Robert ever behaving in such a doting fashion. She allowed herself to be settled in her chair by him and returned his coat with a sigh of relief. She sipped at a glass of champagne and looked about her.

It was like being at a play to see such a splendid collection of society disporting themselves on the large, circular floor, in its centre the massive fireplace which looked more like an organ loft that had been designed with the additional purpose of holding up the ceiling. Kitty said as much and Lord Robert looked at her with admiration. 'Why, you have the truth of it. It was intended to hold the orchestra, only the necessity for some form of heating meant the music had to be placed to one side.'

Complacently Kitty noted the orchestra that was

even now producing lilting tunes to which some of the company were dancing. She was pleased with Ranelagh. She adored its gilded ornamentation, the arches running underneath the boxes, where couples dallied and laughed together. This was a palace made for pleasure and she was determined she would be pleased this evening.

Yet after several minutes Kitty realized she was dissatisfied. All London, you would have thought, provided the multi-coloured throng milling and swirling around the floor. And that was the nub of her discontent. For she had thought Ranelagh Gardens would have been reserved for the *bon ton*, she had expected to see none but the height of society disporting themselves.

Lord Robert looked a little shocked as she made some comment to this effect. 'Why Ranelagh is much more fashionable than Vauxhall Gardens, dear Lady Kitty. There you will find no end of rough and ready fellows. Here are none but that are respectable.'

Yet just below their box was a fellow in the plain clothing of a tradesman or one engaged in commerce, hanging round the neck of a girl who was plainly no more a member of society than was he. And there were others; you might think, in fact, that meeting a butcher or a baker would be no great surprise. Inquisitive faces peered at the boxes, studying their occupants as though they were part of the entertainment.

'Is it not a pretty sight?' exclaimed Lord Robert enthusiastically in her right ear. 'I declare Ranelagh Gardens to be the most enjoyable of London experiences. I only regret it is too early in the season to show you the gardens, which are truly delightful.'

177

Kitty thought of the cold, draughty boat ride from Richmond House and could only be grateful to be spared wind-blown tree alleys. 'I declare I'm vastly amused,' she said languidly.

There was a long pause that Kitty felt no urge to break and Lord Robert appeared unable to. 'How like you London?' he tried eventually.

'Why, vastly amusing,' Kitty replied in the same languid tone.

Again there was silence. 'Why, 'tis Lord Robert,' called a laughing voice and a pert face peered up at their box. 'You've not called upon me a se'nnight, Lord Bobby.'

He coloured and hurriedly excused himself to Kitty. 'An old acquaintance, I will be back in a minute,' he said and scampered out of the box.

Kitty watched bemused as she saw him emerge on the floor to be bussed thoroughly on both cheeks and then full on the mouth by the girl, while her swain, a slight fellow wearing quite ordinary clothes, watched with seeming complaisance. And Lord Bobby seemed right amused by the experience. He appeared animated in a way he had failed to be in her company. Well, there were men, she'd heard, who enjoyed themselves more with women of the lower orders than their peers. Maybe Lord Bobby was one of those.

Kitty's dissatisfaction with the evening deepened. She longed for Thomas Wright to appear but there was no chance of that. She had not seen him since the visit to St Paul's cathedral, after which Emily Kildare had spoken most sharply about the curious way this fellow seemed to dog their footsteps. She hadn't actually called him common, but Kitty had felt the accusation lay unspoken beneath her words. Nevertheless, she had despatched Purity with a note to acquaint him of their plans.

Her maid had returned to say the house was in mourning for Mrs Wright, who had died a few days earlier after a lingering decline. Thomas's mother dead? Kitty's immediate thought had been resentment that he had not informed her of this fact. He'd mentioned that she suffered ill health but nothing more. It was like a door shut in her face. Then she had realized that all the dreams she had built around the longed-for visit to Ranelagh had shattered. She had so hoped that together they could disappear down a dark alley (she had forgot the evening chill) and dally with him in some delightful manner. There, in the darkness of the trees, with romantic music playing, Thomas would say sweet words to her, would draw her to him with protestations of devotion. Oh, if only they could meet on an equal footing. If only he could be asked to Richmond House, how easy everything would then be.

But the son of a tradesman, however well off, could never be acceptable to the Duke and Duchess of Richmond. Nor, indeed, to her own parents. Or could he? Hadn't Emily herself said that parents in this age couldn't force their children into distasteful marriages? Hadn't Kitty the right to choose her own husband?

Collecting herself, Kitty told Purity that no one had a softer heart than she and she felt most strongly for Thomas's grief. In fact she would write him a note, Purity must take it to him. Not at once, though, she was too aggrieved that Mrs Wright could not have remained in this life for a few more days. After all, according to

Thomas, she had been poorly for some considerable time.

When Kitty remembered Tom's manly appearance, she couldn't help but be dissatisfied all over again with Lord Robert's. She would not, in fact, mind if he did not return to their box at all. Which seemed more than possible for he wasn't to be seen anywhere. The Kildares, totally wrapped up in their own happiness, hadn't even noticed that she'd been deserted. Kitty's hand tapped on the table in an irritated fashion. She pushed her glass towards the earl. 'A trifle of champagne would not come amiss,' she said, trying to sound lively and amused.

He was immediately all attention, refilling her glass, but in attending to his wife's was compelled to comment on the charming way a lock of hair kissed her shoulder. Kitty felt isolated, left out of some enchanted world all seemed to inhabit except herself.

'Why, it's the beauty resident with the Richmonds,' said an amused voice beneath their box. Kitty, suddenly radiant, looked down.

'Why, it's Lord Maltravers,' she said in a voice she fancied was sultry enough to attach any man of the world.

Certainly it seemed enough for this one. 'Such charms should have a proper audience. Where is your gallant?'

'Lord Robert? Oh, he allowed the pressing attentions of an old acquaintance to lure him away from my side,' Kitty said, unable to decide exactly how to explain the unacceptable. For surely no escort worthy of the name would have allowed himself to be weaned away from her.

'I cannot conceive how any man could be so foolish as to leave such a delectable person as yourself for another!' exclaimed Lord Maltravers in a laughing voice that yet suggested truth underlay the social flattery. 'Did he dance with you before deserting you in such a cavalier fashion?'

Kitty giggled suddenly. 'I called him my cavalier earlier, when he lent me his cloak against the cold.'

'Then the fellow is not devoid of all social graces. But you have not answered my question.'

'I am happy to sit here, thank you,' Kitty said primly, thinking she certainly was not.

'I cannot believe that, I shall come and claim you,' Lord Maltravers said and disappeared. Only to arrive at the back of their box not long after. 'Come, dance with me,' he said, holding out his hand in the most obliging manner.

Kitty glanced at Emily.

The Earl of Kildare was now whispering in his wife's ear and Emily's attention seemed totally his.

Well, why not go with Lord Maltravers? If Emily was so lost to her duties by her mother's guest, Kitty could please herself. And, after all, what right had Emily to object to Lord Maltravers if he was acceptable to the duchess?

Kitty laid her little hand upon the black velvet sleeve of her new escort and allowed herself to be taken down to the floor. 'Where is your companion?' she asked curiously, then was cross with herself for betraying that she had noticed him earlier.

'Ah, then you saw the lovely Leonora,' Lord Maltravers said, looking down at Kitty from his great height. 'She and I are acquaintances of long standing. I chanced upon her in a party and wooed her away from her squire for a quiet chat.'

'Then you are here on your own?' suggested Kitty in a throwaway voice.

'Why, no, in a party of several friends. But we have no lien on each other, each is free to amuse himself in whatever fashion takes his fancy.' The voice was full of amusement and Kitty was by no means sure that she wasn't providing most of the entertainment. This was not to her taste.

''Tis vastly good of you to introduce the little provincial miss to the delights of London,' she said demurely but with just a hint of provocation.

'Provincial miss?' Lord Maltravers repeated ironically. 'Is that how you see yourself? I think not.' He'd made no attempt to draw her into the dance and Kitty could only feel he was reluctant to enter into an activity where they would be separated as often as brought together by the interlacing of the steps.

Keen dancer that she was, Kitty found herself happy to linger by one of the arches. Lord Maltravers was much more to her taste than Lord Robert. Let him disport himself with his lowly admirer, she had the attentions of someone infinitely superior.

Yet, there was something about this tall man that made her feel less than completely comfortable with him. She couldn't quite rid herself of the notion that he was laughing at her. Then, just when she had decided this was the case, he said something that made her feel that he did, indeed, admire her.

'La, I think you are acquainted with the whole of London,' Kitty said, piqued, after a lady had smiled at

him in a most provocative way and she had suffered
the sight of him returning greeting after greeting.

'Ah, you have it to rights, pretty Kitty. Acquaintances they are. I have moved around the world too
much to form close friendships. The days are gone
when I was on terms with real friends, such as the
duchess and your mama.'

'I have never heard Mama mention your name,'
murmured Kitty. She found it impossible to regard the
tall, handsome man at her side as one with the gener-
ation to which her parents belonged. Why, they were
past everything, had retired from life. Whereas Lord
Maltravers . . .

'Have you not?' He glanced down at her, his face for
once inscrutable. 'And will you, I wonder, mention me
to your children when you become safely married and
start to raise a brood?'

Kitty had the uncomfortable feeling that she had
lost some vital part of their conversation. 'I hope that
we shall still be friends,' she said firmly, unable to
decide if his remark was intended to convey the fact
that she was not to consider him in the light of a swain.

'Do you?' Again that raised eyebrow, that sense he
was laughing at her. 'I wonder. I wonder if I will remain
in England,' he added in a low voice that seemed to be
addressed to himself rather than to Kitty.

'You say you have been abroad,' Kitty said in a light
voice, determined to show that she could converse in a
sophisticated manner about matters unconnected with
herself. 'I would so enjoy hearing of your experiences.'

'Would you indeed? Why, then, I have to tell you
that Paris is a place that can offer the most satisfying
of experiences, if you can withstand the hygienic

drawbacks; that Vienna can be indigestible and Venice has the soul of a whore and an appearance to rival the most beautiful woman in the world.' He glanced down at her with a rueful smile. 'Will you, I wonder, travel?'

'Oh, I should like it above all things,' Kitty said. 'Tell me more.'

'More? You are insatiable, I think.' His hand tightened slightly on her arm and a quick thrill passed through Kitty. It was as if their relationship had suddenly deepened, as though she'd been admitted to an inner place of his person. Oh, she thought, to be wooed by such a man! Beside him Tom's dashing image lost some of its glitter.

She laughed, exhilarated by their surroundings and his presence. 'Tell me about Venice.'

Sets were forming for a new dance. He glanced down at her. 'Shall we?' he said. Without waiting for her consent, he drew her onto the floor. Whilst they stood, waiting for the music to start, his deep, caressing voice described the beauties of the city that floated on water. But that small, private moment between them had passed. It seemed he had retreated from her in some way.

She felt let down. The music started and she moved gracefully through the steps, placing her hand in his as they met, feeling it released as they parted in the movements of the dance. The magic of being with him, though, had been lost. She found her attention wandering to the dancers around them.

Then could not believe her eyes. She missed a step and had to concentrate on regaining her place in the set. When she was able to look again, she couldn't see the person who had caught her gaze. She finished the dance in a torment.

As she curtsied at the end, Lord Maltravers bowed and said, 'Something has disconcerted you, I think?'

'Why no, some trouble with my shoe, merely,' she murmured, looking up at his height. Then an 'oh' of incredulity escaped her.

It had been Thomas she had seen. Her Tom, now in a box straight in her line of vision, bending over a girl of quite surpassing beauty!

Chapter Seventeen

Once Ned had promised he would take Fanny to Rane-lagh Gardens. Then he'd married Lucy and any suggestion Fanny might accompany them on such an expedition had become ridiculous. Sam, the young master carpenter who had wished to marry her, had said he'd take her, but their relationship had finished before the promise had been fulfilled.

Since then no opportunity had come her way.

Now, at last, she was to visit, and with as attractive an escort as she could have dreamed. For Richard Thompkins walked beside her while Canaletto and McSwiney led the way, no doubt discussing tomorrow's visit to Richmond House.

Dusk was gathering as Richard arranged for a hackney carriage to take them to Chelsea. Already lamps had been lit outside some of the larger houses. As they jolted along, Fanny saw the sun slipping down beside the great abbey of Westminster, the red disc just discernible through the smoky haze.

'Signor Canal seems fortunate to have Mr McSwiney to arrange his commissions,' Richard Thompkins said to Fanny as the two older men talked in rapid Italian on the other seat of the carriage. 'Perchance I should take advantage of the offer made me this evening?'

Fanny, too conscious of the warmth of his body sitting beside her, felt complimented that he wished to consult her in this way. 'Mr McSwiney's words are perhaps said more easily than his performance sometimes warrants, Mr Thompkins,' she said softly.

'Please, call me Richard. After all, we are fellow apprentices, are we not?'

Fanny felt inordinately pleased at this invitation.

'So,' he added thoughtfully, 'McSwiney has the typical Irishman's propensity for exaggeration.'

'But you already have a commission, I think you said?'

Richard smiled at her through the gloom and Fanny delighted in the way the creases round his eyes deepened and one side of his wide mouth lifted a little more than the other. Richard Thompkins was someone she sensed had depths of character that it would take time to appreciate. She forgot that she had decided the demands of her career meant she had no time to spend on getting to know young men.

'Yes, indeed. Through an acquaintance of my guardian's I am entrusted with a portrait. I commence in a few days. I confess I am more than a little nervous, it is so important I do well.'

But he didn't look nervous. Fanny wondered if he was one of those lucky souls who had perfect confidence in his ability. 'You have finished your apprenticeship, yet you choose to take lessons from the signor,' she commented in some wonder.

'I am yet a tyro,' he said deprecatingly. 'I know how far I still have to go. And ever since I saw a painting of

187

Signor Canal's, I have desired to learn from him the secret of how he captures light and uses it to achieve his effects. When I heard he was in London, I determined to apprentice myself in some way to him. You can appreciate my feelings and ambitions, I am sure, you have such a nice ability yourself.'

He was sweetly earnest and talking to her as if they were on a social and professional level. Yet, from his bearing, his address and his clothing, Fanny knew he came from a background far above her own.

'Tell me about your guardian,' she suggested. 'You say you have no parents?'

The red disc slipped completely below the skyline, the flush of sunset turned to a charcoal grey with just a hint of blue. Soon link boys would be lighting the well-off on their journeys through the metropolis, their torches flaring shades of yellow-gold in the gathering gloom. Now it was impossible for her to make out Richard's expression as he said, 'Alas, no, I never knew my parents and my guardian, too, is dead. I am alone in the world!'

The dramatic statement was made in a quiet, even voice.

'I am sorry for you,' Fanny said impulsively. 'I, too, am an orphan but I have a brother. We have comforted each other often since our parents died. Have you no brothers or a sister?'

'I was a single child and my guardian knew little of the ways of children. He was, I think, uncommonly strict.'

'Did he encourage your artistic aims?'

Richard laughed harshly, startling Fanny. 'He did not! There was a talented practitioner living not far from us in Derbyshire who gave me lessons. When my guardian discovered that I had the ambition to practise my art in a way beyond that of a dilettante, he barred him from the house. I had to employ the most devious of stratagems to continue my painterly education. But then my guardian died and left me in possession of a reasonable income and so I was able, thanks to the introductions of my friend and mentor, to apprentice myself to Mr Hayman and train to become a portrait painter.'

'What determination,' Fanny cried, impressed by his dedication. 'Your painting must mean much to you.'

'It's everything,' Richard assured her. 'I think it is to you as well.'

'Oh, yes! I think it comes from my father. He was an engraver, as is my brother, and his great delight, whenever he had the time, was to sketch views. My brother, too, is skilful in landscaping. Do you have your talent from your father?'

'I don't know who my father is.'

'You don't?'

'No, nor my mother either. I was discovered as a baby on a church doorstep and my guardian adopted me. The church was on his estate,' he added, as if by way of explanation.

'How terrible!' Fanny said with quick sympathy. 'Not to know where you come from must be . . .' but her voice trailed away because she could not conceive how it must be.

'It is,' said the blank voice beside her. 'And my guardian never failed to impress upon me my fortune in having him take pity on my orphan state.'

Fanny could conceive just how galling that must

have been to a sensitive lad. 'But he left you the means to fulfil your ambition.'

'Yes, I suppose I must be grateful for that. I did not realize, though, that I should have gone to Italy to study; it is difficult for a painter in England to be taken seriously without that background.'

Fanny was silent. Deeply as she respected Canaletto's genius, she had not realized that studying Italian painters and technique could be so vital.

'But Mr Hogarth', said Richard in a brighter voice, 'is of the opinion that we English artists should have our own school.'

'Somewhere we can study painting?'

'Oh, as to that, he and others already run a studio at St Martin's which I have attended. No, by that he means a school of English painting, a style that is recognized as being unique to this country, not founded on that of the Italians, or the French.'

'Why, how splendid! Don't you see, you could think of yourself like a new school, one that owes nothing to any other! Your characteristics are not inherited from your parents but are what you choose.'

'Why, Fanny, I think that is the most creative thing anyone has ever said to me about my background, or lack thereof.' Richard sounded surprised and, try as she might, she couldn't hear any pleasure in the surprise. 'I think you are a most caring person and I am delighted we are to visit Ranelagh Gardens together this evening.'

Canaletto and Owen McSwiney had finished their Italian conversation. 'Fanny, I think you enjoy yourself, yes?' said Canaletto, tapping her on the knee.

'Oh, yes, signor.' Her agreement was heartfelt.

When they arrived at Chelsea, there was a line of carriages queuing to drop their passengers at the gardens and they had to wait, but Fanny didn't care. She was floating in a bubble of pleasure. Everything contributed to her happiness: the closeness of the carriage, the ribald jokes Owen McSwiney was telling, Canaletto's high-pitched laughter, Richard's lazy chuckle, the jingle of horse's harness, the slight sway of the carriage, all were a total delight to her and none more so than the feel of Richard's thigh against her own, a touch that seemed to burn through the layers of her skirts and petticoat.

Fanny was almost disappointed when the time came to step down from the carriage and enter through the lantern-lit gardens into the great Rotunda itself.

She turned to Richard, 'Have you ever seen anything so pretty?'

He laughed. 'I've visited Ranelagh many a time but I think I now see it through new eyes. Your eyes, Fanny.'

Fanny wasn't sure what to make of this but she felt nothing could ever exceed the sheer excitement of being part of such a splendid throng of pleasure-seekers. Her best dress of dimity muslin, prettily corded though the sleeves were, was no match for the gorgeous dresses she saw around her but it hardly mattered. No one would notice her when there were such beautiful and obviously high-born ladies to be seen.

'Well, Tonio,' said McSwiney as they looked about them, 'did you not say we were to look for a very tall lady?'

Fanny realized she had forgotten the main purpose

of their mission. Canaletto would never have agreed to this jaunt if he hadn't wanted to search for Mrs Casement to ask her about the girl who called herself Smith.

'Don't sigh, Fanny,' murmured Richard's voice in her ear. 'We can enjoy ourselves while we search.' His eyes gleamed with fun.

'Shall we split up, signor?' she called to Canaletto. He was lost in studying a group of noisy macaronis, their outfits the other side of fashionability, stocks so high their chins were forced into the air, breeches so tight sitting down must be a sore task, coats so waisted and standing out that their bodies must be corseted and the skirts boned, their faces white with paint and decorated with patches. 'If you and Mr McSwiney take that side of the Rotunda and we this, we will cover the ground more quickly,' she suggested gaily.

Canaletto looked at her solemnly. 'And maybe never see each other again?'

Looking around at the press of people, Fanny realized he had a point.

'We should arrange a box for ourselves,' Richard said. 'We can enjoy some refreshment and then explore, knowing we have a place to return to.'

This seemed a wonderful idea to Fanny but she knew that Canaletto would resent the additional charge.

'It would be my pleasure to arrange it all as a token of thanks for your kindness in taking me on, sir,' Richard said to Canaletto.

'Very handsome of you, my boy,' said McSwiney. 'Tonio, won't that be a treat for us?'

'Wait here, I will arrange all,' said Richard.

'Much money, that one,' Canaletto muttered.

Soon they were ensconced in a box above the crowds with a fine view of the dancers and merry-makers.

'Why, we can see everyone from up here,' Fanny exclaimed in delight. She leaned over the edge of the box. The music had stopped, the dancers were leaving the floor. Fanny scanned them all for a very tall lady without success. She turned her attention to the boxes, bending forward to try to see into as many as possible. Then she clutched at Richard's arm. 'Why, there's a friend of mine,' she said in happy surprise.

In a box not far from theirs sat Mary Butcher with a most handsome young man. She was wearing a green brocade dress embroidered in gold, the neckline so low that her breasts strained against the material as though they would pop out with one unguarded movement. Serving her with food and wine was a magnificent figure of a black man, dressed in an elaborate livery amply decorated in silver lace. He moved with great dignity and unconscious grace between the young man and Mary.

As Fanny waved to try to catch Mary's attention, a girl dressed in rich simplicity stopped below the box and flung up an arm in a haughty style.

'Why, Mr Wright, I declare,' she called up in a languid voice. 'And here I was about to commiserate with you on the death of your dear mama.'

The young man flushed a deep red. 'Kitty,' he said, speaking through a mouthful of chicken and staggering to his feet. 'I, I did not expect to see you here.'

'Why not, when I sent you a note telling you of our plans?' Kitty's bored languor had vanished and Fanny realized that this girl was very angry. Standing slightly apart from her was a tall man of mature years and astonishing splendour. He was watching the scene with what seemed cynical amusement, his eyes flicking from the angry girl to the embarrassed man and then resting on Mary Butcher, quietly placing her wineglass on the supper table, her own eyes wide and questioning.

'Note?' blustered the young man, leaning over the balcony rail, 'I received no note.'

'Thomas, how can you say so when I sent Purity with it and she came back with the news that your mama had died?' The girl sounded as though she could hardly speak for rage. She seemed completely oblivious to the many people who were now watching the little scene.

Then Fanny saw that Richard had left their box and appeared on the floor beside the girl. 'Why, Lady Katherine,' he exclaimed. 'How delightful to find you here.'

'You address me, sir?' she enquired haughtily.

Richard made her a bow. 'Richard Thompkins at your service. I have the honour to receive your father's commission to paint a portrait of you. We met in Cumbria, I think a year or so ago?'

Her manner thawed slightly. 'Mr Thompkins, of course!'

The tall gentleman came forward. 'You are fortunate in meeting friends, I see, Kitty,' he murmured.

The girl waved a languid hand. 'Acquaintances, no more, my lord. Come, will you take me back to my party?'

Thomas leaned over as though he would climb out of the box. 'Kitty, wait!' he called. There was ribald laughter from the crowd that was an avid audience to the little scene. 'Kitty, stay, I can explain!'

'I think we have no more to say to one another, sir,' Lady Katherine said, one hand on the velvet clad arm of her companion, haughtiness back in place.

'But I didn't know . . .' he said despairingly. 'Wait, I'm coming down.'

'Lady Katherine has nothing more to say to you, sir,' the tall man said coldly and led the girl away.

Thomas turned to leave the box and Mary grabbed at his arm. 'You cannot go,' she cried histrionically and the crowd saw that the entertainment was not yet over.

'Unhand me, woman!'

'No, you are mine!' Mary hung on him.

With an effort, he threw her off. 'You fool!' he cried. 'You are a nobody.'

Mary flung herself upon him, tears pouring down her face. 'I am your love,' she declared.

'Love!' he cried coldly. 'What know you of love?'

'I am with child, sir, your child!'

There was an appreciative gasp from the crowd.

'You whore!' Thomas dashed his hand against her cheek, whipping her head round with the force of his blow.

Mary gave a cry. 'Tom!' she cried in quite a different tone of voice. 'You can't!'

'What mean you, can't?'

'You can't desert me!'

'What use have I for a woman with some other man's child?'

Mary swallowed hard and Fanny waited for her to declare that it was Thomas Wright's. Instead she said,

'I'll give the baby away, do anything if you'll still be mine!'

'You're a lying whore!'

'Tom, I speak the truth.' Her face was blanched quite white except for the red patch on her cheekbone where he had struck her.

'I care not,' he said violently, kicking the table so that it fell over, the debris of the meal scattering to the floor. The servant remained standing motionless at the back.

Quite a crowd had gathered now. Thomas reached for his hat and cane. 'Find your own way home, bitch. And look not to see me again.'

'But the child,' Mary implored, her face stricken.

'Send it to the Foundling Hospital. I can have no confidence it is mine.'

'Tom, if you leave me now, I will do such things as will make you regret you did not treat me better.'

'You can do nothing to me.'

'Oh, can't I!' Mary pulled herself up, leaned over the edge of the box and shouted across the crowd, 'Lord Maltravers! Lady Katherine! There are words I would have with each of you . . .'

She was pulled roughly back and Tom fetched her another blow across her face with his cane, his own features contorted with rage. 'Vixen! Shut your mouth or you will be the sorrier for it.'

Mary collapsed again, her show of spirit quite lost.

Fanny waited for no more. She flew out of their box and along the corridor. She was almost knocked over by Tom Wright as he left in a fine fury, followed by the large figure of his servant, his face a mask of stone.

Mary lay on the floor, her shoulders shaking with

sobs. Fanny rushed over, raised her up and tried to soothe her.

After a moment Mary drew away and said in great amazement, 'Fanny? What do you here?'

'Why, Ranelagh is open to all,' Fanny said in a joking way. 'You are not the only one to be brought by a swain.' She hoped Mary would be sufficiently distracted by this to enquire who had escorted Fanny but instead Mary's face crumpled again and she let out a long cry of distress.

'Did you hear his words to me?'

'Yes, he had no right,' Fanny said indignantly. She straightened Mary's dress, pulling up the bodice where it threatened to expose the girl's breast. 'Why did you not tell him you had lain with no other man? That the child has to be his?'

Mary looked at her, wide-eyed, then she pushed down her skirts, avoiding Fanny's gaze. 'Well, there was that one night with his father – but I refused anything more to do with him, for Tom wanted to set me up. You heard me send Mr Wright about his business that morning we met!'

Fanny stared at her friend. Was that what the quarrel on the doorstep of the Wright house had been about? And how could any girl lie with both father and son? 'Oh, Mary,' she said sorrowfully.

'You know nothing of the matter.' Mary flared at her, her face flushed. 'You have never been taken advantage of that way, you do not understand how difficult it is for a girl.'

No, perhaps she didn't.

'Anyway,' Mary tossed her head. 'I will make Tom Wright sorry he treated me so badly. I will tell that poisonous minx of a girl just what a faithless bastard he is. He need not think to find himself welcome there! And if he tries to come back to me – and he will, Fanny, I promise you that, for I can do such things to him – well, I shall have found someone else.'

'I am sure you will have little trouble,' Fanny said gently. She could not condone Mary's chosen path but admired how, even in her distressed, dishevelled state, she was surpassingly attractive, the flame-coloured hair ablaze in the candlelight, her skin glowing and gold-dusted with tiny freckles. 'Is that why you called after that lord?'

A cunning light came into Mary's eyes. 'We have met before. He tried a dalliance with me some time ago. He was mightily taken with me but I would have none of him.' Mary tossed her head. 'He could be as taken with me today and now perhaps I would have him.'

Fanny wondered how she could so delude herself. If Lord Maltravers had wished to take any interest in her, he would have come to her rescue. 'He seemed very taken with Lady Katherine.'

'Why, don't you see, I could tell her about Lord Maltravers as well as about Tom. I have seen that lord take advantage of a girl of good background, almost as fine as herself. Would she consort with him then? And wouldn't he like to pleasure himself with me?' she added pleadingly.

Fanny sat back. 'I think you little better than a street ruffian who would pick your pocket,' she said coldly.

Mary looked at her, astonished. Then a calculating light came into her eyes and she burst once again into noisy weeping. 'Fanny, don't leave me! It's because I'm in such a state, I don't know what I am saying.'

Fanny's heart melted immediately. She took Mary back into her arms and hugged her. 'I promise not to leave you,' she said, trying not to feel desolate at the knowledge this was the end of her treat, that now she would not dance with Richard Thompkins. 'But you must promise to abandon any idea of threatening these men,' she said, her voice sterner than her expression. 'It will not do, Mary, really it will not.'

'My dear,' purred a new voice, 'I think you are in a sad state and I have come to help.'

The box filled with a sweet and captivating fragrance. Fanny's eyes widened at the sight of the tallest woman she had ever seen, sumptuous in gold brocade, her hair an architectural confection.

Even Mary quietened.

'We live quite near each other,' the goddess said gently. 'I will take you home and you can acquaint me with your history.' Her voice soothed while her hands gathered up Mary's mantle and placed it around her shoulders. 'You have a future, my dear, let me assure you of that.'

Mary swallowed a sob and automatically wiped her eyes. She looked at Fanny, 'You will come and see me tomorrow?'

'You would not prefer I should take you home?' Fanny asked, slightly hurt at this easy acceptance of a stranger usurping the role of friend.

Mary looked at the amazingly tall woman. 'I know Mrs Casement, she does indeed live near me. But, Fanny, you must come tomorrow. I have no other friend in the world but you.'

It was a typically exaggerated statement from Mary yet Fanny found herself touched by her insistence on their friendship. 'I will come, I promise you,' she said recklessly. Then, as she watched the two of them move from the ruined box, her wits returned and she realized that Mary's new guardian was the woman that Canaletto sought.

Chapter Eighteen

Canaletto was up early the next morning. His head ached with the wine he had drunk. It had been kind of young Thompkins to provide such generous refreshment but he wished he had not indulged quite so much the previous night.

Thompkins was an interesting young man. He had the talent and persistence to become an acceptable painter, if he was serious enough in his artistic intentions. But announcing he was a portraitist, then wanting to study the art of *vedute*, was that any way to pursue his ambitions?

As he shaved in the hot water Jenny had brought up to him, Canaletto reflected on the previous evening. What a scene there had been! What an idiot girl it was that Fanny had befriended. It had been all her fault Mrs Casement had left before he had had the opportunity to quiz her on the dead girl, and until he learned something of her immediate past he had no way of carrying an investigation into her death further.

For the briefest of moments, Canaletto wondered just why this matter could so concern him. It couldn't just be that she represented what he saw as Fanny's vulnerability, could it? Was this investigation tied up with some feeling of guilt over his relationship with his apprentice? The fact that he'd neglected her artistic education to take advantage of her efficiency in running his affairs?

Or was it that all his life he had been afraid of personal involvements? Twice he had allowed himself to form a relationship with a woman and twice he had been shown he was right to hold back from such attachments. What could be safer than an involvement with a dead girl? Yet life without the demands and delights of love and friendship could be a sterile thing.

Canaletto ran a hand over the stubble on his scalp; it was time he had that shaved as well. Action was what was needed, not inner musings. Fanny had the right idea. It was she who had insisted on continuing to paste up the posters when he had decided that the possible returns were not worth the effort.

Yet he wasn't always indecisive. He'd tried to catch Mrs Casement last night. Only after Fanny had convinced him that speaking with the woman privately would be more productive than a conversation in the social mayhem of the Rotunda had he relaxed and allowed himself to enjoy the evening. After all, they did have his commission from the Duke of Richmond to celebrate. When it was known that the duke had required a view from Canaletto's brush, others would follow. Soon he'd be inundated. Then it would be a matter of finding new subjects for his brush, for there was surely a limit to the number of river scenes the Thames offered. He looked around him at the Rotunda, at its curves and the great central fireplace that arched gracefully up to the ceiling, all offering a stimulating change from the straight lines of most buildings. He looked around to tell McSwiney this, only to find that the Irishman's eyes were closed and a gentle snore wiffled across the wineglass he still had his fingers loosely clasped around.

Then Canaletto's attention was caught by Fanny's delighted laughter at something Thompkins had said and he realized for the first time the dreadful possibility of a serious attraction between them.

He watched the way Fanny leaned towards the young painter, the little muslin ruffles of her sleeves falling back, revealing the sweet curve of her lower arm as she placed her elbows on the table and listened so seriously to what Richard was saying.

'Francis Hayman has agreed with Mr Hogarth to present a painting to the Foundling Hospital.'

'What is Foundling Hospital?' asked Canaletto, deciding the time had come to take part in this conversation.

'A home for abandoned children,' Richard explained. 'A Captain Coram organized it several years ago. There is a splendid new building to the north of London with ample room for the display of paintings.'

'And hospital, it commission paintings? Much money?'

'No, sir, indeed. Several painters, at Mr Hogarth's suggestion, are donating their work.'

'Donating, no money?' Canaletto found it hard to accept that any painter would give away his work.

Richard leaned back in his chair, twirling his half-empty glass of wine. 'Mr Hogarth says that all society will see the paintings and many commissions may follow.'

'Society visit Foundling Hospital? Why?' asked Canaletto.

'It's the fashion,' declared McSwiney, awake again and refilling his glass. 'Lords and ladies give their pledges and all London fights to become governors.'

'Admirable,' murmured Canaletto, still puzzled.

'Patronage for orphans is as essential as it is for painters,' McSwiney continued, waving his glass in an extravagant gesture. 'Society wishes to see what their money is providing and it makes them feel good to see the little ones being brought up in godly ways with proper appreciation of their fortune in life.'

'Fortune!' burst out Richard. 'Sir, I cannot hold that they are fortunate. To have lost your parents, nay, to be given away by your mother or father, how can that be fortunate?'

The young man was too sensitive, decided Canaletto. 'If parents not able to feed and clothe child, then better live in hospital,' he said positively. He had a sudden memory of his childhood. A family dinner, his mother bringing a steaming cooking pot to the table. She'd been a thin, wiry woman who delighted in cooking and whose greatest pleasure was to have her children gathered round the table. Canaletto's father, his fingers still coloured from the scenery painting he was so skilled at, had said prayers, making his son and daughters wait with heads bowed, their mouths watering at the aromas drifting across to them, afraid to ignite their father's uncertain temper. The sun streaming through the window hot on Canaletto's shoulders. His father finally finishing the prayers, swallowing his first mouthful then smiling at his wife and saying 'Bene,' in a voice that brought warmth to her face.

It had all been a very, very long time ago.

'And why should not these good folk view paintings at the same time as they view the fruits of their charity?' McSwiney was saying. 'England has no academy for art, such as France and Venice offer. Where are painters to display their works?'

The man had a point there.

'And how to display that we have talents beyond that of portraiture?' Richard asked. 'Mr Hayman and Mr Hogarth, they are both known as portraitists but each has produced a prodigious work of history painting. Mr Hogarth is all afire to abolish our slavish devotion to foreign artists.' Richard paused, as though conscious this might not be the most tactful of remarks. 'Of course, we must never forget how much we can learn from such as you, signor. That is why I study with you. Anyway,' he hurried on after this sop to Canaletto's heritage, 'the pictures are to be unveiled at a dinner on the first of April. You must attend, sir, it will be an event.'

'I had it in mind to suggest we went together,' said McSwiney, reaching across the table again for the jug of wine. 'You'll come, won't you Tonio? All London will be there.'

Canaletto had agreed.

Now he put on his second-best coat and breeches for his visit to the Duke of Richmond. It would not do to look as though he was trying to rival a possible patron in dress. In Canaletto's experience, however friendly a patron might be, and some were indeed excessively friendly and enjoyed conversing on the finer points of painting and other aspects of art, they preferred a painter to know his place.

Fanny waited for him in the studio with bread and

ale for their breakfast. She already had his workbox ready.

'A fine morning,' Canaletto said, breaking the bread and thinking that soon now he'd be able to afford to add some meat to their morning repasts.

'Yes,' Fanny gazed listlessly out of the window, where the early morning sun was for once visible through the smoky atmosphere.

'I go to duke,' Canaletto reminded her. 'Fanny will work on view.' He expected that to please her. He remembered the intoxicating excitement of his first paintings, the energy he had put into making his views full of drama. The stormy clouds he'd favoured then, the detail of his figures, the care he'd put into painting reflections in the water, so many subtleties of vision he'd employed in those days. And Fanny must be as full of imagination and ambition as he had been.

It was a considerable surprise, therefore, to hear her say hurriedly, 'Signor, I would be most grateful if you could give me leave to visit Mary, Mary Butcher. I promised her last night I would. She has no friends but me.' She paused for a moment. Canaletto ate his bread and considered her request. 'I could visit Mrs Casement also and question her for you about Miss Smith, if you like.'

'No, not talk Signora Casement,' said Canaletto decisively. He didn't want anyone but himself to tackle the delicate task of drawing from the woman everything she had learned about the girl who had acted as her maid before being murdered.

'I would be most circumspect,' Fanny begged. 'People like to talk to me and I have a perfect introduction after last night. After all, you have not yet met her at all.'

Canaletto got a little cross. 'No reason why that should matter. No, Fanny, I talk Signora Casement. No one else. Promise?'

Fanny drew herself up with a degree of hauteur worthy of a society lady. 'If you prefer me not to speak to Mrs Casement about Miss Smith, signor, of course I will not. There is no need to extract my word. But I think if I, another woman, came with you, she would speak to you more easily.'

'Fanny, this woman a courtesan, not suitable you meet.'

'Signor, you forget, I have been in prison.' Canaletto was not likely to forget the time she had been falsely accused of theft or the effort it had taken to get her freed. 'I met all sorts of women in that dreadful place, ah, and men too, malefactors of all kinds. If I can be corrupted, it has happened.'

She looked very earnest standing there, hands on hips, like a little chicken that has decided to defy its parent hen. 'Not suitable,' he said again. 'You visit friend Mary this morning, then work this afternoon. No,' he said sternly as he saw she was about to argue some more. 'I master, you apprentice, yes?'

Her face fell. 'Yes,' she said stonily.

Canaletto felt he had handled the matter badly yet what else could he have done? She was his apprentice, she should be obedient to his wishes.

'I back later,' he said shortly, brushing crumbs off his waistcoat and thrusting his arms into the sleeves of his coat. 'Then we continue work, no? Young Thompkins say he not come for several days, needs time for his portrait commission, but you prepare more pigments, then work on picture of Golden Square, yes?'

'Yes,' said Fanny, still looking obstinate. 'You leave early, signor. Will the duke be up at this hour?'

Was this chit of a girl questioning his judgement? 'Go study viewpoints before meeting,' he said, his displeasure at having to explain himself plain.

Fanny looked a little chastened. 'Your box, signor?' She held it out for him.

Canaletto shook his head. 'Sketchbook only, I not workman,' he said as he left, slipping the book into the back pocket of his coat with a lead writing stylo that Fanny had made sure was nicely sharpened.

Of course he was a workman, he reflected as he made his way out into the street. But he was also a superlative craftsman, one of genius, who had once commanded more commissions than he could handle. Let the Duke of Richmond remember that!

Canaletto decided to walk through Golden Square on his way to Whitehall. It would be as well to remind himself of its features.

He entered the square at its north end and noted the severity of its architecture. Not much here for a painter to turn into an interesting view, it was a hard task he'd set his apprentices. But problems were there to be overcome.

As he skirted the little chains that protected the central grassed oval with its imposing statue, Canaletto's mind returned to the problem of the dead girl's identity. The only reason Mrs Gotobed seemed to have for not believing her name was Smith was the fact that it was so common in England.

Canaletto's career had been founded on the patronage of Joseph Smith, merchant and later consul of Venice. It was a name he therefore had a fondness for. Why should the dead girl not have been a Miss Smith? There were, of course, the initials on the handkerchief Mrs Gotobed had found. Pouf, the girl had maybe had it from a former employer.

It was important to talk to Mrs Casement and frustrating that he had been allowed no more than a glimpse of her at the Rotunda. That glimpse had shown him so striking a woman, Canaletto was certain she would prove no ordinary witness. Surely she would have gleaned vital details from so intimate a servant as a personal maid? Unless, of course, she was one of those women so self-centred they never enquired into the conditions or thoughts of anyone near them unless it concerned themselves.

Mrs Casement, though, had had a fearlessness in her carriage that suggested she had little time for the world's opinion. And her action in taking charge of the distraught Mary Butcher betokened a care for others that boded well.

Unless . . . Canaletto halted at the south end of the square as a thought struck him. Mrs Casement was a courtesan, Mrs Gotobed had left them in no doubt of that. Had she seen an opportunity to take the foolish Mary under her wing and so use her for her own profit? There were many women who not only made a living themselves out of men's lust but arranged assignations for other women and took a percentage of their price.

Had she used Miss Smith, or whatever her name was, in this way? And was she, in fact, as independent as she appeared? After Fanny had left the box on her mission of mercy, Canaletto had seen the distinguished-looking man who seemed to be an escort for the angry society girl who'd caused the scene detach himself for a moment from her side and gesture to someone. That was when the remarkably tall woman had first taken his notice. The two had met for no more than a few seconds, but words had definitely passed between them and they had looked full of purpose. Immediately afterwards, the woman had vanished through one of the arches beneath the boxes. Canaletto, sure she must be Mrs Casement, had gone after but failed to find her. Only later did he hear from Fanny that she'd appeared in the other box. She must have gone up one staircase whilst he descended another. Had there been a connection between the hurried words with the man who had observed but taken no part in the scene and Mrs Casement's swift action in taking charge of Mary?

A servant came out of a house in the southern corner of the square, which had the blinds drawn and mourning greenery hanging round the door. Large and imposing, dressed in a green livery with silver lace, Canaletto recognized him immediately as another of the minor actors in last night's drama and now he remembered Fanny telling him Jonathan Wright's house was here. Thomas Wright, the young man tossed like a shuttlecock yesterday evening between the two girls, must be the man's son.

Jonathan Wright was the man who had hit Betty Spragg. Like father, like son? The servant appeared to be going the same way as Canaletto, down the Haymarket. As the painter stepped carefully amongst the horse droppings, ruts in the road and bargaining farriers, the air heavy with the smells of horses and hay and the sounds of commercial activity, he wondered about the Wright household and the role Mary Butcher had played there.

Gradually he realized that more and more people seemed to be travelling in the same direction as himself and that he had lost sight of the servant. He reached Charing Cross, where he saw crowds lined the road along the Strand to the east and down Whitehall to the south.

'What is reason for people?' Canaletto asked an inoffensive-looking man at his side.

'Do you not know?' the fellow looked astonished. 'Why Lord Lovat, the rebel, is being taken to his trial before the lords in Westminster Hall. Been happening most days for more 'n a week. 'Tis a fine sight.'

'A rebel?' Canaletto was puzzled. 'What rebellion?'

'Where you from, then, that you don't know of the Scots what attempted to put Charles Stuart on the throne?' demanded the man. He was dressed in workman's clothes – moleskin breeches, a shirt that had seen better days and a worsted jerkin. 'The Duke of Cumberland saw them to the rights, marauding buggers.' He spat upon the ground. 'Don't hold with no foreign king meself but the Hanovers be no worse than a danged Frenchman and when all's said and done that's what their precious Prince Charlie is. And a Catholic!' His scorn was deep.

Vaguely Canaletto remembered some talk of rebellion against the king of England by the barbaric Scots some year or two back. King across the water, that's how they referred to Prince Charles. The details, though, escaped him. 'This Scotsman is coming this way?' he suggested.

'Aye, that he is. I'd watch your purse, a press like this gives your whoreson thief an easy opportunity.' The man spat again

This made Canaletto even keener to escape the crowds, for he had no interest in the procession of a rebel Scottish lord. He forced his way through the throng and across the road, slipping down beside Northumberland House. The buzz of the crowds faded as he made his way through Scotland Yard and the remnants of the palace of Whitehall to the Privy Garden and thence to Richmond House, alongside the Thames.

Already Canaletto knew this area well. Just beyond Richmond House was the new Westminster Bridge, which had been the subject of his first painting in England. Not the one he was now working on but a more traditional view.

Canaletto was sure that the duke's idea would be for another traditional river scene. After all, downriver of Richmond House the Thames took a right-hand bend to the east that offered a view of the London skyline dominated by the great dome of St Paul's, the cathedral built after the city had so nearly been destroyed by fire some eighty years previously.

Canaletto wondered that that imposing edifice had been the only great building to emerge from the devastation. The lack of impressive architecture in this huge, bustling city was sadly disappointing. There were no prospects such as Venice offered, the English seemed to build not with style but for comfort, convenience and commerce.

Here was Richmond House, for example, the home of one of England's premier peers. Canaletto knew it well, but he had wanted to come early this morning to check that there wasn't some aspect of it he had overlooked. It would be good to suggest to the duke an alternative to the river view to make a pair of paintings.

Depression settled over him as he surveyed the large but otherwise unimposing building before him. It was built with classical simplicity, no doubt about that, but to the painter's eye the simplicity lacked substance. Where were the ranked colonnades, the extravagant pediments, the ornate balconies? Was this the home of a man who was grandson to a king? Who moved in the innermost of court circles?

Canaletto was not at all certain what the position of master of the king's horse meant, but McSwiney had left him in no doubt about the status the duke enjoyed. 'A royal intimate, Tonio! And a patron of the arts, a collector. This commission will be the making of you in England.'

Would it? Canaletto was wary by now of promises made by Owen McSwiney but Richmond had been one of his first patrons in Venice and the man was undoubtedly rich and influential. All the more important, then, that he should be able to approach him with the idea for a view that would astonish. One that would interest much more than yet another river scene.

Could this plain house furnish the material for a stunning painting?

Canaletto surveyed it again. It was not only the building itself but its setting that was unimpressive. He looked around the Privy Garden. It lacked both proportion and elegance. There wasn't even a great deal of greenery, though that was a minor detail that could be repaired in the painting. It was a public, not a private area, despite the name. People hurried through, intent on business. A couple of dogs sniffed warily around each other, a carriage rumbled carefully across one of the pathways that criss-crossed the area.

Then Canaletto noticed a couple under a tree and recognized the man as the Wright servant. There was an agitated air about both him and the girl he was with that intrigued Canaletto. He walked nearer to them, clicking his fingers at one of the dogs to see if it would come to him – an animal gave a good excuse for walking without obvious purpose. The dog paid no attention, so Canaletto adopted the anonymous expression he used whenever he wished to become invisible. This plus his small size allowed people to overlook him almost entirely.

As he drew nearer the couple, he could see that a fierce argument was in progress. The girl was as attractive as her companion. A turban of pristine white complemented finely sculpted features and her skin had the sheen of a newly opened dark-hued chestnut. Her dress was white also and she had a white shawl fastened round her shoulders against the chill morning air. Together the pair presented a pretty picture.

Canaletto eased closer to them. As he strained his ears, the girl started hitting the man's chest with clenched fists. 'But not to give him the message, to let my mistress go there, John, and see him! See your master with that, that *woman*! And then Lady Kildare was so cross with Lady Kitty, said she had disgraced herself and them. They came straight back here and now Lady Kildare's maid has told me she intends going off this morning without Lady Kitty. How could you do that to my mistress?'

The man caught her hands and held them against his waistcoat. His face was as full of passion as the girl's. 'What better way to cure her of her madness?' he demanded. 'He is not worthy of her attention. All he is after is her wealth and her position. You must have told her this, Purity?'

Canaletto noted the good diction and grammar, so much better than his own. This was an educated man. Was he a slave, or a free man? Both were common in London. The trade so many merchants had made their fortunes in had brought what seemed a multitude of coloured servants to England. Society ladies had black pages and black maids. Many had been given freedom and plied a trade or remained as paid servants but many others were still in bondage. Canaletto lounged against the railings as though he had all the time in the world and tried to look as though he contemplated eternity whilst waiting for a friend. His attention, though, was focused on the couple, whose attention was solely for each other.

Purity hung her head. 'My mistress is headstrong, she will not listen.'

'So, you see?' The fury had left John's voice, it was gentle now.

And Purity, heedless of any curious passer-by, laid her head against the broad chest and said no more.

'The Wright household is in uproar,' John said as his arms closed around her slim back. 'There's trouble over money. The master has spent and spent since arriving in London. Setting up the house, carriage, clothes, servants and more. He has neglected his business to dally with females and gamble and he has made pledges to charities and others to establish his status that he can no longer fulfil. He either needs to rescue his business or for Thomas to marry a fortune. Tom sees your mistress as a money bag, nothing more.'

'Nothing?' Purity raised her head and looked at the man's face. 'She is very handsome.'

John's arms tightened around her. 'Not nearly so handsome as her maid.'

Purity laid her head back on his chest and closed her eyes. 'Oh, John, what is to become of us? How will we meet now?'

John's face tightened. 'I will arrange something. Trust me, there are ways. I have been made an offer.'

'What?' Purity looked up hopefully.

'I cannot say. It is,' he paused, 'it is distasteful.' The dark voice resonated dislike. 'But it may enable us to be free to live together.'

At that Purity gave a small cry, flung her arms around his neck and pulled his head down to hers. He strained her to him and Canaletto could tell instantly that their embrace was more than carnal. The way she drew back and gazed at him, her hand lightly caressing his cheek, the way he smiled into her eyes, the two of them lost to the world, said that here was a meeting of minds as well as bodies.

Then Purity freed herself. 'I must go. My mistress will never believe it took so long to give you her words for your young master. You do remember them?'

John laughed, 'They are not many. "The Lady Katherine Manners thanks Mr Thomas Wright for his enquiries but begs to inform him he need no longer consider himself acquainted with her." I will carry that back and such ructions there will be,' he added in a satisfied tone.

The girl gave him a last kiss, evaded the hands that would hold her again, then ran straight back to Richmond House.

Canaletto quietly melted away into a different part of the garden. When he turned round, John had gone.

Canaletto felt sympathy for the couple. It was difficult for a servant to form a relationship with one from another household, it almost always led to new jobs having to be found somewhere they could work together.

Over the wall that separated the Privy Garden from Whitehall came the noise of a procession, no doubt that of the rebel lord. Then Canaletto realized that if there was to be a trial by the lords, the Duke of Richmond would no doubt be at Westminster Hall and not at home waiting to greet a newly commissioned painter.

Canaletto felt expectation drain from him. The duke had forgotten him. Had he forgotten the commission as well?

Chapter Nineteen

A little earlier that morning Charles Lennox waited in Cheapside, further back along the procession route from the Tower of London, in the thickest part of the crowd. People were restless, jostling, exchanging badinage, as active as birds wheeling and cawing above a rookery.

Lost amongst a forest of taller men and women, Charlie's heart thumped painfully. How long before the carriages came into sight? Five minutes, ten, half an hour? Would that be long enough to lose his nerve? Or long enough to convince himself he was up to the job?

What would happen if he didn't fulfil the part he'd been given, he durstn't think.

Every night he'd spent at Ma's nest, his sleep had been disturbed by dreadful dreams. Chased by a terrible travesty of a woman with snake's heads for eyes, along unlit passages filled with unknown creatures that raked him with their claws as he ran, Charlie had woken with sweat pouring off him, his pulse racing. And each time he'd woken, he'd thought he was in the boys' dormitory in the Foundling Hospital.

Then he'd groan as it all came back to him. He was sleeping on straw in Ma's attic room, the door locked, strange noises rustling and creaking all around him. He didn't know how many other creatures shared his accommodation, but each morning he woke with a new set of flea bites that itched intolerably during the day and prevented him sleeping properly at night.

The first night he'd been given a bowl of thin soup and a piece of dried bread, then taken up the narrow stairs and flung into the dark. The door had slammed behind him and he'd heard bolts slide into place, locking him in. 'Don't even try to escape,' Anaconda had shouted to him. 'You 'aven't an 'ope.'

Charlie had picked himself up from the floor and immediately searched for a window or chimney. Not only might they provide a way of escape, he badly needed somewhere to piss. But the dormer window had been boarded up and there was no fireplace. All he found was a rough bed of straw and an earthenware pot that seemed to have lost its handle and part of its rim. No matter, it at least answered one of his needs. Then he tried to make himself comfortable on the straw until, itching and scratching, he'd fallen into an uneasy sleep then been woken by the first of the nightmares.

He'd had to guess when morning arrived, so little light came through the chinks in the window planks, and it had seemed an age until Bella had unlocked the door and led him down to the room where he'd first met Ma.

There he'd been given another piece of even staler bread followed by his first lesson in pickpocketing. When he failed to use his fingers lightly enough he was beaten. The canings he'd had from Mr Birchem had been nothing to the way this lash cut into his back and he'd cried out – only to have Ma tell him in a terrible high-pitched whisper that it would be the worse for him if he couldn't keep his mouth shut.

Back he'd been sent to the attic and its rustling dark while Anaconda and Bella went out, 'on business'. Much later Charlie had been brought down again for a lesson with the slithering snakes. Desperately afraid of being bitten, he'd nervously jerked a hand in and out of the writhing mass. Anaconda and Bella had both laughed. Then Anaconda had lifted the biggest snake and wrapped him around Charlie's neck.

Rigid with fear, the boy had stood there while the head insinuated itself along his chin, the darting tongue reaching out for his ear. He felt the fangs on his lobe, gave a long cry of anguish, seized the snake and threw it down. 'I'm poisoned!' he yelled, then rolled his eyes desperately, waiting to die.

Bella and Anaconda shouted with laughter and Ma cackled.

'You'll not die, son,' said Anaconda. 'That's a python, 'e kills by squeezing and 'e's not large enough to deal wiv you that way. But no need to tell anyone.'

'That'll be your part in our little show,' said Bella. 'While everyone's looking at you with the snake, I'll be relieving them of their knick-knacks.'

Anaconda replaced the snake around his neck and this time, realizing that he wasn't going to die, Charlie stayed quite still and let the reptile wander around him. After a little he realized that it wasn't slimy, the skin was dry and quite warm and the sensation of the sinuous body against his skin wasn't at all unpleasant.

'Look frightened,' Bella cried.

'Or Anaconda will beat you,' scratched out Ma.

That frightened Charlie again all right. Then it was back to the pickpocketing lessons and more beatings before he was given a morsel of pie and returned to the attic.

The days slid into one another until Charlie could hardly remember any other existence.

One afternoon the lesson seemed to go rather better and Bella said, 'We might make a right little lay of you, yet.'

'Nah,' Ma spat out. 'An Adam Tiler at best.'

'What's an Adam Tiler?' Charlie ventured, feeling for once that the atmosphere was a little warmer towards him.

'Someone who distracts the cull,' explained Bella cheerfully. Then, as Charlie looked no wiser, 'Look, you're a right-looking cove, gold watch chain, silver buttons an' all and you're walking along a crowded street. Then along comes a small boy, all cheeky like, wiv a dirty face and dirty 'ands and asks yer for alms.' Charlie looked blank. 'For money, dolt! An' the cull doesn't want anyfink to do with yer. So yer paws at 'is nice clothes, an' 'e gets in a right state and shouts at yer to be orf. So then yer runs around 'im, thumbing yer nose and being cheeky. Well, by that time, 'e 'asn't an idea in 'is 'ead but to get away from yer. An' it's not until 'e's way dahn the road that 'e realizes 'is watch and chain is missing.'

'But I haven't taken it?' suggested Charlie, worried but unable to believe that they really thought him capable of such dexterity.

'Course not! It's me wots done it, which 'e never notices as all 'is attention is on you, the Adam Tiler.'

It took several more lessons before Charlie took in

exactly what his part was to be. First, though, there was an outing with the snakes.

Outside Ma's nest for the first time, any thoughts Charlie might have had about escaping were erased by Anaconda taking him to see a corpse lying carelessly beside a midden heap. Anaconda had said, 'See what can happen to those who think they can escape?' forcing Charlie to look at the dead man's face. A scar ran down one cheek and suddenly Charlie remembered the highwayman who had come down the stairs the day he'd arrived.

A man appeared. 'I've sent for the Watch,' he said, eyeing Anaconda with a certain respect. 'That body wasn't there a few hours ago, but 'e's been dead some time, the flies 'ave started.' Sure enough, buzzing around the dead body were a small swarm and above the ripe aromas of the midden heap came a sweetish smell that was worse than any Charlie could remember. He spewed up his meagre breakfast and no doubt the incident helped his performance as the large snake writhed around him, the crowd oohed and aahed and Bella shouted her spiel and collected a veritable shower of pennies, even the odd sixpence. Plus relieving several citizens of their valuables after she'd seen where they kept them.

Afterwards, while Ma was assessing the haul, Anaconda arranged the snake sack in its corner.

'Can they really bite you?' Charlie asked boldly. He had given the matter a great deal of thought.

Anaconda for once was in a good mood, perhaps because Charlie had played his part so well. 'Well, what d'yer think?'

Charlie shook his head. 'I think you've done something to them.'

'Well, well, is that your idea?' Anaconda looked
quite friendly, but Ma banged her foot on the ground
and said in her most steely purr,

'Don't yer tell that child anything yer'll regret later,
you 'ear me?'

Anaconda had shot her a sharp glance, but said
nothing more.

Then Charlie saw another sack, smaller than the
one that formed their act, that hadn't been there
before. 'What's in here?' he asked, moving towards it.

Before he could take more than a step, Anaconda
swooped down and whipped him over to the other side
of the room. 'Don't touch,' he said harshly. Charlie saw
that Bella had gone quite white. 'Take 'im away,' Anaconda ground out and Bella grabbed his arm and
dragged him upstairs. But not before Charlie saw the
small sack undulate in much the same way that the
larger one did.

Another snake performance had followed the next
day, then Charlie had been carefully coached in his
part for today's expedition.

Charlie had never seen so many people as there
were around him now. Crushed together near the edge
of the road, they jostled and jockeyed for position, like
dogs straining after a rabbit. There was a holiday
atmosphere, people hailing each other with immense
good nature, giving way for small children to come to
the front, so that they could see 'the rebel lord'.

The procedure that had been practised hardly
seemed necessary to Charlie. Bella could lift several
wallets without any Adam Tiler's help.

Charlie's gullet was tight with apprehension and his stomach threatened to rise up. What he was about to embark on was a sin. There was no doubt in his mind about that. Sunday after Sunday the foundlings had had the Ten Commandments dinned into them. Thou shalt not steal, said the Eighth. Until now Charlie would never have dreamed of stealing so much as a half-eaten bun. But that was before he had met Ma and Anaconda. His terror of what they could inflict on him fought with the teaching he had received since he was born. Vengeance awaited him.

Looking at the press of people, Charlie wondered if he couldn't just melt away in the crowd and make his way back to the Foundling Hospital. Surely Ma and Anaconda's tentacles wouldn't reach that far?

Then he remembered why he had run away and how important it was to find the Duke of Richmond. If only he could discover his sponsor, surely such a powerful man would make everything right? He would be safe with him, wouldn't he?

Charlie's resolve strengthened. Somehow he was going to escape Ma's evil web. But until he could work out exactly how, he was going to have to go along with what Anaconda and Bella said. He looked around him. Anaconda had melted into the crowd but was bound not to be far away. To his right Charlie could just see Bella, clad today in a plain woollen dress with a dark shawl around her shoulders and wearing a bonnet. Quietly and unobtrusively she was casing the crowd, choosing her mark. All the language was strange to Charlie.

'Watch it, young feller-me-lad,' said a stout gentleman as Charlie, his eyes still on Bella, stepped on his foot. It was said not unkindly but Charlie stammered a terrified apology and moved rapidly further away.

And now Bella retied the strings of her bonnet, the signal that she had identified her mark. She was standing behind a middle-aged man dressed in a respectable-looking brown coat and buff breeches. He turned to look down Cheapside and Charlie caught the hint of a ribbed silk waistcoat and the flash of a gold chain. Definitely a man of substance.

Charlie sidled closer to him, remembering the reaction of the man whose foot he'd stepped on. If Bella had been there then, she'd have had the man's purse in a twinkling.

A noise began to filter through the crowd, not quite cheering, not quite booing, more a swelling rumble.

'Yer can't see there, come in front, here,' said an ample matron, grasping Charlie in a kindly way and pulling him in front of her, where he would have a ringside place for viewing the procession.

But a ringside place was the last thing Charlie needed. 'My father,' he gasped, thinking quickly. 'I must find my father.' He slipped easily round to the other side of the sober-suited gentleman.

The sounds of the procession grew nearer and the crowd's murmurings stronger. Cries of 'Whoreson rebel' and cheers for King George mingled with boos and Charlie saw that some of the crowd were getting ready to throw rotten vegetables. Any moment now it would be time for him to jostle the brown-coated gentleman.

Charlie's throat tightened. He couldn't do it!

Then he remembered Ma, her encrusted face, her

cobweb hair, her jellied-eel eyes, her harsh screech. He saw again the corpse of the highwayman who'd tried to double-cross her. There weren't too many more days left of the procession, Bella had said, they had to make the most of the easy takings offered by the crowd. So Charlie had to make his debut.

Yet there was that Eighth Commandment. Stealing was a sin.

The first carriage was passing by. Now was the time to do it.

Like lightning the various arguments flew around Charlie's mind. He wasn't going to do the stealing himself, he wouldn't be the actual thief, so surely it didn't matter?

A stern voice that sounded remarkably like Mr Birchem's told him not to be so stupid. He was part of a gang, he would be as guilty as any of them, whether it was his hand that relieved the man of his watch or not.

Panic paralysed Charlie. Every instinct in him told him he had no option but to tread on this man's feet and let Bella's light fingers do the rest. But his limbs wouldn't obey.

The procession was passing. A carriage containing an elderly, heavily built man received some thrown vegetables. He bowed to the crowd and the cheers and boos swelled ever louder. Charlie had to act!

Suddenly the restraints were off. Charlie leaped up, pretending to try to see the last of the procession, then landed on the man's foot and dug his elbow into his stomach.

'Oouff!' ejaculated the man.

'Watch out, she's after your watch,' hissed Charlie and, as had been decided beforehand, followed up with a loud, 'Sorry, sir,' in a piping voice and disappeared into the crowd.

Behind him he heard a tremendous commotion. No doubt the mark had caught Bella at it. Charlie couldn't help breaking out into a grin. That would teach her! Then the grin faded. Where was Anaconda? What would happen when the snake charmer caught up with him?

Charlie knew he mustn't let it happen. He thought rapidly. His only hope was to get away from the procession route. He dived down one of the little alleys and found himself in a courtyard. Memories of being caught by Anaconda in a very similar place haunted him but he had little choice. Trying to look nonchalant, he swaggered across it and into another courtyard, then another. It all looked too like Ma's surroundings. He could almost imagine hearing her screech float down from one of the wretched houses. He had to get away from this district.

Charlie started to run. Faster and faster. Across roads, through more courtyards, leaving the sounds of the procession far behind him. He'd had no idea London was such a large place. It seemed to go on for ever. Then, all at once, he found himself in a large meat market. Sides of animals hung from stalls, huge joints covered trestle tables. Blood ran in channels across the ground and lay in pools on the tables, flies wallowed in the pools and buzzed around the meat. The smell of blood hung in the air, coppery and heavy. Huge men in blood-spattered clothes hauled sides of beef and sheep around as though they were sacks of feathers.

Charlie stopped, appalled and fascinated.

'Come 'ere for some nice steak?' asked a woman with a red and fleshy face just like a joint of beef.

Charlie shied away in horror. This could be someone who knew Ma.

'No, no!' he cried and took to his heels again.

The smell of blood followed him long after he had left the market far behind. Surely, he thought, Ma's arm couldn't reach this far? He had no idea where he was. He only knew that from the faint gleam of the sun he was travelling west. And still he hadn't run out of streets. Just how large was London?

Tired at last, convinced that Anaconda couldn't possibly follow him this far, his side stabbed by the worst stitch he'd ever had, Charlie slowed right down. Where was he to go now?

He stopped a kind-looking woman. 'Excuse me, madam,' he said with every bit of politeness he could muster, in just the way the foundlings had been trained to address the gentry who came to look at the hospital and its children. 'Excuse me but do you know where the Duke of Richmond lives? I'm his godson, you see.'

The woman looked at him with a very odd expression. 'Godson, did you say, dear?' Charlie was suddenly conscious that his jacket had been torn in his fall the day Anaconda had caught him, that his face was dirty and his shoes looked a disgrace.

'Yes,' he said staunchly and looked her squarely in the eye.

'I think you belong on the parish,' she said in a kindly way. 'Come with me and I'll see if I can find the constable, he'll know where you should go.'

Chapter Twenty

Canaletto approached the door of Richmond House with something like panic. Was it even worth knocking? Now that the commission looked as though it might have disappeared, he realized just how desperately he needed it. He grasped the shining brass doorknocker and gave it a splendid bang.

The door was opened by a dignified manservant, who seemed unsurprised at his name, took him into a small reception room and announced that the steward would be with him shortly.

The steward? Canaletto looked around the room. It was obvious to him that the house had not long been built and that the design and decoration had been carried out with care and taste.

The steward arrived promptly, a thin, slightly stooping man with eyes that looked as though they took in everything they lighted on. 'His Grace the Duke of Richmond regrets he is unable to be here himself, he has to attend the trial of Lord Lovat,' he announced.

Canaletto gave a swift nod. At least he had not been forgotten. 'Today look at prospects, later suggest viewpoints to his grace,' he said graciously.

'Fine,' the steward said briskly. 'The duke suggested I show you the view of the river, he feels it could make a most attractive aspect for one of your famous pictures.'

The steward led him to a door that gave onto a broad terrace with lawns sweeping down to the water's edge.

Canaletto assessed the scene. To the left was the St Paul's-dominated panorama of London. The great bend in the river gave interest to the water and the many church spires fretted the city skyline most attractively. Craft travelled up and down and across the river. To the right was the less populated area of Westminster that was now expanding at such a rate. It was an attractive view, in many ways it offered greater interest than the other.

Canaletto turned round and studied the façade of Richmond House. Would a viewpoint from the other bank of the river offer merit? 'That place,' he indicated a residence of equal standing that stood on the White-hall Palace side of Richmond House. 'Belongs to?'

The steward, patiently following Canaletto's wanderings around the terrace, said, 'The Duke of Montague, sir.'

The 'sir' pleased Canaletto. 'Hmm,' he said. Then, 'Inside, please, view from windows, yes? Up there?' He pointed to the first floor, the piano nobile, where the main reception rooms undoubtedly were.

'Of course, sir, follow me.'

Canaletto was led up a suitably imposing staircase to a large salon that overlooked the terrace. He looked out of the windows to his left and then to his right. He had already discarded the notion of a view from the opposite bank. To include another, similar structure, would detract from the importance of Richmond

House, not what his patron would desire. No, better to offer the onlooker a prospect from the windows, it implied ownership and the view would be so splendid it would rebound on the owner. That would please the duke far more. Yes, he could produce a worthy river prospect, one that might stand comparison with the best of his Venice *vedute*.

Canaletto sighed and ran a hand over the blue damask draperies that hung by the window. For the first time he felt his age. Was fifty so old that he could lose interest in what had been for so many years the chief impetus in his life? For the first time water, boats and architecture were failing to fuel his creative urge. Was it that the painting he had embarked on back in his studio had eaten up all his freshness of vision? Canaletto turned back to the steward. 'Other view?' he suggested.

'Other view?' the man repeated a little blankly.

'The garden.'

'Garden?' Could this fool only repeat what was said to him?

As if to prove that he had some intelligence after all, the steward said, 'You mean a view of the Privy Garden, sir?'

Canaletto nodded with relief. 'Privy Garden, yes,' he agreed.

'Of course, sir. Come this way.'

They went out of the salon, then into an inner drawing room decorated in yellow and through to a larger drawing room which, like the first salon, was hung in blue damask. The walls held a large quantity of paintings, all hung in gilt frames carved in a simple but effective Greek key pattern. The house, in fact, was furnished in a style that was rich but restrained. In Venice everything was a riot of curlicues, gold paint and velvet, usually faded. So much there belonged to the past. Here was every sign of recent expenditure on a large scale. Nothing could be classed flamboyant yet the chimneypiece was an immensely fine piece of marble carving, that of the chairs was equally distinguished and the two portraits of what surely must be King George II and his late Queen Caroline were superb pieces of work. And then there was the ceiling. Canaletto leaned back to appreciate to the full the fine painting of clouds and gods and goddesses disporting themselves in heaven. He began to feel confident of actually receiving the full price for his paintings.

He looked again at the picture frames. This was a connoisseur who liked to stamp his ownership on his possessions, to clothe his pictures in a livery just as he did his servants.

And here was a servant, standing on a stool and cleaning the square window panes, swinging the heavy lower sash into the room by some form of hinge and using a leather to achieve a bright shine on the glass. No livery for her, though, just a simple calico skirt and bodice topped by a white apron.

She paused as they entered and looked at the steward, 'Would you have me finish later, Mr Preston?' she asked.

'Careful with the drips, girl,' he said sharply but not unkindly as her leather looked in danger of staining the carpet.

She blushed and hastily wrung the leather out into her pail.

'You may carry on, Martha,' the steward said and

took Canaletto to another window, which looked as though it had already been cleaned.

Immediately the painter was captivated. Here was a view totally different from his usual *vedute*. The skyline was one of roofs and chimneys, more ordinary than church spires or Venetian palaces, but with their own interest. Before him was the Privy Garden, through which circulated a captivating variety of folk, including the military, and the odd carriage. Directly below was a partial view of the Richmond House yard. Canaletto could see a maid carrying a load of laundry across to the outhouses. And on the left was the sight he had wanted to see from above, the amazing Holbein Gate.

Canaletto had admired the gate on many occasions. It was elaborate, incorporating roundels, carvings and battlemented towers. It dominated the approach to Westminster from the city, once it had controlled the traffic. Now? He looked more closely. 'Please,' he turned to the steward, 'why road go round gate?' He'd never thought about it before.

The steward came and stood beside him at the window. 'Ah, sir, that is because of all the development around parliament and the abbey.'

'Ah,' said Canaletto, thinking he understood, 'the new bridge, eh?'

'Well, sir,' the steward said diplomatically, 'the bridge has yet to open and even before building commenced, the traffic was causing too much of a crush for the gate. There was a proposal to take it down but then Mr Vanbrugh urged that it was too great a treasure to lose and so it was decided to remove a piece of the

Privy Garden and create a road around it. You can see, sir, the line of the garden wall now?'

Canaletto nodded.

'It used to be right up against the gate. Disgraceful the way the garden became then, sir, all neglected, rubbish everywhere, when it had been such a pleasure!' The man's manner had warmed from its previous formality. 'When it was Her Majesty's garden, fifty years ago, I'm told it was beautiful, parterred and in each little square of grass was a statue. And such a sundial as was never seen with so many ways of telling the time. It must have been quite a sight. All gone, now, sir.'

Canaletto looked out of the window and attempted the impossible task of visualizing the garden as it had been. 'But it neat,' he pointed out.

'Oh yes, sir. His grace the duke made representations, got the area cleaned up. It's nice enough now. But nothing to what it once was,' he sighed.

The maid finished her window polishing, picked up her pail and stool and carried them carefully out of the room.

Canaletto drew nearer to the window, his hands on the panes either side of his head, nose against the glass, heedless of the polishing so recently carried out, and drank in the view.

Already his mind was deciding where a building needed to be moved, a skyline altered, a perspective adjusted to make a perfect composition. And yet another part of his mind remained fascinated with this bird's eye view of so many elements of London's rapidly expanding identity. He might even, he thought, be able to introduce a tiny sliver of the Thames, to remind the viewer of the city's principal means of transport.

'Where is the Countess of Kildare?' asked an imperious voice.

Canaletto turned. Coming through from the inner drawing room holding a length of silk in her hand was a pretty girl of around seventeen years. He recognized her immediately. It was she who had started the scene at Ranelagh the previous evening. And behind her hovered the lovely servant he had seen in the garden.

'The countess has gone out, Lady Katherine,' the steward said with perfect civility, yet Canaletto felt there was more distance in his manner than a house guest warranted. For surely this must be a house guest.

'When will she be back?' demanded Lady Katherine without any sign of graciousness.

'I am unable to say, my lady.' The steward did not sound in the least regretful he could not be more informative. From the floor below came the jangle of a bell.

Lady Katherine sighed impatiently. 'I need her advice,' she said, tapping a kid-shod toe on the Turkish carpet that stretched over almost the whole of the polished floor. 'Inform me the moment the countess returns, Preston,' she ordered.

The steward gave her a nod of acknowledgement.

Lady Katherine tossed her piece of silk over her maid's arm. 'Tell that fool of a modiste I shall not be able to make a decision on the new dress today, Purity.'

Canaletto admired the supple little dip of Purity's knees and the graceful way she inclined her head as her mistress swept past her. Swept past only to come to a full stop in the doorway. 'Why, Lord Maltravers,' she said pertly. 'Have you come to see her grace, the duchess?'

Canaletto stared. It was the tall man Mrs Casement had had those few, purposeful words with the previous evening. He came forward easily, followed by a footman.

'Why, no,' Lord Maltravers said with amusement. 'I have called on the Lady Katherine, if she is receiving?'

'Ah, now, there's a question,' she said playfully, then held out an imperious hand. 'I really think she might be, Lord Maltravers.'

He bowed over her hand, then she waved him into the drawing room. 'Preston, some ratafia?'

Canaletto was amused by the way she totally ignored his presence. It was impossible to feel insulted by this chit of a girl. But he was becoming more and more interested in the scene that had been enacted at the Rotunda. How involved was this interesting aristocrat with Mrs Casement?

'May I offer Signor Canal some refreshment?' murmured the steward.

'Thank you, that would be most welcome,' Canaletto said graciously.

'Can we have the honour of being in the presence of the great Canaletto, painter of Venetian *vedute*?' Lord Maltravers asked. He spoke in a pleasant manner, as equal to equal. Close to he was revealed as louchely handsome, with a strongly lined face, pouches under his eyes and heavy eyebrows that gave his face a sardonic look. He moved with the athleticism of a man who exercised frequently.

Canaletto made a leg and swept a bow. 'I am poor painter,' he murmured deprecatingly.

'Oh, I find no interest in painting,' said Lady Katherine with a hint of pique that the attention should have slipped away from her. 'I can see all the pretty views I want from my window, I do not need a painting on the wall. Better by far to have mirrors that can reflect light, don't you agree, my lord?' She looked up at him through her eyelashes. They were not very long and Canaletto thought the trick did her a disservice.

'To be reminded of a visit to one of the fairest cities in the world can never be anything but a total delight, especially when the view comes from the brush of one as skilful as Signor Canaletto. You, my dear Lady Kitty, have not yet had the experience of travelling to the cultural capitals of Europe. I envy the lucky man who may open your eyes to their charms.'

Lady Katherine opened wide her eyes. 'I vow, my lord, you make it all sound most exciting. I pray my escort will be someone who has all your knowledge and wide experience.' She gazed full at him. Then added peremptorily, 'The refreshments, Preston?'

'At once, Lady Katherine,' the exemplary steward said without a flicker. 'May I show you to the ante-room downstairs?' he said to Canaletto, managing to convey exactly what he thought of both Lady Katherine and Lord Maltravers and also that he would have liked to have served wine to Canaletto in the drawing room.

Canaletto followed the steward out. He would have valued more words with Lord Maltravers but he knew women such as Lady Katherine were determined to exert their authority and he had no desire to be dismissed like a servant.

When the steward would have shown him into the ground-floor ante-room, he said, 'Signor Preston, I am craftsman, rather like yourself. Can we not take refreshment together?'

'I shall be honoured, sir,' the steward said. 'Mrs Marrow, the housekeeper, and I usually take some ratafia at this hour in my parlour, if our duties allow. Follow me.'

The steward's room was on the ground floor, behind the elaborate hall and ante-room and, no doubt, a dining room. Once through a door at the back of the hall, they went along a corridor hung with two lanterns. Smells wafted enticingly from a kitchen set even further back.

Mr Preston opened a door and ushered Canaletto into a simple but commodious room, amply furnished with chairs upholstered in worn but serviceable leather, hanging cupboards, conspicuously locked, and some deal tables. A fire burned in the grate and a copper coffee pot stood nearby. Canaletto also noticed that the candlesticks were brass. The duke obviously respected his servants.

'If you will be happy here, sir, I will order ratafia to be served to Lady Katherine and his lordship and then ourselves.'

Left to himself, Canaletto made himself comfortable in one of the chairs and waited in a state of pleasurable anticipation. After a few moments, the door opened and in came Purity. 'Oh, sir, I beg pardon, only I thought to find Mr Preston and Mrs Marrow here.'

'They attend,' Canaletto said, hastily rising to his feet. 'Will you not sit?'

She had brought sewing with her, a silk petticoat that had a rip at the hem. Placing a length of clean calico on one of the tables near the window, she seated herself beside it and arranged the petticoat so that she could work on the hem in the most efficient way. Canaletto watched with a good deal of pleasure as she held a needle up to the light and threaded it with silk to match the petticoat. For a moment he wished he was a painter of figures, he would love to capture the line of her small, high breasts, the bloom of her skin, the sweetness of her mouth, the clarity of her eyes.

'Morning.' A female of far less prepossessing appearance entered and took a chair near to Canaletto. Dark hair was scraped back under a spotlessly white cap, her back was ramrod straight, her black dress of some good quality material.

Canaletto rose and bowed. 'Signor Canal, at service,' he said gracefully. 'Duke wishes painting of view,' he added.

'Of course,' the gimlet-eyed female said with perfect comprehension. 'Her grace mentioned as much. Mrs Heartsease at your service. I am the duchess's personal maid.' It was said with a quiet pride that demonstrated her own view of her standing in the household. 'Have been ever since she was married.'

Had she indeed?

'Here we are,' said the steward, coming through the door with a tray on which was a filled decanter of wine and several glasses. Behind him followed a woman of mature years and a figure as straight as Mrs Heartsease's. Introduced as the housekeeper, Mrs Marrow, she settled herself beside the fire. Her bones seemed joined with creaking hinges and her face looked as though she didn't understand what laughter was, so set were its lines. She would run her little kingdom with rigorous efficiency, Canaletto decided.

'Will not Miriam join us?' she asked Purity after acknowledging Canaletto's presence. 'Lady Kildare's maid,' she said graciously to him.

'She performs a duty,' Purity said, biting off the end of her thread.

'Ah, indeed! It will be a sad day for us when Lady Emily leaves for Ireland,' sighed Mrs Marrow and Mrs Heartsease nodded agreement.

'And we shall miss your presence, Purity,' said Preston in a fatherly way. 'I understand Lady Katherine will return home then.'

She flashed the steward a small smile. 'Our stay here is a great pleasure,' she assured him. Mrs Marrow looked as though it wasn't such a pleasure for her.

'Where Lady Katherine live?' asked Canaletto guilelessly.

'In the north, sir, in Cheshire.'

'The north? Very cold?' Canaletto felt his flesh goosepimple at the thought. He so missed the sun of Venice. It could be bitingly cold in the winter but in the spring the sun came, ah, such sun!

'Indeed it can be, sir,' Purity said with feeling. 'It is so very damp, the chill enters your bones, it is like sitting in a bath surrounded by ice.' She shivered graphically. 'But sometimes the summers are warm,' she added with a smile that would have melted the largest sliver of ice.

'No doubt you'll be used to the sun,' Mrs Marrow said to her with a touch of tartness. 'Seeing as how it's always hot where you come from. I finds it uncomfortable when it's really warm. Makes me right sweaty.'

Mrs Heartsease looked distressed at such talk but Purity smiled agreement. 'We wear fewer clothes in the West Indies and the houses are designed so that the air flows through them,' she said. 'Whereas here I hate it when a door is left open, particularly in winter.' A slight pause then she added with a sigh, 'There are so many doors at Kiddington Park.'

'It's a problem,' agreed Mrs Marrow. 'Some folk never seem to know a door can be closed as well as opened. But we never lack for fires in the winter, whether we are here or at Goodwood.'

'That's his grace's country seat,' explained the steward.

'Seat?' Mrs Marrow sniffed. 'Little more than a lodge, it is, can't understand why the duke's so uncommonly fond of it.'

Canaletto was always interested in gossip and servants knew so much. All the secrets of the boudoir, the quarrels between husband and wife, the tensions of family life, the skeletons of the past.

Over the next few minutes he listened to the charms of the duke and the duchess and their delightful children, responding with an interested but not inquisitive air. This allowed him to ask in a very natural way, 'And, Miss Purity, does household where you live have many children as well as Lady Katherine?'

She finished her seam, bit off the thread and laid aside her needle. 'Nay, sir. None of her brothers or sisters has survived beyond five years of age. The Countess is now with child again but I know the doctor has faint hope of a happier outcome for it.'

'I hope you will not mind my speaking so, Miss

Purity, but I have seldom seen a young miss so conscious of her own importance,' Mrs Heartsease said with a complacent pressing together of her lips. 'The duchess, bless her soul, would never allow her daughters to speak in such a way as she.'

'Indeed not,' supported Mrs Marrow. 'They are the most natural and delightful of young ladies and a pleasure to serve. We are quite one family here,' she said with great satisfaction to Canaletto.

'I understand two daughters are now married?' Canaletto said tentatively.

The steward's lean face took on an even more reserved look. 'Lady Caroline is now allied with Mr Henry Fox.'

'The affair has caused great unhappiness to the duke and duchess,' Mrs Heartsease said primly.

'Lydia, you are too nice,' protested Mrs Marrow. 'It has been a tragedy! For Lady Caroline to choose someone so far beneath her in lineage . . .'

'And politically against the duke,' added the steward.

'Mr Preston, Mrs Marrow, you are too free,' burst out Mrs Heartsease, small patches of red flaming in her cheeks as she gave a speaking look towards Canaletto and Purity.

'Tush, madam,' said the steward. 'I say no more than society! There is not a member but has said it all. And told how Lady Emily's first act as a married woman was to visit her sister.'

'And how Lady Caroline rejoiced at being united with her,' Mrs Marrow said sentimentally. 'I can imagine it all! Such a loving family as they are.'

Canaletto dwelt for a moment on a loving family

that allowed itself to be alienated from its eldest child by an imprudent match. But no doubt the English aristocracy, like the Venetian, allowed its sons and daughters little choice in the all-important matter of allying them in marriage.

'Very important who the milordi marry,' he said carefully. Then he gambled that as a foreigner he might be allowed a pertinent question if it didn't concern the Richmond family. 'Lord Maltravers wait upon Lady Katherine. He suitable perhaps?'

Purity examined her mending and said nothing.

'That one!' exploded Lydia Heartsease. 'When I remember the trouble he caused all those years ago!'

'Indeed?' murmured Mr Preston, his face a study of barely concealed curiosity.

Lydia Heartsease collected herself, pursing her lips as though regretting they had allowed words to escape that should not have been said. 'Of course, Mr Preston, you weren't part of the duchess's entourage then, were you? I forgot you joined us only after the duke returned from abroad. And you, Mrs Marrow have only been with us some ten years.'

Purity started to slip her needle through another part of the hem that looked to Canaletto's eyes as though it did not need repair, and kept her eyes modestly lowered.

'So, the Lord Maltravers knew your duchess that time?' prompted Canaletto.

'Indeed, all the young bucks were after my mistress,' Lydia said complacently. She appeared to have lost any desire for circumspection. 'Prowling round they were, like dogs after a bitch on heat. And she, poor girl, married to a man only seen once before he abandoned her for three years. Was it any wonder she enjoyed their attentions?' A dramatic pause.

Mr Preston nodded wisely, Mrs Marrow looked as though this was a tale she had heard before and Canaletto sensed that little of Purity's attention was devoted to her seam.

'Of course, I do not say she encouraged any of those young men,' Lydia Heartsease said deliberately. 'Any more than did her friend, the Lady Charlotte Manners, who became the Countess of Cheshire, the mother of your mistress, Miss Purity.'

Purity raised her lovely eyes from her sewing and sent Mrs Marrow a glance that was impossible to read.

'And Lord Maltravers, he danced attendance on duchess and friend?' asked Canaletto displaying, he hoped, an interest that was neither too keen nor quite disinterested.

'Indeed, until Lady Charlotte's parents became aware of the connection and whisked her home.' Another dramatic pause. 'I learned from the duchess herself that Lady Charlotte's parents knew of some scandal connected with Lord Maltravers that had not yet reached London.'

'And yet her grace receives him now?' asked Mrs Marrow, to whom this information was apparently news.

The duchess's maid shrugged her shoulders. 'He married another, not so well connected and of advanced years but with some fortune. They went abroad. Lady Maltravers died recently and the duchess sees no reason why she should not receive an old friend. Any scandal is many years in the past.'

Mrs Marrow held out her glass, 'A drop more, I

think, Mr Preston, since you were so kind as to bring in a well-charged decanter.'

The steward hastily apologized for allowing her to sit without refreshment and filled Lydia Heartsease's and Canaletto's glasses also but Purity shook her head with a smile when he offered her more.

'Lord Maltravers', said Canaletto musingly, revolving the glass by its stem, 'seem interested in young Lady Katherine.'

Lydia Heartsease gave him a penetrating glance from her steel grey eyes. 'You say he visits with her, sir?'

He nodded and looked towards the steward.

'I hope, Mr Preston, you will inform the duchess when she returns,' Lydia Heartsease said sternly. 'I do not think her grace would consider Lord Maltravers, however respectable his reputation these days, a suitable connection for a girl of Lady Katherine's youth and station in life.'

At that Purity looked up. 'Forgive me, Mrs Heartsease,' she said, 'but I would be most grateful if you could advise me on a matter?'

Lydia looked positively gratified at the request. 'Any service I can give, I'm sure,' she said graciously. 'You have an intelligence I have not usually met with amongst your kind.'

Purity looked less than gratified with this remark. It took her a moment to decide to continue. 'It's difficult sometimes for me to understand relationships amongst society,' she said in her soft voice. 'Take my mistress, Lady Katherine. Would it be considered *comme il faut* were she to form a connection with a young man of reasonable fortune, at least, he may have a reasonable fortune, but with a hosier for a father?'

The three senior members of the Richmond household stared as though she had suggested introducing a lion into the nursery. 'My dear Miss Purity,' said Mr Preston when he had recovered himself. 'A member of the aristocracy to form a connection with trade?' He inspected the mother of pearl buttons on his waistcoat as though they might be tainted. 'It happens, of course. We all know of situations where a pressing need for funds has made it necessary for a fine family to marry into some rich merchant or industrialist's family. In the Lady Katherine's case, however, her family do not need recourse to any such measure; she is endowed with a considerable fortune. I am confident the earl would look upon any such suggestion with extreme disfavour.'

There was silence for a moment, then Mrs Heartsease said to Purity, 'I would suggest you advise your mistress to forget any such possibility.' After a small pause she added, 'If passing time with Lord Maltravers could turn her inclinations from such an unsuitable attachment, it perhaps might be a good idea.'

'A thousand pities neither the duchess nor Lady Emily are at home this morning,' Mrs Marrow said positively. 'I do not like the idea of a girl of such tender years being alone with such a man.'

'I will enquire whether further refreshment is needed.' Mr Preston rose. 'Signor, I am at your disposal if you need any further examination of, what did you call it, a view?'

Canaletto rose. 'Most kind. However, I think

perhaps return another morning? For sketching? To present duke with suggested prospects?'

'At any time, signor.' Mr Preston was all civility.

Purity rose, gathered up the mended petticoat, dipped a little curtsy and departed with a murmured farewell.

Lydia Heartsease watched the door close behind her. 'I don't know how it is with you, Mrs Marrow, but I find it difficult to see so many strangely coloured folk in London. Nothing wrong with that girl,' she added hastily. 'I believe in her own country she was a princess and she has been well educated. But it's not right.' Her lips clamped themselves together. 'I've heard of black men marrying white women. What is to happen to their progeny? I ask you?'

No one had an answer.

Canaletto bowed to her. 'Madam, most pleasure talk with you, and with you,' he bowed to Mrs Marrow. The housekeeper simpered as she acknowledged the courtesy. Mrs Heartsease seemed to think no less was due her position.

At the door Canaletto paused and turned back to the duchess's maid. 'Know where Countess Cheshire's family reside?' he asked deferentially.

'Oh, they are all dead now,' she replied without hesitation, 'but they came from Derbyshire.'

Chapter Twenty-One

Fanny had pinned the bit of paper Mary had left with her address to the studio wall. It was almost covered now by the sketches for the view of London through the arch of the new Westminster Bridge that Canaletto had fixed up there and Richard's for his Golden Square painting.

Fanny released the address then stood looking at Richard's work. How much more polished his sketches were than hers. The drawing was swift and assured, not tentative with second thoughts. She lifted the covering material from his painting and studied that. Again, to her mind he handled the paint in a much more skilful way than she did. Last night after they'd all got back from Ranelagh, Richard had shown his work to Owen McSwiney, who had been most complimentary. Fanny had wanted to bring out her own work but Canaletto had hurried the two other men out of the studio saying it was time they all got to bed. But it hadn't been that late, still short of midnight, she was sure. They had left Ranelagh Gardens before the dancing had finished, again it had been Canaletto who had said they must leave before the crowds took all the carriages and boats.

Fanny bit her lip as she felt a frustration burn in her breast. Was it because she lacked talent that Canaletto was so short with her, was shutting her out of his life? Of course, she was only his apprentice but who was it who had saved his life on his arrival in England? Not once but twice? Who was it who made that life comfortable? Cheered him up in his frequent moods of depression? And there had been times he'd acknowledged she had a talent worth nurturing. But how much nurturing had he done?

As Fanny left the studio, setting out for the Covent Garden area, her steps were fired with all the agitation she felt against Canaletto. How dare he tell her she must neither talk to nor accompany him while he talked to Leonora Casement? After all, who was it who had pasted up the greater part of those posters that had brought her to his attention? She almost decided to demonstrate her independence and visit Mrs Casement.

After a little, though, Mary's predicament drove all else from her mind. She must be woefully upset by the scene the previous evening. To be treated so! How could any man behave that way?

Then Fanny realized she also wanted to talk to Mary about the confusion of her own feelings, for who else did she know who might understand the pain and delight she felt in equal measure in Richard's presence?

Last night each of the men had danced with her, McSwiney flinging himself into the movements with abandon, Canaletto neat and deft but having to be steered through unfamiliar steps, Richard graceful and assured, handling her as though she was something precious. When his golden eyes met hers in the rhythm of the dance, she had felt something melt within her.

Never before had any man made Fanny feel this way. Was it love? But she knew so little about Richard, how could you love someone when you couldn't share their thoughts or know anything of their philosophy of life? What had he and she talked about last night? After that extraordinary scene it had been her friendship with Mary. Richard had found it difficult to believe Fanny could like her so much. 'You are so different,' he'd said. 'She cannot have a thought in her head beyond men, whilst you are dedicated to your work.'

Fanny had thought that made her sound dull and boring. 'Mary is fun, makes me laugh,' she said shortly. Which seemed to close the matter and after that the conversation had remained on such impersonal topics as painting. Fanny had not found it at all satisfactory.

Maybe Mary could explain what was happening and counsel her on what her behaviour should be.

Fanny found Mary Butcher's rooms without difficulty. A middle-aged woman with a pursed mouth and narrow eyes flung out slops from a pail into the courtyard alleyway and told her she'd find Mary on the first floor. 'Though if she's up it'll be a miracle,' the woman said with a raucous laugh. 'Likes her lie-in that one!'

Ignoring this, and stepping carefully over the runnel into which most but not all of the slops had fallen, Fanny found the entrance, climbed up the narrow stairs to the first floor and knocked on the door.

There was no answer.

No doubt Mary was still asleep. Fanny wondered whether to leave her undisturbed. But she'd promised to visit and she didn't know when it would be possible to come again. She knocked again, louder this time. Still no reply. She tried the door and found that it was unlocked. Silly girl, she should know better than to leave her door open to any who would call.

Fanny gently pushed the door open. She found herself sniffing curiously. Above a stale odour of the face powder and violet-scented toilet water that Mary used was a curiously metallic smell, heavy and potent. As she entered, Fanny shivered, the room was very cold, Mary could not have lit a fire that morning. Then she was inside the room and screaming. Screaming so hard she couldn't stop.

Mary was on the bed. A sheet was trailing on the ground, blossoming with great brownish-red flowers. Her nightshirt was rucked up, displaying her shapely white legs, which were twisted oddly, and the white gown was splashed with the same red as the covers. But it was the face that made Fanny scream and scream. It had been slashed from either side of her staring green eyes to her red mouth and again from each nostril to the corners of her lips, which were drawn back in a terrible grimace as though she was resisting some terrible force.

Fanny sank to her knees beside the bed and clamped her hands to her mouth, smothering the screams. Her eyes were wide as wide, riveted to Mary's figure. It was the blood that smelt, she realized, all that blood. So much blood! It dripped from the gaping wounds on her face and had poured out of what must have been a larger wound in her body.

As her screaming died away, Fanny stretched out a trembling hand and touched Mary's leg. She didn't really know why. It was as though she believed that, if she touched her, a spell would be broken. That Mary would sit up and laugh, then wipe away some stage make-up and say, 'How I frightened you, don't you think I played a splendid part?'

But nothing happened. The leg was cold and stiff. Then Fanny knew that Mary really was dead.

For a moment she sat there, her head against the silk of the bed curtain, her mind unable to take in all the implications of what she had found.

There came a knock at the door and before Fanny had time to scramble to her feet and prevent entry, Leonora Casement was in the room without having waited for a by your leave.

The same sight as had greeted Fanny stopped her immediately inside the door. But there was no screaming. Mrs Casement's eyes widened, her hands gripped themselves so that the knuckles whitened and she gave one horrified gasp, that was all. 'Mrs Porter below said she heard screaming. I take it that was you?' she said without expression.

Fanny nodded, completely unable to utter a word.

Mrs Casement approached the bed. She was dressed in a loose sack of purple silk with a matching wrap, her hair intricately arranged, a patch in the shape of a coach and horses on her right cheekbone. She stood looking at Mary's body for a long time. Then, 'You found her.' It was a statement rather than a question.

Fanny nodded.

'Poor girl.'

Fanny thought how undignified Mary's body looked, the arms outflung, the legs apart and crooked. She tried to bring the limbs into some sort of order but they resisted her attempts to move them. She gave up, catching her breath in a strangled sob.

Mrs Casement gently moved her aside and drew the coverlet up from the bottom of the bed. It was unbloodied and presented an almost respectable image to the room. Then she went to the door and called, 'Someone, whoever, come,' in tones of great authority.

Standing behind her, Fanny saw a small woman come up the stairs. She was elderly with thin hair, protuberant eyes and a chin that ran into her neck; she was dressed in a plain brown wool gown, unadorned save for a white kerchief at the neck. 'What is it? Is aught amiss?' she stammered as she came up.

'I'm afraid there is. You must send for the constable.'

'The constable?' The woman looked shocked.

'Are you deaf? There has been foul play here and the constable is needed. Find some lad or other or go yourself.' Mrs Casement sounded impatient.

Still with mouth agape, the woman dipped a small curtsy and scampered down the stairs again.

'Well, my dear,' said Mrs Casement, turning into the room again, 'you have had a very nasty shock.'

Fanny felt no inclination to dispute this statement.

'I found cognac to give Mary yesterday.' The majestic figure went over to the dressing table furnished with a silver-backed toilet set and a small mirror. 'Yes, here are the glasses still and the bottle.' She went to a cupboard on the wall and looked inside. 'There appear to be no others.' She poured generous amounts of brandy into the two that were on the table and handed one to Fanny. 'Here,' she said, thrusting one of the glasses at Fanny. A little of the brandy spilt and Fanny saw to her surprise that the woman's hand shook. Not as self-possessed as she appeared, then.

Fanny sipped at the brandy and wondered whether this was the glass Mary had drunk from. The idea brought the image of Mary as she had last seen her, fiery, determined and so distressed. 'You brought Mary back here last night, Mrs Casement?'

'Please, call me Leonora and, yes, I did.'

'How was she?'

'Upset still, she felt the world well lost for love.' Leonora looked thoughtful. 'In many ways she reminded me of myself at that age. I, too, once thought my life was ruined for the love of a man but I learned how to make the best of things and a pretty job I made of it too.' She looked around the room, 'I told Mary that this was nothing to what, if she handled things aright, she could look forward to. I think by the time I left she knew she still had a future before her.' Leonora swallowed the brandy in one gulp and poured more into the glass. 'That callow fellow must have come back after I left and done this.'

'Thomas Wright?'

'Who else?'

Fanny drank some more of the cognac and felt it begin to warm her. 'Did you see him?'

Leonora shook her head. 'I helped her to bed, said I would call this morning, and left. I must have been home by ten of the clock.' She took a few jerky steps, as though she needed to work off some emotion. 'What a tragedy! Such a lovely girl. With my help there was nothing she could not have done.'

'And you really think it was young Mr Wright as stabbed her? Why should he?'

Leonora stopped her pacing and shrugged. 'She was interfering with his wish to form an alliance with young Lady Katherine Manners.' She seemed to have no doubts about the matter.

'But her face,' objected Fanny. 'Why should Thomas Wright want to cut her about like that?' She was sure Leonora Casement must have the truth of the matter but why should two girls have been mutilated in the same way – unless, of course, it had been done by the same man? 'Do you know him?' she asked and was just about to follow up with an enquiry about Miss Smith, the girl Mrs Gotobed had sent to her, when the constable arrived.

He was a large and corpulent man with a flattened nose. Once he must have been a powerful figure, now he was long past his heyday. Nevertheless, seeing no one but women to deal with, he took charge.

Such was his officiousness, Fanny had no further chance to question Leonora Casement for she removed herself at the earliest opportunity. She hadn't told the constable she believed Thomas Wright had killed Mary. Instead she gave him her name and announced that the magistrate knew where she resided should anyone wish to question her.

Intimidated by her manner, the constable vented his need for someone to display his authority to on Fanny.

By the time she was allowed to make her way back to Silver Street, the effect of the brandy had long ago faded and she was exhausted.

She opened the studio door and there was Canaletto, sitting at the table in the best of the light, sketching. He looked up, impatience on his features. 'Fanny, what time is this? Do you and Mary think you can spend the whole morning gossiping when there is work to be done?'

'You are a cruel monster,' poor Fanny wailed, 'and I hate you.' She burst into a torrent of noisy weeping.

Chapter Twenty-Two

Canaletto was overwhelmed by Fanny's news. It took a little time to get the details, what with Fanny being so overwrought and refusing brandy on the grounds she had already had a glass and weeping enough to fill the Grand Canal.

Canaletto regretted exceedingly having been so curt with her on her arrival but, really, was he supposed not to have missed her? Not to have wondered at her leaving the studio for a whole morning, not even preparing his meal? But when he realized what had happened, he went out and found an urchin to send for a meat pie and ale. Then he came back and listened to the full story.

'So this Signora Casement think that young man stab her?' he said finally.

Fanny nodded. Her cheeks were flushed and her eyes red with weeping but she had calmed down. Not so far that she had apologized for her outburst but Canaletto felt he would be unwise to press the point. 'But, signor, surely the same man as killed the girl you found must have killed Mary. Could that have been Thomas Wright?'

'Why not? If involve with one girl and get with child, why not two?'

Fanny sighed and looked doubtful. 'But to kill them, sir? And mark them in such a way.'

'You are sure the marks same?' Canaletto pressed her. He had to be certain of this.

Fanny sighed again but impatiently this time and went and got a copy of the poster. 'Signor, this is how Mary's poor face was cut.' Carefully she drew a series of strokes that matched those on the girl that Canaletto had found. He trusted both Fanny's powers of observation and her memory and there was no doubt in his mind that the killer must be the same in each case.

He rose. 'I go see Signora Casement,' he said. For a moment he was worried that Fanny would once again want to come with him but it seemed that she was too exhausted by all she had been through that morning. He looked at her closely, noting an unfamiliar lethargy. 'Perhaps a sleeping draught?' he suggested.

Fanny immediately sat straighter on her chair. 'No, indeed, signor,' she said indignantly. 'I am no society miss with an attack of the vapours. I shall be myself by the time you return.'

Well, she was young and maybe she would indeed be his old Fanny but Canaletto doubted it. She had had a profound shock and it would take some time before she had absorbed its effects. There was nothing, however, that he could do for her but allow her to rest or to work, as she chose. He set out.

The directions provided by Mrs Gotobed proved impeccable. Canaletto climbed to the first floor of a tall house in Covent Garden itself and knocked at a door leading off a narrow landing.

When it opened, Canaletto found himself gazing up at possibly the tallest woman he had ever met, her height emphasized by the elaborate hairstyle she was wearing, the hair drawn up over what must be a frame of some sort and arranged in powdered curls and twists. Her loose robe, such as was worn by society women in the morning, was of a vibrant purple silk decorated with ruching, frills and flowers made from the same material and scattered across its generous folds in a careless manner. She was not a beauty, her features were too irregular, but, with fine skin, large grey eyes and a full mouth, skilfully reddened, she gave the impression of beauty. Altogether a highly desirable combination of artifice and carelessness.

She gazed down at him, her right eyebrow raised in enquiry.

Canaletto sketched a slight bow, all that the landing would allow. 'Antonio da Canal, at your service, signora. This morning you discover my apprentice, Fanny Rooker, with body of dead girl, yes?'

Mrs Casement looked sad. 'Indeed, that melancholy event did take place.' She took a fine lawn handkerchief from some pocket about her person and dabbed with great care at each of her eyes.

'I wish talk with you about this, please? Maybe enter?' Canaletto was tired of gazing up at this amazon.

Mrs Casement shrugged. 'I do not know what your interest is, sir, or how I can help but by all means come in and speak with me.' She backed away, allowing him to enter a room suffused with a seductive perfume.

There was a huge bed hung with damask curtains of a rich red, a matching coverlet pulled up over bed-clothes and a pile of pillows, the arrangement looking as though it had been somewhat hastily achieved; a dressing table liberally supplied with silver-topped bottles, silver-backed brushes and a silver mirror, a long stool at the end of the bed and a small couch, just capable of seating two people.

Canaletto glanced at the magnificent creature who had seated herself on the couch and then arranged himself gracefully on the stool. Again that right eyebrow raised itself in a droll manner and he felt something of a coward.

'Well?' said Mrs Casement. The word came out in a low purr that was somehow highly suggestive.

Canaletto fought to keep his mind on his reason for being there and to find the English that was threatening to abandon him completely. With something of an effort he took Leonora, for so he was invited to call her, through the events of that morning and the previous evening as related by Fanny. Her voice was deep with a distinctive timbre that was very seductive and he had to work hard at remaining in control of the questioning. He listened to a series of answers that matched the details his apprentice had recounted.

'Last night,' he said finally, sticking out a leg and leaning forward a little. 'Last night you talk with tall, distinguished man.'

'Why, sir, I talk with many such,' Leonora smiled at him.

'This was man who,' Canaletto spent a moment searching for the correct word, 'who escort young lady so upset with Signor Wright.'

Leonora looked thoughtful. 'Indeed, I find it difficult to identify who it is you refer to, sir.'

Canaletto looked straight at her, met wide eyes which returned his stare with deliberate incomprehension and knew it would be hopeless to try to extract anything further from her for the moment on that particular point. He felt in the inside pocket of his coat skirt and brought out a copy of the poster. 'Believe signora know this girl?' He presented the poster.

Leonora took the piece of paper and quickly scanned it. 'Ah,' she said. 'Anne Smith. Yes, indeed.' She looked again at the poster. 'I see you offer a reward for information. May I ask what is your interest in Miss Smith?'

'I find Miss Smith dead in same way Mary Butcher dead,' he said in a level voice.

Leonora never moved. It was as though she had been frozen, like Lot's wife, into a pillar of salt or some other lifeless material. 'Indeed,' she finally managed to murmur.

Canaletto felt triumph, he had gained the ascendancy. He must be careful not to lose it again. But almost at once he felt it slipping away as she said, 'And what is your interest in the matter? Merely because you had the misfortune to stumble across her corpse?' It was the tiniest touch of disbelief in the voice that goaded Canaletto.

'English have poet who say, "no man is island", no?'

'Ah, John Donne. Yes, that is right. So, you are touched by this corpse, you feel a citizen's duty to discover who did the dastardly deed, is that it?' Again that note of incredulity.

'Perhaps it done by same man kill Mary.'

'Thomas Wright?' Leonora sounded incredulous.

'Maybe he know Miss Smith?'

Leonora opened her mouth but nothing came out. She shut it, then made another attempt to speak. 'As to that, sir, I could not say. I knew little of Miss Smith's acquaintances. Indeed, nothing in fact.'

'You did not like Miss Smith?'

That was better. There was a small movement as Leonora adjusted her position on the couch. 'You are provocative, sir. I had no feelings towards Miss Smith except as a fellow human being.'

Ah, now he had her on the defensive. Protest as she might, Canaletto knew that Leonora had had no love for Miss Smith. Now to find out why.

'She work for signora, yes?'

A languid hand stroked the silk of her gown. 'For the shortest of times, yes.'

'How short?'

A slight wave, 'Maybe two or three weeks, no more.'

Canaletto brought out a notebook from his pocket and his lead stylo. 'Perhaps give detail, yes?'

The large blue eyes narrowed slightly. 'You are very persistent, sir.'

'When meet Miss Smith?'

A resigned shrug of the graceful shoulders. 'It must have been quite four weeks ago. I had lost my maid.' The barest of pauses before Leonora continued, 'I had mentioned to my laundress, Mrs Gotobed, that I needed someone to help look after my clothes and hair' – one hand automatically reached up to pat the elaborate hairstyle – 'and Miss Smith appeared one day claiming she had all the skills and was in need of a position. She produced what looked like a first-class reference, she seemed a pleasant person, her dress was simple but clean and I decided I could do worse than allow her an opportunity to prove her worth.'

'Reference? Who gave reference?'

Leonora frowned. 'Let me see, it was from some-where in Derbyshire. I remember that because I have a friend who spent much time there. Near to Buxton. But I have forgot the name.'

'You did not write to reference?'

'No. In my experience, one woman's standards are not another's.'

'But if reference forged?' suggested Canaletto. 'It may be that Miss Smith not Miss Smith?'

'Now that would not surprise me,' Leonora con-fessed. 'And if I am honest,' she added with such transparent openness that Canaletto was sure that she was hiding something, 'I suspected something at the time. The girl was so well spoken, far above her dress. But her reference was presented on an impeccable let-terhead and if she had the ingenuity to forge it, well then she would surely have the ingenuity to serve me well?'

'Such ingenuity can be turned against employers,' suggested Canaletto, wondering now just what sort of person Leonora Casement was. Could she have hoped to catch out her maid and turn the knowledge to her own advantage?

She looked soulful. 'Indeed, sir, you have more sense of these things than I. I had merely hoped to help a poor girl who had obviously met with bad luck.'

'What happen? Miss Smith steal from you?'

'You could say that, yes.' A glance down at her skirt, the hands playing with the ruffles.

'Money?'

'No, nothing of intrinsic value, yet, perhaps, in the end, it was.' With which elliptical utterance, she once again fell silent.

Canaletto was bored with this verbal fencing. 'She stole what?' he asked baldly.

Mrs Casement communed with herself then sighed, 'One day a letter came for me. Oh, letters come often, you understand,' she added as though Canaletto stood in danger of misunderstanding the extent of her popularity. 'Anne Smith usually received them at the door and brought them to me. On this day she seemed strangely reluctant to hand over the communication, I had to speak quite sharply to her. Later I found that the letter had disappeared and when I asked if she had taken it, she denied seeing it again, suggested that it might have been left in the pocket of a petticoat I had sent that day to the laundry.'

'You, though, sure it had not?' hazarded Canaletto.

'I am not in the habit of treating my correspondence so carelessly,' Mrs Casement said sharply.

No, this was a woman who would be careless of little in her life, Canaletto was sure of that. 'May ask, your letter, who from?'

Leonora looked haughty. 'A personal friend, sir.'

'Signora, the maid, Anne Smith, she is murdered. Mary Butcher also killed in same way. Is not important find out why? And who?' Canaletto persisted.

Leonora Casement rose and walked round the couch in an agitated manner. Some of her extraordinary self possession had disappeared. 'As to Mary Butcher's murder, I believe, as I told you, Thomas Wright is responsible. I have no knowledge of the other. The gentleman you refer to is someone of standing, he can have had nothing to do with either death. He has been abroad for several months, has but recently returned to this country.'

Canaletto decided a different approach was needed. 'Signora, I no wish to upset such lovely lady,' he said soothingly. 'Perhaps, instead, tell what happen after letter disappear?'

Was there a hint of relief on her features? She certainly sat again on the couch, smoothing her gown as though smoothing agitation from her manner. 'For a couple of days nothing happened. Other than that Anne seemed brighter in spirits than she had at any time since she had started working for me.'

'She good maid?' interposed Canaletto.

Leonora gave a low, throaty laugh. 'Not the worst I have had but definitely not the best either. She could handle an iron, knew how to care for my clothes, but at dressing my hair she had very little skill.'

Canaletto looked at the elaborate hair arrangement she wore like a crown.

She raised her hand and played with a long lock that lay on her right breast, resting like a flower artfully disarranged by a Dutch painter in a still life. 'I now employ a craftsman in the art of coiffure, I find it more effective.'

Canaletto could only guess at how often the man had to be called to repair the damage a gentleman admirer could cause to the arrangement whilst expressing his ardour.

'So,' he murmured, meeting Leonora's gaze and encountering a wealth of understanding in her eyes. 'For couple days, Anne Smith happy, yes?'

Leonora nodded.

'And then?'

'Then a letter arrived for her.'

'Signora see letter?' Canaletto could not help allowing a certain eagerness to creep into his voice.

Once more a play with a ruffle. Yes, madam had certainly seen the letter. 'I asked if it was for me and when Anne said no, it was for her, I insisted she show me the direction,' Leonora said firmly. 'It was indeed for her.'

'Signora recognize hand?' asked Canaletto.

Leonora shook her head, a little reluctantly it seemed. 'The inscription was in capitals. It may have been . . . but I couldn't say.'

'May have been by same hand sent letter stolen by Anne Smith?' suggested Canaletto.

Leonora gave a graceful inclination of her head that indicated agreement. 'That evening she announced she needed to go out, to meet someone, she said. I never saw her again.'

'Wonder what happen?' asked Canaletto.

Leonora shrugged. 'The girl had the soul of a whore. I could tell. I assumed she had found a protector.'

'And protector was friend who sent the letter,' suggested Canaletto, making a tremendous effort to get the grammar right so that there should be no misunderstanding over what he was suggesting.

Another shrug.

'You seen him since?'

'Yes.' Just the one, brief word.

'Last night, at Ranelagh?'

She was silent.

'Please, signora, that night Anne Smeez,' Canaletto cursed the English 'th', so difficult for speakers of more liquid languages to cope with, why should it let him down now when he'd mastered it several times already? He tried again, 'Anne Smith, she killed. This protector, maybe nothing to do with death, but maybe know something.' He leaned forward, almost begging her. 'I think it is Lord Maltravers.'

She did not deny it.

'What sort man this Lord Maltravers?'

Leonora looked tired, the lines around her eyes had deepened, new ones had appeared either side of her mouth. She shrugged her shoulders. 'A man of passion,' she said wearily. 'I would not think little Anne Smith had the experience to keep him interested for long. Men such as he demand much from their amours.'

'Needs woman like signora to satisfy such a one,' suggested Canaletto, his tone carefully admiring. 'I can tell you offer everything any man could desire.'

Leonora gave him a smile that had more than a hint of calculation. 'Say you so, sir? Perhaps we can spend some time together and you can judge the truth of those words?' Somehow she managed to let the silk of her robe disarrange itself in such a way that a curve of well-shaped breast offered itself to his gaze. At the same time a pointed foot peeped out of the hem, idly twisting this way and that so as to show an exquisitely turned ankle.

Canaletto felt a sudden jolt of lust. Standing, Leonora would tower over him, sitting down it seemed that most of her length was in her legs for she appeared more normally proportioned. He had a vision of those legs, as shapely as any limbs on a Grecian statue if the ankle was anything to go by, unencumbered by clothing and knew that this was a state he had to experience. Still, caution was ever his middle name.

'Signora, you do me honour,' he murmured. 'I shall send word perhaps?'

A faint smile, as though she doubted the honesty of his intentions. 'Do that, sir, I shall receive you with inordinate pleasure. That is, if I am free at the time you propose.'

'Of course, signora,' Canaletto bowed. 'Perhaps together sample delights of London?' Here he was, had been in London nigh on a year and he knew little of what it offered for pleasure. Too much of his time had been spent working and worrying. The work had dried up and he was tired of worrying.

A smile curled her mouth into lines of a most pleasing attractiveness. 'We shall go to the playhouse, sir. Later on, when Vauxhall Gardens open for the summer, we may go there, you will appreciate its charms, I know.'

Canaletto felt slight alarm. Was she already talking of the summer, looking on a dalliance of several months' duration?

What was he getting himself into?

Chapter Twenty-Three

Charlie was horrified at the idea he should be brought before a constable. 'Thank you, ma'am but I've 'membered where I'm to go,' he blurted out and started running once again.

The stitch came back.

Then he was in another market, but with plants, fruits and vegetables this time, and the market area was bounded by a little wooden fence. Charlie sank down on a post at one of the corners and tried to think what he was going to do.

After a bit, his breath came back and he became aware that he was very hungry. He stood up, tried to make himself look as respectable as possible, then started walking through the market. Would it be stealing if he helped himself to a carrot or one of those slightly withered looking apples?

He stood by a stall displaying beautifully arranged cabbages and leeks, carrots and turnips and those apples, which were now wafting a hint of their sweetness to his nostrils. Charlie's mouth watered. He waited until the woman behind the stall had finished making a sale to a respectably dressed matron, then, rounding his eyes and looking as pathetic as he knew how, he said, 'Would you have an apple to spare, missus? I don't have any money. But I could run an errand for you if you had one.'

The woman laughed. 'You're a one, you are. Where you come from?'

Charlie thought quickly. Lies were a sin, not quite as bad as stealing but almost. 'I haven't a home any more. I'm on my own and I'm looking for a job.'

'Lovely carrots,' the woman bellowed with astonishing force as a neatly dressed lady hovered over a nearby stall. 'Sweet as sugar, they is, won't find no better in the whole market.' But the customer was uninterested. 'Job is it?' the woman said thoughtfully in an ordinary voice again. Then, 'Finest cabbages in the country!' she bellowed in another direction and this time attracted a buyer.

Quick as a flash, Charlie picked up the best-looking cabbage he could see. 'Won't find no better than that,' he announced with a winning smile. 'And here's another,' he added, picking up a larger one.

The sale made, the vegetable woman selected an apple and gave it to Charlie. 'Born salesman you are,' she said. 'Don't mind if you want to hang around, I'll see what I can let you have at the end of the day.'

Charlie quite enjoyed himself touting the wares, rearranging the stall and generally making himself useful. He only had one scare. 'Isn't that the uniform of the Foundling Hospital?' said a well-dressed customer. 'I'm sure I recognize it.'

'Cast off,' said Charlie promptly. 'Not nearly smart enough for a foundling now.' Which was, he told himself, the absolute truth. 'I know one of the nurses and she gave it to me.' Which, again, was nothing less than the truth.

The lady looked sharply at him but only said to her companion, 'Such good work they are doing there, rescuing those poor mites from the perils of poverty.' They placed their purchases in baskets carried by their servants and moved away.

'What was it she said?' asked the vegetable woman suspiciously. 'Foundling Hospital?'

'Wouldn't I like to be somewhere like that, given regular meals and a comfortable bed at nights,' said Charlie, almost convincing himself he meant it.

It seemed to satisfy his temporary employer, whose attention was in any case claimed by another customer and Charlie fell to weighing out two pounds of apples, finding the right weight without difficulty.

'Read, then, can you?' the woman said admiringly. 'Write too, I bet.'

Charlie remained silent, not wishing to disabuse her of this notion.

Charlie got handed a rather odd-shaped carrot towards the end of the afternoon and earlier there had been another apple.

'Well, lad,' said the woman after Charlie had helped her dismantle the awning above the stall. 'You've been helpful, can't say you haven't.' She thought for a bit then handed him a small coin. 'That's for you. Wish I could offer you a job but I shan't be coming again until next week.'

Charlie swallowed his disappointment. He had so hoped that she would take him in.

'Not to worry,' he said jauntily. 'I got lots of friends.' Which he had, back at the hospital.

He watched her trundle her cart away; she lived,

she'd said, in a village to the west of London called Chelsea.

Then he looked around and for the first time noticed a large church. Perhaps he could bed down there for the night. He went over. On one of the pillars was a small poster that caught his eye. He looked more closely then stood transfixed. It was a picture of Mrs Pleasant, his teacher from the hospital. He studied the poster more closely and carefully spelled out what it said. The word, reward, struck him powerfully. He was a little puzzled as to why a reward should be offered for anyone who knew who this was a picture of but there was much that was puzzling about the adult world and for Charlie it was enough that he might stand to earn some money. A little more study enabled him to work out where he was to go to get the reward.

Where was Silver Street? Charlie ran back to the market. The man who had the stall next to Abigail's was still there, trying to get rid of the last of his produce. Summoning up his politest address, Charlie asked him for directions.

Bob waved a hand towards the west. 'Through there. Keep north of the big church spire, St Martin's that is – used to be fields until back along – find Golden Square and it's just north of that, you can't miss it.'

That proved to be over-optimistic but, after enquiring of several passers-by, Charlie found Silver Street. The poster had said Mr Canal could be found at a Mr Spragg's, cabinet maker. The houses didn't have hanging signs, but Charlie found the workshop quite easily.

He peered round the door, sniffing the fresh, resinous smell appreciatively. It was a place that looked wonderfully busy, with sawdust and curls of wood all over the floor and pieces of wood everywhere. A tall man was carving what looked like a chair back, a graceful fretwork of curves emerging from the wood held in a vice. In another part of the workshop a much younger man was sanding what looked like a chair leg.

'Can I help?' The older man paused in his work as he saw the boy.

Charlie edged nervously towards him.

Then a woman swept into the workshop from a back entrance, her full skirts brushing the curls of wood shavings, her arms waving around like a wind-mill, one of her hands clutching a piece of paper. 'That whoreson bugger has cancelled his chairs and table!'

Mr Spragg put down his little chisel. 'What whoreson bugger, Mrs Spragg?' he asked, brushing down the seat of a chair for his wife.

Mrs Spragg sat down heavily and raised her eyes heavenwards. 'That miserable son of satan, Jonathan Wright. And he says your workmanship's to blame.'

'My workmanship?' exclaimed Mr Spragg with a great shout, then fell to coughing. 'There's nothing wrong with my workmanship,' he spluttered, heaving and choking.

Charlie saw a jug covered with a piece of cloth on a bench at the back, wooden mugs turned upside down beside it. While Mrs Spragg wailed and Mr Spragg struggled to stop his coughing, he poured out some ale and gave it to the carpenter.

'Ah, thanks,' said Mr Spragg as he gradually got his voice under control. 'Good lad.'

Mrs Spragg had her apron over her head and was

rocking back and forth. 'We're done for, we're done for,' she kept saying.

'Nay,' spluttered Mr Spragg. 'Man's a right son of a bastard. But if 'n he'll not order, there's others as will.' But he didn't sound too sure about it.

Mrs Spragg dropped her apron and Charlie could see she was crying.

Mr Spragg seemed to notice him properly. 'Here lad, what's it you want?' he asked in a not unkindly way.

Charlie came forward, suddenly conscious that his uniform, now slept in for several nights, was horribly crumpled and torn in more than one place and his face was no doubt as dirty as the hands he tried to hide by plunging into his pockets. 'I'm, I'm . . .' he stuttered.

'Spit it out, lad.'

'I'm looking for a Mr Canal,' he finally managed to get out.

'Signor Canaletto?' shrieked Mrs Spragg. 'What can a lad like you want with Signor Canaletto?'

'Mrs Spragg's upset,' Mr Spragg said soothingly. 'Something has disturbed her.'

Charlie had seen that. The 'whoreson bugger' had been responsible. Charlie squirrelled the words away.

'Mr Canaletto's through the arch, in the studio,' said Mr Spragg. 'But he went out some time ago and I'm not sure he's returned yet.'

'But what does that rugamuffin want with the signor?' insisted Mrs Spragg, passing the large handkerchief that Mr Spragg had given her over her face.

'None of our business,' said her husband with finality.

Charlie escaped quickly. He found the studio exactly as promised. Chickens pecking around his feet,

Charlie knocked, at first timidly then with more force. At last he heard light feet approaching.

It was opened. A woman stood there. Just for a moment, Charlie was overcome by a wave of nostalgia for Mrs Pleasant. For she had the same sad eyes and coppery hair that sprang out in curls around her face and a small waist. But this woman had a smudge of paint on one cheek and was holding a paintbrush in her hand. 'Yes?' she said briskly.

His curious eyes looked beyond her into the studio. Even though the day was dull, this room appeared drenched in light that fell from windows in its roof as well as its walls and was reflected back from white-washed plaster. This light had an intensity that made Charlie feel more alive than usual. Then he saw a wooden stand holding a half-completed painting.

Ignoring the woman who had opened the door to him, Charlie went over to the picture.

A sky bluer than any he had seen over London was fluffed with white clouds and two birds flew up over chimneys that belonged to houses arranged round a square. The houses were only half finished and the statue surrounded by grass in the middle was only a sketch but he recognized the square he had just come through. He looked at the glistening paintwork and tentatively put out a finger towards a carriage that only existed on the canvas.

His hand was gently taken. 'Don't touch,' she said warningly. 'You could smear it.'

'I've been there,' he said wonderingly. 'It's just like that.'

At that moment the door opened again and a small man appeared. 'Ah, Fanny, you paint, that is good,' he said, taking off his jacket and wig and putting them on the end of a long table.

'Signor,' said the woman eagerly, 'how went your meeting with Leonora Casement? Did you learn aught?'

'Later,' he said, putting on a loose coat and a velvet cap from a hook on the back of the door. 'Who is this?' he asked, looking at Charlie.

'I don't know,' she said. 'He arrived a few minutes ago. When I asked him what he wanted, he just came over and stared at my picture.'

'You like paintings?' the man asked.

Charlie nodded vigorously. 'Like them with people best. Pictures with them doing things, like Mr Hogarth and Mr Hayman do.'

'Boy know Signor 'Ogarth and Signor 'Ayman?' Charlie wanted to laugh at the funny way the man spoke, but knew it would not be good manners. At the hospital you were always being told you had to be respectful and pretend not to notice when people were odd, like when they had a huge carbuncle on the side of their nose, like Mr Briggs, the porter. Charlie thought a funny accent probably fell into the same category.

He nodded. 'I helped them put up their pictures,' he said proudly.

'Where put up?' asked the man again, quite sharply Charlie thought.

'At the hospital,' he said simply.

'Hospital?' queried the man.

'Signor,' interrupted the woman, 'should we not ask why this young man is here?'

Charlie liked 'young man'. He thought it sounded much better than 'lad'.

'Right, Fanny.' The man dragged out a stool from beneath the table, sat on it so his eyes were on a level with Charlie's and said, 'Why come?'

Charlie fiddled with his fingers. His mission suddenly seemed difficult. It wasn't that Mr Canal, he was sure this man had to be Mr Canal, was at all frightening. His eyes were very penetrating but with his velvet cap he looked reassuringly informal.

'I expect you're hungry,' Fanny said. She went to a cupboard and brought out a piece of bread and some cheese. She put them on a plate, found a knife and then led Charlie to the table. 'Help yourself,' she said encouragingly, pulling out another stool.

He forgot why he'd come. He pulled apart the bread, stuffing it into his mouth, cut off a large piece of cheese and ate that as well. Had he ever felt so hungry before in his life? The joy of the taste and solid comfort of the bread and the sharpness of the cheese was immensely satisfying.

'Poor thing,' said Fanny, seating herself beside him. 'You're starving!'

'He is, what's that word, urchin?' said Mr Canal. He looked quite disapproving. Charlie stopped eating and tried to arrange his battered clothing more respectably. 'Better look to silver, Fanny.'

'I'm no thief,' said Charlie indignantly. 'Anyway,' he added, glancing around, 'can't see no silver!'

'We have none,' Fanny assured him. 'Signor Canal is teasing you.'

Charlie looked suspiciously at Mr Canal. Perhaps that was a twinkle in his eyes, perhaps he wasn't quite as stern as he appeared.

'Name?' It was shot at him.

Charlie automatically stood, abandoning the food. 'Charles Lennox, sir,' he said.

'A good name,' Fanny said encouragingly. 'You're probably called Charlie, though, aren't you?'

He nodded.

'Why you come?' Again it was shot at him. Charlie wanted to talk to Fanny, she seemed much more sympathetic than Mr Canal, but he knew he had to address the man. He pulled himself even straighter, then fished out the half poster that he'd pulled off the church pillar. 'This says there's a reward for anyone who can tell about, about . . .' He faltered as he looked down at the torn face.

The bit of paper was snatched from his hand. 'Knew her?'

'It's Mrs Pleasant, sir.'

'Mrs Pleasant? Who Mrs Pleasant?'

Charlie was nonplussed by this.

Fanny pulled him down to sit beside her. 'Signor Canal wants to know how you knew Mrs Pleasant.' She paused, looked at him carefully, then added, 'You liked her very much, didn't you, Charlie?'

'She was very nice,' he blurted out, conscious tears were trembling in his eyes. 'She used to kiss me.' Then he added hastily, 'but only when no one was looking! Teachers don't kiss boys.'

'And what did Mrs Pleasant teach you?'

Out of the corner of his eye, Charlie saw Mr Canal sit back. It looked as though he wasn't going to interrupt. Charlie found this encouraging.

'Reading. At the hospital,' he added.

'And what sort of hospital was this?'

'For us boys – and girls,' he added generously. 'Only we don't see much of them.'

Fanny's face cleared. 'I know, signor,' she said joyfully to Mr Canal. 'Charlie is from the Foundling Hospital.'

Mr Canal nodded, his gaze never leaving Charlie. 'And this woman,' he tapped the torn piece of paper now lying on the table between them. 'You say work as teacher at hospital?'

Charlie nodded carefully.

'How long?'

'She left ages ago, sir.'

'Ages? What is ages?'

'Charlie, how many Sundays since you last saw Mrs Pleasant?' asked Fanny.

Delighted to have some way of working out what the man wanted, Charlie said quickly, 'Oh, 'bout four or five.'

'Four to five weeks,' mused Mr Canal.

'And had Mrs Pleasant always been there?' asked Fanny.

This time Charlie reckoned he knew what was being meant. 'She arrived after me,' he said carefully.

'And you came, when?' Fanny sounded very patient but Charlie could see that she wasn't happy with how he was explaining things. 'How long have you been at the hospital,' she said, as though to make matters clear.

'For ever,' Charlie said, astonished. After a bit more questioning, Fanny said, 'So, Charlie, you all moved to the new hospital building about two years ago and it was after that that Mrs Pleasant came and taught you how to read?'

Charlie nodded.

'Why she leave?' asked Mr Canal. 'That is question.'

Charlie had no answer.

'Foundling Hospital, they must tell,' said Mr Canal.

'You will go there tomorrow,' Fanny cried. 'And this time I come with you. I want to help and you know your English is not perfect.'

Charlie saw the painter's face darken, just the way Mr Birchem's did before he announced he was to cane a boy for impertinence.

Then the door to the studio opened and a tall man dressed in a worn velvet suit appeared. 'Tonio!' he cried, 'The duke wishes to see your sketches. The trial is to finish tomorrow, you are to attend him when he returns from Westminster Hall. A great honour, Tonio! He could have received your ideas from my hand, but he has sent word that he wishes to see you himself. No doubt my pressing the unique nature of your presence in these shores has had something to do with this.'

Slowly Mr Canal let out a long breath. 'So,' he said to Fanny without expression, 'cannot go to Foundling Hospital, must prepare sketches for Duke of Richmond.'

'You know the Duke of Richmond, sir?' Charlie asked excitedly.

'Signor Canal has been commissioned to produce two paintings for the duke,' Fanny said.

'The duke is my godfather,' Charlie said.

He saw none of them believed him. Why was it nobody would believe him?

'So he must be able to apprentice me to a painter,' Charlie went on.

Mr Canal looked searchingly at him. 'You draw, boy?'

'Draw?'

Mr Canal looked at Fanny, who found some used paper and a piece of charcoal. He pushed them towards Charlie. 'Draw,' he commanded.

Charlie looked at the paper and the piece of charcoal and didn't know what he was supposed to do with them. 'Please?' he said.

Fanny drew her stool close beside him. 'Charlie, why do you want to be apprenticed to a painter?'

He looked at her with relief. 'Want to paint pictures, like Mr Hogarth and Mr Hayman. And I don't want to go for a sailor, which is what Mr Birchem said I would have to.'

'Hmm,' said Mr Canal. 'One reason good, other reason bad.'

Charlie looked at Fanny.

'He means that you should want to be a painter because that is what you want to do above all else, not because you don't want to do something different,' explained Fanny.

Charlie thought about this. 'You mean like I liked Mrs Pleasant because she was, well, nice and kind, not because she wasn't Mr Birchem?'

Fanny laughed. 'Well, that is one way of putting it.'

'Exactly,' said Mr Canal. 'Draw!' he pushed the paper and charcoal nearer to Charlie.

The boy stared at them, still unable to work out what he had to do.

'Do you not use writing implements at the hospital?' asked Fanny gently.

He shook his head. 'We don't learn to write.'

'But you can read!' Fanny nodded towards the piece of poster, still lying on the table.

Charlie nodded, looking anxiously from one to the other.

'Why do they not also teach you to write?'

'They say we won't need to write in our station in life.'

There was a small silence. Then Fanny said, 'Well, Charlie, look at this tankard.' She drew it towards him. 'What Signor Canaletto would like is for you to draw it with this charcoal on this piece of paper.' She made a small mark on the paper.

Charlie looked at the tankard and then at the paper. Slowly he drew a line and then another.

Mr Canal rose. 'When shall I attend the duke?' he asked the newcomer.

Charlie hardly heard, he was lost in the difficult art of trying to capture a three-dimensional object in two dimensions. He reached out towards the tankard and felt its roundness, its volume, and looked back at the page. What was there was all wrong but he didn't know how to make it right. He tried again, in a free corner of the paper, squinting at the tankard, trying to convert it into a flat object. His tongue between his teeth, he heard nothing of what was going on around him until the tall man slapped him on the back.

'Taking your apprentices young these days, aren't you, Tonio?'

Mr Canal took the piece of paper from him.

'I can't make it right, sir,' Charlie said. 'How do I make it round? I mean, look round, like it does?'

Mr Canal's expression seemed kinder. 'Question good. Eye sees but brain doesn't. Brain tells you how to draw but eye must educate brain.'

Charlie didn't feel things were much clearer.

'Mug round, yes? But at this angle, eye see oval at top, not round as brain say it is.'

Swiftly Mr Canal drew the tankard on the back of the paper and Charlie watched, excited beyond measure as he understood what the man had said. 'Oh, sir, yes!' he blurted out.

Mr Canal looked at him. 'You artist I think. You work hard, you become painter perhaps.'

Charlie gazed back at him hungrily. 'You will take me to see the duke, won't you, sir?'

Chapter Twenty-Four

'I cannot decide!' wailed Kitty Manners.

The bed in her chamber was covered with clothing.

She looked at herself in the long cheval mirror and pulled a disconsolate face, flipping disdainfully at the lace ruffles of the green brocade bodice she was wearing.

'It is most becoming,' declared Emily Kildare, sipping at a cup of hot chocolate and swaying the toe of an elegant foot clad in scarlet kid.

Purity, standing by the bed, her arms holding yet another garment, said nothing.

'This could be my image for posterity,' complained Kitty. She started to pull the bodice off. Purity laid the robe she was holding on the bed and came forward to help. 'Perhaps we should take some changes with us,' she suggested in her low, musical voice. 'Allow the artist to decide.'

'Why, an excellent notion,' declared Emily. She finished drinking her chocolate, put down the cup and rose. 'Now I must leave you. I go to visit my sister Caroline and play with her delightful Stu. I long for the day when I shall have my own baby boy.' She glanced down at her waist with just a touch of satisfaction. But Kitty didn't notice.

'Oh, babies,' she said petulantly. 'It seems that is all anyone can talk of these days.' Dressed only in the constricting corset that pushed her breasts up high, a fine linen petticoat and small cages suspended over each hip to hold out her skirts, she looked at the garments on the bed. 'Which shall I wear, Emily? And what shall I take?'

The Countess of Kildare gave the laden bed a quick glance. 'White is appropriate for a young girl,' she said judiciously. 'You looked most pleasing in that gold the other night and I think,' she paused, assessing the bounty spread upon the coverlet, then said decidedly, 'Yes, the pink; I think you should take that with you but wear that sky blue, it suits your eyes. Purity, see she wears the blue, I am sure any artist would appreciate her in that.' Without waiting for a response to her diktat, she left the room.

'I suppose I should accept her advice,' Kitty said a little sulkily.

Purity was already clearing away the unwanted garments. 'Lady Kildare has an eye,' she said briefly.

Kitty wrapped her arms around herself and stood in front of the fire. 'I never imagined London would be so cold,' she shivered.

Purity brought over a petticoat with an embroidered front panel and expertly tossed it over Kitty's head. 'Young Mr Wright has sent you another missive,' she said in a tone devoid of expression.

'Tush, I will have nothing more to do with Tom,' she said petulantly. 'He insulted me, flaunting that woman before my eyes.'

'He did not know that you would be there that

evening. The servant I gave your message to mislaid it,' murmured Purity, arranging folds.

Kitty put both hands on her tiny waist and studied her reflection. 'Am I not to care that a man who courts me addresses his attentions to another at the same time?'

Purity brought over the bodice and skirt of deep cerulean blue. 'Men have feelings women know little about,' she said, turning Kitty so that she could tie the lacing down the front.

'Say you so, Purity? And how, pray, do you know these things?' She twisted so she could see how the straight folds of material hung from her shoulders down her back to the ground. 'Is it Brute that teaches you?' She clapped her hands together, her attention suddenly focused on her maid.

But Purity sat her down and started to arrange her hair.

The door was opened to Kitty and Purity by a man-servant resplendent in a scarlet livery. He looked at the two girls as though not quite sure what to do with them.

Purity said, 'The Lady Katherine Manners for Mr Thompkins.'

'Matt, you bring them up to the studio, you great lummox,' said an exasperated voice. Richard Thompkins appeared behind his large servant's shoulder, laughing. 'Ladies, you must excuse us, we are only now getting our household together. Matt, look to the basket,' he added as the wicker container of additional gowns was placed inside the door by the Richmond footman.

'Thank you,' Kitty said to him. 'Mr Thompkins will tell you when you may return for us.' Then, as the footman looked doubtful, added haughtily, 'Her grace said you were to be at my disposal this morning.'

'Shall we say two hours?' suggested Richard Thompkins. 'Come, ladies, follow me.'

He led the way up a wide marble staircase that curved upwards to a generous landing. Leading off the landing were several imposing polished wood doors with ornate architraves. Kitty wondered, though, that such a magnificent setting should be so sparsely furnished. No more than one chest and a high-backed chair in the entrance hall and a side table on the landing.

The painter flung open one of the doors. 'My humble studio,' he said with deprecating charm. 'Now that I have finished my apprenticeship and hung out my sign, as you might say, I need to provide my sitters with a background fitting for their quality. What say you, Lady Katherine?'

Kitty wandered about the room, fingering the draperies of rich brown velvet generously arranged around a sort of stage opposite the windows, 'It is quite delightful, Mr Thompkins.' On the stage was a carved and thickly gilded chair. Half a column stood beside it. Other props were lined against the wall, a Roman bust, a table holding a number of leather-bound books, a globe of the world, a classical statue, a basket of fruits made from wax. Between the stage and the window stood a large easel and on it a canvas. Kitty touched it with a curious finger. It had been covered all over with grey paint. She wondered at such preparation.

Richard smiled at her action. 'We call that priming. It evens out the canvas and provides a base for adding the paint that will capture your beauty.' He bowed to her. 'And in here', he opened a door connecting to the next room, 'I have arranged matters so my sitters may change their clothing, if they should so desire.'

Kitty saw the room was furnished with a screen in one corner, a chaise longue, a table with a mirror and several chairs. 'Like you not this?' She removed her overmantle and pirouetted provocatively in her cerulean blue gown.

The painter gazed assessingly at her. Kitty felt like a piece of meat arranged on a butcher's counter. Not that she knew too much of such matters but surely that summed up the sensation she had of some piece of flesh up for sale?

'You are quite ravishing,' he said simply.

Kitty was immediately reassured, both as to her own attractions and the painter's appeal for her. 'I was not sure which gown I should wear, so we have brought others for your inspection.' With a graceful wave of her hand, she indicated the wicker basket that Matt had placed on the floor of the studio.

'Come, let us see how we shall arrange you,' Richard Thompkins held out a hand.

Kitty allowed herself to be led up to the stage and sat in the ornate chair. She fluffed out her skirts as the painter stood back and looked at her. He drew the curtains more fully behind her, stood back again and looked dissatisfied.

He stood Kitty with an elbow on the half pillar,

then arranged her holding her arms up to a classically shaped urn placed on a larger pillar; she hoped this pose would not be adopted, it would be immensely tiring to keep her arms in such a position. Then the painter tried seating her at a table looking at her own reflection – an idea the painter seemed to like and Kitty herself thought that contemplating her own beauty might not be too distasteful, but in the end this idea was also rejected. A book was handed to her and a pose experimented with her reading. Kitty frowned, 'I do not read,' she said decisively.

Finally Kitty was placed once again in the chair. Richard turned to Purity, 'Please, will you come and stand behind Lady Katherine?'

Purity looked anxiously at her mistress.

'I cannot know what Mr Thompkins has in mind but let us follow his instructions,' said Kitty, not at all sure she wanted to share her portrait but disinclined to say so until she knew exactly what was intended.

Reluctantly, Purity stood stiffly behind Kitty.

Richard studied the effect and his expression lightened. 'The contrast between the depth of colour of the maid and the pale translucence of the mistress is very effective,' he said positively.

Kitty liked 'pale translucence', it suggested delicacy, an ethereal quality that was flattering. Then she glanced up at her maid hovering over her. 'Wouldn't it be even more effective,' she suggested, 'if Purity was to be kneeling at my feet, perhaps offering me,' she glanced around at the various stage properties lined against the wall, 'those fruits?'

'A brilliant idea! Loveliness offering beauty fruits of the divine.' Richard darted across and took up the basket of wax fruit. 'Here,' he thrust the basket at Purity. 'Offer this to your mistress.'

Purity hesitantly obeyed.

'Just a little more towards Lady Katherine, please.'

Purity shuffled forward on her knees so that the basket pressed against Kitty's legs.

Kitty tried to imagine how the finished picture would look. Purity in her tobacco brown dress, her lovely black features against the blue of her mistress's skirts, her African features contrasted with her own very English looks.

'I think I should be dressed in white,' she said.

'Perfect,' said Richard.

Kitty retired with Purity and changed her gown.

'That is perfection,' murmured Richard as she re-appeared. 'Please, will you take your positions again.'

Kitty sat on the carved chair, Purity knelt before her and offered up the basket. Richard retired behind his easel, placed a large sheet of paper on the canvas and began to draw. 'I will prepare a sketch of the arrangement I have in mind. This will be a painting all London will talk about. A study of two continents.'

'The savage contrasted with the civilized,' said Kitty complacently.

Richard glanced up in an absorbed way. 'Quite,' he said absentmindedly as he continued sketching.

Just as Kitty was beginning to think the holding of a pose was extraordinarily tiring, the servant Matt entered. 'There is a Lord Maltravers, says he waits upon Lady Katherine Manners,' he said in a confused way.

'Indeed?' said Richard in a lively manner. 'Send him

up, we will ask his opinion on the composition of the portrait.'

He had come! Kitty felt triumphant. She adjusted the line of the muslin scarf over her bodice so that the swell of her breasts was visible, then saw Purity looking at her with sardonic understanding. 'You must be weary holding that basket,' she said briskly, lifting her skirts and letting them fall again for the pleasure of hearing the swish of the silk and seeing the sheen of the material as it settled into its soft folds.

Richard looked up from his easel. 'A moment more, Purity, then you can relax.'

Retaining the set of her head towards the painter, Kitty glimpsed rather than saw Matt usher in the tall aristocrat and felt her heart begin to beat faster. Oh, Tom Wright was attractive and aroused the most exciting sensations in her but this man was altogether meat of a different kind. Those deliciously decadent yellow eyes with the world-weary pouches beneath them, the lines driven into his face, who knew by what dissipation – oh here was a man of experience who could teach her delights the callow Tom could only hint at. At that moment Kitty determined that she would make this languid aristocrat hers.

'My lord, welcome to my studio! We are most honoured by your presence.' Richard went forward, hand outstretched. He was attractive too, in a more sophisticated way than Tom but a world away from Lord Maltravers. He was as tall, though, and had as straight a nose. Perhaps in years to come he might be worthy of the attentions of a girl like herself. Kitty pointedly retained her posture and deliberately did not look round.

Purity put down the basket, arched her back and stretched her arms. Kitty noted with surprise that they trembled.

'So, it is beauty herself,' Lord Maltravers said, making a leg and giving her a deep bow. As so often with this man, Kitty had the impression that he was laughing at her but it no longer made her feel uncomfortable, on the contrary, it raised darting tendrils of excitement deep inside her body that were totally delightful.

'You will be an excellent painter indeed, Thompkins, if you can do justice to the charms that are now before us,' he said, with that ironic twist to his voice that set him apart from all other men. 'Good heavens,' he added in a quite different tone and leaped forward with astonishing rapidity as Purity gave an odd little sigh and slipped off the stage.

Kitty watched in confusion as he picked up her maidservant. 'Is there somewhere I can lay her down?' he shot at Richard.

'In here, my lord!' Richard opened the door into the changing room and Lord Maltravers strode through.

Kitty trailed behind.

'Do you have sal volatile on you?' Lord Maltravers demanded, laying Purity on the chaise longue and smoothing down her skirts with a hand that seemed very practised.

'N-n-n-no,' Kitty stammered. 'But maybe Purity has, in her reticule.' Anxious to be seen as appearing concerned, she rushed over and opened the drawstring bag that hung from Purity's waist.

'Should we not loosen her bodice?' asked Richard.

But Lord Maltravers was already undoing the lacings.

Kitty's fingers, fumbling in the bag, came across a little cut-glass vial and drew it out. 'Here,' she said thrusting it at him.

He unscrewed its silver top and waved it beneath Purity's nostrils. 'Give her air,' he said as Kitty leaned forward, very conscious of his nearness.

Then the strong, ammoniac smell drove her back.

Purity stirred. Her eyelashes fluttered. She gave a long sigh and then opened her eyes and looked around her in a very puzzled way. 'What happened?'

'You fainted,' said Lord Maltravers prosaically.

'Fainted?' Purity sounded puzzled. 'I never faint.' She dragged herself up on the chaise longue to a sitting position and put a hand to her forehead. 'I feel most odd,' she said in a way that made Kitty afraid she would faint again.

Richard brought forward a glass that he had fetched from somewhere. 'Here,' he said, 'a little cognac will help.'

The attention of the two men was entirely focused on Purity as she took the glass with an unsteady hand that spilt a little. They watched as she drank some of the spirit, spluttering as its fire hit her throat.

Then she noticed the unlacing of her bodice, thrust the glass at Lord Maltravers and attempted to repair the disorder of her dress. 'You are very kind,' she said in a voice that still sounded odd to Kitty. 'I don't know what happened.'

But Kitty was suddenly quite sure. She remembered too many occasions with her mother. 'You are with child!' she said accusingly.

Chapter Twenty-Five

Fanny woke that morning still full of the shock of finding Mary's murdered body.

The night before McSwiney had taken Canaletto off for a discussion about the views he was to prepare for the Duke of Richmond. At least, that was the idea. Fanny knew, though, that one drink would lead to another and it would be late before Canaletto returned. Meantime she gave Charlie a thorough washing and removed his clothes, wrapping him in a large towel until they should be clean.

He submitted willingly enough, enlivening her with tales of life at the hospital. Just as she was wondering where he was to sleep for the night, Daniel had come into the studio to see if the boy had found them.

Fanny had been surprised at his concern, though it had to be admitted that Charlie Lennox was very engaging. Those very dark blue eyes, the fair hair with its double crown that wouldn't stay down, the alertness of his face, they made you want to hug him. 'You can bed down with Adam in the workshop,' Daniel had said, catching sight of the boy nodding off at the table. 'Come and see the chair I'm working on.' Hand around the boy's shoulders, coughing as he went, he'd led out a very willing Charlie. 'I'll see he gets something to eat,' he said to Fanny.

The strains of the day caught up with Fanny. She finished rinsing out Charlie's clothes, cleaned her paintbrushes and palette, put the studio to rights, found some bread and warmed some milk for her supper then went straight to bed, falling into a deep sleep almost immediately.

In the morning, she went over to the workshop. Charlie was sitting astride one of the carpenter's trestles, kicking his toes in the wood shavings, absorbed in watching Adam and Daniel at work.

'I trust he is not troubling you?' Fanny said.

Daniel shook his head and frowned at a small knot in the chair leg he was shaping. 'He's fine,' he said briefly. 'Leave him be.'

So Fanny returned to the studio to find Canaletto was up and already working at his sketches. 'Fanny,' he said, 'please to go to Foundling Hospital and find out what happen to Signora Pleasant?'

'Me?' Despite her remark the previous day, Fanny was staggered. One moment she wasn't allowed to talk to Leonora Casement, the next, it seemed, she was to be given this enormous responsibility. 'On my own?'

'Indeed,' Canaletto said without looking up. 'Fanny eager, her English so good, so Fanny go.'

Fanny's heart sank. She would not be forgiven for that remark for some time! 'If I was a gracious lady,' she objected, 'then I might be told something. But someone as humble as I will not hear anything of the truth.'

'Gracious lady not be told truth,' Canaletto immediately rejoined. 'Hospital directors not want scandal, say everything good. Fanny pretend wants job, talk to those who work as nurses and teachers, then hear truth.'

He made it sound very simple. And she had begged to be allowed to help. The enquiries were even more important now. However much she doubted her abilities, Fanny realized she had to go. She held out her hand for money for the journey, put on her mantle, tied on her wide hat, knotting its ribbons in a neat bow beneath her small chin, added a pair of mittens, picked up her reticule and set out.

Jostled and crushed by several large personages in a public carriage, she was not sorry to alight at what seemed the northern extremity of London. Here estates were being built, large, substantial houses for the gentry and newly rich. Here the all-pervading smoke that hung over London was hardly discernible. It seemed a pleasant place to live but very far from the commercial areas around the City, or the fashionable parts around Westminster. Fanny thought on the whole that if she couldn't live in Fleet Street, her home for most of her life, she preferred Silver Street to this pleasant but distant area.

The driver had set her down at Red Lion Street and she had to ask a passer-by how to find the Foundling Hospital. After that, it didn't take her long to make her way to the wide avenue that led to the impressive building, its stone still white and sparkling in the spring sun, as yet untouched by the pollution of London's coal-filled air.

The porter on duty at the wrought-iron gates was an ample individual with a large carbuncle on his nose. He was dressed in a warm brown coat with a muffler round his neck, it was a raw and unpleasant day.

Fanny rubbed her hands together. 'Chilly, in't it, sir?' she smiled up at him. 'But you looks properly clad enough. Me mother always told me I should wrap up warm.'

'Well, and what can I do for a pretty lass like you?' he asked jovially.

Fanny cast down her glance, shuffled her feet a little. 'Well, it's like this,' she started in a tentative manner. 'Me mother have heard there might be a job for me at the hospital. I'm right good at looking after children and I knows reading and writing.'

'A job, is it?' The porter looked thoughtful.

'Thing is, I'm not sure I want to work so far from everywhere, know what I mean?' Fanny warmed to her act, 'You live in if'n you work here, don't you?'

'It's comfortable,' the porter assured her, then had to excuse himself for a moment as he opened the gates wide to allow a carriage and horses through. 'Gentry,' he told Fanny, looking at the highly polished rear of the carriage as the beautifully groomed horses carried it up the gravelled drive. 'Makes 'em feel good to see the little uns being looked after and prepared for a godly and productive life.'

'Does they have much choice in their lives?' Fanny asked nonchalantly. 'I mean, can't be much they can do, is there?' she said, thinking of Charlie, so desperate to be given the chance of training as an artist.

'All sorts of plans for them there are. Girls will be servants, of course. Boys will go for sailors and soldiers mostly but I've 'eard some of 'em will be apprenticed to trades.' The porter closed one side of the gate, moving with portly steps, apparently not at all discomposed at having to talk to a young girl. 'When you thinks what they've been rescued from – the gutters, starvation and worse!' he said with distinct relish. 'Course, you as a nicely brought up girl, won't know nothing about that.'

Fanny wondered if she was looking perhaps a mite too respectable. 'Me sister was taken advantage of,' she said gloomily. 'Turned out her young man was married already. Told her a pack of lies while he was sweet-talking her. Mother was frantic. Said she'd ruined herself and brought disgrace upon us all.' She shuffled her feet again. 'Her baby died and now she's gone north to me aunt what married someone in the iron business. But that's why I felt I might like to work here.' While she'd been talking, she'd thought of Mary. The story might so easily have been hers.

'An' you could do a lot worse,' the porter assured her.

'Would there be a nurse, say, or a schoolmistress who might have a moment to tell me all about conditions here?' she peeked up at him through her lashes.

The porter hesitated then smiled broadly. 'You go up there.' He pointed to a long, classically ordered building lined with brightly polished windows. 'Ask for Mrs Rutter and say that Mr Briggs sent you. She'll tell you what it's like.' He looked Fanny up and down with what seemed whole-hearted appreciation. 'An' I 'opes you likes what she tells yer. We can do with a bright little face like yours around 'ere.'

Fanny thanked Mr Briggs with a demure smile and followed his advice. One level of her mind was still numb with the shock of Mary's death but on another level she was beginning to enjoy the challenge and excitement of this expedition which she saw as a crusade – for learning something about Mrs Pleasant would surely lead to finding Mary's killer.

Mrs Rutter turned out to be a large lady, even more ample than Mr Briggs, her gown simple but well made, her scarf and apron very clean and nicely ironed. She, too, carefully looked Fanny up and down. 'Job is it? Well, I don't know what Mr Briggs told you but at the moment we're fully staffed. Had you come a few weeks ago, there might have been a chance as we needed a new schoolmistress, but we found someone and now, far as I knows, there ain't no need for more. But', she added, giving Fanny another assessing glance, 'vacancies do come up. You could leave your name and direction.'

They were talking in a generously proportioned hall. Behind doors, Fanny could hear the sound of children chanting their letters. There was a smell of polish and soap. It felt a place that was well ordered and run with efficiency. Fanny wondered how home-like it was for the abandoned children who lived there. 'Thing is,' she said in a confiding manner to Mrs Rutter, 'I'm not sure as how I'd feel comfortable here. That's why Mr Briggs told me to speak to you. Said you'd sort of let me know what it was like, like. Said no one could do it better.' She looked pleadingly at the woman.

'Did he?' Mrs Rutter looked gratified. She glanced around the empty hall, as though checking who might or might not come upon them. 'Tell you what, it's time I took a break from checking the cleaning of the dormitories anyway. Usually have a cup of tea at around this time, I does. Several of us gets together in the housekeeper's room, in fact. You come and sit with us and we'll tell you what it's like. You'll soon see you couldn't do much better than work here.'

'Oh, Mrs Rutter, that's just what I'd like,' Fanny said in gratified tones.

Soon she was sat in a ladderback chair in a comfortable room lined with cupboards. The housekeeper was a woman with a hooked nose, prim mouth and neat hands that added tea leaves from a flat spoon into a pot as though each leaf was a flake of gold. 'Miss Rooker, is it?' she asked, her voice as precise as her hands. 'Let me introduce you around.'

The nurses were mostly mature women. However there was at least one as young as Fanny, a Miss Marvell, and Fanny moved to sit beside her, asking what had brought her to the Foundling Hospital.

'I helped bring up ten brothers and sisters,' Miss Marvell said in a soft voice. 'Then Sara, the next sister, was old enough to take over and father said it was time I started earning and gave them some money, so I got a job here.'

'Best thing she could 'ave done,' said Mrs Jones, a large woman of mature years. 'Like one big family we are 'ere.'

'The children are pleasant to be with, then?'

'Little lambs,' said Mrs Rutter.

There was a murmur of agreement but Fanny suspected a show of some sort for a visitor. She could not believe that a collection of as many young children as there seemed to be in this hospital were all sweetness and light, or could be well behaved all of the time. 'It is not necessary, then, to watch them in case of escape?'

'Escape, indeed not!' the housekeeper said vehemently.

'But . . .' said Miss Marvell, then fell silent before the look that was sent her.

From which Fanny gathered that nothing was to be said about Charlie Lennox's disappearance. 'Then you truly seem one happy family.'

There was general agreement. Mrs Rutter said in a tone of deep meaning, 'Of course, there is some 'as thinks themselves better than they ought to be.'

'Them as has influence with the governors,' agreed another ample woman. 'Like you know who!' She nodded at her fellow nurses.

Was this a reference to Mrs Pleasant?

'Do such people stay long?' asked Fanny with a great show of innocence.

'Longer than they should,' said someone gloomily. 'Mrs Dancer is still with us. Hugger-mugger with the governors, she is. Never know what she says about any of us!'

Fanny could see she had to take a hand otherwise she would be here for the entire tea break without hearing what she'd come for. 'Me mother knew someone as works here, only she hasn't heard from her for some time. Said I should ask about a Mrs Pleasant.'

Immediately glances were exchanged between several of the women. 'Friend of your mother's, is she?' asked Mrs Rutter carefully.

'Not a friend, exactly,' said Fanny with perfect truth. 'More like an acquaintance.'

'Just as well,' said Mrs Rutter with emphasis. 'No better than she should be, that one.'

'I liked her,' said Miss Marvell nervously, blushing at her presumption. 'Always nice to me she was.'

'Oh, very pleasant, Mrs Pleasant was,' sneered someone else. 'Especially to the toffs.'

'The toffs?' asked Fanny.

'Aristocrats and gentry what is interested in our work,' said the housekeeper with a glance around at the others that suggested they should mind their words. 'It's their money what keeps us going, so it's only right they should have the run of the place, see the good job we're doing,' she added in a warning tone.

'My mother said she didn't think she was working here any longer,' Fanny said in an innocent way. 'But she didn't know why she'd left.'

The housekeeper pressed her thin lips together. 'Nothing to do with us, her departure.'

'Oh, come on, Martha,' one of the younger women said. 'We all know why Penelope left. If she'd stayed another month, everyone would have known her condition. And don't we try to keep the innocence of the little ones?' she added piously. 'Aren't they brought up in the fear of the Lord and to read the Bible?'

Mrs Rutter and the housekeeper both drew in a sharp breath.

'Reading the Bible's one thing but mixing with those above your station is something else,' said a thin woman with a wart on her left cheek below a drooping eye. She sounded at once censorious and envious.

'I liked her,' Miss Marvell repeated, her cheeks flaming with her boldness. 'She was, well, she was fun.'

'Missed her social diversions,' said Mrs Rutter.

'Social diversions?' enquired Fanny.

'Come down in life,' said Mrs Rutter portentously. 'She wasn't used to teaching youngsters, not that one.

She'd been brought up with a governess, one of the gentry she was. Fallen on hard times.'

'Had she been married or was she just called Mrs Pleasant as a courtesy?' asked Fanny.

Mrs Rutter sniffed. 'I asked her once and all she said was her history was sad and she'd not talk about it. Well, we don't stick our noses where they're not wanted and if your mother really knows 'er, you wouldn't 'ave to ask. Just what is your game?'

The atmosphere had changed. The women now looked suspiciously at Fanny.

She realized she had to do something. 'Well you may question me,' she said, dropping her eyelids in a demure way. 'Mother has been going out of her mind. You see Mrs Pleasant came to her for a job, must have been just after she left here, said she was skilled in seamstressing. My mother's a laundress and needed someone to help with the mending,' she added, inspired by what Mrs Gotobed had told them. 'But she thought there was something not right. I mean, like you, she thought there was something shifty about her. I mean, why should a well-spoken woman like she was be asking for a job as a seamstress?' She looked pleadingly round the group of women and saw she had their attention. 'So me mother says she doesn't 'ave no job. When, in fact, she 'ad. And then,' Fanny paused dramatically, aware that all eyes were now on her. 'Then she 'eard that Mrs Pleasant, or whatever she was called, well, she was dead, murdered!'

'Murdered!' shrieked the housekeeper. 'Never!'

Mrs Rutter looked very serious. 'Are you telling the truth, girl?' she demanded.

Fanny began to feel a little nervous. 'She was knifed,' she said, 'stabbed to death.'

'And she'd told you she'd been working at the Foundling Hospital?'

'My mother certainly knew she had been,' Fanny said, wondering whether she should have adopted a different story. 'That's why she wanted me to come here, because she felt guilty that she hadn't given 'er a job. She thought if she had, the woman might still be alive.'

'I don't see that,' said the housekeeper. 'Brigands, thieves and murderers are everywhere these days. Person is lucky not to be murdered in his bed!'

This was absolutely true. Fanny felt she had to be more precise. 'Mother was told Mrs Pleasant had been, well, marked about the face in a curious way,' she said, conscious of the interest she was raising. 'It seemed . . . it seemed deliberate. You say Mrs Pleasant had contact with some of your gentry visitors. Could she have met one of them during her time off? Could she, perhaps, have wanted to continue the connection after she left here?' Her tone was light but suggestive. There was no doubt as to what she was implying. She wondered whether to introduce Thomas Wright's name.

'There was one visitor I saw her in close conversation with,' Miss Marvell said eagerly. 'A most distinguished man, a lord, I am sure, so impressive a figure, so aristocratic his manner.' That didn't sound much like the young Mr Wright.

'I saw her talking to more than one on more than one occasion,' said another equally eagerly. 'And she was most anxious to take her time off, it's little enough we get,' she added with a look at the housekeeper.

'I think', said Mrs Rutter magisterially, 'this is not a matter we should discuss further. I think this is something Mr Birchem should be acquainted with.'

Fanny was torn between feeling this was the time for her to exit and excited anticipation at learning more.

Five minutes later she was seated in another room, small, furnished with a desk, a bookcase and a few chairs. It appeared the office of an official who needed to accommodate the occasional visitor.

Mr Birchem was a large, solid man with a pleasant face, who exuded an air of authority. He looked worried. 'I am most concerned with what I have heard,' he said to Fanny, seated in a leather chair in front of his desk. 'Distressed that Mrs Pleasant has met such an untimely and horrible death, of course,' he added hastily.

But Fanny guessed that the matter most concerning him was any possible connection to the hospital. She had enough knowledge of the world to be aware that this place ran on charitable funds. Scandal could mean no more money. No more money, no more hospital. For one of its staff to have been impregnated by a visitor, even, perhaps, murdered by one, could be disaster. No wonder this man was worried.

'However,' continued Mr Birchem, 'I am puzzled by your concern. You say your mother knew Mrs Pleasant? I understood she had no relatives or friends in London.' His voice was stern.

Fanny was tempted to tell him the truth. Then she realized that that truth would implicate Charlie, who would undoubtedly be reclaimed by the hospital. She shrugged. 'She met her after she left here, sir,' she said and looked him in the eye. 'She told my mother she came from somewhere in the west of England.'

'Now I know you lie,' he said. 'Mrs Pleasant came from Derbyshire.'

'Is that not in the west of England?' asked Fanny, her voice all innocence, her mind storing away the fact he'd let drop. If, indeed, it was a fact. For might not Mrs Pleasant have lied about her background?

Mr Birchem looked at her suspiciously but Fanny maintained her guileless expression and eventually he let his gaze drop. 'What know you of her death?' he asked in a low voice.

'Very little, sir. Merely that she was stabbed and her face violated with a knife.'

He flinched and Fanny felt a surge of triumph as she realized that this man had had feelings for Mrs Pleasant.

Had she returned them?

Various wild suppositions ran through her head. Most were connected with Mr Birchem discovering a passion for Mrs Pleasant that was unrequited.

Then she thought of something else, something that was much more probable.

Chapter Twenty-Six

After Fanny had left on her errand, Canaletto tried to
work on his sketches. The one for the view from the
terrace provided him with no difficulty but the other,
looking over the Privy Garden towards Charing Cross,
presented a number of difficulties.

Normally Canaletto had no difficulty in focusing his
mind on any part of the creative process. Ideas came
fluently to him, his mind enjoyed adroitly changing
perspectives, moving buildings and combining several
different viewpoints to provide a satisfactory picture.
For the viewer it would appear to be a faithful repro-
duction of a familiar scene, only close scrutiny would
reveal the changes that had been necessary. Today,
though, he found it impossible to keep his concentration fixed on the problem of bringing together the
Privy Garden, the Holbein Gate, the Banqueting Hall
and the skyline of Charing Cross. Instead he kept wondering what Fanny was finding out at the Foundling
Hospital.

That she would discover something of the history
of Mrs Pleasant he had no doubt. His faith in Fanny's
ability to fulfil any task was boundless. But now he was
beginning to regret that he hadn't gone in her place.

His mind was too full of questions about the two murders.

Then, as he reviewed yet again what he knew of the first murder, he realized there was something he could do without waiting for Fanny's return.

Canaletto abandoned his sketching, found Matthew Bagshott's card and set out to talk to the surgeon who had examined the body of the first victim.

The card said his rooms were behind the Rose Tavern in Russell Street, just east of Covent Garden Market.

The Rose Tavern was easily located, more difficult was Goose Alley, where Canaletto had to look for a golden ball. By enquiring of several passers-by he eventually managed to locate a dark, narrow and muddy lane running behind the tavern. There was a chilly wind blowing and a sudden burst of rain sent him huddling against a doorway. He found the architecture of so much of London oppressive; narrow streets and overhanging storeys cut out the light, such as it was, but there were occasions when it was useful.

The flurry of rain passed and now he could see there was indeed a golden ball hanging over a shabby doorway. It led into a narrow corridor, open to the weather, with a further door at the end. Out of this came what looked from his clothes to be a merchant, stowing a bottle of something into a back pocket of his voluminous coat and breathing wheezily. He ignored Canaletto, squeezing by him as though the painter was some inanimate obstruction to be negotiated with as much speed as possible. The back door banged closed behind him.

Canaletto sighed. He tapped at the further door. No

one came to answer. He tried the handle and it opened
onto a small, dark hallway with several doors, a couple
of chairs and stairs leading upwards. An anatomical
print on the wall proclaimed that here was the place to
come for someone who understood the workings of the
human body.

A door opened. 'Can I help you, sir?' said Matthew
Bagshott, his height looming above the painter. 'Ah,
Signor Canaletto, is it not?'

'I impressed with surgeon's memory,' Canaletto
said, removing his hat and giving a small bow.

'Not much good as a physician without one. Have
you come to consult me as a patient?' Keen eyes
studied Canaletto's face.

'No, there is new body.'

'Is there indeed! Come in, man, tell me all.' He
threw wide the door.

Canaletto entered a small room furnished with a
desk liberally piled with papers and a large, stone
pestle and mortar, two armchairs, one in front and one
behind, and a nicely worked cabinet with glass doors
above displaying varied bottles and packages and
narrow drawers below. In a corner hung a skeleton.
Two more anatomical diagrams hung on the walls. The
room had a nice air of masculine comfort allied with
professional purpose.

'Sit down.' Matthew waved a hand towards the chair
in front of the desk. 'You say someone else has been
killed? Another girl?' He sat himself down, drew a
piece of paper towards him and dipped a pen into the
large and imposing-looking inkwell that sat in the
middle of the desk. 'I have not been asked to examine a
corpse, when was it found?'

At that moment there came a heavy knocking on the outside door. Before Matthew could do more than rise, the door of his surgery was opened and a small boy entered, his clothes worn but serviceable, his face reasonably clean. 'Got this to give you,' he said without ceremony, dumping a letter upon the physician's desk. He waited until a coin was tossed to him, gave a large grin and disappeared.

Matthew picked up the letter and broke its seal. 'I think I can guess the import of this,' he said. 'Yes, I am summoned to examine the body of a girl killed by a knifing.' He tossed the paper on his desk and picked up a case. 'Come, we will go together.'

It was not far to the carpenter's where Canaletto had found him the morning he'd gone to the magistrate's house. They walked rapidly, not bothering with idle conversation.

The carpenter's workshop had the door open wide to let in as much light from the overcast day as possible, as well as generous amounts of damp and chilly air. 'The body's here?' demanded Matthew.

The carpenter, bent over a small coffin, his mouth full of nails, his eyes squinting, nodded.

They went through to the back room. There on the table was a slim form in some white garment with a huge, dark stain flowering out from the chest area.

Canaletto went straight to the head of the table. He ignored the tangle of red-gold hair and the staring green eyes and studied the cuts, obscene across the fine skin and classically moulded cheekbones. Yes, Fanny was right, the face appeared to have been lacerated in exactly the same way as that of the girl he'd found the night of the storm.

Matthew gave an exclamation of disgust. 'Looks as though this is indeed the work of the same madman.' He picked up the edge of the bloody nightshirt. 'It appears she was in bed when her killer appeared.'

Canaletto nodded. He peered more closely at poor Mary's face, pulled down an eyelid, rubbed his finger over an undamaged area, then finally lifted off a neat round patch from near the ravaged mouth.

'She made up,' he said. 'See, salve on cheeks, kohl on eyelids and,' he held out his finger, 'beauty spot!'

'Expecting a lover most like.'

Canaletto explained about the scene at Ranelagh Gardens. 'Perhaps she too upset to clean face.'

'Or perhaps she reckoned the young man would return and apologize for his behaviour.' Using a knife from his case, the surgeon cut off the garment and displayed the rigid limbs. The stab wound was plain to see. Matthew tried to lift one of the stiff legs. 'Rigor mortis in place. When did you say she'd been killed?'

'Fanny, apprentice to me, found her yesterday morning, perhaps ten of the clock or little later. She say body stiff then. How long body take become stiff?'

Matthew pursed his lips. 'Difficult to say, sir. So much depends on the individual, his size, condition, state of health, the temperature of the air. Science in this matter, as in so many others concerning the physical state, cannot be exact. Usually some twelve hours or so, less in a hard winter, more in summer. It's all to do with the cooling of the bodily temperature. Then the rigor will remain in place for perhaps two days when weather is cold as now.'

'Twelve hours?' repeated Canaletto. He worked back from when Fanny had visited Mary. 'So, she killed maybe late evening. Perhaps soon after return from Ranelagh?' Canaletto was thinking that whilst his little party had been enjoying themselves, dancing, drinking wine, eating chicken, this sorry creature was being killed.

Matthew Bagshott commenced examining the wound. 'As to that, sir, I cannot say. It is impossible to fix time of death even within several hours, there are so many variables.'

'Was knife same as other one?'

'I will need my notes to be certain but it looks possible.' He picked up a hand and inspected it closely, then selected a smaller knife and ran it beneath the nails. He looked at the point. 'It doesn't look as though she put up much of a fight, I can see no traces of skin, alas. I would like to think her murderer had been marked in some way.'

Canaletto would have liked that, too.

The surgeon stood back a little and surveyed the body. 'Did you say this girl was with child?'

'So she say. Mr Bagshott tell how long?'

The surgeon frowned as he ran a hand down the stiff stomach. 'I cannot feel anything but with the rigor mortis it is difficult to say. Perhaps if it is in very early stage . . . I shall have to open up the body before I can tell.'

Canaletto tried not to remember what the other girl's body had looked like as Matthew Bagshott had carved his long cut. He had no wish to be present at another such operation. He gave a deep sigh. 'Probably not important. Interesting both girls murdered in same way were with child?'

Matthew was looking carefully at the girl's limbs.

'Physicians do not examine living bodies enough, in my opinion. We look at the eyes, the face, the tongue, we take a pulse, often we bleed, too often I think. But it is not considered either necessary or *comme il faut* to inspect our patient's naked limbs. Yet surely there is much to be learned from feeling for enlarged organs in the stomach region, for tenderness or growths?'

Canaletto had no wish to consider the matter. The very idea of even a man he respected as he respected Matthew Bagshott feeling around his person was repulsive in the extreme.

'However, I remember when my wife was with child – yes, I had a wife and child until the fever took them from me.' He brushed away Canaletto's clumsy attempt to express sympathy. 'It was a long time ago, yet I remember the changes her body underwent, particularly around the breasts. I cannot see any such signs on this girl. But the question can soon be settled.'

Before Canaletto understood what he intended, Matthew opened the case he had brought with him, selected a knife, and drew a long cut from just above the navel to the groin.

Canaletto turned away in revulsion. Then forced himself to look again and found himself fascinated to watch the physician pull back the sides of the stomach. Then the sight of a ghastly arrangement of innards and organs threatened to turn the girl into a collection of offal.

'If there's a child in that womb, I'll change my profession,' said Matthew. 'But we'll just make sure.'

Canaletto moved over to the window and refused to look.

'No, nothing. This girl was fooling herself. It

happens, women can reproduce all the symptoms except the foetus itself.'

Canaletto considered what this development could mean. Had Mary been fooling herself or had she been trying to convince her lover he had a duty to her?

But could she have expected Thomas Wright to marry her? Was it instead that she feared losing him to the girl who'd been walking on the arm of Lord Maltravers? From what Canaletto had seen of Mary Butcher, she was silly enough for either scenario.

Matthew Bagshott straightened up. 'I need to retrieve my notes on that other girl, then examine this one more closely. However, I am almost certain that both were killed by the same man. Never in all my days in this business have I seen faces mutilated in just this way.' The point of his knife rested beside one of the facial cuts. Canaletto avoided looking further down the body. 'And so I shall report to the magistrate.'

Canaletto thanked the man, 'Perhaps we meet soon not over a body, yes?'

'I would like that,' Matthew Bagshott said. 'I shall hope to hear then that you have discovered this vicious malefactor.'

'You investigate bodies, I deaths,' Canaletto managed a smile as he left.

From the carpenter's workshop he walked to Mary's lodgings, having obtained the address from Fanny the previous day. He realized as soon as he was there how near the rooms were to Leonora Casement's. Coincidence, or some design?

He knocked at the downstairs room and had words with the occupant, a small, fluttery woman quite unnerved by the tragedy. Canaletto presented himself as a close friend of the dead woman anxious to uncover her killer, a role which drew forth tremulous sympathy and an overwhelming willingness to help without being able to contribute any pertinent information.

'Hear nothing in evening?' pressed Canaletto.

She shook her head. 'No, nothing. I fell asleep quite early, you see. I do, sir, not so young any more.'

Canaletto ignored what sounded a plea for sympathy as he wondered if perhaps that meant there had been nothing to hear? That Mary had known her attacker and not realized she was in danger until too late to cry out?

He excused himself and went upstairs, past Mary's room. He tried the door but it was locked. On the next floor the room was occupied by a woman who, despite the fact it was now late morning, had obviously just arisen. Her hair, an extraordinary shade of red, hung in meagre locks onto the shoulders of a dirty calico wrapper that flowed around a body that was, to judge by her collarbones and wrists, too scrawny to be desirable. Her face was narrow, the nose crooked, probably as the result of some accident, her eyes too close together. She could be aged anything from mid-twenties to mid-thirties. Her face said that life was hard and she could be just as hard.

She looked at Canaletto and her expression changed. 'Why, sir, please enter,' she said with a smile that was no doubt intended to be welcoming but betrayed the fact that most of her teeth were missing.

Canaletto realized with horror that she assumed he was a client desirous of her services. 'Please, signora, I want question you on killing of my friend, Mary,' he said hurriedly.

The woman's face settled back into its previous lines of discontent. 'That cow!' she said. 'Thought herself too fine for me. I could have told her, few years on, she'd be no better than me. I had her youth, her looks, once. Time takes all and gives you nothing. Well, it's no use your questioning me. I was out all last night, didn't get back until after one of the clock. Right profitable time I had of it too,' she added with a lewd look. 'Old Mother Parsons on the ground floor, she may have heard something. Shocking business, even if that Mary was a cow,' she added. 'Shan't sleep easy in my bed from now on.'

'Alas, Signora Parsons say she sleep, not hear,' Canaletto said.

'Oh yes, Mother Parsons sleeps all right. Has a nightly appointment with the gin shop. Take more than the dead to wake her up!'

So the evidence of Signora Parsons was worth nothing, not if she spent the evenings in a gin-sozzled state.

'You heard nothing and saw nothing,' Canaletto said, preparing to leave.

'Ah, well now, I didn't say I saw nothing,' she said coyly. Then looked worried. 'I wouldn't like him to get into any trouble though, such a gentleman as he is.'

Chapter Twenty-Seven

Fanny returned to the studio in the early afternoon and found Canaletto sitting where she had left him, working on his sketches.

'All most interesting,' he said after she had related the results of her morning's visit.

Fanny felt disappointed. He didn't seem nearly interested enough in what she'd had to tell him. Nor had he congratulated her on the way she'd handled what had after all been a very tricky assignment.

'Don't you think it might be possible that Mrs Pleasant lay with Mr Birchem and that he then dismissed her?' It seemed obvious to Fanny, just the sort of thing men would do. 'And then he killed her?'

'Why?'

'To prevent her telling anyone he had been involved with her.'

'I think not. Does not fit in with details Leonora, Signora Casement,' he corrected himself, 'tell me. She say girl happy till she see letter Signora Casement get from Lord Maltravers.' Then Canaletto realized he had not told Fanny of his meeting with the courtesan yet and proceeded to tell her what he had learned.

So, Canaletto was calling Mrs Casement by her Christian name, was he? Fanny had a moment's ridiculous vision of her small master with the imposingly tall courtesan. Then banished the wayward thought as she considered what he'd told her. 'Lord Maltravers! He could fit the description of a man Mrs Pleasant was seen with at the hospital. And Mary told me that she had met him while she was working in the country, that he had been, well, interested in her. She said she knew some scandal about him, that she might threaten to tell others unless he befriended her. Mrs Casement was there at the time,' Fanny ended with a small gasp.

'Lord Maltravers spoke with Signora Casement at Ranelagh,' Canaletto seemed to be thinking out loud. 'Before she went to box. They know each other.'

'And, signor, we did not see Lord Maltravers after Mary had left with Mrs Casement,' Fanny said excitedly.

Canaletto was still thinking. 'And man you spoke with at hospital said Mrs Pleasant came from Derbyshire?'

'Yes, sir.'

'Leonora Casement said girl had reference from Derbyshire. I heard recently someone else lives Derbyshire,' mused Canaletto.

'Why, sir, Mary Butcher! Mary told me once she had commenced to work for Mrs Wright in Derbyshire. It may have been there she met with Lord Maltravers.'

'No, not Mary,' said Canaletto, wrinkling his forehead then striking at it with the palm of his hand, a gesture Fanny felt was unnecessarily theatrical but was no doubt the result of his being a foreigner. He tended to the dramatic every now and then.

'But is it not a coincidence, signor, that the two girls

killed in the same way, both with child, had each lived in Derbyshire?'

'Ah, Fanny, Mary not with child.'

'Not! Signor, are you sure?'

Fanny listened as Canaletto told her of his visit with the surgeon to see Mary's body. She didn't want to think about what he was telling her but her imagination could picture the scene as vividly as if she was there.

'Poor Mary,' she said when he'd finished. 'But, signor, I am sure she believed in her condition.'

'Surgeon say 'tis possible,' Canaletto agreed. 'But also possible she try to keep lover who wishes leave, no?'

Fanny saw the force of this. 'You think he might have killed her because of this? Mrs Casement believes this to be the case.'

But Canaletto's mind had gone back to the previous subject and he was walking around the studio muttering, 'Derbyshire, Derbyshire.'

Fanny thought of something else. 'Mrs Truscott, who lives in Golden Square, her companion mentioned she came from the same area as Mr and Mrs Wright. That means she must have lived in Derbyshire. It was Mrs Truscott who wanted me to show her my work only you made me cancel the arrangement,' she added with a touch of bitterness.

'Indeed?' Canaletto stopped stalking around and stared at Fanny. Then he clicked his fingers together. '*Perfetto!*' he said. 'Fanny go now! Go to Signora Truscott with paintings. Come, I show what to take.'

'But, sir,' protested Fanny, 'it may not be convenient for Mrs Truscott to see me now.'

Canaletto paid no attention, he was sorting through the little collection of work that Fanny kept in a corner of the studio, drawings and sketches for the most part but there were one or two small paintings as well. Then he went to his own work and added another sketch. 'Go now,' he said. 'I tell you what to do.'

Fanny approached Mrs Truscott's house with no confidence that she would be seen. To cancel one appointment then to turn up with no attempt to make a prior arrangement was not a way to do business.

Indeed, the servant who opened the door to her appeared equally doubtful that Mrs Truscott would be at home to Miss Rooker. The man wasn't tall but he managed to look down his long nose in a way that suggested Fanny was not the sort of visitor who would normally be made welcome. He bid Fanny wait on the doorstep while he enquired, as though she was some sort of tradesman who couldn't be allowed in the house.

Fanny waited, the collection of work under her arm, wrapped in a cloth, getting heavier and heavier. Then, after a remarkably short time the door was opened again. 'Mrs Truscott will be happy for you to be announced,' he said, in a manner a trifle less lofty than that he had used before. He stepped back and Fanny swept in with as much dignity as she could command.

The hall was not large but it had pleasing proportions and an elaborate cornice. The floor was of black and white marble squares and against one wall stood a marble table with two bowed legs of gilded wood. On the walls were several engravings of Roman ruins. Fanny would like to have studied them and compared them with her brother's work but the manservant had started to climb the stairs and she had to follow.

He opened a door on the first floor with a flourish and announced, 'Miss Rooker, madam,' in supercilious tones.

Mrs Truscott was sitting in a wing chair upholstered in dark red damask. Her unpowdered hair was a silver grey that looked very well against its rich colour. Her hands were busy with a piece of crewel embroidery, an elaborate arrangement of stylized flowers in autumnal colours. Opposite her, knitting a bead purse, was her companion, Patience Partridge.

Mrs Truscott nodded in a pleasant way. 'We were wondering how to employ ourselves this afternoon. We finished reading Mr Fielding's latest work yesterday and had neglected to furnish ourselves with a replacement. The weather is too inclement to venture forth in search of a book or, indeed a new hat, an enterprise usually replete with entertainment.'

This was all said with a droll look. Fanny felt immediately at ease with Mrs Truscott and less than happy with her assignment.

'Come, my dear, over here. James,' she said to the manservant, still waiting by the door. 'Bring over that small table and place it near my chair so that Miss Rooker may show me her work.'

Grudgingly, or so it seemed to Fanny, the manservant brought over a three-footed round table that Daniel Spragg would not have been ashamed to have owned as his handiwork, and arranged it in front of Mrs Truscott.

'Thank you,' she said. 'Now, that will be all until I ring for the tea tray.'

The man disappeared.

Fanny slowly approached Mrs Truscott.

'I am not a dog, I will not bite,' said that lady in a lively manner. 'Put your burden on that chair and show me your work piece by piece.'

Fanny did as she was told and eventually forgot the purpose of her visit in the welcome appreciation that was given to her sketches and paintings, carefully placing each on a chair on the other side of Mrs Truscott as her hostess asked to see the next. At last she said, 'That is all, madam.'

'Why, no, it is not! I see another sketch,' said Mrs Truscott, peering over at the wrapping still lying there.

Reluctantly Fanny brought over the last drawing and laid it on the round table. She didn't know whether it would stimulate a reaction but if it did she knew that what followed would be a shock to her kindly hostess. She almost hoped the sketch would go unrecognized.

At once, though, it was apparent that Mrs Truscott had known the girl, for she gazed at the drawing as though she could not credit her eyes and it seemed her figure shrank in size. At last she tore her gaze away. 'Where did this come from?' Her voice was old and quavered.

'Is it someone you recognize?' Fanny asked as gently as she could.

Mrs Truscott's companion rose and came over. She picked up the sketch. 'Why,' she said in shocked tones, 'it is Penelope.'

'You did not do this sketch,' Mrs Truscott said in

accusing tones. 'It is quite different from your work. Who did it and why have you brought it here?'

'Signor Canaletto, my master, he drew it.'

'Why?' The word was shot at her with the crack of ice breaking in winter.

'Who is the drawing of?' repeated Fanny and this time she looked at the companion.

'Penelope is Mrs Truscott's granddaughter.'

'Tell me, I must know, where did your master see her? I so wish to find her.'

Never had anything been more difficult to say than the words Fanny had to utter. 'I am right sorry, madam, but I am afraid your granddaughter is dead.'

Mrs Truscott clutched at the arms of her chair, her eyelids closed. It was as though she was willing herself to remain upright. 'I have hoped against hope never to hear those words,' she said at last. She let out a sigh like the expiration of a dying bird.

'Oh, Nancy, do not despair,' fluttered the companion. 'How many times have I heard you say hope can never be relinquished?' She wrung her hands together, her eyes rolling around their sockets. 'How do you know that this wicked girl is telling the truth? It could be a plot, all a farrago!'

Mrs Truscott looked straight at Fanny. 'Are you telling the truth? Do not toy with me. If you have some nefarious purpose, I wish you to tell me immediately.'

'Oh, madam, indeed I would never try to delude you in any way!' Fanny reached into her reticule. 'My master told me that if you recognized the dead girl, I was to show you this further sketch. He said it might prove to you that he told the truth.' She handed over a small piece of paper.

Mrs Truscott took it with a hand that trembled. 'I recognize the ring,' she said finally. 'It is, it was, Penelope's.' For a long moment she said nothing and Fanny waited. 'You must tell me all,' she said at last. Then, 'No, not you, your master, he must acquaint me with every detail.' Putting both hands firmly on the arms of the chair, she rose to her feet. Gone was all the liveliness Fanny had seen before. 'Take me to him.'

'Signor Canaletto said if you sent for him, he would come immediately,' Fanny said quickly. 'He thought that you would want to speak to him.'

'It would be intolerable for me to wait while James went for him,' said Mrs Truscott, 'Patience, my wrap!'

Patience Partridge was already on her feet and halfway out of the door and in a very short time she had returned with a warm mantle. 'Are you sure, my dear? 'Tis very cold out, you know, you remember we decided we would not venture forth.'

Mrs Truscott said nothing, merely gave her companion a look that had her holding out the garment to wrap around Mrs Truscott's shoulders. A pair of mittens was produced and a walking cane also. This Mrs Truscott brushed aside. 'Tush, Patience, I do not need a stick, I have told you many a time.'

'You remember when you slipped on the pavement, dear?'

'It was freezing and I did not see the ice. Put it away,' Mrs Truscott said impatiently. She seemed to have recovered from the shock Fanny had dealt her. She held out her hand. 'Come, Miss Rooker, you shall give me your arm and take me to your signor.'

Chapter Twenty-Eight

Canaletto was so engrossed in his drawings, he did not hear the door open. Not until Fanny said, 'May I present Signor Canal, madam?' did he look up.

He saw a woman of advanced years who held herself erect and seemed active. She had a face any painter would want to try and capture with its dark blue eyes, soft fair skin that was threaded with innumerable lines yet remained attractive, and silver-grey hair arranged into a soft style that was elegant yet suitable for her age, topped with a lace cap. She looked stern and as though she was holding herself with iron control. He knew immediately that she had recognized the sketch and that the connection had been close. He regretted the fact but could not help being filled with anticipation for what she must surely be about to tell him.

He scrambled to his feet. 'Signora Truscott, yes?' he said, advancing with his hand outstretched.

She placed hers in his and he bowed over it, not quite touching the mittened fingers with his lips. He could feel the hand tremble, as though her control was imperfectly imposed.

'Signor,' she said as he straightened himself, 'Miss Rooker tells me that my granddaughter is dead.'

'Please,' he said, indicating one of the studio stools for her to sit. She sank onto it with as much dignity as if it had been a chair in her drawing room. 'Grand-daughter?'

Mrs Truscott clicked her fingers at Fanny. 'The sketch, Miss Rooker.'

Fanny gave the drawing of the dead girl to Mrs Truscott. She laid it on the studio table, her fingers lingering on its surface, as though she would caress the ink-drawn lines. 'This is, must be, Penelope Bardolph, my granddaughter.' Her fingers clicked imperiously again. Fanny produced the little drawing of the ring. 'I also recognize this. It is of a ring I gave her for her seventeenth birthday.' Her voice shook and she closed her eyes.

'Signora, permit me, a little cognac?' Canaletto went to the corner cupboard and took out his prized bottle of French brandy, poured some into a glass and offered it to his visitor. He admired the way she took it without demur, drank a little and composed herself again. This was a woman of extraordinary control.

He drew up another stool and sat himself opposite her. In the background he saw Fanny attend to the fire then sit quietly on her bed, listening with keen attention.

'So, signora?'

'Sir, I came to hear how you know my grand-daughter is dead.' Her back was as straight as his painting stick, her voice now as steady as his own.

Gently he told her of his discovery, omitting both the damage done to the face and the fact that the girl had been with child.

'There was no identification, no knowledge who

girl is,' he finished. 'So I draw sketch and Fanny organize printing – poster.' He looked round at her.

Fanny had already gone to the chest where they kept painting supplies and brought out a copy of the poster. She gave it to Mrs Truscott.

Mrs Truscott laid it beside the sketch as though to compare the two. Then looked up at Canaletto. 'Why were you concerned?' she asked. 'You did not know this girl, she could have meant nothing to you. Why go to such trouble?'

How to explain? 'I have apprentice,' he said, glancing at Fanny. 'I think, maybe she meet such, such monster.' He spoke with a certain force and he felt rather than saw her look at him. 'Now another girl killed as well, in same way.' He drew a deep breath. 'Signora, I have to say, these not ordinary killings. Both girls' faces slashed.' He grabbed the poster and the pen he'd been using and drew in the cuts that had so disfigured the dead face.

Mrs Truscott viewed the result without visible sign of emotion.

Canaletto gave her the details they had learned about her granddaughter. As he told her that she had been working at the Foundling Hospital, Mrs Truscott's hand, lying on the table, clenched. 'Oh, the stupid, stupid girl,' she said.

'I think, maybe, granddaughter have child that is given to hospital?' Canaletto offered the suggestion gently but with conviction.

The eyes looked straight at him without flinching. 'Sir, you are, I think, a man of understanding.'

It was a compliment that Canaletto felt he did not deserve but he remained silent. He waited while Mrs

Truscott thought for a moment. When she spoke again it was with decision.

'To understand the relationship between my grand-daughter and myself, and so the history of how she left my care and protection, I have to tell you about her mother, my daughter, Hester.' She glanced down and brushed at the folds of her skirt, as though dislodging a smidgen of dirt. 'I am a woman who has always been accustomed to obedience from those around her. My husband, a man of means, died shortly after our daughter was born. It was left to me to raise her. She was,' another moment's hesitation before she continued firmly, 'Hester was a headstrong girl. I attempted to discipline her, to make her aware of the behaviour expected from someone in her station of life. I have to say that my success was only moderate.' There was a wealth of unspoken information behind the way the words were clipped out. Canaletto had a vision of a girl with all her mother's iron will and her own views on how life should be lived. They must have had battles royal.

'It was something of a relief to me when Hester married. She had early displayed tendencies . . . well, let us say I was delighted when her passions found a suitable outlet. Her husband was a young man of good family with a great fondness for my daughter. Soon they had a daughter of their own, Penelope. Then, alas, my son-in-law was killed in a riding accident. I wanted Hester and Penelope to come and live with me. Hester preferred to maintain her own residence.'

Again Canaletto was aware of unarticulated battles.

'Some two years later it was brought to my attention that Hester's behaviour was such as to cause concern. Gossip reached my ears. I visited her, not, I have to say, at her invitation, and soon found that she was with child. She refused to tell me who was responsible. She was unrepentant and intransigent. I left. Five months later I returned for her lying in, again uninvited.' The voice was caustic, no trace of regret there. 'It was a difficult birth and my daughter died. The child too.' An index finger smoothed her eyebrow. Canaletto noted the movement.

'What a tragedy,' burst out Fanny.

'Indeed,' said Mrs Truscott coldly. 'But if the child had lived, I could not have acknowledged him. Death and oblivion were a better end for a bastard.' It was almost as though she tried to convince herself of this.

'So, Penelope grows up,' prompted Canaletto as the story seemed to have stalled for a moment.

'Quite!' agreed Mrs Truscott, gathering her forces once more. 'Again it gives me great regret to have to say that early on I saw the same defects in her as I had seen in her mother. Headstrong, forward, too fond of pleasure. However, there was something else in her that gave me a certain hope, a softness, a warmth that her mother had lacked. No doubt she inherited it from her father.' Again that movement of the finger across one eyebrow. She was denying something here, Canaletto sensed it. Had Mrs Truscott herself some warmth she felt was a weakness? Had it been Mr Truscott who had given her those rigid standards of life? Or her own parents? Parentage had such an influence on a child.

'I had hopes', Mrs Truscott continued, 'that Penelope would contract a match with the son of a neighbour. Then her path crossed that of an aristocrat of doubtful character who had often been in the neighbourhood. He was staying, as usual, with our friends the Earl and Countess of Russell. The acquaintanceship between us is not close, but we dine with them. Lord Maltravers seemed very taken with Penelope and she with him.'

At the name, Canaletto let out a sigh. It was as if he knew exactly what she had been going to say.

'I saw immediately he was not a man to be trusted. The countess made us aware as soon as she saw the way things were going that he was married, though his wife was something of an invalid and travelled little. There was no future in any sort of relationship and so I told Penelope. But short of locking the girl in her room, I could do nothing. In the end, I even did that. But it was too late. Lord Maltravers left the district but by then Penelope was with child. Sir,' now her voice shook and held a note of appeal, 'she was unrepentant. Her only regret was that he had had to abandon her. But even that she excused by saying he owed it to his wife. To his wife! The man is a blackguard. I took her abroad and she gave birth to a son in France. I wanted him to be adopted by some bourgeois family there but Penelope beseeched me not to. Eventually I persuaded her it would be best for the child to become a foundling at the new hospital that had recently been set up in London. There he would have a good and Christian upbringing and be prepared for life. I had seen what excesses the anticipation of an inheritance could do to a young man and was convinced that a sober, righteous life without great expectations would be a kinder fate.'

'All this you tell granddaughter?' asked Canaletto.

'Ah, no. To her I merely pointed out that public acknowledgement of a bastard was impossible for one of her background. Eventually she saw the strength of my arguments. I arranged for the child to be taken to the hospital and it was one of the first to be accepted.'

'And then?'

Mrs Truscott had fallen silent, her gaze on the sketch of Penelope, her expression unreadable. She looked at Canaletto for a moment as though wondering who he was. 'And then Penelope and I resumed our life in Derbyshire. But she was changed. Joy was no longer her companion. She abandoned her art – she, like her mother, was exceedingly skilled – and refused to resume any sort of social life. She devoted herself to our local school, teaching young children their alphabets and numbers, taking soup to those who were indisposed or needed charity.'

'She pined to see her son?' suggested Fanny.

'Yes, Miss Rooker. Lamentable as the situation was, that was what she wanted. I did all I could to distract her attention, to suggest she saw eligible young men, to promise that once she had a family of her own she would forget him. It was of no avail. She began to talk of visiting the Foundling Hospital. I had made it my business to follow their work, to discover their methods, and I knew it would be impossible for her to identify her son. I told her this and eventually I understood her to have accepted it.

'Then Lord Maltravers paid the Russells another visit. Penelope once again came to life. Only to discover he was not to stay for long. He was merely pausing for a few nights. I begged Penelope to consider her reputation. Thanks to my prompt action in taking her abroad, it had remained intact after his previous attentions but she might not be so lucky a second time.

It made no difference to her. He left and the following day I found Penelope had gone also.'

'With him?' Canaletto asked.

'I feared so. I called on the countess. For once in my life I begged someone's help,' the proud voice hardly faltered. 'She knew nothing, or so she told me. She had the grace to admit it had been a mistake to agree to Maltravers's request for a few days' accommodation, but their friendship was of many years' standing and it was difficult for her to refuse, especially as she understood that Penelope no longer moved in society. She told me he had gone to the continent, I gathered his circumstances were not such as to sustain his style of life in England any longer. His wife, whose inheritance he had squandered, still lived but remained at his country estate in the north, a chronic invalid. There was no hope for my granddaughter and she had forfeited any further concern for her on my part.' Her tone was impatient. 'So I banished all reminders of her from my life. But it proved harder to forget her than I had imagined.' The faintest note of surprise in her voice. 'I decided I must remove myself to London, away from bitter memories and create a new life. So I acquired my house in Golden Square, applied myself to music, art and other diversions. Occasionally I travel to Paris or Vienna and study the passing crowds.'

She would never admit she had hoped to see her Penelope in those passing crowds. But beneath her adamantine front, Mrs Truscott was bleeding, her loss of both daughter and granddaughter a continual wound she refused to acknowledge. Until now.

'You did not consider she might have applied to the Foundling Hospital for a position?' asked Fanny.

Mrs Truscott shook her head. 'I had shown her the hopelessness of any such action.'

How convinced she was of the rightness of her actions, Canaletto marvelled.

'She perhaps felt a mother would always recognize her son,' Fanny said in a soft voice.

'What a sentimental notion,' Mrs Truscott said impatiently.

'She was certainly not living with Lord Maltravers when she was killed,' Canaletto said. 'If, indeed, she ever had been. Fanny, how long had she been working at the Foundling Hospital?'

'Three years.'

'And how long since she left your home?' he asked Mrs Truscott.

'Three years.'

He spread out his hands. 'So. She could not go to continent with lord.' He did not add that Mrs Truscott could have discovered her granddaughter had she thought to visit the hospital. He knew that this tough, intelligent but bigoted woman would be bitterly aware of the fact.

Mrs Truscott said nothing.

'You do not ask how I know granddaughter work at Foundling Hospital,' Canaletto pointed out.

Mrs Truscott raised an eyebrow.

'Poster put around area where I find body,' Canaletto said. 'Boy come who say he know lady.'

'Boy?' queried Mrs Truscott, raising her eyebrow a little higher.

'Some seven years old, one of first foundlings in hospital I think,' Canaletto continued in a quiet voice.

Mrs Truscott said, 'I think there were many

children taken in that first night. Many, many children.' Her voice denied the possibility Canaletto was suggesting. He looked towards Fanny and made the slightest of movements with his eyes towards Daniel's workshop. She slipped out quietly behind Mrs Truscott.

'Understand,' Canaletto said soothingly. 'He say granddaughter called Mrs Pleasant.'

'Indeed? My granddaughter once had a governess of that name.' Mrs Truscott unbent a very little. After a moment, she added, 'Did this boy mention aught of Mrs Pleasant?'

'He very fond of her. He say Mrs Pleasant kind to him, talk to him.' He paused then said, very deliberately, 'The boy wishes become painter, artist.'

Mrs Truscott stiffened again. 'Indeed? Ambitious!'

Canaletto nodded. 'For one unable write, he show promise.'

He could see Mrs Truscott fighting emotion. Then behind her he saw Fanny shepherd young Charlie into the studio. 'Ah, here Master Charles Lennox. Charles, Signora Truscott visit us.'

The boy's appearance had improved radically since his arrival at the studio. Fanny had washed him and cleaned, pressed and mended his clothes. His fair hair shining and brushed neatly round his well-shaped head, he came forward. 'Pleased to meet you, ma'am,' he said, his voice high but steady, his good manners instinctive as well as trained. He gave a small dip of his head.

'Humph,' said Mrs Truscott, her eyes scanning his every feature.

Fanny stood back but she was watching Charlie's effect on their guest as carefully as Canaletto.

'You are called Charles Lennox? It is a famous name.'

'Yes, ma'am, the Duke of Richmond is my god-father.'

'Indeed!'

'And the signor is to take me to meet him.'

Canaletto had promised nothing of the sort. Glancing at Fanny, he saw where to place the blame for this unexpected piece of news. She shrugged her shoulders and spread out her hands. 'It seems only sensible, signor,' she said.

He was amazed at her obtuseness. 'Madness, Fanny. First thing duke do – send Charlie back to hospital.'

'Perhaps that would be best, signor,' said Fanny. 'How else is he to survive in London?'

'The girl has sense,' Mrs Truscott said, her voice cold. She rose, 'I thank you, signor, for your information. I trust you will keep what I have told you this afternoon confidential?'

'I citizen of Venice,' Canaletto said simply. 'Am honourable.' He offered his arm, 'Will take Signora Truscott to home.'

He almost expected her to refuse. Instead, she laid a gloved hand on his arm and nodded to Fanny. 'Miss Rooker, I was impressed with your talent. I may contact you again now I know where to find you.' Then she picked up the sketch of her granddaughter. 'You are a skilful artist, signor.'

Fanny came forward with a couple of boards,

slipped the drawing between, tied all up with ribbon and handed it to her.

Yes, thought Canaletto. Once he'd had as much talent for depicting people as he had had for limning buildings. Once character had shone out of his paintings. No longer, he knew that. Many years ago he'd perfected the art of painting figures with such economy it took no more than a few quick strokes of his brush, forced to such measures by the pressure of commissions. How could he turn away the many orders Consul Smith obtained for him? He had growled and objected as much as he'd felt able but in the end the glitter of the money, and a sense of duty to the man who had brought his career to such a successful point, had forced him to utilize short cuts. Even with his father and his nephew to help him, he'd still struggled to keep up with the demand.

Despite the circumstances, it had been a pleasure for him to polish up his rusty skills and produce a work of such character as that sketch.

And it had proved its worth.

It looked as though Lord Maltravers had visited the hospital, perhaps as escort to some society lady who had an interest in the work. There he had met again Penelope Bardolph, known as Mrs Pleasant. Judging from Mrs Truscott's account, she would have been overjoyed to see him. Had she met him outside the hospital, lain with him? Allowed him to get her with child for a second time? Whatever, once again, if Leonora Casement's account could be trusted, he had deserted her by disappearing to the continent. Cast out by the hospital, Penelope had found work with Mrs

Casement, and seen a letter from her lover. She must have contacted him. Had he decided she threatened him in some way and needed removing from his life?

Why, though, mutilate her face?

Chapter Twenty-Nine

'That lady did not seem to like me very much,' Charlie said as the studio door closed behind Mrs Truscott and Canaletto.

'She was thinking of other things,' Fanny said gently. 'She had just had some very bad news.'

'About Mrs Pleasant?'

Fanny nodded.

'She's dead, isn't she?'

'I'm afraid she is.'

'I thought she must be.'

Fanny studied his downcast face. Were those high cheekbones and straight nose inherited from his mother or his father? The wide-set eyes and determined chin were, she thought, very like the drawing of Penelope Bardolph but how could one be certain from a sketch? She tried to remember what Lord Maltravers had looked like but it was difficult to equate that long, aristocratic visage with the childish face turned up to her.

'The duke won't really send me back to the hospital, will he?'

'What else can he do?'

'Take me into his household.'

'But then wouldn't all the boys in the hospital leave and seek their godfathers?'

Charlie thought about this. 'Bartholomew and Simon and James don't know who their godfathers are,' he said doubtfully. 'So they wouldn't want to leave.'

From which Fanny gathered that there were others who would go at the first opportunity and that Charlie understood what she'd told him. He had a very quick intelligence.

'Would you like to go and help Daniel again, Charlie?'

His face brightened immediately. 'May I? He allows me to brush away the shavings. And Adam says he will take me out tonight, that is why I came back, to see if you agreed.' He'd been well trained at the hospital.

'As long as you do not fuss Adam and you behave yourself,' Fanny said with a smile. He ran off excitedly.

Fanny started tidying up in the studio. The light was almost gone now, there would be no more work today. There was not much to do, neither Canaletto nor she had done any painting. As she straightened his drawing tools and dusted around the table, she thought about what they had learned from Mrs Truscott.

By the time Canaletto returned, she had decided that the case was solved.

'Oh, sir, it must be the lord, must it not?' she said the moment he entered the studio again. 'Now we know that he was connected with Mrs Pleasant, that is, Penelope Bardolph.'

Canaletto sat himself down at the end of the studio table and picked up a pen, studying the nib as though to check whether it needed trimming. 'This lord, this

Maltravers, a good name, no? Bad, what is word English use for something wrongly done?'

Fanny thought, 'A defect, signor? Or a flaw, a fault?'

'Yes, so – Lord Bad Fault!' Canaletto gave her one of the wide smiles that came so seldom. 'Good, no?' Then he grew serious. 'This man cause much trouble. Seduce Signora Truscott's granddaughter. Perhaps he reason why Penelope leave Signora Casement. Except, I do not think she leave. Not take things. Only the signora say she leave. Signora Casement tell of letter Penelope receive. Is true? Or is what she want me to believe. Complicated, no?'

'Signor! You do not think that Mrs Casement could have anything to do with the killings?'

'She tall woman, very strong, I think. Strong enough to stab girls with knife. In Venice we say poison is a woman's weapon but knife can be also.'

Fanny sat down on her bed with a thump. This was a completely new idea, one that she found difficult to take in. 'Do you think she could be an agent of Lord Maltravers?'

'Ah, Fanny, interesting thought. Perhaps first killing because she fear lord taken from her. But Mary? I think not. But maybe what Lord Maltravers say to her concern Mary. Maybe he worried she could tell the Lady Kitty truth about himself, prevent him making match with rich young aristocratic girl.'

'Signor, Penelope Bardolph was with child, do you think it was Lord Maltravers's child and that is why he killed her? Because she wanted him to marry her?'

'Maybe, Fanny, maybe. Before Signora Truscott tell her story, think I know who killer is, now not sure. Too many things not fit. Yet,' he paused for a moment then continued, 'maybe perhaps make them fit, like picture.'

'Are you sure both girls were killed by the same man? So many grievous crimes are committed. Perhaps Mary, being distraught, met someone, brought them back and they killed her.'

'Too many things same,' Canaletto said. 'Cuts to face, stabbing same place, maybe same knife. No, Fanny, same man do this.' He rose and reached for his hat. 'I need make visit. Then meet with McSwiney and friends.'

A moment later he was gone. Fanny didn't know anyone who could move so quickly and quietly as Canaletto.

She sat where she was, feeling deserted and lonely. All at once grief for Mary overwhelmed her. She hadn't known her long but her liveliness and good looks and the defiance with which she faced life had all been immensely attractive. Fanny had felt more than once that she would like to have the same attitude, to be able to reach out and take what she wanted without worrying about anyone else. But she knew she could never be like that.

There came a knock on the door. Maybe Canaletto had returned, maybe he wanted to share the evening with her. Fanny hurriedly dug the heels of her hands into her eyes and wiped away the tears. 'Come in,' she said.

But it wasn't Canaletto who entered, it was Richard Thompkins!

Chapter Thirty

'Why, Fanny, whatever is the matter?' Richard came over, knelt by the bed and took her cold hands in his own.

His golden eyes, sparkling with a warmth she hadn't seen before, looked up at her. He brought a bustle and excitement into the quiet room that for a brief moment overlaid the terrible pictures she had of Mary's death. He'd taken off his hat and his wig was not quite straight, the tight rolls of powdered hair higher on one side of his head than the other, gave the handsome face a skewed look that made it the more endearing.

Fanny found herself putting her hands on either side of that face and lowering her lips to his. His mouth was cool with the chill of the March bluster and she could taste a faint flavour of strong spirit.

For a moment he remained quite still and time seemed suspended. Then his arms came round her body and he held her tight.

Fanny felt her heart swell. It filled her ribcage so full it seemed either she would suffocate because she couldn't draw breath, or her body would burst. But at the same time she wanted the moment to last for ever. This was a totally new experience. Kisses from other young men had been clumsy things, aimed with more eagerness than skill, heralds of outbreaks of passion that always proved embarrassing since they failed to arouse similar feelings from herself and meant she had to fight to preserve her virginity. At this moment, she would willingly have yielded all.

Richard, though, drew back. Gently he removed his arms.

Fanny felt deserted. Her eyes flew open. He was still there, balancing on his haunches, looking at her with – with what? What had she done?

Fanny hurriedly fought for composure.

'Something has upset you,' he said, still breathing fast but more in command of himself than she was.

All the despair and sorrow flowed back, even more strongly. 'Mary's dead, she's been killed,' she jerked out, tears starting again.

'Mary?'

'My friend, the girl who was at Ranelagh when we went there, who had the fight with her young man.'

'Ah, that girl!' Impossible to say what he had thought of Mary's outburst but he obviously remembered the incident.

A sudden, vivid picture of Leonora Casement's arm closing around Mary's shoulders that evening came to Fanny. Had it been protective? Or a declaration that the woman was about to control the girl's life – and her death?

Fanny shivered.

Richard sat himself on the bed next to her. 'I remember you went to her help, she was a close friend?'

She nodded. 'We'd only recently met but I liked her and she didn't have many friends.' Nor, Fanny thought, did she. Since moving away from Fleet Street, she'd seen little of her old circle. Only now did she realize how much she missed the pleasant evenings she'd spent, gossiping, playing silly games, enjoying friendship; or making a visit to the playhouse or in the summer visiting one of London's many pleasure gardens to gossip and listen to music. Instead she'd become totally involved with her life as Canaletto's apprentice. And what had it brought her?

Mary had seemed to offer a friendship that would reintroduce some of the companionship she so badly missed. Fanny became aware that a part of her grief was for herself as much as for Mary.

'I am sorry,' Richard said softly. He lightly caressed the back of her hand where it lay in her lap. 'I've been visiting in your neighbourhood, an old family friend. And now I'm on my way to spend a convivial evening at an acquaintance's. Come with me.'

'Oh, I would love to,' said Fanny, suddenly lighting up. 'But I do not know your friends, will they not think it odd?'

He smiled at her. 'Why, the world and his wife is welcome there. You will soon forget your pain.'

Had he invited her to accompany him a few days earlier, Fanny would have been dazzled. Even now the invitation was tempting but, 'I am not minded for gaiety,' she told him.

'You are not thinking you should be here if your master should return?'

'I am Signor Canaletto's apprentice, not his housekeeper,' she said sharply.

'That's good! There is more to life than work.

344

Come,' he said coaxingly, 'a night amongst congenial company will lift your spirits.'

Fanny allowed herself to be persuaded.

'Splendid,' Richard rose. 'I will find you a chair.'

Before Fanny could say she was happy to walk, he'd left the studio.

She took off her smock and looked down at her dress, remembering how so many of the women had been dressed at Ranelagh and the fashionable silks and satins she had seen in Mary's wardrobe. Fanny had no hoops to hold out her skirts, no embroidered petticoats or high-heeled shoes. She went to her box and took out a fine lawn apron worked along its border with ivy leaves. On her simple, dark green dress, she hoped it looked well. She brushed her copper curls and added a little lawn headdress made with looped folds that Betty had once given her. 'It adds dignity,' she'd said. 'Sets off the colour of your hair.' Fanny studied her reflection, then removed the headdress. She hadn't noticed any such wear at Ranelagh.

Then Richard was back to say the chair waited.

Fanny hadn't often enjoyed the comfort and ease of riding in a sedan chair. Richard walked beside her as the chairmen carried her over the muddy streets and London's litter. She could see his tall figure through the side window, the classic profile, the head held high, hat back on, his dark brown velvet coat gleaming with gold buttons. Every now and then he would address a remark to her. She thought there was never another young man in the whole of London that was finer.

The chairmen walked with confident steps, seeming to make light of their load. They crossed Piccadilly and finally came to a stop in front of a house in St James's Square. Light poured out of the windows, there was the buzz of conversation and the sound of music.

Fanny grew nervous. Was this their destination? The chair was carried into the house and set down. Richard opened the door. 'We are here,' he said.

There was nothing for it. Fanny placed her hand on Richard's outstretched arm and alighted.

'Evening, William,' Richard said to the footman seeing out the men with the chair.

'Evening, sir,' said William. 'May I take your hat? And your mantle, madam?' Fanny allowed him to remove her outer covering.

The hall was graced with a number of marble statues. From it rose a curving staircase. A large glass lantern hung in its well, lit with several candles. At the top of the landing stood a small group of fashionably dressed individuals with glasses in their hands. More lanterns of similar style spilled light onto the powdered hair of the women and the small but elaborate wigs of the several men. One of them caught sight of the newcomers. 'Why, Richard, you have come! Splendid!'

Fanny went up the stairs with as much aplomb as she could manage, her hand clutching Richard's arm, feeling the strength of his muscles as they moved upwards together. At the top a footman offered a glass of some cordial.

'Why, here's a pretty thing,' said one of the men, raising an eyeglass to survey her from top to toe.

'Gentlemen, may I present the artist, Miss Fanny Rooker,' said Richard with a flourish. 'Fanny, this is Bartholomew Manning and Frederick Peters. I regret I have not the pleasure of the acquaintance of the rest of the company.'

Introductions were made. Fanny was very aware of the way the men looked at her and the contemptuous glances of the women at her dress. It was quite obvious she was considered something of a curiosity. She bitterly regretted accompanying Richard. This was not going to be the evening of pleasant chat amongst friends that she had envisaged.

But Richard seemed to notice nothing amiss. He led her into a large drawing room looking over the square. A vast chandelier lit the scene, the light of its candles reflected again and again by sparkling lustres hanging from the graceful curves of the metal branches. Mirrors on the walls reflected back yet more candles, flooding the room with a soft, wavering light. In it the skin of the women glowed, not only their faces but their flagrantly displayed bosoms also. Only on Leonora Casement had Fanny seen more flesh displayed. But these women were no courtesans, they were ladies of fashion, their eyes everywhere, curiously watching others whilst talking animatedly themselves.

'Fanny, let me introduce Mr Francis Hayman, whose apprentice up until now I have been.' Richard pulled her through to the far corner of the room where stood an engaging looking man of similar height to Canaletto. Indeed, Fanny found it strange Richard could have seen him across the throng from where he stood, then Mr Hayman let out a high-pitched laugh that she remembered hearing before. There could not be two people with the same bray!

'Sir, may I present the artist Fanny Rooker, apprentice to Canaletto?' Richard said yet again.

'Canaletto, eh?' Hayman bowed over Fanny's hand. Not very low but low enough to gratify her. 'Another of the foreign painters that blight the existence of those of us who strive to establish an English school.'

Fanny was taken aback. 'Sir, Canaletto is a master. I am fortunate to learn from such an able practitioner. Indeed Richard comes to him for lessons.'

Hayman turned a satirical eye up to the much taller young man. 'You do?'

'It's his way with light,' said Richard, seeming undaunted.

'We can all learn from such masters,' agreed someone else. 'But let not our English commissions go to them. Let them return to their native lands and not take our business.'

'And talking of business,' broke in Richard, 'I have to tell you this morning I made a prodigious start on a portrait that will take London by storm.'

'You will be fortunate to retain both your sitters,' said a voice from behind them.

Richard wheeled and flushed slightly. 'Lord Maltravers! I did not know I would see you here this evening.'

'Nor I you, young Thompkins. But there seems nowhere one does not meet with artists these days. Quite the professional men,' he added sardonically.

It was Fanny's first sight of Lord Maltravers close to and he could only be described as imposing, dressed in a moleskin grey coat heavy with silver lacing, a white satin waistcoat embroidered in silver and grey beneath, lace ruffles at his cuffs. He made the rest of the men in the room seem drab by comparison. His face with its world-weary lines and lion-gold eyes drew the gaze of every woman.

'Did your first session go well, Richard?' Fanny asked, suddenly aware that Mary's death had quite driven from her mind the fact that he was to have started his portrait that morning.

'Two sitters?' commented Hayman at the same time.

Lord Maltravers flipped open an enamelled snuffbox and took a pinch, his lazy eyes on Richard. 'One white, one black, both quite divine,' he drawled. The snuffbox was replaced in his coat pocket and a lace handkerchief brushed away any trace of the powder from his clothes.

'You should see the effect of an English pearl set next to the ebony jewel from Africa,' Richard said earnestly.

Francis Hayman's eyes flickered. 'Indeed?' he said softly. 'Richard, my boy, you could indeed set London in a storm with such a portrait.'

'A pity you treated them like such inanimate objects,' said Lord Maltravers in his drawl.

'What mean you, my lord?' Richard asked stiffly.

'Why, of course, that you kept them holding their pose for such a length of time that one of them fainted.'

Richard flushed angrily. 'It was not my fault. There were, well, there were other factors.'

Fanny wondered just what had happened.

Lord Maltravers raised one of his dark eyebrows. 'So it seemed,' he murmured. 'And that is why you will be fortunate to see again your ebony jewel – a clumsy image that,' he added languidly. 'Wood can never be a precious gem.'

Richard ignored this. 'You mean, sir?'

'Why, that Lady Kitty means to turn her off.'

'Turn her off?' repeated Richard.

'As she told me herself, someone in her position cannot have a slave in her entourage who is in an interesting condition.' The voice was silky smooth.

'Why, that's cruel,' Fanny burst out.

Lord Maltravers looked at her. 'You hold with bastardy?' he enquired, his voice pleasant and interested.

'No, sir!' Fanny said with feeling. 'And I pity anyone who has to grow up with that sin on their soul, it must be a sore distress in life.' She thought of Charlie, hardly able yet to understand what being a foundling meant, then was conscious of Richard standing rigid beside her. She'd forgotten he did not know his parents either. Had he been a bastard? Had his mother had to abandon him because she had been cast out from her home? 'But surely some suitable arrangement can be made? Perhaps Lady Kitty means to ensure her maid is looked after until her lying in.'

'I think not,' Lord Maltravers said, again in that pleasant, interested voice. 'Purity – such an ironic name, don't you think – is to go. Lady Kitty was quite definite.'

'I would thank my lord not to bandy a lady's name about in public,' Richard burst out.

The little group around them had swelled, others drawn in by the sense that something interesting was taking place. There was a rustle of anticipation. All eyes looked at Lord Maltravers.

His expression was impenetrable but his eyebrow rose again. 'If you were not such a boy, I might ask for satisfaction for such a remark,' he said pleasantly.

There were a number of indrawn breaths and anticipation flickered keenly across several faces.

Fanny placed her hand on Richard's arm, 'I regret I have recollected a previous engagement. Would you be good enough to escort me home?'

For a long moment he ignored her as he gazed furiously at Lord Maltravers. They were of a height, both with noses that gave an expression of superciliousness but Richard's face was contorted with anger whilst the older man maintained his composure.

Fanny shook his arm. 'Richard, please, I need to return home.'

'Take her someone, anyone,' a man at the back of the crowd called out. There was a murmur of laughter.

Richard's face darkened still more, Fanny could see him struggle with himself, then he turned to her, 'I am yours to command,' he said stolidly. He looked back at Lord Maltravers. 'This is not finished, my lord.'

'No? I rather think it is.' Lord Maltravers turned very deliberately and walked to another part of the room, hailing an acquaintance.

Richard flushed painfully and would have gone after him but Fanny hung onto his arm. 'Richard, please!'

So then he shrugged his shoulders, 'The privilege of birth,' he sneered.

'Be careful,' said Francis Hayman. 'As a portraitist you will rely on the goodwill of such as he.'

Going home, Richard stalked grim-faced beside Fanny's chair. Back at Silver Street, he helped her out, paid off the chairmen, then said, 'Fanny, forgive me, I am in too much of a temper at what that man said. I cannot stay with you further. I had meant to give you a pleasant evening; instead, you see me humiliated.'

'No!' Fanny cried. 'You were not humiliated. That

man's behaviour was uncalled for. You protected your honour, nothing more.' Then felt she had to add, 'But your Mr Hayman is right, it could be dangerous to cross swords with Lord Maltravers. I would not care to see you dead,' she added lightly.

'I was so out of temper I could not think.' He picked up her hand and kissed it in a courtly fashion. 'Now, I think you have saved my life.'

'It may not have come to that,' Fanny said. 'But I remember my brother getting in a fight once with a boy much bigger than himself. He had not intended it but others goaded and urged the two of them until there was no alternative.'

He kissed her hand again, his lips cool against the warmth of her skin. 'You are my guardian angel,' he said.

Chapter Thirty-One

When Canaletto left the studio, he went back to Golden Square. It was dark now and the square was quiet, though light spilled from many a window and at least one house had a carriage halted outside. He headed across the square, towards the south-west corner, noting as he went that Mrs Truscott's house had its curtains drawn. A faint chink of light from the first floor suggested that she and her companion were sitting there together, maybe sewing or reading quietly.

Canaletto turned over in his mind once again the tale she had told. That history had something to do with the killings, he was sure. It had been her grand-daughter, Penelope, whom he had found murdered in that foul alley, and the second victim had come from a house only three doors away from hers. No longer living there, it was true, but nevertheless the connection surely had to mean something.

Reaching his destination, Canaletto wielded the heavy brass knocker that gleamed brightly in the light of the lamp mounted above the door. The door was opened by the tall, powerful figure of the servant he had seen in the Privy Garden.

'Signor Canaletto of Italy to speak with Thomas Wright,' he said with a careful hauteur.

'Certainly sir, would you please wait in here whilst I see if young Mr Wright is at home?'

Canaletto was shown into a room just off the narrow hall. The servant lit two candles with a taper brought in from the hall then retreated.

Canaletto looked around. The room was too dark for his purposes. He took one of the candles and lit two pairs of wall sconces. Then found two more on the mantelpiece and lit those as well. He would have liked to ignite the fire that was prepared in the grate, the night was very chilly, but drew back from this as too bold a move.

Then he waited.

He thought he could hear raised voices from the floor above but it was difficult to be sure as a carriage was passing outside. Then he heard steps coming down the stairs but they were heavy, not the light tread one might expect from a young man.

When the door opened, however, there indeed was Thomas Wright, wig discarded for a velvet cap with a neatly turned up brim. That was the only detail about him that was neat. His stock was awry as though he'd tugged at it, a long brocaded nightcoat over his waist-coat and breeches was scattered with snuff and badly creased, his eyes were bleary and his chin shadowed with stubble.

He stood in the doorway, clutching the handle as though reluctant to enter. 'Mr Canaletto, is it?'

'Signor Antonio da Canal from Venice, Mr Wright,' Canaletto said reprovingly, ignoring the fact that he'd given his common name to the servant. He made a slight leg; this youngster qualified for neither a full bow nor an 'at your service'.

'And what brings you here, Mr, that is, Signor Canal?'

'I carry sad news for you, I think.'

Thomas looked wary. 'Sad news?'

'Your friend, Mary Butcher, she dead.' Canaletto watched carefully to see how this was received, even in the extra light he had created he had to concentrate hard to see the young man's expression.

Thomas flinched, Canaletto was sure he'd flinched, but it was not the reaction of someone hearing news for the first time, rather an automatic reflex, as the knee jerks when it is hit. Then he gave a theatrical gasp. 'No!'

'You did not know?'

'Indeed not! This is shocking news, sir.' His eyes bulged slightly in his effort to appear truly surprised. 'Tell me how and when she was killed?'

'Killed?' Canaletto pounced. 'Why killed? Why not she just die?'

Thomas raised an unsteady hand to his head and came further into the room. 'You must forgive me, sir, my mind is awhirl. The news is so sudden, I had heard of no illness, I naturally assumed she had been killed in some accident. Heaven knows, and heaven must regret, such tragedies are a common occurrence in our city.'

It was a notable recovery.

'I regret to say, Mary Butcher stabbed to death.'

Another histrionic gesture. 'Stabbed! Sir, this is most shocking! Who can the malefactor have been?'

'Who indeed?' Canaletto said in sepulchral tones. 'Does Thomas Wright know of aught reason friend Mary should be stabbed?'

'Why, no, sir. No reason at all,' Thomas said with

vehemence, shutting the door behind him. 'She was a gentle, lovely person,' he added piously.

It wasn't the way Canaletto himself would have described Mary but perhaps allowance had to be made for partiality. 'Most attractive,' said Canaletto.

Thomas suddenly seemed to take a grip on himself. 'May I ask, sir, how you know of this death?'

'I investigate killing,' Canaletto said simply.

Thomas's eyes bulged again. 'Investigate?' he said, the word coming out as a squeak. 'By what authority do you investigate?'

'Miss Butcher family friend,' Canaletto said firmly. 'Friend my apprentice, Miss Rooker.'

'And that gives you authority to investigate?' The emphasis on the last word showed Thomas's incredulity at this state of affairs.

'Why not? Mr Pitt place extreme confidence in Antonio da Canal,' Canaletto said, confident the name of the paymaster general would give him the necessary authority in this young man's eyes.

'Mr Pitt?' Thomas was indeed awed by the name. 'In that case, sir, I understand.'

Canaletto did not think it necessary to mention that it was a previous case Mr Pitt had enlisted his help to solve. An enquiry at Mr Pitt's office from the young Wright would be dismissed without ceremony but he was confident Thomas would never think of making any such overture. For the first time Canaletto began to feel sorry for poor Mary Butcher, could she have done no better for herself than this sorry apology for a young man?

'What would you with me?' Thomas suddenly

demanded. 'I had no part in Mary's death. I was nowhere near her place two evenings ago.'

'Again I ask, how you know when Mary killed?' Canaletto said softly. Anger was building up in him at this man's lies.

Thomas reddened. Several times he made to speak and each time thought better of the idea. Then he collapsed onto a chair. 'I do not know what to think!' he cried, sinking his head into his hands. 'You confuse me.'

'Person your description went to Mary's lodgings two nights ago around one of the clock,' Canaletto said slowly. The time-soiled trollop above Mary's room had been most definite. It had been the gentleman responsible for Mary's support, she said. 'Her gallant' had been the phrase she used. 'Seen him often,' she'd added. She'd been returning from a night on the town, had someone with her. As they approached the lodging house, she'd seen Thomas leaving. 'In a hurry,' she'd added.

Thomas dropped his hands and looked up, his face racked with agony. No trace now of the debonair young man-about-town Canaletto had seen at Ranelagh. 'I was seen?' he asked in a hollow voice.

Canaletto nodded sternly.

Back went the head into the hands as Thomas struggled with himself. Finally he raised an ashen face. 'I did go,' he said slowly and almost inaudibly. 'We'd had some small disagreement at Ranelagh Gardens.'

Small disagreement! Canaletto remembered the fight, the outrage shown by the aristocratic young girl on discovering him with another woman, the despair Mary Butcher had displayed. He grew even angrier with the young man. He had no principles, no loyalties nor any idea how a man should conduct himself.

'You kill her!' he accused Thomas.

'No!' Thomas shouted. 'I did not! I went to give her money I had collected from here.'

'Pay her off?' enquired Canaletto silkily. 'Then decide kill is cheaper?'

'No!' shouted Thomas again.

The door opened and in came a much older man. 'Tom, what is this? Who is this person?' he demanded. He was also dressed in a long nightcoat with a velvet cap upon his head, though this was some draped affair not dissimilar from Canaletto's own. His heavy and florid face was so similar to Thomas's, he could only be his father. His voice was slightly slurred. 'I cannot abide shouting.' He stood unsteadily in the doorway, holding a glass of what looked like brandy.

Canaletto said nothing.

'Well, sir?' demanded Mr Wright of his son.

'Mary is dead,' Thomas said with a gulp. 'Stabbed to death.'

His father gazed at him, he seemed stunned by the news.

'Signor Canaletto thinks I did it!'

'Good riddance!' Mr Wright swallowed half the glass of cognac. 'Expensive nonsense! I told you to get rid of her. Glad you saw sense.'

'I did not kill her!' shouted Thomas again. 'She was already dead when I arrived. It, it,' he gulped, took the glass from his father's hand and drained it, 'it was terrible. So much blood. I have never seen so much blood.'

'Be a man, sir! Now perhaps you can concentrate

on the business. If we're not to end up in a debtors' prison, I need you. Fool you may be but you have some talent for persuading the gentry to purchase our hosiery, though sometimes I think your slave has more knowledge of the business than you. And give up your prattle of this rich young aristocrat, none such will have a dolt like you for husband!'

Mr Wright turned to Canaletto, 'And you, sir, can leave. I want no more of you in this house.' He went to the fireplace and pulled on a rope that hung there.

'Father, he has Mr Pitt's authority,' said Thomas.

'Then he can come by day with an official notification and I'll be happy to speak with him. As for you, you'll say nothing more, understand me, boy?'

It seemed Thomas did for he slumped further down in his chair and gazed mutely at his feet.

The servant appeared at the door. 'You rang, sir?' His voice was colourless.

'John, show this, this intruder out! And do not let him back inside without some official business. You should never have let him enter and I'll make that plain to you later, understand?' There was a heavy threat behind the words.

Thomas looked up. 'Father, Brute is my servant, you should not speak to him so.'

Mr Wright cuffed his son heavily about the head, knocking off his cap. 'Damn you to hell, boy, you don't question me! Everything in this house is mine. Now that your mother is no more, you'll do as I say or leave without a penny to your name.'

Thomas scrabbled wordlessly on the floor for his cap.

Canaletto walked steadily from the room. As he

reached the hall he turned, 'I prove who kill Mary Butcher and law take course,' he said with great solemnity. Then he took his hat and swordstick from the servant who appeared to have two names and left.

Outside Canaletto drew his cloak warmly about himself as the damp air struck chill around his neck. The square was deserted now, no waiting carriages. He looked about him nervously, took a firm grip on his stick and walked swiftly back to Silver Street, emotions crowding upon him.

The facts that he had elicited that evening had pointed directly at Thomas Wright being the murderer. But what reason could there be for the young man wanting to kill Penelope Bardolph? Unless – Canaletto turned and looked again at Mrs Truscott's house. She came from Derbyshire and so did the Wrights. Could they have known each other? Could there have been an attachment between Penelope and Tom Wright?

Thinking hard about this possibility, Canaletto returned to the studio. It was empty. No light burning, only a damped-down fire, and no Fanny. Well, he had said he would be meeting McSwiney, it was only a desire to discuss his meeting with young Thomas Wright that had taken him back to the studio.

No sign of young Charlie either. However, from the workshop Canaletto could hear laughter and the boy's excited voice. No doubt playing with the apprentice. They sounded happy enough.

A movement attracted his attention.

A bald-headed man in a long coat was slipping quietly round the corner of the house, back into Silver Street. Canaletto strode quickly under the arch and, by the light of one of the sparse number of house lamps, saw the man moving swiftly away towards the notorious district of Seven Dials.

Was he a thief? Canaletto hurried back to the studio, lit a candle and checked the contents. Everything seemed to be untouched and in place and the door had been locked. The man might have just been relieving himself in the strip of garden.

Canaletto dismissed him from his mind and turned instead to the question of whether he should go out again to meet McSwiney as had been arranged. But it had been a casual invitation, the Irishman trying to get Canaletto out to socialize. Canaletto didn't like socializing. He decided he would rather stay here, drink a cognac and wait for Fanny. She would probably not be long. He made up the fire, stood watching the flames for a little then went to the corner cabinet.

Armed with the bottle of brandy and a glass, Canaletto settled himself on one of the stools and automatically reached for pen and ink, pulling a piece of paper in front of him. But his thoughts were for the problem of who had killed Mary Butcher, not for what he was drawing.

Lost in thought, he had no idea how much time had passed before the door opened.

'Signor!' Fanny said in tones of great surprise. 'I thought you were to spend the evening with Mr McSwiney.'

'I changed my mind,' he said simply. 'You have had a pleasant time?' he asked courteously, noting flushed cheeks and an unusual air of excitement about her.

'Richard Thompkins took me to see some friends of his,' Fanny said in a level voice.

'Richard?' Irrationally, instead of feeling pleased for

her, Canaletto was irritated. Then he looked at her more closely and noticed she was wearing an embroidered apron and had dressed her hair with particular care. 'I trust it was an enjoyable visit,' he said in a strained voice. Then found himself spluttering with anger as she related details. 'They insult Italian painters?'

'Not insult quite,' she said hastily, sitting on a stool. 'They feel it is time to be recognized in their own right.'

'They idiots not to learn from masters of paint,' he said contemptuously.

'And so I told them, signor.'

'Fanny did, eh?'

'Oh, yes,' she assured him.

'You would like a little brandy?' he suggested.

Fanny shook her head, 'I will heat myself some milk, thank you, signor. You have done a fine job with the fire.' She arranged a small pot on a trivet beside the merrily burning mixture of coals and logs.

Canaletto watched her with a great deal of pleasure. 'Very fine company?' he enquired carefully.

Fanny blushed. 'I thought so until I saw Lord Maltravers, then I realized they were not so fashionable. He was so fine and has a considerable air. I, though, was a dowd.' She handed him one of the tankards.

'Lord Maltravers? He there?' Canaletto ignored any necessity to reassure Fanny on her appearance as he pounced on this unexpected development.

'Yes, and I think he is a man who will have his own way over any matter. He spoke most cruelly to Richard. And, oh sir, a most interesting and shocking thing.'

Canaletto added more brandy to his glass and listened carefully as Fanny told him the tale of Richard's first sitting for his portrait commission. 'Girls who get themselves with child without securing the father in marriage are indeed foolish but to be turned off like that, is that not dreadful?' Fanny spoke with deep feeling.

'You English so, so censorious,' Canaletto said. 'Surely Duke of Richmond son of bastard?'

'Ay, sir, but he was a king's bastard,' said Fanny earnestly. 'That is different.'

'Is it?' Canaletto looked at her. So bright in so many ways, so conventional in others. 'So, there is another girl with child,' he said.

'I hope this one will not be murdered,' Fanny said with a fleeting smile at such a ridiculous notion.

It was a wish Canaletto heartily concurred with. He wasn't sure whether Mary's condition, or lack of condition, played any part in her murder or not but there was a strong probability it had. He realized he had not told Fanny of his visit to the Wright household and proceeded to do so.

'Thomas Wright was there the night she was killed?' cried Fanny. 'Why, then, surely he must have killed her?'

'So I thought,' admitted Canaletto. 'And with Derbyshire connection, perhaps he acquainted with Penelope Bardolph. Perhaps Signora Truscott mistake granddaughter's lover. Perhaps was Thomas Wright.'

'She seemed very definite,' said Fanny doubtfully. 'Could Penelope Bardolph have told Thomas she was coming to London, to the hospital?' Then she gave a small cry, 'Of course, Jonathan Wright told Betty and me that he is one of the hospital governors. He must visit there and he would have known she was working there, perhaps he even ensured she had the job.'

'If he see girl there, why not tell Signora Truscott?' asked Canaletto.

'Because Penelope asked him not to?' suggested Fanny. 'Or some other reason?'

Yes, thought Canaletto, there could be a very good reason for not informing Mrs Truscott where she could find her granddaughter.

'And, signor, Mary said she lay with Jonathan Wright. Only once, she said, but you never knew when Mary was telling the truth.'

'Maybe Thomas Wright or his father the lover of both Penelope and Mary,' Canaletto said slowly. 'Maybe kill both. But why cut face?'

Fanny stared at him, excitement draining out of her. 'Oh yes, the cuts!'

Canaletto looked down at his piece of paper and saw that he had drawn the faces of the two girls as he had seen them laid out waiting for the surgeon's knife. Two sweet young faces, each brutally slashed in an identical way. Fanny came and studied them over his shoulder.

'I cannot forget what I said when you first showed me sketch of cut face,' she said slowly. 'They look like a letter.'

He agreed. 'Maybe girls killed because they loose women. Go with more than one man. If only cuts draw "h", for there is English word for loose woman, yes?'

'Whore,' said Fanny in a whisper.

'But cuts definitely not show "h".'

'Signor, whore is spelt with a "w" before the "h" most often. I know because there is a play called

The Honest Whore. I have not seen it but I have seen a playbill with it written,' Fanny said with great authority.

Canaletto drained his brandy. 'Is there such thing as honest whore?' he asked himself ruminatively. Was Leonora Casement, for example, honest?

Chapter Thirty-Two

It was Betty who brought up Canaletto's hot water in the morning. Canaletto found Daniel hacking his lungs out whilst trying to plane a piece of wood, Adam the apprentice holding the end of the plank steady over the trestles. Sitting on another trestle was Charlie, chipping away at a little block with a small knife.

'Sorry see you looking so poorly,' Canaletto said to Daniel.

The cabinet maker took a deep, shuddering breath and said, 'I'm done for, signor. Last night the bloody flux, spent the night on the pot, today me lungs. It's London's plaguey smoke.' Indeed, once again, the city was shrouded in the pall that constantly hung over the chimneys. 'And my work's not what it was,' Daniel added, sinking onto a stool and wiping his sweating face with a large handkerchief.

'Never!' said Canaletto with conviction. 'Daniel craftsman superb!' He brought finger and thumb together in a gesture of excellence.

'That whoreson bugger Wright has cancelled his order on account of it,' Daniel said gloomily.

'Not so,' said Canaletto. 'I find last night he no money. Cannot pay.'

It was as if Daniel hadn't heard. He looked as

though he had had no sleep at all and his hand was trembling. 'Charlie, get me gin, there's a good lad,' he said, producing a penny out of his pocket. Charlie took it carefully. 'There's a place you can get it just round the corner from here,' Daniel added and gave directions.

Charlie disappeared out of the workshop.

Canaletto viewed his landlord's frailty with despondency but failed to find anything to say that would raise his spirits.

After a moment or two Daniel picked up his plane again. 'Hold the wood firm,' he told Adam, 'and keep those big hands out of the way.' Long curls of shaving started to fall to the floor.

Then Charlie was back, his face as pale as Daniel's. 'S-s-s-sorry, sir, I can't get your g-g-g-gin,' he said, stuttering in a way Canaletto hadn't heard before.

'Why not, boy?' he asked him. 'Daniel very kind, small thing to do for him.'

Charlie flushed, the fair skin colouring to the roots of his hair. 'C-c-c-can't say, s-s-sir.' He looked miserable.

Canaletto went to the door and walked quietly to the edge of the street and looked each way. Leaning against a building towards the left was a figure that looked very much as though it could have been the man he'd seen the previous evening. Certainly the long coat seemed the same and the fellow's bare head. As he looked, the man seemed to sense he was being watched and very casually loped off round the nearest corner.

Canaletto went back and beckoned Charlie out of the workshop. 'You frightened by man with long coat, perhaps he seek you, yes?'

Charlie started to shake, he looked terrified.

Canaletto put a hand on his shoulder. 'Important tell me everything. Do not be afraid but must tell,' Canaletto insisted. He took him through to the studio, where Fanny was cleaning up after last night, humming a little to herself. She smiled at Charlie, then the smile faded as Canaletto sat the boy on a stool and repeated that he must tell him everything.

Finally Charlie brought himself to speak but it took a little time for Canaletto to make sense of his story.

'So, man with snakes? And girl who pick pockets? And old woman?' It didn't sound too desperate to Canaletto but, then, he wasn't a boy of seven. 'This not good, but you not with them now.'

'They'll take me back, sir,' Charlie cried, his eyes terrified. 'You don't know them! They said no one ever gets away. They know everyone. There was a man they said they'd find and they did and they killed him.' His fear was plain to see. 'I asked the way to Silver Street in the market, p'raps they traced me through that.'

'What you think, Fanny?' Canaletto asked.

Fanny wiped her hands and put the crockery back in the cupboard. She looked pale and frightened herself. 'I think everything Charlie says could be true, sir. There's all sorts of gangs around London and there's people have spies everywhere.'

Canaletto nodded. She spoke no more than the truth. And such people only kept control through fear. Let one escape and others might think they could do so as well.

'We go to Watch,' he said decisively. 'Tell them.'

'Little they can do,' Fanny said soberly. 'Not against villains like these. They have to be caught first and who's to do that? A few elderly men? No, sir. Charlie has to be sent away, that's the only thing.'

Canaletto looked at the boy. He was a bright lad, pleasant to have around, full of life and with a definite artistic talent.

Was he really at risk? In Venice there had been villains aplenty, even with the strict official control that was exercised there. Here, where officialdom seemed lax to say the least, who knew what villainy could thrive?

'Charlie come with me to Duke of Richmond this afternoon,' he said.

Charlie looked both gratified and apprehensive. 'But you said he'd send me back to the hospital.'

'There is better place?' Canaletto asked gently. 'Gang not reach you there, I think.'

Fanny looked as though she was about to say something; Canaletto caught her eye and shook his head in warning. She pursed her lips and turned to Charlie. 'You can help me grind some pigment,' she said gently. 'It will be good practice for you.'

He looked up at her with hope. 'You mean I might be able to become an artist after all?'

'I don't know but if you tell the duke that is what you want to do, maybe he can help.'

Canaletto felt despair. It was no kindness to raise hopes in the boy. He could imagine what the great Duke of Richmond would think of the presumption of a foundling boy to become an apprentice to such a craft as painting. Maybe if he'd wanted to be a printer or even a carpenter. He looked at Charlie, 'Would you like work as Daniel does? Be apprenticed as Adam is?'

Charlie thought for a moment then nodded

vigorously. 'Look, sir, at what I do now.' He handed over the piece of wood he'd been chipping away at in the workshop.

Canaletto turned it over in his hands. It was, or would be, a carving of a man. Very simple, rough even, but the body was emerging out of the wood. It would be a thousand pities if the boy wasn't given an opportunity to fulfil his artistic talent.

'Bring with you to Richmond House,' he said, giving back the little figure. 'Now, I write letters. Fanny, find boy to take messages, please.'

Later that afternoon Canaletto set out with Charlie and Fanny for the Privy Garden and the duke's house.

Charlie looked around them nervously as they made their way but there was no sign of the fellow who had been lurking in Silver Street. 'Anaconda can follow anyone and not be seen,' Charlie whispered to Canaletto, clutching at his hand. Fanny had pressed his clothes and he looked more than respectable in his brown drugget coat and breeches, both decorated with red flashes. Fanny had trimmed his hair as well and the dark blue eyes looked out from beneath a neat yellow fringe.

Fanny herself was equally neat in her green gown with embroidered apron and a pale shawl around her shoulders. She carried Canaletto's sketchbook and the two finished drawings of scenes to show the duke.

They entered the Privy Garden. 'So much of interest,' Fanny said happily to Canaletto. 'And the Holbein Gate, I don't think I've ever looked at it properly before. It is indeed magnificent and something different from your river views.'

That made him apprehensive. Yes, the picture he had sketched was very different from his usual vistas. Would the duke agree that it would make a suitable picture or would he insist that a Canaletto must have water in it? In which case the view from the terrace must surely find favour.

On arrival at the house, they were shown into an ante-room. 'The duke will soon be returned from Westminster Hall. It is anticipated the trial will be over today,' said Mr Preston. 'Would you care for some refreshment while you wait? A glass of ratafia, perhaps, and some milk for the lad?' Only one short glance at Charlie had betrayed his interest at his presence.

Canaletto accepted the refreshments gracefully.

The drinks arrived and were consumed. Fanny and Charlie began to lose their awe at their surroundings. 'Look at that chair,' Fanny said breathlessly. 'Such damask! Such gilding! And so wide! Well, the skirts fashionable ladies wear require it so. And some of the gentlemen's coats are almost as wide. Charlie, isn't that a lovely landscape on the wall?'

The picture in question was a rural view that Canaletto allowed was attractive enough but not to be compared with continental masterpieces. He wondered if this was an example of the English school Fanny had talked of. But Canaletto was more concerned that the duke had not yet arrived. If his plans were to be carried through, there was not much time left.

Then from outside they heard a commotion. Charlie ran to the window. 'I can't see!' he moaned. 'But there must be several carriages.' They could hear the rattle of coach wheels, the metal harsh against the stones of the road, the jingle of harness and the clopping of hooves of many horses, but the wall of the Privy Garden prevented them having a view. Jeers and catcalls from what sounded like many people drifted to them also.

'My Lord Lovat is returned to the Tower,' said a voice behind them.

Canaletto turned.

A middle-aged man had entered the room without ceremony.

He was pleasant faced with a longish nose and high forehead, his bagwig neat with side curls. His eyes were weary. 'We have pronounced sentence on him.'

The duke went over to the window and looked out where there was nothing to see. 'I was called back from hunting the fox to hunt a man. Much as I dislike the fellow's politics, he is a noble gentleman and it has given us no pleasure to condemn him to the executioner. Such, though, has to be the fate of traitors. Now, Signor Canaletto, I understand you are to paint me a view of my terrace? My old tutor, Thomas Hill, is convinced it will be a fine addition to my collection.' He looked curiously at Fanny and Charlie. 'You have come with an entourage, signor?'

'Your grace,' Canaletto made a fine leg and gave a low bow. May I present apprentice, Fanny Rooker. Fanny carries Canaletto's sketches for your grace.'

'You are welcome, Miss Rooker.' Fanny, looking a little awed, bobbed a curtsy and handed over the small portfolio, just in time to divert the duke's interest from Charlie.

The duke took the folder eagerly and placed it on a table, untied the strings, extracted the two sketches and placed them side by side. He looked from one to the other, nodded at the one of the terrace, then held up the other. 'This is something different,' he said to Canaletto.

Canaletto said nothing.

'The Privy Garden indeed. Alas, it is now a nothing. Fifty years ago, before the great fire in the palace, I understand it was indeed a glory. I cannot think that this will make a picture worthy of your talents, signor.'

The trouble was, thought Canaletto, the man was too used to the view from his window, no longer saw its unique charm. 'I think, your grace, if we take a look at actual scene?'

The duke thought for a moment then gave a little nod. 'Excellent idea. Come.'

The duke led them up the stairs and into the drawing room. 'You have noted my small gallery, signor?' He waved a hand at the paintings on the walls around them.

'You are connoisseur, I think,' murmured Canaletto.

'Indeed, yes,' the duke said with a note of enthusiasm. 'And I am keen to support our national talent. You maybe saw a landscape downstairs?'

Canaletto nodded.

'That is by a fellow I discovered down in Sussex, near my estate at Goodwood. Pleasant is it not? Remarkable technique!'

Canaletto murmured something polite.

'Now,' said the duke, 'let us look at this viewpoint of yours.'

They gathered round the window and Canaletto

started to point out how the intricacies of the Holbein Gate balanced the massive simplicity of the Banqueting House, how both contrasted with the informality of the garden and the interest of the townscape in the distance, each roof separately delineated.

'Sir!' squeaked Charlie suddenly. 'Sir, you told me to say if I saw that man, the one I'd seen with Mrs Pleasant?'

Canaletto turned his attention to the scene. Were all his preparations about to bear fruit?

'What is this?' enquired his grace.

'A matter of murder,' said Canaletto, scanning the garden, the afternoon light beginning to fade. For a moment he could not see anyone he recognized, then, approaching the house, came the figure of Lord Maltravers. 'This he?' he asked Charlie, pointing.

Charlie nodded. 'I saw him with her twice.'

'Murder?' commented the duke, raising an eyebrow. 'I think you must explain yourself, Canaletto.'

But Canaletto was eyeing the foreshortened figure of Lord Maltravers. Could Charlie be quite certain of his identification? And then he saw another figure of much the same height hurrying away from Richmond House, Richard Thompkins. 'Charlie, are you sure it wasn't that man?'

The boy shook his head vigorously. 'It was him,' he said, pointing at Lord Maltravers again. Then, coming through the gate to the gardens from Whitehall, Canaletto saw Thomas Wright, walking with hurried steps, his face alight with anticipation.

'Have you seen that man before?' Canaletto asked Charlie.

'No, sir, never,' the boy answered unhesitatingly.

Now Canaletto was sure. Seeing all three of his suspects together, having Charlie identify Lord Maltravers, had made so much plain.

The duke intervened. 'I asked for an explanation,' he said haughtily. 'And I would also like to know why there is here a foundling from the hospital.' He looked sternly at Charlie, the great lord had replaced the affable gentleman.

Charlie gazed beseechingly at Canaletto.

'What is your name, boy?'

Charlie seemed to realize he was on his own. He looked straight at the duke, 'Charles Lennox, sir.'

The eyebrow rose even higher. 'Is it, by God!' He looked keenly at the boy. 'And what, Charles Lennox, are you about here?'

Charlie looked at Canaletto, who gave him the tiniest of nods. 'I'm your godson, sir, and I don't want to go for a sailor,' he blurted out.

'You don't, eh?'

'No, sir. Water and me don't suit,' he added with a quaint solemnity.

'No? And how have you found that out?'

'When I was little, I lived in the country, near the sea, and I was taken on a boat.' Charlie's face contorted till he looked as though he was sucking on a lemon. 'It was terrible, sir. I thought I was dying. I wanted to die,' he added simply.

'And who told you you would go for a sailor?' enquired his grace gravely.

'Mr Birchem and Captain White, sir.'

'Mr Birchem I know, but Captain White?'

'He came to talk to us, to tell us what a splendid life we should have on board a ship like his,' Charlie said with a touch of desperation. 'He told us it would be all my hearties, splice the mainbrace and jolly Jack Tar. But it wouldn't be jolly, sir, it wouldn't!' Charlie looked despairingly up at the duke. 'That's why I wanted to come to you, sir, you being my godfather and all.'

'Indeed?' said the duke sounding a little nonplussed. He turned to Canaletto. 'And how is it you have the lad with you?'

''Tis all a part of the murders, your grace.' Canaletto drew a deep breath and summoned his best English as he embarked on as succinct an explanation as he could of the discovery of Penelope Bardolph's body and subsequent events.

Early on in the story, the duke sat himself down in another of the damask chairs Fanny had admired, his eyes never leaving Canaletto's face, his fingers lying still on the gilded arms of the chair. Fanny remained standing behind Canaletto. Charlie quickly got bored and transferred his attention to the window again.

When Canaletto arrived at Charlie's part in the history he was relating, the boy grabbed at his arm. 'Look, sir, look! It's Anaconda!' They all looked, the duke twisting in his chair to see out of the window.

Fanny gasped. 'Oh, signor!'

Twilight was now beginning to fall in the Privy Garden but there were still many people wandering through and seated on the ground not far from Richmond House was an outlandish figure with a striped bandanna round his head, a long brown open coat billowing out around him. He played on a pipe. In front of him was an open sack. Out of its mouth rose a collection of heads, waving curiously in the air, their sinuous bodies executing a sinister dance. By his side was another, much smaller sack, tied tightly at its neck.

'Snakes!' breathed Fanny.

Around the snake charmer had gathered a small throng of people. Clearly up to the window came a concerted gasp as the man discarded his pipe and thrust his hand into the writhing mass. Two women brought hands to their faces in horror but he seemed untouched by the darting tongues. He lifted a snake high above his head, its body hanging and twisting as it tried to bite his arm. The crowd gasped, oohed and aahed. Even the sentry who commonly stood guard in the garden had wandered over to see what was happening.

'Oh sir, he's come to get me, he has!' wailed Charlie.

'How is this?' asked the duke. 'Why should anyone come to get you?'

Canaletto placed an arm round Charlie's shoulders and held the shaking body close to his as he repeated the story Charlie had told him that morning.

The duke's face grew dark. 'This is appalling,' he said. 'Appalling.' He turned to Charlie. 'Come here, Master Charles Lennox.'

Canaletto gave him a little push towards the duke. Reluctantly, the boy advanced a pace.

The duke waited. Charlie took another step closer.

'Now you see the folly of leaving the hospital,' the duke said sternly. 'There you are fed, educated and protected. You are lucky to be among those so cared for.'

Charlie gazed back at him, obstinacy written all over his face. These were words he had obviously heard before and valued not.

'Had you not left the hospital, you would not have fallen amongst these villains. You see why you must go back? You understand?'

Charlie glanced towards the window, then slowly nodded his head.

'I am glad to see you do.' The duke's expression relaxed a little. 'Now let us turn our attention to the matter of your future. I have to tell you as a governor of the hospital that whilst we think the sea offers a great career to boys like you, it is not the only prospect that can be placed before you.'

Charlie started to look a little hopeful.

'We are looking at apprenticeships of various kinds. When the time comes it may be possible – may, I say – for you to follow a career more to your liking.' He paused, considered for a moment while Charlie gazed at him with dawning expectation, then said, 'What wish you to do in life?'

'A painter, sir, like Mr Hogarth and Mr Hayman.'

The duke first looked startled and then roared with laughter. 'Do you indeed, young Charles Lennox? I think you presume too far.'

Canaletto decided it was time to take a hand. 'Charles shows skill working with wood, your grace. Maybe apprentice to carpenter?'

'Ah, now that sounds a more suitable ambition.' He looked kindly at Charlie. 'I cannot approve your truancy from the hospital and no doubt Mr Birchem will have words to say to you but you have enterprise, young Lennox, you do indeed! George, my elder son, has your spirit. Indeed, I regret to say he has too much at times. Would you believe he set fire to his tutor's hair and then put it out by boxing his ears? Now, I shall call for my steward and arrange for the arrest of the snake charmer. We cannot allow that sort of behaviour to run rampant in London or particularly the Privy Garden.' He rose and went towards a bell pull.

But before he got there the door opened and in came a woman of the first rank, dressed in a rich gown of green silk, a cloud of muslin scarf around her bosom, ruffles at her elbows, her hair dressed with exquisite simplicity. Her soft, charming face wore a harassed look. 'My lord, at last,' she said, going straight to the duke. 'I am so pleased to see you are returned, my love. We are in such a commotion. Everyone calls claiming Kitty wishes to see them but I can get no sense from her and they have all had to be sent away for Kitty is beside herself. Neither Emily nor I can make her see reason and we need you to bring her to her senses. It is this wretched business of her maid, Purity.'

The duke took her hand. 'We have visitors, my dear. May I present Signor Canaletto, who is to produce more *vedute* for us, his apprentice, Miss Rooker, and,' he turned and beckoned Charlie forward, 'my godson from the Foundling Hospital. You remember we attended his christening all those years ago?'

'Indeed,' the duchess murmured. 'I am happy to see you, signor,' she said to Canaletto. 'We greatly admire your work and I am sure it will be a profound pleasure to have more of your views on our walls,' her politeness was rather spoiled by the distracted way in which she spoke, her attention quite obviously with the matter that had brought her into the room. 'I regret, however, that I must remove the duke.'

It was too late. Into the drawing room marched the girl who had made the scene at Ranelagh, dragging by the arm the servant Canaletto had seen in the Privy Garden. An immensely fashionable girl followed them crying that Kitty musn't do this.

Lady Kitty paid no heed to her or to the others. Perhaps in the darkening gloom of the room she didn't notice Fanny and Charlie standing inconspicuously by the window, or Canaletto dropping quietly back to join them. She marched imperiously up to the duke, pulling the unfortunate maid behind her.

'Your grace,' said Lady Kitty, flinging the other girl to the carpet with astonishing force, gasping with the effort, 'Purity must be beaten!' Her appearance was singular. She was dressed in the sort of loose gown intended for informal morning wear, and her hair needed a great deal of attention. Perhaps she had been preparing to change for some evening festivity.

The maid lay collapsed on the floor, her dark head bowed. A cloak was fastened at her neck and opened out over a simple black dress and white apron. In one flung out hand she clutched a piece of paper.

As Canaletto took in the scene, he realized she had lost the sheen of health and happiness that had been hers when he'd seen her in the Privy Garden with her African lover. Her skin was now ashy and her eyes dull and swollen.

'What is this?' demanded the duke. 'Beat Purity?'

Kitty stamped her foot. 'She is with child. I have dismissed her and now I find her sneaking out for some assignation with her lover!' She spoke with supreme contempt.

'Katherine, explain yourself,' the duke said coldly. 'You speak of dismissing your maid but also of objecting to her leaving. This is not rational.'

'I did not give her permission to leave on the instant,' Kitty complained. 'I have a dance to attend this evening, she is to dress my hair! She refuses, she must be beaten.' She sounded as though there could be no other alternative.

'Kitty, my dear,' started the duchess.

'Madam, you asked me to handle this,' said the duke. 'Lady Katherine, while you are under our house you will obey our rules. We do not beat our servants. If necessary they are reprimanded and shown the error of their ways.' He spoke very sternly.

Kitty gave a small cry, like a puppy whose tail has been trodden on, and took a step back, her hand at her mouth.

'As for your maid, if she is with child indeed, that is a sore offence. I understand your need to dismiss her but not, I think, quite yet. And I am sure you will wish some arrangement made for her welfare. Purity,' he said in a not unkindly way, 'give me that piece of paper.'

She looked up with bleary eyes which hardly seemed to take in what he had said. Then she relinquished her hold on the paper.

The duke took and read it. 'Who is this fellow who asks you to meet him in St James's Park after sunset? Surely you cannot think this a respectable assignation or one that is safe?'

'It is John, he knows I am in desperate trouble,' Purity said in a voice so low they all had to strain to hear it.

'It is not signed.'

'But it is him, I know it! Who else would it be?' Purity demanded, looking up with her first display of life. 'What else can I do, your grace? He is the only one who cares for me,' she said pitifully.

The duke's daughter looked as though she would refute this but before she could speak Canaletto stepped forward. 'May I, your grace?' he asked. Without waiting for permission, he whipped the paper out of the ducal hand.

'Sir,' protested the duke with great hauteur. 'What mean you?' He made as if to snatch the paper back.

But Canaletto retreated a few paces and finished scanning the short message. 'I know your desperate condition,' it read. 'Come to me at St James's Park, by the trees on the left as you enter from the Horseguards' Parade, after sunset and I will bring you hope.' As the duke had said, it was unsigned. The writing was in very black ink, an elegant, italic hand not too dissimilar from Canaletto's own.

It was writing he had seen before and instantly recognized. 'In hand of dead girl I tell your grace of, I found torn piece paper with writing exactly same.' He waved the note. 'Scrap only have two phrases, "This evening" and "help you". I sure it part of letter making assignation also.'

The duke's manner altered entirely. 'Upon my word!'

'That girl was with child and second girl been murdered, she say with child also but not.'

'Not?' repeated the duke in some perplexity.

'Not,' said Canaletto firmly.

'I don't understand,' Kitty said stamping her little foot again. 'What mean you with all this talk of murder?'

'Indeed, I should like to know,' agreed the duchess.

Purity said nothing, she sat with head bowed hopelessly.

'This man commit murders, I cannot say why,' said Canaletto carefully. He felt he now knew why but it seemed too incredible a motive to place before this assembly. How could he explain the common denominator that linked three girls from such different backgrounds? A gentleman's daughter, a lady's maid and a slave from Africa, all placed in the same jeopardy. How much reliance could he place on a betraying gesture and even if it meant what he thought, did the rest follow? But now that the killer had moved again, action had to be taken. 'It is important we capture.'

'Whoreson bugger,' said Charlie from where he leaned against the window.

'Charlie!' said Fanny in horror.

'They never taught you that at the hospital,' said the duke severely but Canaletto could see there was a twinkle in his eye.

'But he is a bad man, isn't he? If he kills?'

'Yes, Charlie, he is,' said Fanny.

'Then you must catch him.'

'We will,' said Canaletto with finality.

The duke looked very sceptical. 'Signor, I know not whether you have the right of it or not but one thing is certain. Purity will not leave this house. She will dress her mistress for the reception, then remain in her room. I will send men into the park to discover who it is who waits for her and why.'

Such power! Earlier the duke had talked of apprehending the snake charmer so that he should not be able to threaten the young foundling who was his namesake. Now he spoke of capturing the writer of the note. But what would that achieve? It wouldn't prove the person they captured was a killer. Or, in fact, that he meant any harm to Purity. He could easily complain he was merely pursuing his own business, that anyone was at liberty to walk in the park. There would be no grounds to hold him, even by ducal authority.

'Your grace,' said Canaletto urgently. He had to stop this action, already the duke was pulling a bell rope to summon his servant, but he was unable to think what should be done.

'Signor!' Fanny came forward, her face alight with purpose, 'I understand the matter, I think. You believe if Purity meets with her correspondent, he intends her harm?'

Canaletto nodded.

'Let me go and meet with him,' she said. 'The duke's men can be near at hand. Then if whoever it is threatens me, they can apprehend him and you will know that that was his intention.'

Canaletto was amazed that she had followed his thinking so exactly. But he couldn't let her undertake such a dangerous mission. 'He has knife,' he said. 'So easy stab you and disappear before men can arrive.'

'Quite!' said the duke. 'I applaud your courage, Miss Rooker, but it will not do.'

'How else are you to prove anything?' demanded Fanny, her cheeks pink with her presumption.

The other girl came up to her. 'I am Lady Kildare, the duke and duchess's daughter,' she said. 'I think you are so brave. What is your name?'

'Fanny Rooker, your ladyship,' Fanny gave a little bob.

'Surely if we can guarantee Miss Rooker's safety, it

will mean we can discover if this man means Purity ill or no?' Lady Kildare continued.

'No guarantee of safety possible,' cried Canaletto agitatedly. If the Richmond family were going to approve of this mad plan of Fanny's, he could not see how he could stop it. And he knew, none better, of the coldness of this killer. Of the bitter hatred he must have for the girls he stabbed to death then mutilated. 'W' for 'whore' drawn on their faces for the world to recognize, if the world were quicker to pick up the point than his dull brain had been, he thought bitterly. 'This man so skilled with knife,' he protested.

'He has stabbed before?' asked Emily.

'Twice,' said Canaletto in despair.

'Where? In the heart, the throat?' Emily drew her finger across her neck, her expression so lively and intelligent, Canaletto had to forgive her the dramatic gesture. He showed on his breast where the killer had attacked his two victims.

Lady Kildare's eyes widened. Then she clapped her hands together. 'I know, Father, if we give this brave girl George's fencing jacket under her cloak, then she will be safe.'

The duke shook his head. 'It would not be strong enough. Fencing swords have a protective button against the point, against a sharp knife the jacket would be useless.'

'How about leather?' suggested the duchess. 'I am sure one of the grooms has a leather apron.'

'No,' said the duke, his expression clearing, 'I have it – George's breastplate. Steel would meet steel.'

'Father, that is perfect!'

'But what if he should then go for her throat?' cried

the duchess. 'The breastplate would give no protection there and I for one would never forgive myself if he succeeded in his foul plan.'

Even Fanny looked hesitant at this suggestion.

But Lady Kildare had another idea. 'Master's collar! It is leather and studded with metal. It would deflect any knife. Jem,' she said to the servant who entered at that point, 'fetch Master.'

Jem disappeared again.

'I cannot agree with this plan,' Canaletto said agitatedly. 'Fanny too vulnerable.'

Fanny came and placed a hand on his arm. 'Suppose we do not ensure that this man can be stopped, how many other poor women might he not kill?'

Purity staggered up from the floor, using a chair to help. 'John does not intend to kill me, sir, he does not!'

'Do you recognize the writing as belonging to this John you speak of?' asked the duke.

'Your grace, I have never seen his writing, but who else would write to me in this way?' pleaded Purity.

Jem arrived back leading a large and panting dog that wagged its tail in friendship. Lady Kildare ran to it and took off its collar, slipping the leash around its neck in an extempore fashion. She handed the dog back to the servant, who took it away again, and brought over the collar to Fanny, trying it on around her neck. 'See, it fits!' she cried.

'What a fuss is this,' said Lady Kitty sulkily, sitting herself down on a couch with a thump. 'All about a maid!'

Nobody paid her any attention.

'Signor, surely this would make it safe?' pleaded

Fanny, removing the collar and turning it over in her hands. 'Mary was my friend, if I can do something to catch her killer and avenge her death, then perhaps she can rest in peace.'

Canaletto thought of the stiff, naked body of the violated girl and found he could understand why Fanny was so full of purpose.

In came another servant, carefully carrying a taper with which he proceeded to light the wall sconces and branched candlesticks that stood on tables, though he ignored the imposing chandelier. Some of the gloom disappeared but the flickering light threw into relief worried eyes set in anxious faces. 'I apologize for the delay, your grace. Will there be anything else?'

'Yes, Andrew. Fetch Lord George's breastplate.'

'Your grace?' The footman looked goggle eyed at the instructions.

The duke said nothing, merely gave him a long look. The footman flushed in embarrassment and retreated. 'And, Andrew . . .'

The footman turned, 'Your grace?'

'Purity was delivered a note this afternoon. Find out who by.'

'I know, sir. One of the scamps who are always asking for errands brought it to the back door. I just happened to be in the kitchen at the time,' he coloured slightly but continued steadily. 'I asked who had given him the note, for we do not like to receive anything into your grace's house without knowing from where it has come. He said a tall gentleman gave it to him.'

'That was the only description?'

'Yes, your grace.'

The duke dismissed him.

For Canaletto another little piece of the puzzle clicked into place.

Lady Kildare went to Purity. 'We need your cloak, my dear.' She gently unfastened the clasp, removed the heavy folds from around Purity's shoulders and brought it over to Fanny, enfolding her in it. 'It is a pity your hair is so bright. Not a pity for you, of course,' she added hastily. 'But Purity is so very dark and even with the hood up,' she demonstrated, 'one can see that you are not she.'

Canaletto looked at Fanny's pale skin and the bright strands of hair that stole out from underneath the dark hood. Even in the dark it would be quite evident she wasn't the African maid. He looked across at Purity, wondering if perhaps she could be persuaded to don the breastplate and dog collar. No, it was obvious that she was in no condition to face whoever her attacker turned out to be.

'A wig, perhaps?' suggested Fanny. 'And maybe if I rubbed my face with a little coal dust?'

Canaletto could not help but disapprove of all this play-acting. He felt that it demeaned his investigation. He looked out of the window. The snake charmer seemed to have disappeared and people were hurrying away through the gathering darkness. Soon dusk would have fallen. And someone would be waiting for Purity in St James's Park.

Chapter Thirty-Three

Fanny felt very frightened as she stepped out of Richmond House and went slowly down the front steps and into the Privy Garden.

The breastplate was uncomfortable, larger and more inflexible than stays. It fitted quite well, the young Lord George seemed much her size but he was longer in the body and they'd had some difficulty fastening its straps at the back over the gathers of her skirt, till Canaletto had exclaimed irritably, 'Does not matter, front is what matters.' He was told it was no use if the breastplate slipped. Finally they'd managed it. Fanny felt her breasts pressing against the unforgiving steel and for once was grateful nature had not endowed her more generously in that region.

The breastplate forced her to walk slowly and very upright. How had a man fought in such a garment, she'd wondered as they'd fitted it on her. But more worrying was the dog collar. Masters, the mastiff, had a larger neck than hers and even though the leather had been tightened to its shortest limit, it slid around her neck. It smelt of dog, a peppery and oily dirt that was most distasteful. It was heavy, too. Between the collar and the breastplate, Fanny felt dragged down.

The officer of the Watch had been sent for by the

duke. He had also assembled footmen and stable boys armed with stout staves and a blunderbuss to follow Fanny at a short distance. Canaletto had already left with the duke. They intended to see if they could identify a waiting man and remain at a convenient distance without alerting the fellow. The duke had his sword and a pistol, Canaletto his swordstick.

Mr Preston, the steward, was in charge of the household men. Fanny felt she could trust him to keep the correct distance between them and her, not so far they would not be able to rescue her should she need it, but not so near that they would alert anyone waiting for Purity.

She stood at the bottom of the steps of Richmond House for a moment, pulling the cloak around herself and allowing her eyes to adjust to the dark. There was no moon and the night was dark indeed. Candles lit the windows of the buildings beside the Holbein Gate. The wall of the Privy Garden hid the houses in Downing Street and the other streets in Whitehall but Fanny knew there must be light there as well. The thought removed some of her feeling of being alone on this venture. She was in a populated area, not a deserted country road.

Skirting a small fence, she started off across a patch of grass. The sentry had left his post, the box stood empty to her right. To her left was a small stand of shrubs, leafless now but soon they'd be displaying new leaves. She'd seen dogs playing there when they'd first arrived but now all the animals had gone. As had the people. There was no one in the garden.

Then a coach rumbled past and in the faint glow from its lights, she thought she saw someone crouching behind the bushes. Someone answering a call of nature? Or waiting for Purity? Her attention distracted from where she was walking, Fanny stumbled over a large stone and, hampered by the breastplate, couldn't prevent herself falling.

She lay winded for a moment, then slowly and carefully got herself to her feet.

Mr Preston was there as she became upright again, giving a hand to her elbow, his voice concerned as he asked if she was all right.

'I am fine, thank you, Mr Preston,' she said in a low voice, adjusting her hood, which had fallen off her head. This was bound with a dark scarf that hid all her hair, no short black wig being available in the Richmond household. Fanny couldn't imagine how she looked, she'd refused the offer of a mirror after Lady Kildare had enthusiastically daubed her face with coal dust, carefully brought in a silver porringer by a junior footman, who'd watched the operation with an amazed expression and seemed to have difficulty in containing his giggles. She clutched at the steward's arm and whispered, 'I think there is someone hiding in those bushes. I shall see if it is perhaps the man we seek.'

Before he could prevent her, Fanny walked swiftly over the grass towards the bushes and started parting the budding shrubs.

Then she screamed with shock as a man dressed in a long robe hit her across the face, knocking her to the ground with the force of his blow, and slipped by her. But, right behind, were Mr Preston and his men. With a halloo and cry, they were upon him.

Then there was consternation as the figure showered his attackers with the contents of a sack.

Hunting cries turned to screams of fear and anguish. 'Snakes,' cried one. 'I'm bitten,' cried another. They stumbled and fell about and, straining to make out what was happening in the darkness, Fanny saw the snake charmer slip away, through the gate of the garden into Whitehall.

Fearfully she once again managed to get herself upright and stood trying to work out what was best to do. Get nearer the scene of panic-stricken and struggling men she durstn't. Not if there were snakes!

Then the door of Richmond House was flung open and an elderly man with a torch appeared, followed by the housekeeper with another torch and Charlie.

The lights illuminated a scene of chaos, of men sitting on the ground, nursing an arm or a leg, their faces terrified, their eyes wild as they tried to see where the snakes were going. Others were dancing around trying to avoid the slithering mass of writhing reptiles.

'Don't worry,' screeched Charlie. 'They've all had their fangs removed. They can't harm you!' He pounced on one of the snakes and picked it up, holding it near his face, allowing the fangs to dart out towards his neck. Fanny marvelled at the way he could bring himself to touch it, let alone seemingly allow it to bite him.

'The boy's right,' said the steward after a moment. 'Calm yourselves, there is no need for panic.'

But it took some time for order to be restored and each man to realize he had suffered no ill effects. One of them hurried to the back yard of the house and returned with a sack. Fanny couldn't bring herself to help as, aided by Charlie, they gathered up the snakes.

'It was Anaconda, come for me, like I said,' hissed Charlie to her. 'But I'll be all right now and I'll protect you.'

Which reminded Fanny of her mission. 'I must continue to St James's Park,' she said to Mr Preston.

'Indeed, miss, his grace and Mr Canaletto will be wondering what is keeping you.' No anxiety about her safety, Fanny noted. Did that show the confidence he had in their ability to protect her?

'We'll be right behind you,' he said reassuringly.

But several of the men were too overcome with fright and still insisted they had suffered poisonous bites, so now it was only Mr Preston, two of the footmen and Charlie who followed behind. Fanny had tried without success to get Charlie to return to the house. Finally, worried by the time passing, agitated at what lay before her, she lacked the will to insist he went back.

A few carriages were making their way along Whitehall as Fanny passed through the gate from the garden. Across the road were the buildings of Whitehall with the massive Holbein Gate to her right. There were people getting ready to enjoy the evening. She could see rooms illuminated by candles. On the other side of those buildings was the darkness of St James's Park. Fanny felt very cold.

She crossed the road, aware of Mr Preston holding the blunderbuss, waiting with his two footmen and Charlie for her to get ahead. She looked about as she went in case the snake charmer was still around but she could see no sign of him. There were so many arches and nooks and crannies where a person could lurk in the dark, though, that she had no confidence he had indeed gone. Would Mr Preston keep a careful enough eye on the boy?

Fanny passed through the arch of Horse Guards Parade and emerged on the wide open parade ground. Ahead of her was the long triangular sweep of grass, bisected by the almost equally long canal, that made up St James's Park. At the point of the triangle stood Buckingham House. All around its perimeter and the canal were trees, planted by Charles II and now in their maturity. Fanny paused to acclimatize herself to the darkness and found herself reflecting on the strange fact that Buckingham House was in the possession of an illegitimate son of the Duke of Buckingham. Here was someone else who had not been prevented by bastardy from joining society.

As she stood, the immense darkness in front of her became more and more terrifying. The silence oppressed her. The Whitehall traffic was muffled, no birds sang in the darkness, no children ran, shouting, no dogs were being called. There was only wind soughing gently through the trees. What waited for her out there? A killer? And where were Canaletto and the duke? The hard steel of the breastplate pressed on her and she tried to feel reassured by its impenetrability. Then she touched the leather collar, heavy and solid. But what if he stabbed her between plate and collar? What if he used his knife to slash her face?

Fanny shivered. She almost turned and went back to the safety of lights, people and Richmond House. But the ghost of Mary Butcher seemed to rise in front of her.

Drawing the cloak more closely around her, Fanny walked forward.

And now the darkness was not, in fact, absolute. As she left behind the houses around the parade ground with their lamps and splashes of candlelight, the night seemed to lighten. She could discern the little picket fence that ran around the rows of trees. Some said this was a pleasure ground for lovers, that that was what King Charles had intended when he'd laid the parkland out after the manner of the French. It was still the playground of the court. One of the royal homes, St James's Palace, was somewhere off to her right. No doubt the duke and duchess found the short distance from their own home convenient when they had to attend court.

Fanny realized these stray thoughts were to keep her mind off the idea of someone waiting for her amongst the trees. She looked at them stretching to right and to left. How was she to know where to go?

Common sense told her no one could expect Purity to venture far. If someone was waiting for her, it must be amongst this stand of trees across from the wide pathway, separated from the gardens of the Whitehall properties by green sward.

Nervously Fanny crossed the pathway, clacking across the small stones in her patten shoes. No need now for them, they were needed to lift her above the debris of London streets; here, in the royal park, there was little rubbish and the mud from the last rain had dried out. But she'd donned them automatically and felt no desire now to take them off. Besides, the sharpness of the stones through her thin soles could be painful.

Keeping her mind on such matters, Fanny approached the trees. 'John?' she called out in a low

voice. Purity had a wonderful resonance and roundness to her voice. Fanny couldn't imitate it but she
dropped her voice as much as she could. 'John,' she said
again, 'are you there?' She stood on the edge of the
trees and turned this way and that, clutching the cloak
round her, making sure the hood hid as much of her
face as possible. 'John, I am afraid,' she called out
softly.

Something stirred amongst the dark trees.

Fanny gasped, hand to her mouth. There was
someone there. Her heart raced. Any moment now
she'd know who it was.

A tall figure, cloaked and wearing a large hat,
detached itself from the dark trunks that stood like so
many soldiers.

'Purity?' a voice breathed in a harsh tone. Harsh but
anonymous. So anonymous it was impossible to tell
even if it was male or female.

Fanny couldn't bring herself to move or utter anything further. She stood as though nailed to the spot but
her eyes darted anxiously around the gloom, trying to
discover Canaletto and the duke.

But she could only see this tall, dark figure
advancing on her. Where were Mr Preston and the
footmen? Surely well back across the parade ground.
Every instinct told her she should run as fast as she
could, back to them.

'Purity,' the figure said again and now it seemed
almost caressing. 'You are with child.' It was a statement not a question. 'You are bringing a bastard into
the world.'

Fanny peered, trying to see below the enveloping
cloak. She had only seen the Wrights' servant once but

she remembered a much more solid figure than this appeared to be.

'John,' she whispered, 'please, say it is you.'

'Nay,' the figure said in a low chuckle, and now Fanny saw that the face was covered with a mask. 'Not your African lover, you whore.' There was vicious force on the last word.

The masked form was almost upon her now but what with the hat and the mask, Fanny could not recognize who it was. The only feature she could see was the nose. And now she knew. No doubting that long, supercilious organ. It was Lord Maltravers, as she had suspected all along. Canaletto had set him up this afternoon to be recognized by Charlie.

Fanny's heart failed her, her frail defences would be useless against the tall, languid aristocrat, cosmopolitan man of the world, experienced and ruthless. Then it was too late to think because her arms had been caught and dragged behind her and one strong hand anchored them there. Fanny saw that the other held a knife. She screamed as it was driven towards her ribs. 'Die, whore! Never bring a bastard into this world!'

The knife hit the steel with a force that drove it back into the assailant's hand. There was a surprised grunt. Fanny screamed again as her hood fell back, revealing that despite her darkened skin, she was no African girl.

'What in hell's name,' said a voice quite different from that which had been used before. The knife was raised again as Fanny fought to release herself. Again it came down, this time glancing against the collar. Fanny felt sudden sharp pain as the blade caught her shoulder beneath the line of the breastplate. 'God's teeth!' the assailant said.

'Have at you, man,' said Canaletto's voice. '*En garde*,' said the duke's, and Fanny was abruptly released.

She must have lost consciousness then for the next she knew she was on the grass, the ground cold beneath the cloak. People were shouting. She was aware of a breeze across her face, then of Canaletto kneeling beside her, waving his hat. 'Fanny, Fanny, all right?' he said, sounding extremely anxious.

Fanny sighed, 'Yes, signor, I think so.' She struggled to sit up, wincing as the wound in her shoulder dragged. People were running with torches from Horse Guards Parade. Through the gloom Fanny could see the duke, sword in hand, Mr Preston and a footman holding down a wildly thrashing figure and Charlie dancing around them in excitement. 'He's trying to escape, he's trying to escape,' he squealed. 'Don't let the whoreson bugger escape.'

'Your grace,' shouted one of the torch bearers, puffing and panting as he ran up. 'Your grace, are you all right?'

Fanny's head ached, which was puzzling because she couldn't remember being hit there. She pulled off the scarf that had been tied so tightly around her copper-coloured hair and used it to push down the breastplate to stem the flow of blood where the knife had caught her.

'Now,' said the duke. 'Let's see what villain we have here.'

The steward and footman held the struggling figure tightly by the arms. With his sword the duke knocked off the wide-brimmed hat then used his hand to whisk away the mask.

Fanny gazed in horror. 'Richard!' she gasped. But the nose had belonged to Lord Maltravers. How strange, the two of them had identical noses! Little flecks of foam escaped his mouth. His gaze lighted on her and he let out a groan. 'Fanny,' he said despairingly. 'I nearly killed you!'

'Blackguard,' ground out the duke. 'Scoundrel!'

Fanny scrambled to her feet. 'Why, Richard, why? Poor Mary and that other girl. It can't have been you that killed them, surely?' But she knew he had. There had been no mistaking the ferocity of his attack. Involuntarily she put a hand to where her shoulder had been cut.

In the flaring torchlight Richard's eyes were deep-set, shadowed, impossible to read. His mouth curled. 'Women like them! They bring bastards into the world to fight for their existence. I know the lovelessness of being brought up without parents, the bitterness of gratitude that's extorted from you every day by those who reckon you owe them unfailing obedience.'

'Take him to the Watch,' instructed the duke through gritted teeth.

'We hear first what he say,' urged Canaletto. 'Must know why.'

The duke looked as though this was far from necessary, then he gave a nod of his head.

'You speak of your guardian,' Fanny breathed. 'But he gave you everything.'

'He *gave* me nothing. I had to earn everything. And when my precious guardian found I wanted nothing but to paint, not as an amateur but to study as a professional, he threatened to cut me out of his will.' His lips drew back in a ghastly grin. 'A riding accident wasn't difficult to arrange.'

Fanny couldn't believe that the delightful young fellow she had known and felt such emotion for could be this bitter man or that he had extracted such terrible vengeance for his sterile upbringing.

Then the grin faded and he seemed to come to himself. 'Oh, Fanny,' he groaned, 'you have no idea what my life was like. The beatings, the sermons, the lack of any feeling for myself as a person. I couldn't let that happen to someone else.'

The torchlight flickered and threw strange shadows. The branches of the trees moved erratically in the wind, they seemed alive.

'What sort of life would an abandoned child have? I heard Mary say she'd give her baby to the Foundling Hospital.' The young man almost sagged between his two holders. 'I went there with Francis Hayman to see where his picture should go. I saw the children, regimented, given succour but no love, no understanding. Then I found Penelope was working there as a teacher, Penelope, whom I'd known all my life. When I realized that she had condemned her own son to life in such a place, I was outraged beyond anything!'

'Did you speak much with her?' asked Fanny, thinking of the poor girl who had so cut herself off from family and friends. What must she have thought to see someone from her home?

'She begged me not to tell Mrs Truscott where she was. I promised her and then she seemed pleased to talk with me.'

Richard had grown quiet now and stood straight.

'Only a few days later she sent me word she had left the hospital. I arranged to meet her and she told me she was again with child and by the same man. She hoped he would provide for her. I knew he would not,' he spoke with supreme contempt. 'Lord Maltravers has no money, he lives on his wits, looks to make a famous marriage. I could not let her bring another unwanted child into the world.'

'You write note,' said Canaletto. 'You take knife, artist's knife for cut pigments, work paints, and meet her, then stab her,' he made a graphic gesture with his hand. 'Then cut her face.'

'She was a whore,' the bitter voice said. 'I wanted the world to know that.'

'And you did the same with Mary?' Fanny breathed, horror-struck.

'Another whore! When I heard at Ranelagh that she was with child and was to give it away, I knew she could not live.'

'She was not with child,' said Canaletto sternly. 'If you had waited a while, you would have found this. And what about Purity?' he asked. 'How could you know she would not bring up her babe? The father loves her.'

'She was being dismissed from her position, how could she?' Richard's voice was bitter. 'Whores the lot of them. As was my mother.'

'How do you know that? Did someone tell you her name?' demanded Canaletto.

Richard laughed, a desperate, strangled sound. 'My guardian told me how she'd pleasured herself with no thought for the consequences. He told me that to make me grateful he'd given me a home and a name.'

'She died giving birth to you, if I have the matter right,' Canaletto said. 'I believe Lord Maltravers is your father, Mrs Truscott your grandmother and you have murdered your half-sister.'

One of the torches flared up and showed Richard's disbelieving expression. 'That cannot be true!' he said despairingly.

Canaletto grabbed hold of Charlie and pulled him forward. 'And this is Penelope's son, your nephew.' Richard gazed horror-struck at the boy. 'You have killed his mother.'

'We've heard enough,' instructed the duke. 'Take him away.'

The two men started to march him off but at that moment Charlie gave a great cry.

So involved had they all been with what was being said, no one had noticed a figure in a long, loose garment creep silently up to where they stood under the trees, a small bag held in his left hand. 'Here's for you, my bully boy,' he cried. He took something small and wriggling from the bag and advanced on Charlie.

'It's Anaconda, come to get me,' he screamed, running around the group so that Richard and his two captors were between him and the sinister snake charmer.

'I'll get you all right,' Anaconda said in a low, evil whisper. 'You'll learn no one deserts Ma and me. No one!' He evaded the thrust of the duke's sword and ran after the boy. In the light of the torches, they could all see the snake in his hand, a 'v' clear on its head. He waved it towards those who would capture him. The eyes of the snake glanced wildly around, seeking someone to fix his flickering fangs into. 'This one isn't like the others, this one'll kill you,' he hissed at them.

Those who had been about to apprehend him, fell back.

Mr Preston raised his blunderbuss but Anaconda was too near to Charlie. If he fired it, the spraying shot could catch him as well. The weapon was lowered.

Fanny wanted to tell Charlie to run but in the dark how could he evade this terrible man? He'd fall and then the snake would bite him and that would be that. Surely someone must be able to stop him? The duke had drawn his pistol and he now took aim.

'Run!' shouted Fanny at last. 'Run to Whitehall, Charlie.'

But Anaconda was advancing. Gripping the hissing snake just behind the head, he held it out towards Charlie, who seemed mesmerized.

The duke fired.

Nothing happened but the click of a hammer hitting uselessly on the firing plate. The duke swore, threw the gun away and drew his sword.

Anaconda laughed and held out a long arm towards him, advancing the poisonous, hissing head.

The duke made a few, wristy movements with his weapon but it was easy to see it wouldn't be possible for him to lunge without coming within range of the snake. He tried slashing at the arm instead. Anaconda gave a contemptuous laugh as he leapt back out of range but also a little away from Charlie.

Fanny ran and grasped him, pulling him against her, feeling his terror-stricken shivering. The enormity of Richard's crimes had filled her with a strange sense of fatality and a fearless determination to save the boy.

'You'll not harm him,' she said to the charmer. 'I'll not let you.' She wrapped her cloak around them both and faced Anaconda and his hissing snake, clasping Charlie in her arms, feeling the warmth of his trembling body against her legs. Could a snake bite through the material of her cloak? She had no idea and durstn't think of the possibility.

'Fanny!' she heard Canaletto cry.

'A pox on you,' snarled Anaconda and lunged forward towards her.

'No!' cried Richard with a great shout. Taking his captors by surprise, with a superhuman effort he loosed himself from the restraining arms and flung his body against the snake charmer's, dashing him to the ground. The two of them rolled over and over in the grass.

Everyone followed, the men with torches holding them high in an effort to illuminate the scene. All, though, that could be seen was Richard wrenching at something, giving a great cry and then flinging it away. The snake sailed through the air and landed at Canaletto's feet. He jumped back then drew his swordstick and slashed desperately at the ground. 'It's dead!' he cried and lifted his weapon with half the striken reptile hanging uselessly from it.

'Look to them, men,' cried the duke. Richard now straddled the snakecharmer, forcing his arms flat along the ground.

Fanny crouched, cradled a wildly sobbing Charlie in her arms and tried to soothe him.

In a moment the duke's men had both malefactors under control. Richard leaned heavily on his captors, a curious smile on his face. 'I will not trouble you long,' he said, his eyelids heavy.

'Aye,' spat out Anaconda, struggling uselessly. 'You killed the snake too late.'

The duke pushed up Richard's sleeve on his right arm and directed one of his servants to bring the spluttering torch near. There they all could see the livid bite.

'Faugh!' exclaimed the duke. 'The hangman's robbed!'

Epilogue

'Hurry, signor,' said Fanny. She started cleaning the last of the brushes she had been using, working the spirit into the bristles.

Canaletto carefully added the final touches to the figures he had been painting. He had had the luxury of time to attend to every tiny detail of the landscape and architecture and now attended to the figures that brought the view to life. The picture was good, he had no doubt about that.

'We must not be late,' Fanny urged him.

He handed Fanny his palette and brushes and stretched his arms. 'I ready. Soon we go, yes?'

'Yes, signor,' she said with a touch of exasperation.

But for once he was delighted to hear Fanny express something other than numb acceptance of life.

He had done everything he could to stimulate her. He had encouraged her to complete her painting of Golden Square, carefully guiding composition and technique, had given her stretches of grass and road in his picture to paint, had even sent his laundry to Mrs Gotobed. Fanny had obediently done all he'd asked, taken every piece of criticism to heart, working so hard he feared for her health, giving him all the support he could wish for and proving so apt a pupil he could not but feel guilty at his earlier lack of instruction.

Her heart, though, had not been in any of it. To Canaletto it was as if he lived and worked alongside some clockwork doll. Where was the bright, opinionated girl who had so often caused him pain as well as pleasure? He had begun to fear she was gone for ever, lost in that dreadful scene in St James's Park.

'See,' he said, 'I finish the figures now.'

Excited, she came over. 'Oh, signor!' She came closer. 'Why that is Jem and Andrew searching in the bushes, is it not? The duke's footmen?'

Canaletto nodded. 'They look for Anaconda. And you see John is standing guard on the other side of the bushes?'

Fanny looked at the figure of the African servant and nodded, delighted. 'Anaconda can be found in Newgate any day,' she said scornfully. 'He will be there a long time, thanks to the Duke of Richmond bearing witness against him. I only wish his accomplices, Bella and that dreadful old woman Charlie told us about, could be there too. But I am glad you have painted the bushes in leaf, so much more attractive. Oh, and is that not Lady Kitty and Lady Kildare walking with the little girl? Is she Lady Kildare's small sister?'

'I thought duchess like that.' Canaletto wondered if her grace would recognize either of her daughters, he used figures to bring his views to life, not to offer portraits.

'And there's the duke himself!' Fanny pointed to the figure standing in the yard of Richmond House, a corner of which appeared in the bottom right of the painting. 'And Mr Preston bowing to him. Who else have you put in?' She peered at the other figures. 'Why, there is Mrs Gotobed, sitting with some laundry beside her. And isn't that Charlie?' she said with a delighted smile looking at a small boy pulling along a middle-aged man. 'But who is he with?'

'That is surgeon, Matthew Bagshott. Someday you meet, very good fellow.' He rubbed at a little paint on his hands. 'I go get ready now, we must not be late,' he gave her a sideways glance.

'Signor, that is what I tell you!'

'So Fanny be ready when I come down, yes?' he goaded her.

She sent him a speaking look that said her readiness was not the problem.

He smiled to himself as he left the studio.

All day the June weather had been beautiful, the air sparkling in a way it so seldom did in London. No doubt the fact that the only fires needed were for cooking had had something to do with it. Canaletto had worked in shirtsleeves and his lightest smock and he wasn't looking forward to donning waistcoat and jacket for their evening engagement, not to mention his wig. Today he hadn't even worn a cap on his bald head.

There was a large cart standing under the arch that led to Silver Street. Adam staggered out of the workshop with a load of wood. Canaletto looked at him, dismayed. He had forgotten that the cabinet maker was to leave so soon. 'You go with Daniel?' he asked.

'Aye, sir,' Adam said dolefully. He dropped the wood onto the cart with a resentful thump.

'Not like to go to country?' suggested Canaletto.

'Leave London? Bury myself where nothing happens? Don't know how I'm to go on, that I don't.'

'Jenny go too?'

Adam's eyes bulged in frustration. 'No, she don't! Mrs Spragg say she has no need of servant in country.' Without the income lodgers brought, she probably couldn't afford her. Poor Adam.

'Perhaps stay, work for cabinet maker who comes here instead?'

'But my articles!' Adam puffed, heaving the last piece of wood onto the cart. 'I'm indentured to Mr Spragg.'

'Ah,' said Canaletto in understanding.

'Two more years afore I'm finished. If I'm still alive then!' He disappeared back into the workshop.

Canaletto went upstairs to his rooms wondering how Daniel and Betty would take to living in the country and also how this new ownership of his accommodation would work out. Daniel had assured him the arrangement with the studio and his lodging would continue but Canaletto had little confidence things would remain the same. They never did and he would miss his landlord.

It was due to Canaletto that the decision had been taken. Worried about Daniel's condition, he had asked Matthew Bagshott to come and examine him. The surgeon's diagnosis had been that his lungs and stomach were weak and that the London smoke was having a deleterious effect on them. He should leave town for the country, he said. Now the Spraggs were on their way to Goodwood, near Chichester, and a job at the Duke of Richmond's country seat.

Half an hour later, Canaletto and Fanny set out together to walk to Golden Square. 'We pretty couple,' said Canaletto, taking her arm through his, noting the care with which she had brushed her hair. 'New gown, I think.'

Fanny looked down at the full folds of the sprigged muslin. 'Mrs Casement told Thomas Wright I should have Mary's things. I have not had the heart to wear any before this, no, nor the opportunity. They are all so fine.' She gave a delicious giggle that warmed Canaletto. 'A most curious arrangement holds out the skirts.' She released her hand from his arm and lifted the material on either side of her hips to demonstrate the shape of the little cages that provided support. Then slipped her hand back again, 'I feel a proper lady with them!' she said confidingly.

'So you look,' he assured her. 'We are to visit at Wright house first, I think?'

Fanny nodded.

The door was opened by John but gone was his livery. Instead he wore a business-like looking buff jacket and breeches of plain linen.

'Mr Canaletto, Fanny!' he said with a beaming smile. 'Come in. We await you.'

He took them through to the rear of the house. In a comfortable room next to the kitchen was Purity. She came towards them with a new confidence, carrying her gently swelling belly before her like a flag.

'Purity, I am so glad to see you,' said Fanny. 'Or should I call you Mrs Okuboko now?'

'No formality between us, please,' said Purity. 'I regret it has not been possible to invite you here before but there has been so much to attend to.'

John served them with glasses of claret. 'Nothing but the best for you,' he said.

'Mr Wright's business prospers then?' suggested Canaletto.

'Since he has taken John to help him, it has,' said Purity. 'Such a to-do there was when John presented him with the offer he had received from one of his rivals.'

'They recognized your worth?' said Canaletto.

'I had run so many errands for Mr Wright, been involved with him and Master Thomas in so much of his business, I knew every detail,' John acknowledged. 'Another hosier wanted me to work for him and said that if the Wrights tried to prosecute me as a runaway slave, he would arrange legal representation. He was confident we would win the day, opinion in England is changing.' John gave a low, rumbling laugh. 'Mr Wright was so angry! Accused me of so many things and swore he would prosecute me. But thanks to you, sir,' he acknowledged Canaletto, 'and your intercession with the duke, everything was brought to a happy conclusion. I now have my freedom and a position in Mr Wright's firm. And my beautiful wife,' he held out a hand to Purity, who clasped it tightly and smiled at him.

'And you?' Fanny asked her.

'The Earl and Countess of Cheshire, Lady Kitty's parents, gave me my freedom as a wedding present,' she said quietly. 'The position of slaves in England must alter soon. Moves are being made and we shall help wherever we can.'

'And Lady Katherine?' asked Fanny. 'What has happened to her?'

'Ah,' said John with another of his rumbling laughs, 'she has met her match.'

'She has gained her heart's desire,' said Purity with a slight smile. 'She is now Lady Maltravers.'

'And a merry dance he is leading her,' said John.

'You remain in touch?' asked Fanny with a slight air of surprise.

'The Countess writes to me and I have heard from Lady Kildare, who is now Duchess of Leinster, the earl having been made duke,' Purity said. 'The newly married Lord and Lady Maltravers visited Leinster House in Ireland shortly after their marriage. But John does not have the right of it, I understand Lord Maltravers is run on a tight rein.'

'But he has the control of her fortune,' protested John. 'He will not long allow her to rule the roost.'

'I think they both have determined tempers,' said Purity. 'It will be a stormy marriage but maybe each needs the other. He could be a steadying influence in her life and she provides him with the funds he needs.'

'Quite May and December,' murmured Fanny.

'Hardly December,' said Canaletto sharply.

'And steadying is not quite the word I would use to describe my lord,' said John. 'But, as you say, he is advancing in years and no doubt has put his wicked past behind him.'

Canaletto would have no truck with all this, Lord Maltravers was some ten years younger than himself. 'I heard from Leonora Casement only the other week that Lord Maltravers has not ceased his connection with her,' he said severely. Then he glanced quickly at Fanny, but she had not seemed to make the obvious connection over his reference to Leonora. Still, thought Canaletto, it was time he ceased his visits to the woman, she was too voracious, too demanding. And now that Lord Maltravers was back in her life, she would have other diversions.

'Say you so!' breathed Purity. 'Then I feel for my erstwhile mistress. I am sure she believes that my lord has no other interest than her.'

Canaletto felt he had said enough. 'And the young master, Thomas?' he asked.

'He has certain business talents but little desire to practise them,' John said. 'He finds it difficult to adjust to my new status but I think we will eventually make something of him.'

After hearing of John and Purity's joy in looking forward to the birth of their child in October, Canaletto and Fanny took their departure.

'There is a happy couple,' said Fanny contentedly as they made their way along the stone pavement to Mrs Truscott's house. 'I trust we may find the same felicity here.'

The taciturn servant showed the two of them up to the first-floor drawing room. There were Mrs Truscott and her faithful companion, Patience Partridge. And there was Charlie. 'Fanny, Fanny,' he shouted excitedly as they came in. 'And signor, oh how pleased I am to see you. I have left the hospital! How is Daniel?'

'Hush, Charles,' snapped out Mrs Truscott. 'Do you not know better how to comport yourself?'

A chastened Charlie fell silent. He was no longer in the Foundling Hospital uniform but wore black silk breeches, a white shirt and short black jacket. 'You look most handsome,' said Fanny. 'You must be very happy to be with your great-grandmother.'

'Yes,' he said a trifle doubtfully, 'but I do miss my friends from the hospital.'

'You will soon make more,' Fanny said encouragingly.

'Oh, yes,' said Miss Partridge. 'We are to return to Derbyshire, Charles will find lots of comrades there.'

'Indeed?' Canaletto turned to Mrs Truscott.

'I think it wisest,' she said quietly. 'London is no place to bring up a boy these days and if we were to remain here, I would always be worried that those dreadful villains he fell in with would discover and take their vengeance on him.' Canaletto saw from the way her glance fell on the boy that she was genuinely fond of him.

'A problem to free him from hospital?' he asked. Charlie had been returned to the Foundling Hospital after the events in St James's Park but afterwards Canaletto had visited Golden Square and told Mrs Truscott all he had learned.

'Not a problem, more a tedious process,' she replied. 'He has only just been released into my care.' Canaletto took the glass of ratafia her servant offered him. 'It was not difficult to establish my relationship as I was able to swear to the clothes he was dressed in when delivered to the hospital and a scrap had been pinned to the paper I had written witnessing that he had been baptized and that his name was Barnabas Bardolph.'

Canaletto could not help but think that Charles Lennox would have been an infinitely preferable name for the boy's journey through life.

'I think, though, that we have no choice but to call him Charlie,' added Mrs Truscott. 'I have had to give a written undertaking to maintain him until adulthood and to pay the hospital some eighty pounds for his release.'

'Eighty pounds!' Canaletto was staggered by the amount.

'I have been told it has cost all of that and more to maintain him during his stay,' said Mrs Truscott with a resigned air. 'And now it seems a small price to pay to have Penelope's son with me.'

She had travelled a long way since handing the boy over to the hospital seven years ago, thought Canaletto.

'And you will encourage his artistic instincts?' he asked his hostess, watching Charlie show Fanny some childish effort at drawing at the other end of the room.

A shadow crossed Mrs Truscott's face. 'I see little alternative, signor. Both my daughter and grand-daughter had considerable talent. I have seen the pain caused when my friend, Mr Edward Thompkins, attempted to crush his adopted son's aim to become a professional painter.'

'Ah, then your daughter's son did not die, did he?'

Mrs Truscott repeated the betraying gesture of smoothing her eyebrow that had alerted Canaletto to the possibility she had lied when she had first told him this. Now she seemed prepared to repeat the falsehood. She opened her mouth, then closed it again and drew him nearer the window, away from the others in the room. 'Signor, I feel I can unburden myself to you. You are right, but my daughter died giving birth and there was her other child, Penelope, to bring up. I could not accept the boy into my family without admitting his bastardy. I turned to Edward Thompkins knowing he had no heir and was concerned over the future of his estates. He agreed to adopt Richard and never to tell him of his parentage.'

'And you were friends, so see Richard growing up?' Canaletto said.

Mrs Truscott nodded. 'I was able to maintain contact, allow Penelope to become friends with her half-brother, and ensure Richard had a more than easy competence for life and an acceptable background.' She made it seem a logical choice. 'How was I to know Edward would prove such a disciplinarian?' Mrs Truscott once again smoothed her eyebrow. 'Or that his ideas on how a boy was to comport himself were too strict? That he would make Richard so sick of the gratitude he was forced to acknowledge every day, it would show itself in such a terrible way?'

How Mrs Truscott deceived herself! Not about Richard but about her friend. Such a disciplinarian herself, she must have recognized the same instincts in her friend, maybe she had been drawn to him because of this.

'Signora Truscott engage tutor for Charlie?' asked Canaletto, worried about how the boy would fare with this woman.

She nodded vigorously. 'I know just the man, someone who will enlarge young Charles's education, teach him sporting activities, how to handle a gun and ride, and make him fit to attend school in a few years' time. I am old, Signor Canal, no, do not demur,' she added as Canaletto would have made some graceful denial of this obvious fact. 'Even if I, thanks be to God, enjoy reasonable health, I am far removed from Charles in age. He needs companions, someone to show him how to enjoy all he has missed so far in life.'

'His father, Lord Maltravers, you try for connection?' asked Canaletto.

She shook her head. 'Unwise, I think. He is not a man I can admire or could consider a proper influence on a growing boy. In any case, the question is academic as the man will not admit paternity.'

Lord Maltravers deserved every barb he would receive at the hands of his new wife, thought Canaletto. 'I hope Charles not need know who father is,' he said gravely.

'I agree, signor. If he should require information, though, I will acquaint him with the facts, however unpleasant they may be.' Mrs Truscott paused, her expression painful. 'I have much to make up to Charles, signor, none is more conscious of that than I, nor none how ill-fitted I am to carry out this task. I have made many mistakes in my life, I only hope I can avoid more.'

Canaletto was touched by the way this proud woman had brought herself to admit such difficult facts. 'Signora, Charles lucky to have understanding guardian now,' he said with a small bow. 'I, Antonio da Canal, proud to make acquaintance of such woman.'

Mrs Truscott blinked rapidly.

'When remove you from Golden Square?'

'Tomorrow. I have always maintained my Derbyshire home and I think it sensible to take Charles away from here as soon as possible.'

Canaletto nodded. He felt she was very wise. But he was sorry he would not see the scamp again.

'You and Miss Rooker will be very welcome should you wish to visit the Derbyshire area. It is very picturesque,' Mrs Truscott said gracefully.

Canaletto bowed his appreciation of this invitation. 'Perhaps, most possible,' he murmured.

'And, Miss Rooker, have you noticed the place I have found for your painting?' Mrs Truscott drew their attention to the wall. There hung Fanny's view of Golden Square, the sun highlighting the houses on the western side and casting a shadow from a waiting coach and the statue, proud in the centre. She had bought the picture as soon as it had been finished, paying a price that had rendered Fanny speechless. 'I shall take it with us to Derbyshire. Now, Patience,' she added briskly, 'will you not play for us?'

After a small demur, her companion seated herself at a spinet and played some pieces in an enthusiastic if not particularly skilful manner. Canaletto applauded politely and wondered how long it would be before they could make a graceful exit.

After the little recital, they were led to refreshments, some meat pies, a neat's tongue, candied potatoes, apricots and an almond tart. Charlie, full of high spirits, had more than once to be reprimanded by his great-grandmother but there was affection in her remonstrance and he seemed to accept her strictures in good part. Canaletto thought there was a good chance the relationship would mellow over the years ahead.

'Charlie seems happy,' said Fanny as they walked home a little later, her arm through his, the night air soft and warm around them.

Canaletto nodded but did not wish to add to this statement. They walked in silence towards Silver Street for a little.

'Did you,' Fanny hesitated, as though reluctant to continue, then said, 'did you know who it was who waited for Purity in the park that night, signor?'

It was the first time she had spoken of those events.

'Yes,' he said, thinking how different this evening was from that other one, remembering how worried he had been, not only for Fanny's safety but for her shock when she found out who had been perpetrating the horrendous crimes. 'Thompkins and friends talk whole time of English school of painting, yet Thompkins come to me for lessons. He portraitist yet insist want learn from *vedute* artist.'

'You are a great painter, signor,' said Fanny.

As always, the words warmed Canaletto's heart but he would not allow himself to be too swayed by them.

'I am not portraitist. Yet Thompkins insist on pay much money for lessons. Later Canaletto wonder why.' He was reluctant to admit that at first he had been seduced by the young painter's fulsome praise of his abilities. 'After Mary killed and we discover who other girl was, cuts to face worry me more and more,' he went on. 'Maltravers capable of killing, perhaps. Opportunist, selfish, breaker of women's hearts but I think not twisted in that way. There must be message in cuts if only Canaletto can discover. Before she killed, Mary announce herself with child. I ask myself, who know? Answer, all at Ranelagh. There Leonora Casement, Maltravers, Thomas Wright, John, his servant, and Richard Thompkins. Leonora I think not. She too confident of her powers over men. And what reason has she to kill Mary? No, not Leonora.'

'I didn't think her capable of killing,' Fanny agreed quietly.

'I think killer perhaps more than little mad, will maybe soon strike again. If Charlie recognize man he saw with Penelope at Foundling Hospital, perhaps that man villain. It cannot be servant, I think, but I send letters to Maltravers, Wright and Thompkins to visit Lady Kitty at the Duke of Richmond's house around five o'clock.' Canaletto sighed. 'I think that is what decide Thompkins that night kill Purity. Because he right beside that part of park.'

They had reached Silver Street. 'Perhaps,' said Canaletto hopefully as they turned in under the arch, 'we take cognac?' They had not spent time together in the evenings since that fatal night.

'I would like that, signor. I need to hear the remainder of your tale,' Fanny said, leading the way into the studio and going to the cupboard for the brandy.

So,' said Canaletto when they were settled on the stools, 'Charlie recognize Maltravers and not Thompkins or Wright. I think maybe Canaletto wrong not to think the lord the villain. Maybe cuts to victims' faces some conceit of his. Then, in Privy Garden I see Richard and Lord Maltravers near each other and see similarity. It comes to me like flash lightning make when I find girl's body. Maltravers perhaps his father! I remember Signora Truscott's tale. She lie when say daughter's baby die. She say she not know name of daughter's lover. But could be Maltravers. He sort of man enjoy bedding mother and daughter.

'Then we learn of letter to Purity and I am sure it cannot be milord who send. He can have no reason to kill Lady Kitty's maid. Now I am certain killer choose victims because they with child. He very twisted. I remember Richard very bitter about no parents, that his guardian make him very unhappy. He grow up in Derbyshire, maybe he meet first victim there. He apprentice with Hayman, go to Foundling Hospital with him. If he knew victim in Derbyshire, maybe meet her there without Charlie seeing. Perhaps it is Richard who kill so no other child grows up without parents. Everything start make sense. After I find girl's body, McSwiney go to Artists' Club, maybe tell those there of adventure with Canaletto and that I concerned to find killer. Thompkins hear, he wonder what Canaletto discover about body, decide must be close to me so come for lessons. All connections there. But no proof.' Canaletto reached forward and took Fanny's hands. 'Canaletto not want you to risk life like that,' he burst out.

Fanny returned his grasp. 'Signor, I'm glad I didn't know who it was who waited for Purity out there. I'm glad you didn't tell me.' Neither of them said anything for a moment.

Then Fanny said, 'Do you think Charlie will grow up the same?'

Her face was very worried. Canaletto wanted to reassure her, to smooth away the lines and bring back joy to her eyes. It wasn't possible. 'Many people unhappy, beaten by parents, bad childhood,' he said. 'They not all kill! Charlie good boy, Signora Truscott look after well, I think.'

'Oh, signor, I pray that you are right.' She sighed deeply. 'That was a terrible night, I was devastated when I knew Richard was dying from the snake bite but it would have been worse to see him tried and executed.'

Canaletto relaxed a little. At last Fanny had brought herself to talk about the young painter. He had been afraid she would bury the dreadful events deep within herself.

'He sad young man. Had talent, too.' He smiled at his apprentice. 'English school of painting soon exist.' He had gone to the Foundling Hospital for the unveiling of the pictures that had been donated. He hadn't particularly liked them, derivative and lacking in subtlety, he'd thought. But they'd been well received. He thought the English talent was best demonstrated in portraiture and landscape, not history paintings. 'And Fanny will join their ranks.'

At last she gave him a genuine smile. 'Oh, signor, you really think so?'

'Yes,' he said solemnly. Now, perhaps, she would put the pain of this episode behind her and he could have back the charming, lively girl he had met on his first arrival in London. In future he would not neglect her artistic education. Her view of Golden Square had been very competent and she was now fully capable of helping him with minor details. Soon, surely, he would need her help. McSwiney had sold the view of London through the arch of Westminster Bridge to Sir Hugh Smithson, and now that he had the Duke of Richmond as patron, commissions would at last flood in, the way they had in Venice. Canaletto swallowed the remainder of his brandy and smiled at Fanny. Together they could handle all the business McSwiney would negotiate. She would forget her unhappiness and there would be no time for investigations into murder.

Historical Notes

The Duke of Richmond and his family, Canaletto, Owen McSwiney, William Hogarth, Francis Hayman, Lord Lovat and Edward Rooker are all historical characters. Richmond House, the Privy Garden and Ranelagh Gardens existed much as I have described them. So did the Foundling Hospital, and the second Duke of Richmond did give his name to one of the first foundlings. While he worked in England, Canaletto lodged in Silver Street, now known as Beak Street, with a cabinet maker. All the background details are as accurate as I could make them. Everything else in the book is fiction – but could just as easily have been fact!

JANET LAURENCE

Canaletto and the Case of Westminster Bridge

Pan Books £5.99

Canaletto wiped cold sweat from his forehead. Then he adjusted the set of his wig, and looked at last on London.
What he saw was not reassuring . . .

It is 1746 and famous Venetian artist Canaletto arrives in London, eager to exploit his popularity with English collectors.

But London is a dangerous city. Barely have the painter's feet touched soil than he narrowly escapes robbery and death. Clearly there are people in England interested in him. Unfortunately they want him dead . . .

Then, as London hums with a scandal surrounding the new Westminster Bridge, Canaletto makes the most grisly of discoveries . . .

'A tasty treat.' *Sunday Times*

'Janet Laurence blends fact and fiction in a readable and worthy yarn.' *Evening Telegraph*